CW00459201

PAUSE STOP EJECT

Pause Stop Eject

Scoon Ferguson

wfh

Copyright © Scoon Ferguson 1999

The right of Scoon Ferguson to be identified as the author of this work has been
asserted by him in accordance with the Copyright, Design and Patents Act 1988

This is a work of fiction. Names, characters, places, organisations and incidents are
either products of the author's imagination or used fictitiously. Any resemblance to
actual events, places, organisations or persons, living or dead, is entirely coincidental

All rights reserved. No part of this publication may be reproduced, stored or
transmitted in any form by any means, electronic, mechanical, photocopying or
otherwise, without the prior written permission of the publisher

ISBN paperback 978-1-7392684-0-4
ISBN eBook 978-1-7392684-1-1

First published in the UK 2023 by
What Fresh Hell Books, Northumberland

@wfh_books   wfhbooks@gmail.com

1 2 3 4 5 6 7 8 9 0

A CIP catalogue record of this book is available from the British Library

PAUSE STOP EJECT

PAUSE

"I'M SORRY, I REALLY DON'T HAVE A CLUE."

"Do you work here, or don't you?"

No, I'm just wearing this fucking uniform for a laugh, what do you think? "Yes. I work here."

"Well then."

Well then? *Well then?* "Excuse me, if you don't mind, I've got a lot of work to do."

"Well excuse *me* young man."

Oh that was it, that was *it*. "Listen mate–"

"Anything the matter Thornwood?" barked Lord Tit-head himself.

"No, I'm just dealing with this… uh, *gentleman*."

"What was it you were looking for, sir?"

Cheeky little– "Hey, I said–"

5

"Shelves to be filled, Thornwood."

Lord Tithead turned his back, and the subject was closed.

The cunt! Always ordering people around, constantly poking his nose into other people's business, forever proving his power and authority. Christ, David hadn't exactly wanted to deal with the tight-arsed old fart, but to be told to push off by Scott Watson...

Life as a supermarket shelf-filler was hard.

Fuck that: *life* was hard.

Yeah mother that's right, I've finally woken up to the real world, what you predicted all along, hope you're satisfied.

He returned to where he'd been working before the old fart had started whittering on about alcohol-free lager. And for Christ's sake, what was the point of drinking lager if there was no alcohol in it? What'll be next, non-alcoholic whisky? Apple-free cider? No added hops bitter? Oh yeah that's right, you have to *fit in* don't you? Have to be one of *the lads*, downing your pints and bellowing your laughter, sucking on your tabs and wolf-whistling at all the brain-dead tarts and slags.

Well fuck that for a laugh.

He pushed a final few bottles onto the shelf, chucked the empty box in the general direction of the rubbish pile he'd created at the end of the aisle, then pushed his half-full stock cage along to the next gap in the fixture.

What a life.

Half-seven to midnight, four days a week, enough to make you sick.

Or terminally depressed, whichever took your fancy.

It wasn't as if the surroundings were much cop, either. The place'd only been open a few years, yet still looked as out-dated, cheap and dirty as the local quid-for-everything bullshit discount dump. What with its shelves full of crap no one wanted, its prices shooting through the roof and heading for the stratosphere, a rival company planning a hypermarket down near the river, it wouldn't surprise David if the place went under in a couple of years.

Actually, it would *delight* him if it went bust. Out of a job at last, he'd be able to sit around at home doing bugger all, living off the skinflint government.

Mind you, he might as well be living off the skinflint government, the slave wages he was paid for working his arse off in this dump.

Schweppes' original bitter lemon. A massive gap, the fixture empty, and what had the twat gone and ordered?

Bugger all.

Three cases of own-brand low calorie tonic water, the space for that full to the brim, with several bottles encroaching onto the bitter lemon shelf.

This place was run by a bunch of titheads.

King Tithead and the Prince Titheads, then Lord Tithead, and after him all the little Servant Titheads, their tongues so far up King Tithead's arse...

It was pretty daft the way he got so worked up by it all.

7

Just some part-time work after school, something to line the pockets.

Well that had been seventeen months ago, and here he was still, school out the window after flunking his A-levels, with a future as bleak and depressing as this bloody job.

Suicide seemed rather appealing at times like this.

He smiled to himself.

At least he could joke about it.

His situation was seriously dire, however. He didn't have any hobbies. He wasn't interested in furthering the little education he'd had, couldn't be bothered applying for even more mind-numbing jobs he probably wouldn't get anyway, was hopeless with girls (and boys, come to think of it), all his friends were either frying their brains with a variety of interesting drugs, or had buggered off someplace to start the proverbial new life, and to top it all, his mother had booted him out.

He was currently dossing with some eighteen stone psychopath who had a tendency to rifle through David's belongings and copy down any potentially useful bits of information (bank account number, debit card number and expiry date, insignificant things like that), and even he was getting ready to show him the door: the flat only had two bedrooms, and the psychopath's two girlfriends had shown an interest in moving in, but only if that grumpy anorexic prick moved out.

And that was another thing.

How come some overweight, over-muscled, under-brained dick like him could pull not one but *two* lasses, and get them not only to agree with the arrangement, but who regularly dived into bed with each other, as well as the psychopath?

Life, David Thornwood had come to realise, was one top-notch grade-A pain in the frigging arsehole.

"Thornwood!"

Oh Christ, here it came, learn some manners, respect the customer, blah-de-fucking-blah.

Lord Tithead, also known as Deputy Twilight Supervisor Scott Watson, strode over from the beers fixture, greasy black hair streaked violently backwards, neatly pressed trousers hanging over shining shoes, creamy white shirt ironed and tucked in, supermarket branded tie dangling loose, moronic smile spreading wider and wider and, "When a customer asks us something we aren't sure about, what do we do?"

"Shit our pants," David suggested.

"Eh-uhhh," Watson screeched. "We ask one of our superiors."

"But mate, who would you ask, you bein' manager an' all that?"

"I think you need to learn a little respect, Thornwood." He smacked David over the head with a piece of cardboard he'd been carrying, then waltzed off to annoy someone else.

The quip about manager always got the little shithead. He was one of those hopeless losers who actually believed they could get somewhere in life, and was currently working his way up the shelf-stacking ladder having landed the Deputy Twilight Supervisor position, and was so pleased with himself the title might have been another expression for 'god'.

Sickening really.

Bloody annoying really, actually.

It made David want to turn to some inconceivable act of violence.

Sometimes.

Most of the time.

Of course, the thought had always been there – gonna get that prick, show him who's boss, jump on him after work – but he'd never tried anything. It simply wasn't the way you behaved.

Anyway, there were plenty more fuckers in the world whose charming personalities would be permanently improved by falling onto the business end of a knife.

None sprung to mind more readily than Watson, however.

Well fuck it.

Back to the shit-stained grindstone.

He launched the three cases of tonic towards the steadily increasing pile of back-stock, then dragged the cage along to the canned drinks section. 'Section'. That was a laugh: there was less than six feet of shelving available, every square inch crammed full of crap no one was buying. Oh yes! a miracle! the Coca-Cola fixture was empty, oh hurrah! oh joy!

Oh the little dickfuck who did the ordering hadn't ordered any.

"Wanker," he grumbled, rather loudly for half-an-hour before closing.

One of the checkout lasses was heading in his direction, and he busied himself with some meaningless task as she passed. He tried to ignore the fact she had deliberately moved to the other side of the aisle to avoid him, and also tried to ignore the fact she was damned near gorgeous.

Another one destined to become nothing but a stain on the bedclothes.

But they were so far up their own arses in here, no part-time after school shenanigans for them, no, this was serious work, career-making stuff, set up for life, you listening? no I suppose not, you're always in a bloody dreamworld, never on the same planet, well it makes me *sick* [walk off in opposite direction with head held high].

Bitches.

The keeno pricks he shared the twilight shift with weren't much better. Oh yeah, they all spoke of getting out, leaving this dump behind and fucking off from the north east for good, but when it came down to it they'd do bloody anything to keep their jobs, worked so hard, were so determined to do well, but it was a shithole really, no way were they hanging around, oh yes sir I'll do anything sir, suck your smeg'-drenched cock sir? of course sir.

Pricks.

But it was Watson who got him going the most.

Watson who inspired the homicidal dreams and fantasies.

He took out his supermarket craft-knife, and pushed out the blade.

It was about three inches long.

After a few moments just staring at the gleaming sharp edge, he turned around, abandoning his stock cage, and headed towards the main central aisle. He turned left and started along, head swinging left and right, searching the tributary aisles.

Scott Watson was on biscuits, busy manhandling a young female shelf-filler who obviously just wasn't quite doing her job properly.

"You bash them in like that, no wonder we get complaints. And we want them all faced forwards too, you see?"

The young blonde eyed him warily. "Uh... I guess."

Clamping his sweaty hand around her wrist, he carefully guided her hand – and the packet of digestives it held – towards the shelf.

David stood at the end of the aisle, looking on in disgust.

Why was power and authority so attractive to some people? Couldn't the twat just let her get on with it, learn by her own mistakes? He just had to show her who was in charge, exercise his non-existent authority, had to prove how clever he was, how much more knowledgeable he was.

"There now. Wasn't too difficult was it?" he asked as patronisingly as possible, still gripping the blonde's wrist, still standing over her, above her, staring at her, dominating her.

With a calmness completely contrary to his current state of mind, David called, "Leave her the fuck alone, Watson."

The deputy supervisor spun away from the girl as if she'd suddenly exploded into flame. He turned to David, his face hot, red, for once in his life caught off guard, unprepared, vulnerable.

David advanced slowly towards them. He held the craft-knife down by his thigh, out of sight. He looked at the girl. "Someone wants you in the warehouse."

"Who–?"

"No idea, but it seemed urgent."

With a final glance at Watson, she stepped away, then all but sprinted towards the back of the store.

This delay had given Watson time to recover.

He strode over, smiling a rather more crooked smile than usual, his head tilted at the same odd angle. "Okay fucker." His eyes widened, his hand moved upwards, fingers curling inwards to leave a solitary, accusatory digit pointing directly between David's eyes. "Just *what* was that all about? How *dare* you speak to me like that?"

David looked at him, beyond the finger, beyond the clenched semi-fist, staring straight into those two dark piggy eyes. "I'll speak to you however the fuck I want to, you dirty pervert bastard."

Surprisingly – or not really considering the moronic personality of the wanker – Watson grinned, seemed excited by David's obvious anger. "Is that so, Thornwood? A 'dirty pervert bastard' hey? Now that's something Mr Stonewall will just *love* to hear about, don't you think?"

Mr Stonewall aka King Tithead aka Store Manager, of course. "Shame you'll never be able to tell 'im."

"Oh yeah pal," Watson snapped, now visibly both irritated and amused by the unforeseen and more-or-less unprovoked outburst. "Just how did you work that out?" He shook his head, the anger suddenly outweighing the amusement. "You know Thornwood I've never liked you, and you've just given me the excuse to see you on the fucking doorstep. Ever since you started, you've had one serious fucking attitude problem, yeah? Maybe there're a few people who'd let it lie, maybe reckon you're too good a worker to see the boot, but not me pal."

Stab the fucker. Stab him and shut him up once and for fucking all.

"No way. You'll never stack another shelf once I've finished with you."

Oh just stab him, shut up his clichéd *bollocks waffle shite fucking cack stab him do it–*

"But don't worry," Watson adopted a falsely sympathetic tone, "I'll be with you in the dole queue – with you to laugh and point and rub your fucking face in the dirt *just who the fuck did you think you were talking to*?"

–do it do it do it–

"One of those little tarts, like that filthy fucking slag you sent off? Fancy a bit of that did you?" He shook his head, eyeing David with piercing contempt. "You wouldn't know what to do, where to look, where to fucking start you shit-fucking little cunt!"

–doitdoitdoitdoit–

Watson raised his eyebrows questioningly. "Thought she was all right, huh? Thought I was trying it on did you? Got a bit jealous, hmm? Bit jealous of all the cunt I can get just by fucking existing which you couldn't get with all the cash in the fucking world? Was that it Thornwood? Have I just hit the nail on the fucking head *or what*?"

doitnow DO IT NOW!

His brain seemingly overloading with the enormity of the situation, his adrenaline pumping faster than ever before, his heart beating wildly, breath coming in huge gasps, David raised his arm, glanced down at the wicked blade, looked back up at Watson and–

STOP

–THRUST!

Yet with the movement a scream, his own: "NO!"

Incredibly, he managed to stop his arm – to carry out his own command – with less than an inch to spare.

The tip of the blade was actually prodding his supervisor's shirt.

A clockless moment later, David Thornwood dropped the craft-knife, collapsed to the floor, and started to cry.

THERE WERE QUITE A FEW MOMENTS BEFORE David realised Watson wasn't responding to his arse-licking apologies and meaningless moans.

He was still on the floor, still in a heap, still tugging at the semi-flares of Watson's trousers, the tears still coming, not as uncontrollable as before but still there, streaming down his face and breaking down the barrier he'd built up for most of his life.

He had been proud of his emotionless façade.

But now it had all gushed out – and was still gushing – he'd be blubbing in front of some wooden soap opera before he could blink.

The craft-knife was on the floor in front of him, lying

there as if disappointed it hadn't been put to any particular use.

Everything around him was silent. As if the world had hushed up, its breath held in anticipation of what he would do next.

Himself, he hadn't a clue. What could be done? He'd just kissed his job goodbye, and had no doubt got an attempted assault charge into the bargain.

Apologise and apologise, mumble and mumble: it was all he seemed capable of doing. Yet Watson wasn't responding much. No doubt revelling in the power, the lovely lovely power, towering above that prick Thornwood, the guy damned near licking his boots!

Okay, stand up, show him you've at least got some semblance of dignity.

He pushed himself up onto his knees, his head bent down, his face a portrait of misery. "Look please," he began, not really sure how he would finish, "I just got a bit... carried away, didn't mean anything..."

Deputy Twilight Supervisor Scott Watson did not respond.

Didn't move a muscle. Just stood there, towering above him, frozen. In shock? David didn't think so. The man seemed statue-like.

It was about this time he started to seriously consider the silence. He and Watson hadn't raised their voices that much (there were still a few customers wandering around after all, and we couldn't have them upset by irate shelf-fillers and authoritarian supervisors, oh no perish the thought!), and the biscuit aisle was fairly popular – or as popular as dilapidated supermarket aisles went, anyway – yet the silence which surrounded them now was undeniably eerie.

Even the pigshit-thick Tannoy announcer had given up, maybe realising the customers who had heard her and her shamelessly exaggerated Geordie accent struggling through the list of reduced fresh bread products, were exactly the same customers who heard her when she repeated the announcement thirty seconds later. Mind you, even so, five minutes rarely went by in this shithole without sometwat's better half phoning the office and wondering what time they'd be home for din-dins or whatever. "Fern cull on lie-nuh won fur Mistah Ster– uh, hah-hah, shit uh, Sternwal, thank–" snigger, snigger, "youuu!" Christ, one day he was going to put his fist through every single cheap tinny speaker.

And where were the shuffling OAPs, like alcohol-free man? The half-pissed teenagers, desperate for a final seven-hundred mils before blackout? The fat fuck security guard, wandering around looking as dazed as those he was meant to be chucking out?

There was absolutely no noise whatsoever.

Actually that was a lie: he could still hear the dairy fridges whirring away, and the freezers at the other end of the store.

The lone chattering of a checkout receipt printer.

Just as he looked up and saw Scott Watson staring off into the middle distance with eyes bulging madly, the noise of the printer ceased.

Watson's jaw had drooped considerably, and his hands were starting to come up from his sides. Either he was taking the piss, or there was something very wrong standing right behind David.

Christ this was it, the axe-wielding maniac come to disembowel them all, unless they handed over twenty cases of McVitie's digestives ("–and you fucks better make sure they're the plain chocolate ones, too!").

He spun around on his knees, simultaneously skidding away from the nutcase and grabbing the craft-knife while he was at it, and was so impressed by his own execution of the manoeuvre was rather disappointed when he saw there was no one there.

There was someone in the opposite tributary aisle – coffees, teas, sugars, flours – frozen in the act of picking up the jagged pieces of a broken Horlicks jar, but apart from that, no one.

David turned back to Watson, and actually wasn't really surprised to see the man in exactly the same position as before. He might have found this peculiar, but it wasn't half as peculiar as what he could see down the opposite aisle.

Mr Teas, Coffees, Other Dried Drinks and Home Baking (Sweet) was having a hell of a time. It looked to David like he'd just slid a tray of Cadbury's drinking chocolate onto the shelf, inadvertently triggering a chain reaction, culminating in the demise of the Horlicks fixture.

Tumble tumble, shatter shatter: a lovely mess (and one you got used to in this gangrenous cunt of a job).

Only, not all the jars had collapsed at quite the same moment. No doubt a few had held back, waiting for a more opportune moment to fall (say, the manager walking past, or maybe that smart lass you were trying to impress).

And so here the poor lad was, down on his knees, his fingers gingerly grasping at a dagger-like shard of glass, while directly above him, and more-or-less in line with his head, was one of two final jars of Horlicks, frozen in mid-descent.

David stared at this peculiarity for quite some time.

The jar remained motionless. So did the lad below it. And, when David turned back and looked up, so did Watson.

Quickly he pushed himself into a standing position, determined to get all this bollocks sorted out. It just wasn't the sort of thing you expected on a Monday evening during those few hours of hell known as work.

Looking Watson directly in the eye (and god, the guy wasn't even focusing on anything, wasn't twitching, wasn't trembling, breathing, *anything*), he demanded, "Stop fucking around you prick. Hey Watson, can't you hear me?" He pocketed the knife and started waving a hand in front of his supervisor's face.

Then he leaned back, and threw a punch, his fist stopping perhaps an inch or two from the man's nose.

Lord Tithead did not even flinch.

Aware he was on the verge of freaking out, on the verge of screaming out loud and not stopping until someone told him what the fuck was going on, David turned around and walked along to Horlicks Boy. As he crossed the central aisle, he noticed one of the aforementioned OAPs, gazing disinterestedly at a side-stack of bleach. He, like Watson and Horlicks Boy, was absolutely motionless.

There was something going on here, David decided, and he didn't like it one tiny bit.

Christ. There was another lie.

Truth be told, he thought he kind of *did* like it.

There was a strange sensation inside him, a tingling, the tingling of excitement; his heart too, beating faster, anticipating what could maybe turn into some fun and games, adrenaline once more released into his bloodstream… But what the fuck was he thinking? Surely he couldn't be accepting whatever had happened already? Or was he now merely relying on gut instinct? Reacting as if he had no intelligent mind to contemplate the whys and hows?

He reached Horlicks Boy.

The poor lad was wearing an expression of such pain and misery you half expected a dark cloud hanging above his head.

Instead, a jar of Horlicks.

David reached out and grabbed it.

As soon as he touched it, its weight seemed to increase instantly, and he had to grip it tight in case it slipped. He looked at it, threw it up and down a few inches, confirming it really was just a glass jar full of powdered malt drink.

Then, he held it above the floor, and carefully let go.

It shot downwards and detonated against the hard vinyl flooring like a water bomb, glass and sandy-coloured powder exploding outwards in a really rather decorative starburst.

David was glad he'd stepped out the way.

He wondered if the smash, all the more sudden and shocking in the abnormal quiet, would bring anyone running.

He slowly got down on his knees and looked at Horlicks Boy. He seemed pretty young, but with his twisted face could've been pushing thirty. The moronic military-style haircut didn't help matters, either. David nudged his arm, asking, "You playing silly twats, huh? Huh?" He started pushing harder when he didn't get a response, and Horlicks Boy toppled over sideways.

David leaped to his feet, sure the game was up, sure he'd be knocked out for not being able to take a joke, but Horlicks Boy just lay there, in exactly the same position as he'd been in on his feet, only now resting on his side.

It looked so bizarre, so blatantly physically *impossible*, David stepped over him, his gaze fixed straight ahead, and went to find someone who might know what in fuckery was going on.

As he walked parallel to the combination butchery-delicatessen-bakery, he tried not to notice the motionless girls behind the counter standing around in a huddle, laughter and smiles frozen on all three faces.

He reached the end of the counter, ignored the little grinning kiddie paused about three feet in the air, pushed open a door marked

STA F ONL !

then walked along a short corridor and into the warehouse.

The blonde he'd sent away from the biscuit aisle was there, frozen in the act of chatting to an utter cockhead David only knew (for what reason he hadn't a clue) as Tampon Man.

Tampon Man was smiling cheesily as the biscuit girl no doubt tried to assure him she really had been sent back here by someone, and David didn't have to look twice to see the cockhead's eyes were absolutely unarguably locked onto her admittedly-not-unimpressive tits.

He didn't even bother trying to speak to these two.

But just as he was about to head off in the direction of the security office, Tampon Man stirred.

Or rather, farted.

There followed the sound of some liquescent solid pushing its way through something equally squishy and bodily.

Tampon Man was taking a dump.

In his pants.

David would have burst out laughing were it not so disgusting. There the man was, standing in front of a lass, gaping at her tits and shitting his kegs. He'd probably been on his way to the toilet when Biscuit Girl had stopped him, wondering who needed her so urgently. And now out it all slopped. David could actually see it, a big lump against the arse of Tampon Man's trousers.

Looked like that motherfucker'd been brewing for a good few days.

It was then the smell hit him.

Wrinkling his nose in distaste, he hastily retreated to the opposite end of the warehouse, where the security office was.

But before he reached the door, something else caught his eye. Or rather, some*one* else.

Rick Greenhead, easily the most arrogant person David knew.

The lad did even less hours than David, couldn't give a shit whether his work was up to standard – or even if he did any work – nor if any of the supervisors gave him a hard time. It was an attitude David sometimes wished he shared, but the utter immobility of Rick's belief in himself and his superiority over everyone else made him just that little bit difficult to get on with.

At the moment though, David actually felt sorry for the guy.

It was a wonder he'd seen him, he was so far back in the

shadows. He was leaning against a wall, behind a row of stock cages, his mouth open wide, his eyes shut tight.

Clutched in one of his hands was what looked like a snapped off piece of credit card. He was holding it so tight the area of his skin in contact with the card was stark white.

It was genuinely spooky to see him like that. Rick looked like he'd just watched his entire life collapse in front of his eyes. It frightened David so much he could feel the beginnings of a piss.

But no time for that now.

He wanted to get into the security office, see what the hell was going on, why everyone had given up the ability to move (and Tampon Man the ability to control his muscles), and so it was with something akin to anger he discovered the office door firmly locked.

He rattled the handle a while just for the hell of it, then actually started kicking the door, when the pressure down below built up from tolerable to uncomfortable within the space of a few seconds, and he looked around for the nearest pisshole.

Amusingly, Rick Greenhead's gaping mouth filled his vision and would not budge.

But the image quickly reminded him it wouldn't be the first time he'd hidden behind some stock cages and took a slash against the back wall. What a shame Screaming Rick just happened to be in the line of fire this time.

Ripping open his vomit-coloured shelf-filling jacket and

unzipping his fly even as he crossed the warehouse, he promised himself he'd leave the frozen people alone after this: he hadn't a clue what'd happened here, and no doubt there was a chance the frozens had some deadly disease transmitted by touch, but this piss was either shooting out the end of his cock within the next *five seconds* or it was exploding out his bladder of its own accord.

He reached Rick, and started to remove that part of his body of which he was so proud, oh yes so proud, yes indeed.

Three inches at best – and even then only when squinting, even then only after the fifteen degrees centigrade mark – and never put to any more use than the obligatory call of nature and the addictive old five-knuckle.

He whapped the pathetic thing out, freeing his balls in the process, and moved his left arm to prop himself up against Ricky, using him like a drunk holding onto the wall above a urinal.

He took careful aim, then released. It pattered down Rick's work trousers, and started flooding over and into the remarkably expensive-looking shoes he was wearing. David leaned closer to make sure the footwear was blasted by a direct stream.

The thought came to him he might appear slightly strange to some people, a little bit dodgy, perhaps even (certainly given his first thought of pisshole) verging into full-on predatory sex offender territory, but he found himself not really caring: he was so fucking frustrated, even being a piss pervert would propel him miles ahead of his present position in the sex race.

A little smile came to his face at that.

Yes, that was quite amusing.

Maybe if he–

The sound of shattering glass shocked him so much he not only completely lost his train of thought, but also his balance.

He jerked forwards, his foot slipping in his own piss, and found himself mashing his face against Rick's own, as if he'd gone in for a full-on tonsil-tickle. There was a brief moment as he grunted with pain into Rick's mouth, before the useless fucker must've lost his own footing, and started dropping to the floor.

Had they not been snogging at the time, David might've avoided being dragged down with him; as it was, his dead colleague seemed to be embracing him, pulling him closer for more face-sucking as they both collapsed to the pissy concrete.

"TWATTING HELL!"

"HELP, SOMEBODY HE– oh, oh god–"

Just to top it all off, Rick fucking Greenhead – getting the upper hand yet again – managed to land on top of him with a deadhead-butt to the shoulder. At least he'd been able to twist his face away from him.

"Ah shit, SHIT! Please, what's happening here, HELP ME SOMEBODY!"

Quickly he shoved the clumsy twat off and away from

him, pushed himself into a sitting position, and bent down to check he was still in one piece.

And throughout it all the noise from the shop floor: the screaming, yelling, shouts of surprise, the tumble of knocked-into side-stacks, coming closer, moving towards the warehouse.

Miraculously, his cock hadn't been mangled in the cheap fly of his work trousers. He fondled his balls to double-check them as well, before wiping himself clean on Rick's trousers, then carefully pushing the whole lot back out of sight.

Zipping up and standing up, he kicked Rick the Prick in the head.

It slammed back, completely limp and lifeless (David was reminded of Horlicks Boy, frozen in his position even after he'd tumbled over), and was a couple of inches away from soundly rebounding off the wall.

David tried not to feel disappointed.

He knew he shouldn't be taking his anger out on him – after all, he hadn't asked for someone to piss all over him, even after death (if dead he was) – but all the same, the guy was a smarmy twat, and had most likely done any number of equally humiliating deeds which had yet to be avenged.

With a final glance at his useless piss prop (he noticed the broken credit-card-like object had gone, no doubt lost in the tumble), he straightened himself out, buttoned his shelf-filling jacket back up, then went to see who was making all that racket.

He hadn't taken two steps before the warehouse doors burst open, and a young dyed-redhead dived on top of Tampon Man and Biscuit Girl, pleading with them to help her.

David realised this one was in for a bit of a shock.

She grappled with the two frozens a while, tears streaming down her cheeks, her shoulder-length experiment in colour hanging loose and in her face, before realising they were in exactly the same condition as everyone else she'd no doubt jumped on.

David wondered what the matter was. Seemingly she hadn't realised everyone was frozen, yet was still in one hell of a state. Her clothes looked a bit tattered, too. He didn't think he recognised her. Maybe a year younger than himself (who was nineteen), and perhaps in the sixth form up at the high school. He didn't know what it was about those particular girls, he just seemed to have a knack for recognising them.

As for who she was, he hadn't a clue.

"Oh Christ oh Christ oh Christ." She was stumbling away from Tampon Man and Biscuit Girl, her back to David, and he thought it was about time he made his entrance.

"Surely he don't smell that bad?"

She screamed and leaped into the air, swirling around to face him. There was a moment's pause before she once again practiced for the long jump, and almost crushed him in a suffocating bear-hug.

"Oh please, please help, please…" Her words dissolved into a fresh bubble of flooding tears.

David watched her start to slowly slip down his body, her grip either lost or released. By the time she was at his feet, her arms around his legs, her face against his shins, he was feeling rather uncomfortable. "Hey… er, it'll be okay, yeah?"

"Ohhh."

He slowly moved himself down into a crouching position, giving himself the opportunity to rest his hand on her shoulder. She still had her head pressed against his leg, and he looked down at her hair. Even from this close, some of the darker red colours might have passed as natural.

He liked hair.

Liked the way it felt, the way it simply rested there while just about anything and everything went on within the dome it existed to protect. He especially liked looking at it at times like this. Up close, and without its owner realising you were looking.

Not that there'd been many occasions like that within his lifetime, but those he had experienced, he would never forget. It was the intimacy, he supposed.

Something which seemed to be forever denied him.

He wondered if he was brave enough to touch it. Run his fingers through it. Probably shouldn't push his luck, but it was pretty tempting.

The girl seemed to be sorting herself out now, anyway. He watched as she sniffed, then raised her head and rubbed her eyes awhile, perhaps a little too thoroughly, as if struggling to remember why she'd been so upset.

"I'm… I'm sorry, but…"

"It's all right," he assured her, knowing this sort of stuff was expected of him, "there's no need."

"It's just… I mean before, someone… someone…"

She paused to regain her composure, but for David she didn't really have to continue. Her clothes weren't merely the tatters of the latest fake second-hand eco-warrior fashion.

They had been torn, ripped, grabbed and snatched at.

David reached out and finally touched her hair. It felt soft and smooth between his fingers and against his skin. "I'm sorry."

He watched her struggle to hold back more tears, but he didn't mind. She could cry as much as she wanted. Christ, he felt like bawling himself (the barrier's broken down now, just you wait, the next soap opera you watch you'll drown in your own blubbing).

"What… what happened here?"

"I haven't a clue."

She turned to look at Tampon Man and Biscuit Girl. Their positions were slightly different after she'd jumped on them, but they were still frozen, and Tampon Man still looked like he had a deformed arse. "Why aren't they…?"

"Alive?"

"Moving."

"I'm afraid there's a pretty good chance they're dead."

"I know the girl. She's in the sixth form too."

David allowed himself a little smile of victory, his Smart Sixth Form Lass Radar as fine-tuned as ever. "I knew them all."

"You work here?"

No, I'm just wearing this fucking uniform for a laugh, what do you think? The memory of the old fart seemed bizarrely nostalgic. As if that part of his life was now over. "Not anymore."

"Danielle Eastman."

"David Thornwood."

THEY SAT IN THE MIDDLE OF THE WAREHOUSE gangway for quite some time. The silence of the frozen dead surrounded and engulfed them.

David had little difficulty in describing his experience of the initial freeze (carefully omitting the fun and games with Rick), and Danielle, after a few false starts, managed to struggle through her own tale.

She had stayed back after school, arranging to meet with the rest of her drama class to organise some bollocks or other, and afterwards had headed to the Queen's Hall café with one or two girl friends for a milkshake.

It was in there she first saw her attacker.

"He wasn't particularly creepy, but there was something about him, sure. My friends kept whispering about him being a bit Glittery, but I was more worried about our drama project." She smiled at him, for the first time since they'd met. "It's a bit of a full fail at the moment. Anyway, when it was time to go we all went our separate ways, and I forgot all about him. I live up behind the General, and usually walk through your car park then along by the school. It was there he jumped me."

"You don't have to… well you know. Go into any detail."

"There's not much anyway. We struggled a bit, he tore my clothes, I started yelling. He clamped a hand over my mouth, pushed me against a wall. I was seriously panicking, I mean I've never been so scared."

"It's all right now, though: he's frozen isn't he, that's what happened isn't it, how you got away?"

"Yeah. Just as I thought I'd go mad if he didn't stop pawing at me, just as I knew I couldn't take any more, he stopped moving. Froze, if you like. I didn't hang around to see what the problem was, I got free, then headed straight in here. Freaked me completely with everyone just staring at me, ignoring me, not moving. I think I knocked a few things over, smashed some stuff, tried to get their attention, but… I heard you yelling, no doubt as scared as me and… well, you know the rest."

They were silent a while.

Then: "You really think they're all dead?"

He paused before answering, realising the enormity

of what he was about to say. "I… yeah, I think they're all dead. No idea why, no idea why they've just frozen, but…"

"You said there was a jar of something frozen in mid-air above that kid, didn't you?"

"Uh, yeah."

"Weird." She looked at him. "You think it's just Hexham or…?"

He shrugged his shoulders. She had since let him go, but they were still sitting pretty close. "Haven't a clue."

"What about everyone else in here? You sure they're all frozen too?"

"Not given it much thought. Like I said, I just reckoned someone was mucking about. But wouldn't you think they'd've made themselves known by now?"

"I guess."

"So… what do you think we should do?"

She looked at him, smiling slightly, and shook her head. "I don't know. I'm still pretty freaked out. I… I wouldn't mind going home, getting changed, washed…"

"Oh. Oh right, yeah, should've thought. Uh, do you want me to come with you, or…?"

"You don't think I'm walking past that creep on my own, do you?"

"Christ, sorry, forgot, yeah, no problem." He made to stand.

She put a hand on his knee. "Thanks David. Thanks for being alive."

He smiled. "You too. No idea what I would've done on my own."

They both stood, and made their way past Tampon Man and Biscuit Girl.

Danielle paused next to the blonde, studying her. "She doesn't look dead at all."

"They will do. Soon. You can smell the bloke."

She looked at him, then at Tampon Man. "They seem so… helpless." Returning her attention to Biscuit Girl, she reached out a hand and gently touched her shoulder. "She's… she's still warm. Warm… and alive."

David placed his hand on Danielle's, moved it away. He looked her in the eyes. "Not for long."

Letting go of his grasp, she shook her head once more. "Come on."

As they stepped through the automatic warehouse doors, David asked, "Should we get someone's car keys do you think? It'll save time – if time needs saving."

Danielle still seemed preoccupied by Biscuit Girl. "I don't know. Maybe. But what– oh wow."

It was the grinning kiddie mid-leap.

"That just freaks me out," she whispered.

"Yeah, it is kind'f strange." He walked over to the little guy, waved a hand beneath his tiny feet. "Nothing there."

"Try touching him. You know, lifting him down or something."

Tentatively, David reached out, fully expecting the kid to crash to the floor as soon as he touched it. But even when he had his hand gripped around the kid's arm, it was still frozen. He loosened his grip, pulled at the sweater the toddler was wearing.

It behaved like normal material.

Then he grasped the kid's cheek, and pulled it out. He tried to waggle it back and forth. Although it moved slightly, there was an unnatural resistance, as if it were not flesh and skin, but a thin sheet of lead.

He was about to describe this strange sensation to Danielle when the kid just collapsed.

It hit the floor with a rather unpleasant thud. Both legs twisted themselves beneath the torso.

And there the poor thing remained, as motionless and lifeless as before. However, as David bent to take a closer look, he could see the rigidity had for some reason disappeared. To demonstrate to Danielle, he lifted a miniature arm and then let go. It flopped back down to the floor.

"What in hell does that mean?"

He shook his head. "No idea. Somehow they remain frozen for a few moments after being touched, but then: flump. But nonhuman material – like the Horlicks jar and this kid's jumper – behaves normally the instant you touch it. Fucking weird."

Danielle stepped closer and looked down. "Fucking terrifying."

He stood up next to her, his gaze still on the broken child.

"There's his mother," Danielle whispered.

David looked up at a young acne-scarred lass. She was standing in front of a grocery laden trolley, frozen in the act of (presumably) admonishing her offspring for leaping around. Her mouth was twisted as she yelled the command, and the hand which wasn't gripping the trolley was outstretched, a finger pointing directly at the place the toddler had been.

He walked over to the young woman and took hold of her arm. Like Biscuit Girl and the flying toddler, she was still warm.

After a number of seconds, her arm drooped downwards in his grip, her whole body instantly succumbing to the force of gravity.

He struggled to right her again. "Shit, I didn't mean..." Realising he couldn't do anything now she'd flumped, he tried to dump her on the floor as carefully as possible.

Danielle stepped over to him and said, "Leave her. You were right. They're all dead."

Red-faced and uncomfortable, he stood up and, without another glance at either mother or child, strode off down the frozen food aisle. "The manager's office'll be our best bet: once we've got his keys, we'll just have to find the most expensive car in the car park."

Danielle struggled to keep up. "It's only a few minutes up the road."

"Fuck it. I'm taking his car and wearing it into the fucking ground."

"Christ David, you couldn't've exactly done anything."

He didn't answer.

Reaching the end of the aisle, he crossed the row of checkouts, then headed towards a set of double doors next to the customer toilets. They were marked

STAFF ONLY!

and even that pissed him off: how come it wasn't missing a few letters? Were the warehouse staff and all who used it such a bunch of useless nonentities they weren't even entitled to a new door sign?

He pushed the double doors open, and Danielle scurried in behind him. The manager's office was marked on the left, next to another, unmarked door.

He marched into the room, walked up to the man sitting behind the expansive mahogany desk, and punched him full on in the face.

Danielle let out a little shriek.

Stonewall was still frozen though, so the punch hadn't done as much damage as David would have liked; in fact he'd hurt his fist on the fucker's teeth, and so, as much as he wanted to continue, he ceased the attack before it could properly begin.

"Feel better?" Danielle asked after a few seconds of silence.

David raised his hand, and was dismayed to see it shaking. It looked a bit red, too. He lowered his head, low enough to notice the supermarket manager's desk was actually just a cheap laminated flatpack job. He muttered, "Sorry."

Danielle laughed a little. "It's okay. Guess shelf stacking's not the most satisfying of jobs, huh?"

"That's one way of putting it, I suppose." He looked around, and for the first time noticed his dick-fucking cunt of a Grocery Supervisor, sitting opposite Stonewall, frozen in the act of some serious arse-licking. "Come on, we'll take his car, given me a lift home once or twice, I know what he drives."

Danielle remained silent as he searched for the keys – eventually finding them in his supervisor's right trouser pocket, along with the man's bulging wallet – but then: "Come on David, we don't need that too."

"Might come in useful," he said, busy searching. He smiled a little as he pulled out a clingfilm-wrapped lump. "Hey-hey, the lad wasn't as much of a twat as I thought!" He showed Danielle the sizeable chunk of cannabis resin, then threw the wallet in the face of its owner and pocketed the drug. "Mind you, I suppose there're only two types of people who smoke this shit: dense dickheads with nothing better to do like this wanker, and people with the imagination to get something out of it."

She smiled, almost laughed. "Wow."

"What?"

"Just wondering what the weather's like up there."

"Huh?"

"Nothing. Not judgemental at all. Not that I've ever really thought about it like that."

"Don't suppose it matters much now anyway. You know. If it turns out we're... you know. The only ones."

She looked at him, the smile gone. "You really think that's possible?"

"Well... to be honest, I doubt it. I don't think there'll be many, though. So if we don't find anyone then we might as well be, you know? But the fact we're both still here–"

"Makes it seems likely there'll be more of us."

"Can't wait to get away, huh?"

She smiled again. "It's not that. Really. But... maybe someone knows something. About what's happened."

"Maybe." He jingled the car keys. "Come on. Let's get you home."

They left the manager's office without another word, headed back through the double doors, and started along adjacent to the row of checkouts. There weren't many operators working this time of night, maybe three or four, and all were frozen, most in the act of gossiping to their nearest neighbour, only one of them actually serving a customer.

David realised he'd heard the receipt following this transaction rattling away moments after the freeze.

The customer, a short, scruffy-looking young man, was clutching his purchase, a litre bottle of Virgin Vodka, as if it were a new-born baby.

Danielle seemed not to notice.

They reached the internal automatic double doors, which whirred open. The movement of these doors triggered the outer set, and the two survivors stepped out into the twilight.

They took a few steps then came to a halt.

David caught his breath.

The silence was stunning.

It seemed to hang above the world like some daemonic creature, minute glimmers of noise – music, bangs and clunks, wind through trees – somehow muffled by the non-existence of what would normally be a random drunken Monday evening in the town centre.

"Christ," Danielle began, "that's– Jesus," she exclaimed, lowering her voice almost to a whisper, "it's like I'm shouting at the top of my voice."

"Yeah." David's voice was equally quiet. "I suppose there's a bigger chance we'll bump into someone in this, but it's pretty spooky, like it's the middle of the night or something."

"I just don't know how I didn't notice before."

"You could hardly've been in any state."

Danielle shivered violently. "Let's find this guy's car and get home, huh?"

David nodded.

Since the end of March, the night-time temperature had rarely managed to struggle above five degrees, and this cloudless twilight promised a continuation of the trend.

He led Danielle along the side of the supermarket building, and around the corner to a section of car park rarely used by anyone other than staff (far too far for your average customer to walk). He spotted the battered two-tone Montego parked at an interesting angle next to an over-flowing trolley park. A few of the equally battle-worn trollies had rolled out behind the grocery supervisor's vehicle, and one, its plastic melted and twisted, its metal scarred black, had tipped over, and was resting against a car in the opposite row.

"Flamin' shoppin' trollies," David commented.

Danielle noticed the scorched trolley and smiled. "Ah, the youth of today."

He reached the half-empty row, and started removing obstacles. Danielle was about to help him, but he passed her the car keys instead. "Get the engine going, see if you can find out how the heater works."

"Will you drive?"

"Can't you?"

"Not legally."

"Don't you want to anyway?"

"Not particularly."

"Fine."

She walked over to the car, manually unlocked the driver's door (David recalled his supervisor cursing the fucked central locking), and got inside.

He kicked a final trolley out the way, then decided to

move the torched one too, just in case he had trouble reversing with the stupid angle the Montego had been parked.

Behind him, the car's starter motor turned over an alarming number of times before finally catching. Danielle gave the engine a few revs, then scooted over to the passenger seat.

Having sent the burnt trolley on its merry way towards a dead flowerbed, David went over to the Montego and got behind the wheel.

"You can drive, yeah?"

"Yeah." He yanked it into reverse, dropped the hand-brake, then shot them out the parking space as surely as if there'd been a V12 under the bonnet.

After a shuddering halt, not actually hugely dramatic since they'd only moved a couple of car lengths, Danielle ventured, "Uh what I meant was, you have got a licence?"

"Not that it matters, I suppose." He crunched it into first, gave it a good few revs, and shot away with a pleasing screech-slip-screech sound. "But yeah, I've got one. Thing is, I've never actually had much of a chance to use it, what with getting kicked out the house a month-or-so after passing."

Danielle decided to shut up.

They tore through the car park, bouncing over the raised divider pavements, then slewing around the mini-roundabout and onto the road.

"Hey-hey, I can see I'm going to enjoy this," David said, turning to his passenger and raising his eyebrows.

"Uh," she muttered, "you do realise there's a car in the middle of the road?"

Snapping his head forwards, he let out a little yelp and yanked the steering wheel, screeching the vehicle away from the frozen hatchback with barely a car length to spare. Righting the Montego again, he decreased his speed and said, "Oops."

"Boys and their toys."

He snorted with laughter.

They continued their journey through the east end council estates at a more refined pace, Danielle giving directions as necessary, and they arrived outside the two-bedroomed semi without further incident.

It was with dismay David noticed the lights were on. "Uh Danielle, if there's anyone in there, your family, flat-mates – whatever – well, do you not want me to check or something? I mean, if you think it might be... too much."

She kept her eyes on the house. "I live with my mother and sister. My dad's down south someplace. Both Mum and Michelle should be in." There was an uncomfortable silence before she continued. "But it's okay. I mean, as long as you come in with me. All right?"

"Of course."

She unlocked her door and got out.

Taking the keys with him but leaving the doors unlocked, David joined her on the pavement. "Right then. Ready?"

"I guess." She stepped forwards, removed a bunch of keys from a pocket, then unlocked and opened the front door.

Light and warmth gushed out from within.

Along with a terrible, deafening silence.

Danielle breathed out deeply. "Christ."

"Look, I'd better check… not that I'm exactly looking forward to it, but I don't want you getting any more upset."

She looked at him. "And what about you, David? Who'll do the checking for you?"

His face hardened slightly. "There's nothing to check for." He stepped inside. "Come on. It's warm."

She followed him in, shutting the door behind her.

He turned. "You'd better stay here, but if you hear me freaking out or something…"

"Don't worry."

"Are there any places you don't want me to look, your room or–?"

"You're too thoughtful," she interrupted, smiling. "Michelle and I share. She'll most likely be there. Mum, I don't know." She pointed at a closed door at the end of the hallway. "The kitchen, I suppose. Maybe the lounge."

"All right. I'll check upstairs first. Right. Okay. Here goes." He stepped over to the stairs, and started to climb. About halfway up he paused, breathing heavily.

"You sure about this?"

He nodded. "I'm okay. I'll be fine."

He continued up the stairs, stepped onto the landing, then disappeared into what he assumed was the master bedroom.

It was empty.

Next to that was an airing cupboard, also empty. Glancing back down the stairs, he smiled at Danielle slightly, then tried the next door along.

This was the bathroom.

Where Danielle's sister Michelle was.

Sitting on the edge of the bathtub, naked, her legs spread wide.

She was holding a mirror between her thighs. With her other hand she was reaching down towards herself.

There was quite an intense gaze in her eyes.

David guessed she was maybe twelve or thirteen years old.

He pushed shut the bathroom door behind him.

The bath was full of water and slowly dissipating bubbles. Michelle's underdeveloped breasts were small and pointy.

He wondered if he should put her in the bath. Danielle had expressed an interest in getting clean, but if she went in here and saw her sister's corpse – especially in its current position – who knew how she would react?

But then, if he did move her, Danielle would know: he'd have to wait until Michelle flumped before he could get her into the bath, and even then, would he manage to keep her sitting up straight?

And all before Danielle started to worry and came up to see for herself?

He decided to ban her from the bathroom.

Taking one last glance at Michelle, unable to prevent his eyes from dropping to her delicate smoothness, her sparse dark hairs, he turned around, opened the door and stepped back into the hallway. He closed the door firmly behind him.

Michelle and Danielle's bedroom was empty.

By the time he returned downstairs, the weird churning feeling in the pit of his stomach had started to subside.

Danielle was looking at him worriedly.

"Your sister – Michelle? – was taking a bath. I don't think you should go in. Apart from her, no one."

"My room's okay?"

"Yeah go for it, but remember, the bathroom…" He trailed off, avoiding her eyes.

"Right." She started upstairs.

He looked around. There were three doors off the downstairs hallway: the one at the end Danielle had indicated was the kitchen, and two on the left, opposite the staircase. There was another underneath the stairs, but David just assumed it was a cupboard.

He opened the first door on the left, and stepped into the sitting room. It was smartly decorated and very neat, its curtains shut against the outside world.

It was also empty of the girls' mother.

He noticed a door into the dining room, which he assumed he could also access by the second door on the left in the hallway, but there was no one in there, either. The lights were off, too.

So. The kitchen it is.

He went back into the hallway, and stepped over to the final door. Light spilled out from between door and doorframe.

Grasping the handle, he carefully pushed it open.

BY THE TIME DANIELLE RETURNED DOWNSTAIRS David had organised two mugs of coffee, and was busy hunting for something to eat.

He turned when he heard the door open.

She had changed into dark-blue jeans and an equally dark, cosy-looking jumper, either consciously or sub-consciously using the baggy garment more for protection than warmth. She had tidied her hair, washed the streaks of salt from her face.

David waved at the coffees, the cupboard he'd opened. "Er, hope you don't mind, I just thought we could, you know, do with something." He was genuinely apologetic at having helped himself.

"No problem," Danielle told him, and with those two words, David knew she had been in the bathroom.

Mortified, he could feel his cheeks instantly glowing with heat, but she didn't notice: her gaze was elsewhere, deliberately avoiding his eyes.

Although he knew it would embarrass them both, he had to say something. If they were to see through this nightmare together, they needed to maintain something which at least vaguely resembled a trusting relationship. "You know, I uh, I did advise against it."

This time she returned his stare. "Yeah." She nodded. "Guess I should've paid more attention, huh?"

"Guess so." There was silence as he returned to the cupboard, took out a packet of cakes, and dumped them on the bench next to the drinks. "Didn't know how you took it," he explained, gesturing to the mug of black coffee.

"A little milk and it'll be fine."

He poured in some semi-skimmed from the bottle he'd found in the fridge, stirred it, then passed the mug over. "Listen, let's just forget about it, okay? We can't be falling out over stuff, we need to start thinking what in hell we're going to do next. Yeah?"

She took the drink and nodded again, slowly this time. "Yeah. Okay." The other coffee was sat on the bench next to the kettle, and she clunked her mug against it. "Still friends, David." She turned to the door to the hall, which she'd left open. "Safe to go in the lounge?"

"Oh shit yeah, I couldn't find your mother, she's nowhere, must've gone out or something." He shrugged his shoulders at her look of surprise. "Not in the lounge, not in the dining room, not in here. There's noplace else, is there?"

"Uh no, no," she muttered, shaking her head, obviously puzzled. "She never usually, you know, never goes out or anything, especially at night, I just…"

"Well maybe, I don't know, no news is good news?"

She looked at him for a moment, grabbed the cakes, then said, "Come on. We've got some shit to work out."

David watched her disappear into the hallway, then grabbed his coffee and followed.

She was waiting outside the lounge door, unsure about entering. He gestured for her to go in, and after a pause she gripped the handle tightly, and started pushing the door slowly open.

By the time he reached her, he could see she was genuinely afraid.

He touched her arm. She flinched, slopping coffee.

"Let me," he offered.

Gratefully, she stepped out the way, and waited until he returned with the all clear.

Shutting the door behind them, they each took a seat, David in the armchair opposite the front window and to the right of the dining room door, Danielle curled up on one side of the couch against the hallway wall and to the right of the lounge door.

It was Danielle who realised it first.

"The fucking television!"

David decided to make light of it. "Come on, I hardly think we've got time to worry about the wankers in Albert Square."

Ignoring his lame joke, she put down her mug and reached for the remote control. "There's got to be something on about it, a news-flash, on-scene reporting, Christ the entire week dedicated to it considering how much bullshit they broadcast about Lady fucking Di – and there're how many thousands living here? – god, we'll be on until the next century."

Disregarding her equally awkward humour, David seriously considered the possibility. "You think so? I mean, how would anyone know?"

Instead of answering, she crushed a button on the remote, jabbing it towards the television set as if expecting a laser to shoot out the end instead of an infrared beam.

The television tuned into BBC2.

Shitty snooker.

Live action from the Crucible in Sheffield.

Only, it didn't seem very lively to David and Danielle, and as for action…

They were frozen, too.

Alan McManus and David Gray.

The audience.

Everyone.

Tyne Tees was broadcasting as normal, *Coronation*

Street, as was BBC1, something presented by that personality vacuum Gary Lineker.

Channel 4 was in the middle of the evening news. Jon Snow was frozen solid.

Danielle turned the television off.

"No Channel 5?" David whispered.

"Welcome to Hexham," Danielle replied, equally quietly.

She dropped the remote and picked up a golden syrup cake bar. She tore off the wrapper and started to eat.

David watched her, wondering if she wanted to cry as much as he did. His face felt numb, and the sensation was creeping down his entire body, tingling his skin and chilling his insides.

The entire country had frozen.

He felt like he needed to sneeze: his nose was itching, his eyes starting to water, his mouth dry. The room, previously fairly warm and comfortable, now felt cold and claustrophobic.

The entire country had frozen.

He slurped at his coffee. It had started to go cold already.

Danielle threw the rest of the Lyle's cakes at him. He caught them, removed one, its wrapper, then shoved it whole into his mouth.

It was tasteless.

"What…" Danielle began, "what do you think…?"

"Leh," he replied, spraying cake crumbs. He chewed a

bit more, then took another gulp of coffee. He swallowed. "Let's just say they've tasted better."

She twisted her face. "Not the bloody cake, the... whatever. Freeze. The entire country. The world? You think? Or...?"

He shrugged his shoulders. "Does it matter?"

She stared at him, agape.

"Okay, maybe that came out wrong: what I meant was, do you think it changes our position here? Whether it's just Hexham, Northumberland, the UK, Europe? We're still here, now, we still have to deal with it, what's happening over in America or South Africa or someplace doesn't have much bearing on it, does it?"

"But if they're still all right, they could do something, revert the process maybe, or at the very least get us out."

He looked at her. "You don't read much, do you? Don't watch many films, many episodes of *The X-Files*?"

There was silence before she replied evenly, "What the hell are you talking about?"

"It's nothing specific, but generally when there's some global crisis or disaster, no one gives much of a fuck about anyone except themselves."

She narrowed her eyes, shook her head. "Come off it David, that's just some pervy writer getting his wank fantasies down on paper or on the telly. It's different in real life. People stick together. It's what they do. What they've basically always done."

"You think?"

"Look, just what're you trying to say here?"

"I'm saying we're on our own. Somehow we've survived, we're alive, but as far as we can tell we're the only ones. It's no use headfucking ourselves working out the whys and hows. We're on our own. Everyone else is dead. End of story."

Danielle reached down for her coffee. He watched her drain the mug. When she was finished, she breathed out heavily. "What's the plan, then?"

He shook his head. "I really don't know."

"Do you have anyone you want to–"

Before she could finish, he interrupted, "No."

Lines creased her forehead. "What… no one?"

"What about you?" he asked, ignoring the question. "Do you want to call your friends or something, the rest of your family?"

"Well I was wondering if we should even bother, I mean, the chances of them being alive…"

"Yeah. And even if they did survive, the chances they stayed at home, just waiting for someone to find them…"

She nodded. "Mmm."

"But we probably still should, right?"

She smiled, looking relieved. "Yeah. I mean, we have to try, anyway."

"Anyone specific?"

"Becky. My best friend. Lives up Causey Hill. Haven't seen her the past few weeks, she's been spending all her time with Rick recently."

David stared at her, his goosebumps suddenly returning. "Don't tell me... you don't mean Rick Greenhead?"

She nodded. "Yeah. They've been seeing each other for ages. God knows what she sees in him, the bloke gives me the creeps."

"Jesus," he breathed. Rick Pissy Shoes Greenhead. Would the guy ever leave him in peace?

"Oh yeah forgot, he works with you, doesn't he?"

"Well we're both shelf-stackers if that's what you mean. God, Rick bloody-minded complete twat smarmy git show-off wanker Greenhead. Small fucking world."

She smiled. "What's so amazing?"

"Oh nothing, not really," he said, the image of Rick covered in piss and going in for a tongue sandwich crystal clear in his mind.

"You don't happen to know–?"

"Oh yes," he interrupted, "he's dead all right. Bit weird too, looked like he was screaming his head off when he froze."

"'Bit weird,' yeah, that just about sums him up. Becky was absolutely head over heels, though. Reckoned there was something really special about him."

"Twelve-inch cock, probably," he joked.

"You really think so?"

"Come off it. Well, one way to check I suppose."

"Ugh god, no thanks."

Their laughter soon lapsed into an uncomfortable silence. After a few moments, David stood up. "Let's go check on her, then." He turned around, grabbing the rest of the cake bars from where he'd dumped them. "Take the last of these?"

"Yeah," she said, standing. "Think we need anything else?"

"Actually, I wouldn't mind a coat if you've got one spare, this thing's freezing," he said, gesturing down at the vomit-coloured shelf-filling jacket he still wore.

"Okay. Torches or anything? I don't know, what're we likely to be doing?"

David smiled. "The world is your oyster."

"Shame it's a dead oyster."

"Mmm," he agreed, not really sure how to reply.

"Right, well I'll get some stuff, you might as well turn the car around or something." She opened the door and stepped into the hallway. David followed. "Won't be a minute," she assured him, and disappeared upstairs.

He wondered if she was going to say goodbye to her sister.

He opened the front door and stepped outside.

It seemed even colder than before, if that were possible, and during the time they'd spent indoors, night had truly fallen.

At the driver's door of the Montego, he stopped for a moment, looking up and down the street, the unnatural silence affecting him once more.

He was about to open the door when he heard the dog barking.

It sounded extremely close, but then he supposed in the quiet of the frozen dead, the sound could easily have travelled from the other end of town. He was still wondering what to do about it when the lights in the house winked off, one by one, and a moment later Danielle appeared on the doorstep, clutching a few things in her hands.

She shut the door, locked it, then went to join him. She handed him a heavy ski jacket, almost identical to the one she was now wearing. "I got some more food, couldn't find a torch, but thought these might come in useful." She held up a packet of firework rockets. "You know, use them like a flare or something."

"Right, great." He checked his jacket pockets – transferring his craft-knife onto the car roof, leaving his pens and a roll of tape – before dumping it onto the road. He pulled on the ski jacket. It was slightly small, but anything was an improvement on the vomit-coloured paper-thin shelf-filling jacket. He put the craft-knife into one of the front pockets. Danielle opened her door, and was about to get in when he told her about the dog.

"What?"

"A dog. Barking. It's quit now, but it sounded pretty close."

She looked around. "Do you think we should look for it?"

"I don't know. The sound could've travelled from anywhere. We might be searching for hours."

She nodded. "Yeah. I guess."

She got into the car, and David did likewise. He removed the keys from a trouser pocket and started the engine. The handbrake off, he reversed towards the other side of the road, then shot forwards again, back the way they'd come.

There were more cars on the main street.

He had to weave in and out of the frozen vehicles, their frozen occupants gazing blindly out the windows or engaged in static conversation.

It started to creep him out a bit.

Safe in Danielle's house, it really hadn't seemed as bad as he'd first thought.

Now he realised it was much much worse.

Pedestrians were frozen on the pavements. Frozen in groups outside shop fronts.

The pizza place opposite the bus station had already attracted the attention of a large group of feral-looking lads, as well as a hatchback police car parked in the bus station itself. The officers within would be staring at the group of youths for eternity.

And all around them it seemed life went on.

Lights burned from within buildings, streetlamps cast their horrible orange glow, vehicle headlights blazed. Some boy-racer's bass-heavy tune blasted from one of the cars. The wind rustled the hair of the frozen.

David came to a halt between the bus station and pizza place.

The road ahead was blocked.

He reversed a few feet, then swung the car to the left, driving over the wide pavement in front of an off-licence. The Montego's left-hand wing mirror almost clipped a man frozen just outside the shop, his blue-bagged purchases gripped tightly in his arms, his skin already drained of the colour of life.

Further up the street, they passed a pink Nova hot-hatch from which the latest happy hardcore megamix was blasting.

Weaving the car this way and that through a jumble of frozen vehicles at the Beaumont Street junction, David was inspired by the blasting music to flick on the Montego's own radio.

The automatic search started scanning the bandwidth, static filling the car.

It seemed to get louder with every passing second.

Danielle turned the machine off. "For god's sake David, we don't need reminding."

"I just thought…" He trailed off. He didn't know what he'd just thought. Everyone was frozen. End of story.

He'd said so himself.

They reached the end of the main street and, noticing the Allendale Road junction looked totally blocked, David turned into a side road he knew would take them to Causey Hill.

"Better start giving me directions," he advised.

A few minutes later they were parked in the drive of a large, modern-looking detached house, a world away from Danielle's small terraced council property.

David stopped the engine, and removed the key. One or two lights burned from within, he noticed, as had the lights in most homes they'd passed.

He wondered how long it would be before the electricity ran out.

They both got out the car, and Danielle walked up the rest of the drive and over to the front door. She pressed the doorbell, held her finger there a few seconds.

David hung back a bit. "Should I wait here or...?"

She turned, gestured for him to join her. As she watched him jog over, she said, a little unkindly perhaps, "Do you honestly think they're going to give a shit who I'm with? In the midst of all this?"

"I know. I just thought–" He grimaced. He was going to have to stop this 'just thinking' business.

She turned back to the door. No one had answered. There'd been no sign of movement from within. The door had no handle, you could only open it from this side with a key, but she pushed it anyway in case they'd left it off the sneck.

No such luck.

"I'll check around the back," he offered, and walked over the grass, around the right-hand side of the building.

A trellis-topped fence blocked his path.

He went back around the front, but Danielle must have already gone around the left-hand side of the building, probably quietly chuckling at his mistake.

He really didn't know what to make of her.

Yeah, she was nice enough to look at, and after she'd done herself up at her place looked pretty damned stunning, but he just couldn't work her out at all. One minute she was nice, they seemed to have something going between them, but then the next she acted as if she wished they'd never met.

And of course the fact she'd blatantly ignored him and gone into the bathroom still pissed him off.

She'd been the one scared of discovering a body, wanting him to make sure the coast was clear, he'd told her specifically where her sister's corpse was, yet she'd gone ahead anyway to check for herself.

He felt there was something strange about her, a little weirdness which hadn't yet shown its face, a perversity almost, but it was impossible to tell just what it was.

He could probably cope, though. The world as fucked-up as it was, he had a funny feeling they'd be meeting other survivors who might end up making Danielle look positively angelic.

He wrinkled his forehead.

That actually hadn't been as comforting a thought as he'd intended it to be.

The porch light came on, there was some scrabbling

from within, and then the girl in question flung open the door, her eyes wide, and gasped, "You'd better get in, and you'd better do it *quick*."

The fact she was looking over his shoulder as she spoke had something to do with the speed at which he dived through the doorway.

Behind him, Danielle slammed shut the door, the lock clacking into place.

"What is it, what is it?" he hissed, panicky.

"Over the road," she replied in a whisper, turning, "a light in one of the downstairs windows just went off. I saw it through the fish-eye."

"What were you looking through there for?" he demanded, his heart still beating wildly.

"To see where you were. Didn't know whether you'd followed me or not."

"Oh. Right." He stepped up to the door, took a few deep breaths to try and regulate his breathing, then put his eye to the lens.

The eye which looked back at him was huge, bloodshot, distorted.

He jerked backwards as if he'd just taken a shotgun blast to the chest.

Danielle leaped into the air herself, stifling a scream.

He turned to her, his face bleached white. "There was… there was…"

She looked from David to the door, then back to David again, her eyes wide as she realised what he meant.

"Just behind the… he's just behind the fucking door!" He stepped even further away.

In front of him, Danielle was staring, rigid with fear, as the letterbox slowly opened, pushed from the outside.

From his position, David was able to bend down a little and look through the widening gap, and once more found himself peering into those two horrendously bloody eyes. "Shut it," he whispered.

Danielle moved closer, her arm outstretched. David was wondering whether he'd ever be able to shift his gaze from those hypnotic red orbs, when she slammed the letterbox shut.

There was silence from behind the door.

No yell of pain, no growl of anger.

Nothing.

"Okay, what do you reckon?" Danielle whispered.

He shrugged his shoulders, shook his head, whispered back, "Haven't… haven't a clue. But no one who looks like that gives up easily."

She leaned over to the fish-eye, moving slowly towards it, ready to retreat at the slightest sign of anyone. By the time she pressed her eye to the lens, she still hadn't moved away. "He's… he's gone, I can't see him anywhere."

There was silence.

Suddenly she jerked back and turned to him, screeching, "The back door!"

As one, they turned to the darkness of the downstairs hallway. From beyond, light spilled through from what

David assumed was the kitchen. "Through there?" he asked.

"Yeah," she confirmed, her voice quiet, shaky, "David I didn't shut it, I didn't know whether you were following, I didn't shut the door!"

"It's okay, it'll be all right, I'll just check it out, he'll be long gone." His words were reassuring; his voice as fearful as Danielle's.

The house – the night, the world – was as silent as ever as he made his way falteringly along the hallway towards the light.

Surely the red-eyed guy couldn't have known to go around the back? But if he'd been watching them, he'd have certainly seen Danielle head in that direction then a few moments later appear at the front door…

He stopped in his tracks, realising there was a very real possibility the red-eyed man was at this precise moment carefully choosing the kitchen knife with the longest blade.

And then he heard it: heard *him*.

Shuffling along the kitchen floor, advancing slowly.

And muttering.

Mumbling.

The ranting of the insane.

David turned back to Danielle, who was still watching him intently, and pointed frantically at the kitchen.

She in turn started gesticulating towards the stairs, which she moved towards once she thought he'd got the message.

But it was slightly more difficult than that.

Any movement David made, the red-eyed maniac would be able to hear no problem: the man was deliberately being quiet, yet David could hear him clearly enough. And then the shuffling would turn into sprinting, the mumbling would turn into screaming, the knife would be raised…

He couldn't exactly defend himself against a knife though, could he?

The sweat was really starting to pour, now.

His heart was slamming horrendously.

The shuffling came closer.

Behind him, halfway up the stairs, Danielle was hissing for him to get a shift on.

It was the red-eyed madman's shadow that finally got him moving.

It creeped upwards, slowly engulfing the rectangle of light pouring into the hall, and David decided to just get the hell away and fuck the consequences.

Leaping up the stairs, taking two or three steps at a time and almost knocking Danielle flying, he was having trouble stopping himself screaming out loud, but soon realised he'd made enough noise for the red-eyed psycho to come running, to come lolloping into the hallway, to look around drunkenly, and for him to mutter, "Hey man, way-out…"

David stopped in his tracks.

Danielle stood gaping.

The intruder, the red-eyed maniac, the guy David had just spent the last few minutes crapping his pants about, looked maybe fifteen or sixteen years old, was dressed in blue jeans and denim jacket over a white tee-shirt, and absolutely stank of marijuana smoke.

He was looking around in a complete daze, pointlessly running his hand through the close cropped dirty-blonde almost-ginger haircut he sported.

David looked at him a moment longer, then collapsed to the stair treads and started giggling.

The boy turned to him, jaw drooping low, and started laughing himself. "Madness, huh? Absolute... madness."

Danielle turned her attention from the boy to David, then back to the boy.

"Madness," the boy assured her.

"Jesus... Jesus," David was gasping, pointing.

"Just insane, man. Just... insane."

"We thought... we thought you were some *nutcase* or something!"

"Hey man," the boy said, trying to sound offended, "not me. No way. Nope. Not at all."

"Wait a minute, wait a minute," Danielle said, sensing there was something essential missing from the conversation, "just what the fuck were you playing at?" Although her words were harsh, she spoke like she was commenting on the weather, unsure if she should be annoyed or not.

"I seen yous man, I seen yous. He went around the wrong way!" he yelped, pointing at David. Struggling with another fit of giggles, he moved his finger to Danielle. "And you knew, you knew, yet you said nothing!" This time, he couldn't hold back the laughter.

"For Christ's sake," Danielle muttered.

"I seen yous man, I seen yous!"

"But how…?" David began, leaning forwards, grinning. "How'd you survive the freeze?"

The young lad looked a bit puzzled at that one, but then something seemed to click. "Oh man, is that what it was? A freeze? Hey man, I was seriously tripping out, you know? Couldn't've told you what in hell I did."

Danielle started down the stairs, and walked towards him. He was watching her warily. She stopped about two feet away, leaned even further forwards, and demanded, "You know everyone's dead though, don't you? You know we're so far the only ones left, don't you? You're not too fucked in the head to realise that, are you?"

Not bothering to wait for an answer, she stormed off into the kitchen.

The boy and David exchanged glances.

David shrugged. "She gets a bit… annoyed sometimes."

"Hey man," the boy grinned, attempting to raise his eyebrows in a knowledgeable nudge-nudge kind of way, "if she was mine, I'd let her get as annoyed as she wanted."

David smiled, but said, "I don't think she's anybody's."

"No?"

"No."

"Then how come yous're together? Just mates?"

He wrinkled his face. "Sort of. I'd like to think so. But truth is, we only met each other tonight, just after the freeze."

The youngster shook his head. "What is this freeze thing, man? It sounds kind'f… intense."

"Yeah, you could say that." He paused. "You know what Danielle was saying before? You remember, when she was shouting at you?"

"Uh… about people, like, dying?"

He nodded. "Yeah."

"Whoah."

David watched the younger lad carefully, wondering how he would react. Then he realised there were only two ways you could react to something like that when stoned: get completely paranoid and start tripping off and freaking out, or otherwise just basically ignore it, take everything as it comes, mellow out man. He started smiling again as he remembered his own marijuana-smoke-stained youth.

Then he remembered the deal he'd nabbed off his supervisor in Stonewall's office. "Hey," he said, digging around in his trouser pockets, "what do you reckon of this?" He brought out the tac and threw it down to the lad.

Clutching it between two fingers, the boy's eyes widened (which wasn't actually very amazing, considering how much like slits they were to start with). "Wow, pretty cool ounce man, is that what you paid, fifty smackers?"

David shook his head. "Want to know what I paid?"

The boy looked up expectantly.

"Bugger all."

"Hey man, take me to your dealer."

David laughed. "No, nothing like that I'm afraid. Here," he prompted, his hand outstretched.

The boy passed back the deal, gazing after it longingly. Then he looked up at David once more. "So the babe's called Danni – what about you?"

David smiled. "Yeah, she's all right isn't she?"

"In this town, she's off the scale, man."

David stuck out his hand over the bannisters. "David. Dave. Whatever."

The young lad reached up and took it. They shook. His hand was warm.

"Dustsheet," he said. "I get called Dustsheet." He smiled, shook his head a little. "Just don't ask me why, man."

David laughed, dropped his hand. "I can live with that."

Dustsheet looked around, curious. "So what brings you here, Dave my man?"

"One of Danielle's friends lives here. Becky."

"Becky, yeah." He started grinning. "Her bedroom faces onto the street. She always leaves a little gap in the curtains when she's getting ready. Makes you wonder if she knows I'm out there, huh?"

David stared at him, astounded. "You watch her get undressed?"

"Oh sure," Dustsheet laughed. "She's almost as hot as your Danni."

"Christ."

"Matter of fact, I was up in my room before, watching. She was getting ready to go out someplace. Must've been something wrong though, she was in a right old state. Spending too much time with that dickhead boyfriend, you ask me."

"Rick Greenhead?"

"That's him. Real creepy guy. Kind'f freaked me out sometimes, 'specially after a few buckets. But–"

Danielle coughed to get their attention. She was standing in the kitchen doorway.

"How long've you been there?" David wondered.

"Doesn't much matter," she replied, staring at Dustsheet. "I could hear everything from the kitchen."

"Oh."

"Hey I didn't mean nothing, just–"

"Yeah, whatever," she interrupted, walking past him and stopping at the bottom of the stairs. She looked up at David. "You going to help me search the house, or are you too busy chatting to your buddy here?"

He gave her what he hoped was a meaningful look before answering, "I'll search upstairs. You and Dustsheet can do downstairs if you want, but be warned: you find anyone, they'll be frozen."

"How can you be so sure?"

He tilted his head at an angle. "Come on. The noise we've been making?"

Danielle lowered her eyes, realising. But then: "Unless they've already run away…"

"Well, let's hope so."

"C'm'on Danni," Dustsheet began, rather jovially for someone who'd just revealed he liked spying on her best friend, "let's do what we've got to do."

David went upstairs.

There was a small half-landing near the top, and the rest of the steps, only about three or four, continued ninety degrees to the left. It was even darker up here than downstairs, so he felt along the wall and found a set of light switches.

He flicked them all.

Both the upstairs and downstairs halls were instantly illuminated. He looked around and could see five doors, all of them closed. One of them had wooden slats, and he assumed it led to an airing cupboard. He turned right, and opened the door at the end of the hall.

His heart leaped a little as the bathroom came into view, but there was no one there. He looked at the bathtub, as if expecting to see a little naked girl, her legs spread.

He turned and left.

Coming out the bathroom, the airing cupboard door was to his left, so he turned right, and opened the door of the master bedroom.

The king-size bed was neatly made and empty. The lights were off, the curtains open. He looked out at the rest of the west end estates.

Just looking through the window, he found it difficult to believe the town was dead.

It was only when you heard the silence you knew something was seriously amiss.

The next room along had been turned into a study.

The shelves were piled high with reference books and bulging files. Papers were strewn all over the large desk, almost swamping the old word processor which sat there. Boxes and other junk took up most of the remaining floor-space.

David went around the desk, just to make sure no one was hiding underneath, but he needn't have bothered: there was hardly enough space for someone's legs, let alone the rest of them.

And so he came to the final room, the room at the end of the corridor, the room which looked out onto the street, the room in which the curtains didn't shut properly.

It was locked.

HE'D NEVER PREVIOUSLY HAD ANY PARTICULAR desire to kick down a door in true shit Hollywood action movie style, but now he was faced with having to do just that, he found himself feeling rather excited.

He wondered if he'd be able to make it in one kick.

He looked at the handle. Lever latch and mortice dead-lock.

Great.

Nevertheless, he stepped back, judged the distance, aimed, then booted the door, just beneath the handle.

The door rattled.

His leg damned near rattled, too.

It hadn't been as painful as he'd been expecting –

possibly because he'd known it *would* be painful – but any more blows like that and his leg was likely to seize up.

He heard footsteps from downstairs, then Danielle shouted up, "You all right?"

"Uh yeah," he called. "Becky's door's locked, that's all."

A few moments later, Danielle and Dustsheet joined him in the hallway.

"There's nothing downstairs," she said.

"Absolutely no one, man," Dustsheet echoed.

David shook his head. "No one up here either, 'cept maybe behind this door."

"Most likely definitely: her mother went apeshit if she went out and locked up behind her."

"And like I said, I was watching her when this… freeze thing froze… or whatever it did."

Danielle glared at him, but remained silent.

"Okay," David said, "that makes it all the more important we get inside. Anyone fancy giving it a good kick while I search the garage, you're welcome."

He stepped between them, and went downstairs. As he descended, he heard Dustsheet comment, "I'm not usually one for destruction, but if that's what the man wants…"

By the time he reached the downstairs hallway, there was a muffled thump, followed by a yell of complaint, and David smiled.

He headed through the kitchen into the laundry. Danielle had since shut and locked the back door, but there was a side-door into the garage, next to the freezer, which he took. He felt around the wall and located the light switch

There was an empty space for a reasonably sized car, but apart from that, the place was even more of a junkyard than the study. Fortunately, he didn't have to scan the mounds of rubbish for too long: the sledgehammer was propped up against a pile of overflowing tea chests.

Navigating his way towards it was another matter however, so he was pretty much pissed off by the time he returned upstairs to Danielle and Dustsheet, the younger youth eyeing up the door as if it had just given him a mouthful of abuse.

"Right, stand back," David ordered, striding along the hallway, the sledgehammer raised.

They moved out the way as he advanced. He was about three feet away when he swung the hammer, pounding it through the top-right section of the door.

The smashed panel didn't even snap off, just hung there precariously. David stepped back then swung again, this time trying to aim for the lock.

He hit it square on, just beneath the handle. The keyhole buckled, the wood beneath it snapped apart, the door trembled, but still it did not burst open dramatically.

Once more, he thought, once more…

This time, he brought the hammer down at an odd angle, against and on top of the handle, and the satisfying snap of crunching doorframe preceded the dismal bump of the door swinging open about two inches.

"I'm sure it would've been better in slow motion and widescreen, but hey," Danielle commented, pushed him aside, and opened the door fully.

The first thing David noticed was the splinters and chunks of wood on the floor.

The second thing was Becky.

It did indeed seem like she was getting ready. She was dressed in knickers, bra, and an open white blouse.

It also seemed like she was in a 'right old state,' just as Dustsheet had said.

She was sitting on the edge of the bed, her hands held out in front of her, her fists clenched tight, her head thrown back and her face twisted into such an expression of concentration, hatred, and anger, David was afraid even to guess what her problem might've been.

Danielle hadn't yet moved, her eyes locked onto the sight of her frozen friend, so David dumped the sledge-hammer and stepped around her to get a closer look.

He glanced up at the window, noticing the gap in the curtains, and it was as he was looking back he saw the thing Becky was holding in her right hand.

He widened his eyes and knelt down before her, study-ing the object up close.

It reminded him of a credit card. Or at least part of one: peering even closer, he could see it had been snapped in half.

It didn't take a genius to work out who had the other half.

Rick get-out-my-life-and-leave-me-alone-okay-I-pissed-all-over-you-but-hey-I-was-desperate-and-you-were-dead Greenhead.

Was the guy destined to haunt him forever?

He reached out and made to pluck the card from her grip. He didn't need to counter-balance her fist: she was still frozen, immobile, and after a few moments wiggling and tugging, the card thing came free.

He looked at it.

It was jet black.

Smooth.

Thicker and, David guessed, a little bit larger than a credit card, he didn't think this had anything to do with banks or banking. Its corners were rounded, as were the edges themselves.

He realised he was starting to shiver, even so soon after messing about with sledgehammers and doors. His hand trembled as he turned the card over.

Jet-black smoothness. Uninterrupted perfection.

Except, of course, for the fact it had snapped in half.

He made to examine the wound– the *wound*?

But that was it.

The thing hadn't been manmade.

It was something far stranger – a natural phenomenon, or–? Or what? What else was there but nature and man?

He didn't know.

The card, however, did appear to have bled from the snapped edge.

A matt-black gunk had leaked out, and had started to dry along the length of the snap. When David touched it, it felt tacky, and made his finger tingle uncomfortably.

"Jesus man," Dustsheet whispered from the doorway, behind Danielle, "this is just so… so ex-*treeeme*."

"What is it?" Danielle breathed.

David shook his head. "I don't– Rick. Fucking Rick Greenhead had the other half in his hand. I saw it. Him. He was screaming, looked terrified, afraid, defeated. He was clutching the other half in his fist."

"Oh man…" began Dustsheet.

"There was something weird going on between those two, I told you there was, something downright bizarre, but she wouldn't say anything, just hinted at something magic, out of this world."

David looked at her. "You serious?"

She nodded. "Yeah. I just thought she was exaggerating, you know, but seeing that thing… hell, seeing everything tonight, the freeze, Christ, I feel like I could believe in anything."

"I know what you mean. And this card thing. It's like…"

"In-tennnse," Dustsheet breathed.

David looked at him, agreed, "Yeah." He made to pass the card-like object to Danielle, but she stepped back, bumping into Dustsheet.

"No… something's wrong here, something beyond what's happened tonight."

"But what *has* happened, man?" Dustsheet asked, a little panicky.

Danielle shrugged her shoulders. "We don't know." She shook her head, trying to ignore the fear which was starting to affect them all. "Christ, we really need to work out some plan of action." She looked at David, who nodded agreement. "Let's just get the kettle on, sit ourselves down, and sort things out."

"Okay." David watched her turn around and head towards the stairs. He called after her, "Be down in a minute."

She didn't reply.

Dustsheet moved further into the room, his eyes fixed on the black card. "What is that thing, man?"

"Haven't a clue." He slid it carefully into the inside pocket of the ski jacket.

Dustsheet turned his attention to the frozen Becky. "That face she's pulling doesn't exactly bring out the best in her."

David looked at her.

She seemed so determined, so desperate to go through with whatever it was she had planned. Yet she was scared as well, that much was plain.

In fact, she looked just about as terrified as Rick Green-head had.

He wondered what these two young lovers had shared.

What had brought them to this stage in their relationship? What had they done to scare themselves so much; what was it Becky was so determined to do?

And why? What had filled her with such contempt, what had finally prompted her to go ahead with it?

He realised he would probably never know.

Dustsheet reached out and started fondling one of Becky's impressively large breasts.

He muttered something David couldn't hear, and then a moment later his other hand joined in the fun. After a while, he moved her blouse out the way, and reached behind her to try and undo her bra.

"You, uh… you do realise she's dead?" David asked, as nonchalantly as he could manage.

"Hey man," Dustsheet slurred in reply, then crouched down to lean forwards and press his face to her midriff. It looked like he was trying to kiss her belly-button.

David was counting down the seconds until she flumped, and was actually pretty accurate: he had reached 'two' when she collapsed, her arms drooping onto Dustsheet's back in parody of a lover's embrace, her body falling back onto the bed.

Dustsheet seemed encouraged.

David wondered what the fascination with her belly-button was.

The lad still had his face there, and seemed to be repeatedly kissing her, his head waggling up and down and side to side. She'd trapped his hands when she'd fallen back, but he pulled them free, and started groping her tits again. He paused his slobbering long enough to comment, "Gone all soft babe." He pushed out his legs behind him, positioning himself so his groin was pressed to the floor.

David watched as he started to slowly grind himself against the carpet. "You really don't believe me, do you?"

"Shluh-uh."

"Surely you can't be so stoned you don't get it? Hey man," he gasped, suddenly realising, "if Danielle catches you…"

Dustsheet raised his head. "I'll fuck her too man."

"Will you shite," David snapped, trying desperately to ignore the fact he was unbelievably starting to get an erection. He stepped over and put a hand on Dustsheet's shoulder. "Time to go."

"Hey Dave, what's the problem, she's begging for it."

"She's *dead* Dustsheet. Dead. Kaput. A corpse. Couple hours' time, she'll start to rot. Know what I'm saying?"

Dustsheet seemed to consider this. He stared up at David with eyes not quite as red as when they'd first met. Then he looked back at Becky. Whispered, "But look at her man, she's just there, for the taking. Feel her, she's so warm, she can't be dead…"

David sighed, let go of his shoulder, straightened. "I'll ignore the 'for the taking' thing – just explain the not moving thing."

"That freeze lark man." He turned more fully to David, tried to explain further. "I just, I mean I never dreamed…

You know when I'm watching her? I mean, if I'm on my own, I like, sometimes, you know–"

"Christ Dustsheet…"

"But Dave man, look at her. She's so… I mean, it gets me off so much: *she* gets me off. I've never dreamed I'd get this close to her, you know? Never dreamed."

"But she's dead. She is dead. Dead. Corpse. Dead body. Cadaver. Lump of meat."

Dustsheet ran his hands over her breasts once more, then finally pushed himself up into a standing position. He moved his cock around in his pants, trying to get comfortable. "This is… I could be… five minutes, I mean, less, I'm so–"

David grabbed his shoulder once more and pushed him towards the door, finally starting to feel the disgust he perhaps should have felt the moment he'd realised the little pervert's intentions. "Just get the fuck out."

They joined Danielle in the sitting room in silence.

She looked up at them curiously, almost suspiciously. "Where've you both been?"

"Just had to explain one or two things to Dustsheet here," David said. He sat down on the three seater, Danielle having taken the only armchair. Dustsheet joined him on the couch.

On the coffee table in front of them were three mugs of coffee, the rest of the golden syrup cakes Danielle had retrieved from the car, and a bowl of sugar and bottle of milk for the drinks.

David helped himself, making up Dustsheet's while he was at it. He passed the mug over.

"Want a joint," he snapped huffily, ignoring the coffee.

"Here man, I'm not putting up with this kind'f shit," David warned, dumping the mug back on the table, slopping coffee.

"Come on, we'll get nowhere by bickering," Danielle advised, still curious as to what had gone on between the two youths.

"Want to knock up a joint," Dustsheet repeated, in that same brattish tone of voice.

David quickly swallowed a mouthful of coffee, then snapped, "Whay is anyone honestly stopping you?"

Dustsheet looked at him. A few moments later, despite all his efforts otherwise, he started to smile. "You've got the fucking stuff, man!" He started laughing.

"Come on lad," David said, smiling, his voice softening, "get a grip." He reached into his pocket, brought out the dope he'd nicked from his supervisor's wallet. "Make it as fat as you like."

Dustsheet took the deal, still laughing, and dug out his own wallet. Once he'd laid out on the table the resin, his green Rizlas, pack of Regal King Size, and cheap throw-away lighter, he tried to calm himself down. He reached over, grabbed his coffee, took a sip. "Thanks, Danni."

She raised her eyebrows. "No problem, Dusty."

He got to work.

It was a laborious process, one which took an over-long

length of time, and the end result was rather limp-dickish in appearance, but David decided not to pass comment.

After several attempts with the lighter, Dusty sparked up, and inhaled deeply. "Yous two haven't planned much yet," he observed, exhaling a big cloud of smoke.

"We were waiting for you, I guess," David explained.

Danielle drained the contents of her mug, set it down on the table. She'd already eaten two cake bars. "All right lads, who's got a sensible suggestion as to what the hell we should do next?"

"Mmm," agreed David, "good question."

"Right," Dusty began, twisting his face up and exhaling a stream of harsh smoke, "first on the agenda is explaining to little old me just what the hell's happened."

Danielle sighed. "Okay then. Right. Well, it seems everyone has somehow died. Only, instead of falling to the floor, they've stayed frozen in whatever position they were in when they died. Some people, like you and David and me, well, somehow we survived. And that," she concluded, "is basically all we know."

He shook his head. "Crazy, man. Just… mad." He pointed the smoking spliff towards Danielle, but she shook her head, so he offered it to David.

"Cheers." He took the joint, and sucked in a huge draw. Exhaling as he spoke, he asked, "You think we should head back to the supermarket, check out old Ricky-boy?"

"Prick Greenhead?" Dusty asked.

"Yeah. Remember, he had the other half of Becky's black card?"

"Oh shit yeah, you said." His eyes were wide. "That was just so freaky, that thing…"

"It freaked me out too," Danielle admitted. "Where is it?"

David patted his jacket. "Inside pocket," he explained. After another hit off the joint, he continued, "If we manage to get the two pieces back together again…"

He trailed off, and Dusty started giggling. "Hey man, that's just so way-out."

"But don't you think?" David persisted.

Danielle shrugged her shoulders. "I guess something might happen. Or… have you not thought they separated the thing for a reason? That there was something dodgy about it, and they destroyed it?"

He paused, the joint a few inches from his mouth. He shook his head. "No. No, I hadn't thought anything like that."

"So you don't think it's a possibility?"

He inhaled. "I didn't say that." He blew out a long stream of smoke, then offered Danielle the spliff. "You sure?"

"Christ, pass it here, peer pressure or what?"

"She doesn't have to, Dave man," Dusty advised.

"No it's all right, might as well make the night even more freaky than it already is." She took the joint, curled her hand into an open fist, stuck the spliff between the second and third knuckles of her second and third fingers, pressed her lips to the gap made by her forefinger and the curve of her thumb, and inhaled.

The two lads looked at one another. Dusty was the one who said it. "Bizarre."

They both fell about laughing.

She screwed up one side of her face, then joked, "Yeah hilarious, just because I give a shit what diseases yous might be carrying."

Once more, her and David's definition of humour seemed to be misaligned. "You taking the piss? You can't really get anything from–"

"I know, you moron," she interrupted, exhaling in his direction, "it makes the smoke less harsh…" She shrugged, then suddenly spluttered out a cough. "Or more harsh. Or something."

"Whoah," nodded Dusty. "Ingenious."

She scowled at him, took a few more drags, then twisted her face in disgust. "Ulrh. Anyone want to kill it?"

Dusty and David both shook their heads, so she took another hit, then ground the roach against the inside of her mug, and dropped it in.

She leaned back in the armchair and sighed. "Wow." She paused. "Right. Time for some planning."

"Yeah, man," Dusty agreed.

"Whatever you say," seconded David.

They grinned, and Danielle started laughing, and David couldn't help noticing how damned attractive she was when she smiled.

Dusty shook his head. "What a mad, mad night, huh?"

David reached over for the last golden syrup cake. "Munchies," he declared, tearing it open. He began to take careful bites, savouring both the overwhelming sweetness, and the somewhat strange feeling of his jaw moving up and down. He had wanted to ask Danielle's opinion on what they should do next, he was going to ask soon, to prompt a conversation, but in actual fact just couldn't be bothered.

Eating a cake bar seemed a much more sensible option.

"Come on then," said Dusty, "what's all this planning business?"

"Uh, I think it's when you make a plan," Danielle offered.

Dusty seemed puzzled. "What about?"

"What we're going to do. You know, now we're on our own sort'f thing."

"I could think of—" Dusty began, but David elbowed him, and they started laughing. "Hey man, you've got one dirty mind."

David looked at him. "I'm not the only one." He turned to Danielle. "Okay, let's go back to the original plan: see if our family and friends're all right." She nodded. "Well, is there anyone else?"

"No, not really." She shrugged her shoulders. "I mean, I don't think it's necessary: I'm not really keen on seeing another dead friend."

"Mmm, me too."

They both turned to Dusty, who at once became paranoid. "Uh hey, I've got nothing to do with this you know."

Danielle smiled. "Yeah, we know. We're just wondering if there're any friends you want to visit, or family or something? To see if they're all right."

"Well…" He seemed to consider the proposal for a moment, then spoke in a rather more serious tone than normal. "I guess there's not much chance of them being all right, though, is there?"

She smiled sadly. "No, I'm afraid there isn't much chance."

"Well, I'd rather, you know, rather remember them as they were… But my folks, they went away for the weekend, should be back tonight some time." He lifted his arm, and looked at his watch.

It was the fact he kept staring at it gave David the chills.

For a split second, he thought the little weedhead had frozen. "What… what is it?" he mumbled.

"It's… whoah, I guess this means we're really fucked." He took the watch off, and passed it over.

David looked at it.

Time had frozen.

The digital display was stuck between the seventy-sixth

and seventy-seventh centisecond of the twenty-third second. David could see both of the small digits on top of each other, looking like a semi-transparent number eight.

"How the hell…?" he whispered. He looked up, saw Danielle watching him, and passed her the timepiece.

She grunted a little when she saw it.

Dusty muttered, "This is some freaky shit, man."

David suddenly got up, ignoring a slight dizzy spell, and walked over to the television. He looked down at the digital display of the VCR.

19:53

Frozen. "The video clock's fucked, too."

"So's my watch," Danielle said, looking at it. It was analogue, as opposed to Dusty's digital, and all three hands were frozen. The time was just coming up five-to-eight.

David returned to his seat. Dusty returned his watch to his wrist.

"How can manmade objects–"

"Just don't ask," interrupted David, looking at her. "Better not to think about it."

She nodded. "I guess. But–"

"Yeah, I know." He sighed. It sure was a mindfuck. How could manmade objects, representational objects with no direct connection with the concept they represented, be affected by that very same concept?

He rested his hand against his chest, against his jacket, his inside pocket, what was contained within.

The broken black card had something to do with it, he was sure. It mightn't have been the direct cause, but it was certainly a major catalyst, or at least an essential part of what had happened.

If they could join the two pieces together again, surely something of significance would occur? Or at the very least, an understanding of the night's events?

As if sensing his thoughts, Danielle shook her head and warned, "I really don't think we should go back to the supermarket. I mean, trying to find the other half of that card... surely Rick and Becky separated it for a reason?"

David shook his own head. "Come on. Don't tell me you believe that. There's something about it, something really weird... magical, like your friend said. But Christ, the expressions on their faces... No, I don't think this was something they worked out together. It couldn't've been. Well, I mean, well god I don't actually know what I mean, but I've just got this really strong feeling about joining the two pieces together."

"There the man goes again," Dusty said, "pieces of puzzles, clues and signs, all that. Like some murder mystery or something."

"Well maybe it is, you know?"

"Hey man, after tonight, I'd believe anything."

"Pretty much what I was saying earlier," Danielle said.

"Come on," David announced, standing up, "let's just get down to the supermarket, check out pissy– I mean Pricky Ricky, see if we can find the card, if we get any dodgy feelings we can just leave, otherwise… well, I just think we might as well give it a go."

"What've we got to lose kind'f thing?" Dusty asked, standing.

David nodded. "Yeah."

Danielle pushed herself up. She blinked, held a hand to her forehead. "Whoah."

"Hey-hey," smiled Dusty, "great, i'n' it?" He turned to David. "Come on. You okay to drive?"

"Uh yeah, course."

"Not that there'll be many copper cars out tonight," Danielle reminded them. They were walking out the front door when she asked, "Don't you think we should… well, maybe take along a weapon, or something? I mean, just in case."

"In case what?" Dusty asked.

She smiled humourlessly. "David seems to think it's a dog-eat-dog kind'f world out there."

"Hey," he protested, "I never said anything like that, I was just saying we're most likely on our own, you know? I mean, maybe there *are* a few nutballs out there: Christ, we freaked out when we first met Dusty, didn't we?"

"You know, I'm not really sure about this whole 'Dusty' thing…"

"Yeah but he was off his head, wasn't *deliberately* trying to frighten us."

"Who's saying there's anyone out there who'd want to?"

"Well… no one, but… oh Christ I can't think straight, what was the point in this conversation again?"

"Hey, she's away man, away," Dusty grinned.

"Look, let's just get going, yeah? We see anyone dodgy, we drive off in the opposite direction, okay?"

"Okay," Danielle agreed, still puzzled why she'd brought up the subject of nutballs.

They walked out the house, Danielle shutting the door behind them, and got into the Montego, Dusty sitting in the back seat.

David turned on the lights, started the engine, reversed out the drive, then headed off down the hill.

"Hey man," Dusty told them after a moment, "it's just great riding along when you're stoned."

Danielle turned to David. "Are you sure you're okay to drive?" She felt her forehead. "I didn't have much, but I don't think I'd be able to."

"Well, we'll find out when I wrap it around the nearest lamp-post," he joked, but then, as Danielle's face dropped, reassured her, "It's all right, I smoked so much when I was younger, it'd take a lot to properly affect me nowadays."

He turned onto Causey Hill Road, and started off back towards the town centre. Remembering the main Allendale Road junction was blocked, he slowed halfway down the hill, turned right onto another estate then, at the end of the road, left, back onto the road he'd taken on the way up.

They were mostly silent during the short journey.

But as they turned back onto the main road, and began to pass the frozen vehicles, David could hear Dusty muttering to himself in the back seat, and Danielle began to have second thoughts.

"You know, I really think we should just leave this thing – this black card – alone. Who knows what might happen?"

"It can't exactly do any harm."

"But it can't do any good, either. Everyone's dead. Just by putting two bits of plastic together, we're not going to mysteriously reanimate them."

David squinted out the windscreen.

He'd seen something moving in the darkness.

On the other side of the road. Just opposite the statue in the middle of the Beaumont Street junction.

As the headlights swept over the road, there was a flash of movement, and some blurry shape dashed across the street in front of them and disappeared into the park.

"Hey man, was that–?" began Dusty.

David slammed on the brakes, swinging the car to the left.

The park gates were on the corner of Beaumont Street, but by the time David had thought to chase the survivor he'd already passed the left-hand entrance lane of the junction, and had to drive the wrong way around the central monument, over the white chevrons, across the Beaumont Street pavement, and onto the park walkway.

Dusty grinned with excitement as he was slung sideways in his seat, the tyres slipping a little. He turned to the left, towards the place the survivor had appeared from.

There was a naked frozen lying in a twisted heap on the pavement.

"Hey, guys…" he began, his excitement immediately replaced by fear.

David flicked the headlamps onto main beam, picking out the survivor from the darkness ahead.

Danielle gasped, seeing him for the first time.

He seemed pretty young, was dressed fairly well, but it was difficult to tell anything what with him running as fast as he could, and the Montego bouncing over the uneven tarmacadam of the thin pathway. He was quite a distance away, but obviously no match for a vehicle, so he veered left, off the track, over the grass, and into some vegetation.

David bumped onto the grass and swerved against the bushes, keeping the car parallel. He couldn't see much with the headlamps pointed in the wrong direction, but there weren't many places the survivor could go. They reached the end of the greenery, and he slowed right down to take a sharp left-hand bend into another section of park.

As slow as he was, the saloon still slid a little on the damp, muddy grass.

In the back of the car, Dusty felt the skid more than the others. He had to shout to be heard. "Hey, you know, I'm not exactly sure about this!"

David ignored him, having caught sight of the fleeing

guy. He was heading towards the Sele, an area of sloping common ground adjacent to the park, many times larger, and much more wide open. More to the point, the entrance the survivor was aiming for couldn't be used by motor vehicles.

"I think he's one of those nutcases we were talking about you know!" Dusty called, leaning forwards, his eyes wide, his seatbelt stretched taut.

In one last desperate attempt to catch the survivor without having to leave the car, David headed up the slight incline of the park after him, and would have knocked right into the sprinting young man had Danielle not screeched in terror and yanked on the handbrake.

If she'd intended to slow them in a controlled manner, it didn't work.

The back of the car suddenly lifted up off the ground, and David left his seat and spider-webbed the windscreen with his head.

They'd caught the end of the park wall with the front-right wing, the handbrake having slid the wheels through the muddy grass and twisted the vehicle towards the wall.

Danielle's side of the car was still sliding forwards, slewing the vehicle around to the left, jerking her against the cutting seatbelt.

Behind her, Dusty yelped as he fell back down after headbutting the ceiling, and was crushed against the back of her seat.

There was a high-pitched scream, and Danielle had time

to think they'd caught the survivor after all when her passenger window disintegrated, and something clutched her around the throat and screamed its rage and pulled at her and shook her.

DAVID WOKE WITH THE BEGINNINGS OF AN erection.

He couldn't have been out for more than a few seconds.

Something was screaming.

Yelling.

Danielle was screaming, too, struggling so violently the whole car was wobbling, shaking back and forth on the handbrake.

Behind them, Dusty was making strange little whining noises, as if he were looking at something rather unpleasant.

Christ he hadn't meant the chase to end this way.

He wondered what had turned him on. The crash?

Jesus.

Groggily, he turned to see what Danielle was making such a fuss about.

Her door was open, its window shattered and broken. Something which David vaguely recognised as human was grappling with her, had its arms around her torso and was pulling, yanking with all its might, seemingly unaware she was still seatbelted in.

It had its head between her breasts and was chomping repeatedly on the ski jacket which covered them.

Quickly, blindly, almost without thinking David started punching the mad thing writhing on top of her, punching its head and punching its back, and when it looked up to see who the hell was interfering, David punched its face.

It looked pretty annoyed.

Although it was obviously a human being, David couldn't think of it as such.

There was such an animalistic hatred glowing within its eyes, such an intense expression of base bestial need on its face, there was no way it could be classed as human. It may once have been, but now madness had invaded, a primitive need and hunger had taken over, and blood ruled its mind.

David punched its face again, and yelped as the thing's teeth gouged open his knuckles and splatted blood into the air.

Taking advantage of David's pause for pain, it dived forwards, ignoring its first-choice prize, and going for David with twice as much energy and intensity.

Dusty started bawling.

The thing writhed back and forth on the seats, bucking this way and that, smacking legs against the doorframe, digging knees into Danielle, battering arms and fists against David.

He heard Danielle unbuckle her seatbelt, while the thing on top of them kept battering and punching, and then jerked its head between David's legs and bit at the ski jacket there. Pounding on its head with both fists, dimly aware he was drilling its skull into his own groin, David looked around, panic-stricken, and saw Danielle manage to squeeze free of the flailing limbs, manage to push herself away from the vehicle.

As if the fact she had escaped had given him a new lease of life, he grabbed the thing's head and started battering it against the Montego's steering wheel, jerking up his knees and driving those forwards too, pounding away as the thing's hands clutched at his head and ripped at the wound there.

His strength just evaporated.

It was as if the thing had pressed the shutdown switch.

David collapsed in his seat, drooping, his hands losing their grip on the madman's head, his knees dropping back down, his head falling back. His whole body seemed to shudder as a bolt of pain shot through him.

"Oh god, no no, David get up, wake up, oh…" Dusty's words dissolved into more panicked screeches.

The thing tore itself away from its position against the

105

steering wheel, jerked back into the passenger seat, and regarded David warily.

Then, without so much as a moment's thought as to why its adversary wasn't fighting anymore, it grabbed David's left arm and backed out the car, dragging him with it.

There was a moment when David's legs got caught on the gearstick, but after a good yank, he popped out the saloon and landed on the ground in a heap.

It was then the thing started to rip his clothes off.

It tore at the ski jacket first, and David could only watch numbly as he was jerked around. Eventually the thing freed the garment, and propelled it into the dark of the night.

David tried desperately to regain control of himself, but his muscles didn't seem to be responding. It was as if his body had been coated in some restrictive material. He could only slightly feel his legs and arms, but even then, where there should be pain, there was only warmth.

The thing came at him again, and ripped at his shirt. Buttons catapulted into the air. One of them fell back onto his face.

Then there was something else on his face, a whole load of wet yucky stuff, gushing over his face and into his mouth, and it tasted awful, warm and gunky in his mouth, and then the thing bent over him and crushed him.

Danielle had crept up behind the fucking abomination and slit its throat.

Hell, she'd *gouged out* its throat.

She'd used the craft-knife she'd seen David dump in the ski jacket she'd got for him. Lucky for him the freak had chucked the jacket without bothering to search it.

And now there they both lay: David, motionless on the ground, the freak on top of him jerking around slightly, flooding the place with its life-force, Dusty's incessant yelping slowly diminishing as he realised it was all over.

She remained where she was, breathing heavily.

The bastard freak had really shook her up.

Crushed her breasts. Scratched the side of her face. Not to mention all the bumps and bruises she must've got after it psycho'd-out when David had tried to save her.

Sometimes she wished she'd never teamed up with Dave the Reformed Marijuana-Junkie Shelf-Stacker.

Christ, the entire country had gone to shit, everyone acting like their body temperatures had just dropped a hundred degrees, and here she was with some nutball who drove like he was fucking invincible. She tried not to think what might've happened had she not had the good sense to yank on the handbrake. She was surprised David had even woken up from the bashing she'd seen his head take.

And now this maniac.

Lying on his front as he was, he looked fairly normal, if a little dishevelled.

It was only when you saw his face you knew something essential had left him and gone for one hell of a holiday.

He was unquestionably better off dead, but she nevertheless felt pretty guilty at having killed the only fellow survivor they'd come across besides Dusty, even though it'd been a question of kill or be killed.

She couldn't even think why it had started to strip David. And what had it been up to before they'd found it? Who had it killed? Anyone?

She looked at the craft-knife in her hand. It was so flimsy half of it had snapped off in the madman's neck, and was no doubt still buried there.

But it had done the job.

She bent down and, replacing what was left of the knife in a jacket pocket, started to tug at the nutcase.

He was pretty heavy.

She pulled and yanked, then pushed, and found it was much easier to roll him off. He hit the ground with a squelching sound, wobbled around a little, and came to rest face down.

It was as she was looking at David she realised Dusty had fallen silent.

If she didn't know otherwise, she might have thought David had died along with the madman. He was absolutely drenched in blood. His face especially. She could kind of tell where his own head wound ended and the splatter of the madman's carotid began, but there was so much mess it was hard to distinguish anything.

She went back to the Montego for the bottle of water she'd taken from her house. Dusty watched from the back seat, his eyes wide, face streaked with tears. She tried to smile, to reassure him, but the enormity of the situation seemed to have sapped her of all emotion.

She grabbed the water from the small bag she'd packed, then went back to David.

He was coughing slightly, half awake, gazing up at her through a haze of pain, and she did feel sorry for him, but no one had forced him to shoot off after the madman like… well, like a madman.

And just before they'd left, he'd yet again been whittering on about all that 'we're on our own' crap. Maybe he was more shook up about this business than he made out. Which of course would be exactly what he was doing, bottling everything up, ever so heroic and masculine, either trying to impress her or simply not wanting to upset her.

He'd been pretty sympathetic after she told him about the run-in with the pervert creep, but maybe he'd been in the middle of coming to terms with the freeze, had been more susceptible to emotion.

Even Dusty freaked her out a bit, little doped-up peeping tom that he was.

She knelt down beside David, and started washing his face with the water.

He coughed, and commented, "Like I said, we see some dodgy character, we'll just drive off in the opposite direction."

She smiled, and this time it was a true smile.

"How's Dusty?"

"Er," she began, turning towards the car. Dusty was

there, his face pressed up against the back window. He managed a limp smile. "He'll be okay, I guess."

Once she'd got his face clear of the worst of it, she leaned back, and he pushed himself slowly into a sitting position. He started rubbing his face dry. "Christ."

She stood up, and held out a hand for him. He was a little unsteady at first, and she asked, "You going to be all right?"

"I… I think so. Back then though, when that thing grabbed my head…" He trailed off, shook his head gently, and looked around, blinking. "No permanent damage, I reckon."

"Still going to be one hell of a bump."

"You can say that again." He stepped over to the open passenger door, and sat down heavily.

Dusty was watching him, concerned. "You…" he croaked, "you okay?"

David smiled. "Sure. What about you?"

"Uh, yeah. Fine. Hit my head, but…" He lowered his eyes. "I just didn't know what to do man, just panicked, completely freaked."

"It's okay, it's over. He's dead."

"Danni really… she really killed him?"

David nodded, looking at the blood-washed corpse. "She really did." He raised his eyes, and Danielle met his gaze. "Are you… you know, sure you're okay with this sort of thing?"

"I haven't exactly done it before, you know. But… I

guess so. I mean, he was going to kill you, probably me and Dusty too, so…"

"Maybe we should've taken weapons," Dusty said.

"Yeah. Maybe." He looked around, and noticed the ski jacket on the ground where he presumed Danielle had dropped it after retrieving the craft-knife.

He pictured the broken black card inside.

"Christ I'm freezing," he lied, wrapping the remains of his torn shirt around him. "Could you pass my jacket, Danielle?"

She looked around, located it, and went to retrieve it.

"What now then?" Dusty asked, without much enthusiasm.

He shrugged his shoulders, smiled at Danielle for getting the jacket, then stood to put it on. "I don't know. What if there're more like him?"

"But what was he?" Danielle asked, then shook her head, rephrasing the question: "No I mean, what made him go nuts?"

David zipped up the ski jacket, smiling. "Sorry, I flunked my psychology degree." He patted his chest to make sure the black card was still safe, then sat back down in the passenger seat, feet on the grass. From the back of the car, Dusty let out a short-lived burst of laughter.

Danielle didn't seem impressed by their joking. "Do you have–"

"Oh come on," David interrupted, "why else do you think he was nuts?"

"'cause of the freeze, man," Dusty supplied.

She shook her head. "It can't... it can't be the answer to everything."

"No one's saying it is, Danni."

"But you have to admit, there's something pretty damned fundamental about it all, isn't there?" David patted his chest once more, this time making sure Danielle saw him. "That's why we have to get back to Rick tossing Greenhead, get his half of the card, and see what the hell those two were up to."

"I'm just... Christ, we've had this conversation before, David."

"Right, here's the plan: we get to the supermarket, I go in alone, you and Dusty head off and find us some sort of transport – weapons too, if you can – and get back to the supermarket. I should've found out if there's any point to this weird card thing by then, so if I've turned into some homicidal maniac you kill me, destroy the card, then bugger off for a new life someplace. Otherwise... well, whatever happens happens."

"Philosophical, man," Dusty commented.

David looked at Danielle, wondering what she thought of his spur-of-the-moment plans.

She shook her head in submission. "Okay David, have it your way you know, you seem to be the one calling the shots, but..."

There was a moment or two of silence before Dusty

decided, "It's times like this you could do with a joint, huh?"

David smiled. "Yeah. I don't know what it is, but after that nutcase tried to kill me, I just feel completely sober."

"Look," Danielle began, "why don't me and Dusty head off now, okay, so we've more time to get something half decent, and more time to find some weapons, too."

David agreed, "Yeah. Sounds like the best bet. You'll be driving?"

She nodded.

From the back seat, Dusty protested, "Hey you guys, I'm not far off my seventeenth, I'm sure it can't be that hard."

Danielle made a face. "I think I've had enough boy-racing for one night, thanks."

David watched her, waiting a few moments before speaking. "Danielle, you uh… I'm not sure you realise this, but we wouldn't've actually crashed had you not, uh, you know, not…" He was unsure if he should continue. She was looking at him with a rather worrying glint in her eyes. "Uh well what I meant was–"

"Come on Dusty. Let's get some wheels."

"And weapons," he reminded her, opening the back door and stepping out onto the grass. "But seriously, about the 'Dusty' thing–"

"Right," David interrupted, joining them. "Uh, well, see you at the shop I guess. I wouldn't spend all night trying to find some R-reg Porsche and a small arsenal, I mean, just in case there's something dodgy…"

"It's okay David, we'll be as fast as we can." She smiled. "Take care."

"Yeah, you too. And you see anyone, just run."

"You can count on that, man," Dusty assured him.

"You still got the craft-knife?"

"What's left of it, yeah."

"Okay. Well, see you soon."

With a final nod farewell, they strode off onto the path towards the Sele, then turned left onto a short driveway which would lead them back to the main road.

David watched them disappear into the silence of the night.

He was about to start off towards the superstore when he remembered the bag Danielle had taken from her house, the bag which was still in the saloon. He clambered back in, grabbed it, and had a look inside.

The fireworks she'd shown him were there, as was another packet of golden syrup bars. The bottle of water was still on the ground. She'd used just about all of it washing his face.

Unable to fathom how he might defend himself with a few party rockets and a bunch of cake bars, he decided to leave the bag, and started off back across the park.

Trying desperately to ignore the headache which had been steadily increasing in intensity since the effects of his adrenaline rush had worn off, he stuffed his hands deep into the pockets of the ski jacket, and walked along with his head held low.

As he walked, he followed the twin tracks of the Montego's tyres, and after a few moments of calculation, sighed his weariness out loud.

He had been right.

If Danielle hadn't yanked on the handbrake, they'd have sailed along the grass, parallel to the wall, and ended up in the bushes at the edge of the park. Obviously all that would've depended on his driving ability, but he reckoned he could have pulled off the manoeuvre.

Now, one handbrake skid and swerve in the wrong direction later, they were lucky to be alive.

He wondered about Danielle sometimes.

Well pretty much all the time actually, but this recent carelessness, coupled with the almost barbaric way in which she dealt with the nutcase, made him increasingly certain of his initial impression: there was something not quite right about Danielle Eastman, something just a little off-kilter, something which was starting to feel like a threat to not just the stability of their relationship, but possibly even their lives.

Which was daft.

She'd been a nervous wreck when she'd first jumped him in the supermarket warehouse, hysterical almost.

She just wasn't the death-wish type.

Deciding not to decide, which, if things seemed a little too complex, David always thought was the best solution, he continued on through the park, turning onto the main stretch of tarmac back to Beaumont Street.

The silence was as deafening as ever.

There were a few strange, perhaps even suspicious noises, seemingly extremely loud in the abnormal quiet, and he had to struggle to identify them. Muffled music from somewhere behind him. The crying of animals from all around: barking, mewling, something flap-flap-flapping in the air. And the ancient trees in the park, creaking eerily in the wind.

There were also one or two noises he could have sworn were screams.

But he didn't want to think about those.

He shook his head a little, tried to clear it.

The headache hadn't actually developed into anything more than a dull thudding, and he supposed the joint they'd shared at Becky's had something to do with that.

Shame any other effects had been lost after the encounter with the nutcase.

He looked up from the pathway, and stepped out onto the wide pavement at the Beaumont Street Battle Hill junction.

Immediately his eyes rested on the lump of naked flesh dumped at the side of the road opposite the monument.

From this distance, he couldn't even tell what sex it was, let alone whether he recognised it at all. One of the nutcase's victims, surely. Driving towards him as they had been, they'd probably disturbed him, made him panic.

Deciding against a closer examination, preferring not to find out what might've become of him had Danielle not intervened, he crossed the street behind the statue, then carried on down the main road towards the supermarket.

It was as he was walking through the car park he realised someone was already inside.

And making a lot of noise.

There was the sound of breaking glass, tumbling fixtures, snapping shelves, demented yelling, loutish whoops.

Narrowing his eyes and shaking his head slightly, wondering just how the hell the night could get any worse, he quickly raced over to the front of the building – careful to avoid the motion detectors on the automatic doors – and peered in through one of the tinted windows.

There was nothing to be seen.

At first glance, the place seemed to be in just the same condition as he'd last seen it.

Yet still the noise, the sounds of destruction.

He was staring at each aisle in turn now, trying to see anything even slightly untoward, and it was as he was squinting at his own drinks aisle he saw the stock cage he'd been working literally launch itself into the air and plough through a side-stack of £14.99 Moët and Chandon.

Glass and champagne scythed and splattered in all directions.

David jerked back from the window, eyes wide.

Obviously someone in there was deliberately vandalising the place. But who? And how had they survived the freeze?

Shifting his vision as he had, he suddenly found himself really rather determined never to get an answer to those questions: he hadn't noticed her before, but one of the checkout operators, the one who'd dealt with Virgin Vodka Man, was lying splayed out on her conveyor belt, semi-naked and splashed with blood.

The bottle of booze she'd just sold had been shattered between her legs. The neck was poking up from the mess like the tail of a particularly enthusiastic carrion feeder.

Virgin Vodka Man, his hands now clutching at nothing, remained standing guard.

David stepped back even further. He looked around nervously, all too aware of the vast open space of car park behind him.

He really didn't want to be anywhere near the super-market, let alone inside it.

But Rick Greenhead.

Rick fucking Greenhead and his half of the black card.

Turning to the right, he headed along past the ATMs and around the side of the building, into the section of car park where his supervisor's Montego had been.

A good ten feet of wall separated him from the super-store's loading area, and he'd have to hope someone had left the warehouse door open, but then it would only be a matter of diving in, grabbing the black card from Rick the Prick, and scarpering.

It seemed a sound plan.

If the warehouse door was indeed open.

If whoever was on the shop floor didn't hear him and come investigating.

If Danielle and Dusty didn't burst into the supermarket and wonder where he was.

If–

"Oh fuck it," he cursed, strode over to the wall, and scrabbled his way up onto the top.

From this angle, he could see the main warehouse loading door was shut, but the smaller fire door to the side was ajar. Trying to quash the rising fear in his stomach, he lowered himself as quietly as he could down into the yard.

Walking quickly across the stained and mucky concrete, heading behind the huge storage containers and along the wall, he tried to keep himself as inconspicuous as possible, hoping no one had broken into the security office and was watching him on the monitors. He reached the dock, jumped up the few steps, and raced across the grey cement slabs towards the warehouse fire door.

Light spilled out onto the dock.

Light, and shadow.

There was a shuffling noise from within the warehouse.

David froze, leaning against the wall, his face pressed as close as he dared to the opening of the door.

More shuffling. Perhaps a footstep.

Then tearing. Clothes being ripped. A grunt.

Barely registering his continual misfortune to encounter

Hexham's entire quota of deviants in one evening, he decided to risk a peek.

It was Biscuit Girl.

She was moving.

Jerking back and forth slightly.

David moved his head further around the doorframe and saw just *why* she was moving.

A young, long-haired muscular lad, dressed in a slashed, open chequered shirt and blood, was busy tearing her jeans off with a knife.

His cock was hard, and much bigger than David's. It wobbled as he struggled with a particularly stubborn piece of denim.

David's eyes were wide as he watched. Dimly, he became aware of his heart racing in his chest, his lungs struggling to take in air.

With a roar of satisfaction, Biscuit Girl's jeans were finally yanked away from her, and there she stood in knickers and shirt, still chatting merrily away to Tampon 'So I Like Shitting My Kegs, What's Your Problem?' Man (who was still staring at her tits). David noticed her shelf-filling jacket dumped on the floor, a little further off from where the long-haired bloke had dropped her jeans.

The guy threw his knife down onto the jacket and, after a moment's hesitation, stepped forwards and pushed himself between Biscuit Girl's legs and then inside her. He seemed to have a little trouble getting her underwear out the way and arranging himself, but he was soon thrusting away, his face changing in expression from machine-like psychopath to machine-like psychopath with the horn.

She flumped a couple of seconds after he'd penetrated her, but this seemed only to encourage him, and he took hold of her body around the hips and started jerking her this way and that, yanking her back and forwards in time to his thrusts.

When he started ramming her head against a nearby stock cage, slamming it from side to side, David glanced over at the place he and Rick the Dick had been frolicking in, and guessed if he made a run for it, and was as quiet as possible, he might be able to make it without the long-haired guy noticing. The fire door wasn't open wide enough for him to actually see Rick, so he could only assume he hadn't been interfered with.

David looked back as the necrophile groaned exagger-atedly and increased his speed, dancing about the place and bouncing Biscuit Girl up and down and all around. She bumped into Tampon Man, and the long-haired guy used him like a wall, ramming Biscuit Girl up against him, his hips jerking back and forth spasmodically.

The groan turned into a growl, Tampon Man flumped, and all three ended up on the floor, the corpse-fucker continually grinding away for all he was worth. He started screaming, and when his yells dissolved into words – "OOOH! FUCK! YES!" – David seized his chance, crept the fire door further open, dived through, and stepped quickly over towards Rick.

The King of Smarm himself was lying just as David had left him, in a heap next to the wall, entombed by the pungent stench of drying piss.

The black card was nowhere in sight, so he decided to search Rick's pockets, just in case the lad was hiding the secret to yet another metaphysical mystery. There was a wallet in his trouser pocket, along with a large bunch of keys. David put them both into a ski jacket pocket. Ricky-boy didn't appear to be carrying anything else, apart from the usual shelf-filling shite – craft-knife, Biro, a few other useless bits and bobs – so his eyes quickly darted around, trying to locate the missing half of the black card.

From the warehouse gangway there was a seemingly endless exhalation, a strange mixture of scream, groan and bestial satisfaction, followed by the sound of someone rolling over onto the floor.

David didn't need to remind himself he was rapidly running out of time.

Trying to move Pissy Ricky wouldn't be such a hot idea: the cheap material of the shelf-filling jacket crumpled and crackled at the least interference, David knew, so he didn't even bother. Instead, on hands and knees, he peered beneath the stock cages, squinting into the gloom, searching for anything resembling that which he so desperately sought.

"UUUH!" from the gangway.

And then shuffling. Grunting.

Somebody stumbling around as if in a daze.

There was nothing beneath the cages, apart from the mess of a smashed jar of something or other someone hadn't bothered to clean up.

David turned around, panicky, scanned the area next to the wall. Saw nothing. Leant over for a closer look.

Now the necrophile sounded like he was walking someplace, walking purposefully, walking quickly, towards, towards...

It was as David was about to give up he noticed it.

The black card.

Wedged about halfway beneath Rick's shoulder. He hadn't been able to see it before, but now, leaning over the body slightly, it was in plain sight.

He grabbed it, not even bothering to look at it before slipping it into a pocket.

He turned around.

The footsteps were louder than ever, now.

He needed to get out.

Immediately.

The door was there, half open as he'd left it.

Maybe only ten feet away.

Move.

Had to move.

But the footsteps.

Closer.

Clo–

The long-haired guy stepped into view, continued over to the fire door, and carefully pulled it shut.

Slowly, deliberately, he turned around, and looked directly at David.

His glistening cock was almost fully erect once more.

He grinned.

THEY STARED AT ONE ANOTHER FOR A FEW SEC-
onds, David wondering just how the hell he was going to
get out this time, the long-haired guy no doubt imagining
all the fun and games they were about to have.

Suddenly the necrophile flinched forwards, and David
jerked back, slipping on the damp floor, almost losing his
balance. The long-haired guy relaxed once more, and kept
grinning.

His slick cock was now jutting out in all its erect glory,
David was depressed to find himself noticing. Aware of his
interest, the corpse-fucker jerked his hips forwards and
made it wobble. The grin turned into a laugh.

David glanced quickly behind him, searching for any
means of escape, but the stock cages were jammed tight

together, and by the time he clambered onto them, the psycho would be all over him. Rick remained on the floor, splattered with piss and generally looking sorry for himself. The only way out was blocked by the muscle-bound lunatic in front of him.

The muscle-bound lunatic who was slowly edging forwards, rubbing his red-raw bell-end.

Impulsively, not really thinking what he was doing, David reached down and grabbed Rick the Dick's shelf-filling jacket, hauling the corpse upwards and grabbing it around the waist. Grunting some appropriate I'm-just-a-nutball-same-as-you noises, he proceeded to crash Rick's head against the wall, ramming himself up behind him and pushing him flat against the bricks.

Out the corner of his eye, he could see the necrophile regarding him rather suspiciously, but he carried on mashing Rick's face against the wall, carried on ramming his entire body against Rick's back, carried on ignoring the weird tingling sensation in his groin, carried on wondering what the hell poor Rickster had done to deserve all this, and carried on yelling his scream-grunt-growls.

By the time Pricky Ricky's nose and split lips were leaking so much blood David had trouble keeping the shelf-stacker's face from slipping sideways, the long-haired necrophile decided enough was enough, desecrating corpses might be fun but this was just taking the piss, and it was time for some serious violence.

He let go of his cock and grabbed a handful of David's

hair, yanking him away from Rick, who dropped to the floor in a mess of piss and blood.

David's head wound once more flared up, his yells of falsely demented rage swiftly morphing into screams of genuine pain and terror. Lashing out wildly, using both fists and feet, he was satisfied to hear a few grunts of discomfort, but when the necrophile started dragging him into the warehouse gangway, it was all he could do to remain on his feet.

The hippy corpse-fucker suddenly let go, then dived on top of him with such force they both collapsed to the ground. Managing to avoid yet another bash to the head, David decided to employ below-the-belt tactics.

The long-haired guy's cock was huge and incredibly hard, warm and disgustingly juicy.

David made sure he had a tight grip, then started to snap his hand downwards with as much force as he could manage.

The necrophile clamped a vice-like hand around his arm and stopped it dead.

But he hadn't been quick enough to completely avoid damage.

The scream was music to David's ears.

Actually, it was about three inches from his ears, and damned near deafened him with its high-pitched tones of exquisite pain.

Jerking away as if launched from a cannon, the necrophile seemed to explode in a rapid spasm of horrendously jerky movements, legs dancing back and forth, skinning over the rough floor, fists clenching then unclenching, head rattling from side to side.

Seizing his chance, David pushed himself upright, then stumbled backwards and promptly tripped over the twisted remains of Biscuit Girl and Tampon Man.

Crashing to the floor once more, he was aware of the long-haired guy breathing noisily, yelping in time to each inhalation and sliding around on the floor, but it was depressingly obvious there was little sign of the infamous snapped cock syndrome David had so looked forward to.

He moved into a standing position again, trying to ignore the stink of come and shit wafting off the two bodies, and started immediately towards the warehouse doors, the shuffling and sliding and grunting from behind him an indication the necrophile wasn't about to be stopped by a sudden case of Mr Floppy.

Increasing his speed seemed like a damned good idea, but he was still shaken by the utter horror of the situation, and his headache was now pounding like never before, so he was pretty much stumbling by the time the warehouse doors swung open for him, and he stepped through. He moved over to the delicatessen counter and leaned heavily against it, his breath coming in huge gasps.

Most of the curved display glass of the serve over counter had been shattered, rendering what little food remained beneath this time of night completely inedible. One of the serving girls had been removed from the cosy chat she and her friends had no doubt been having, and was sitting on the back countertop against the wall. Her white coat was open, her legs were bare and spread wide. A once decorative chocolate gâteau, spiked with shards of glass, had been rammed and splattered all over her crotch.

Snuffling there, his face buried in a mixture of chocolate, fresh cream, shattered glass and dead fanny, was a young, shortish-looking skinhead, chomping away like there was no tomorrow.

Reeling away from the counter, previously never having considered more than one person running amok, David glanced back towards the warehouse just as the doors started to automatically close, and was pleased to see no sign of the limp-dicked lunatic. Realising he was obviously still far from safe, he started off down the nearest aisle – paperware and babycare – with the intention of cutting along the main aisle and then up towards the front doors without either skinhead or hippy noticing.

He had just past the New Improved Andrex toilet tissue fixture ('So Thick You Need Less'), when the corpse-fucker stepped out from the central aisle and stood in front of him, blocking his path.

He was erect once more. He had lost the chequered shirt. Gained a pair of black Doctor Marten boots.

He also seemed a lot more surprised to see him than he had in the warehouse.

Reacting instantly, David spun around, and started back down the aisle.

Just as he was about to break into a run, the warehouse doors swung open, and out limped the necrophile, bruised and floppy cock cradled in his hands, an expression of utter contempt on his face. He had put the shirt back on, removed the boots.

David jerked to a halt.

Turned around. Slowly.

There he was again.

The corpse-fucker. Minus shirt, plus boots and hard-on. He was starting to laugh.

Two of the fuckers!

Not even bothering to attempt to try and rationalise the situation, he relied on gut instinct to propel himself up the nearest metal shelving, packs of Kleenex flying every which way. Scrambling onto the top shelf, he risked a glance around, and was dismayed to hear a pair of Doc Marten boots clomping rapidly into the next aisle – health and beauty – and start to scale the shelves. Bottles of shampoo, conditioner, and other hair-care products bounced onto the floor and scattered all over the place.

Meanwhile, the original attacker had reached the paper-ware aisle, and was busy selecting a number of interesting missiles from the baby-food fixture.

The first to fly past David and shatter somewhere was a small bottle of fruit juice.

Keeping himself bent as low as possible, he raced along the top shelf as fast as he dared, kicking the packs of toilet roll out the way where he could, crushing them beneath his feet where he couldn't. There was a growl from behind him as the Doc Marten guy pulled himself up and over the health and beauty strip lighting support grille, demolishing half of it in the process.

In front of David, a can of Heinz baby food detonated against the back wall of the shelf, just about shearing his nose off.

Yelping a little, he continued along to the end, and tried to jump the central aisle.

In his mind, he'd landed heroically on the Beers Wines and Spirits free-standing fridge jutting out from the opposite aisle, but slipping on a bunch of own-brand shit-paper as he did, he managed in reality to simply tumble over the edge of the paperware shelving, and slide down the end-of-aisle promotion shelves, currently employed to advertise a special twelve-for-nine offer on Andrex.

Bracing himself for the impact against the hard flooring, he was confused as to why he still seemed to be dangling in mid-air.

A glance up at Doc Marten Man standing above him provided the answer. He had David's feet gripped in both hands, and was grinning maniacally.

The glass in the left-hand BWS fridge door suddenly crashed apart, and a dented can of puréed dinner found a rest someplace amidst a couple of four-packs.

Doc Marten Man leaned backwards, and, incredibly, started hauling David back up the shelving. Struggling from side to side, David tried pulling himself back down, grabbing onto a shelf and holding on tight. A tin of SMA infant formula sailed out paperware and disappeared down the centre aisle. By now, the underside of the shelf was slicing into David's hands, but he held on and tried again to pull himself down. After a few seconds' struggle, Doc Marten Man above him grunting with his own effort, he had actually started to get somewhere, and so was somewhat put out when the shelf came away in his hands, and he shot back up the shelving as if spring-loaded.

Unintentionally booting his adversary in the face and squawking at the sudden movement, he dropped the shelf, and twisted around in time to watch Doc Marten Man slip on the very same pile of shit-paper he himself had tripped over, and crash down onto the top shelf, which promptly collapsed.

Instinctively letting go of his prize, Doc Marten Man smashed to the floor in a heap of unwinding toilet rolls, twisted metal shelving and brackets – and another can of mashed-up food, which had once again rebounded off the back wall of the shelves.

Simultaneously, David also dropped to the floor in his own muddle of display apparatus and bog rolls (and baby food), and was pretty astounded when he realised he hadn't in fact broken his neck.

There were several grunts and groans from the paperware aisle, followed by another thud of a small tin can, and David wasted no time in getting to his feet and racing off down the central aisle, towards the fresh produce and dairy departments.

The OAP he'd seen before was still there, staring at the side-stack of bleach, only by the look and smell of things, one or both of the twins had emptied several bottles of the pungent liquid over his head.

Jumping over the puddle of semi-transparent liquid which surrounded the pensioner – and trying to hold his breath at the same time – he raced into one of the chilled produce aisles, chancing a quick look over his shoulder for his pursuers.

No one was following him.

Yet.

Turning back the way he was running, he had to dodge both the contents and remains of a shattered and bust-open fridge, and turned so sharply his feet slid out from under him in the leaked water on the floor.

Landing painfully on the side of his left leg, he skimmed through the icy liquid, soaking himself, and crashed into the defunct refrigerator, multipacks of bacon dropping off the shelf and plopping onto his stomach.

Skidding and sliding, he tried desperately to push himself up, sure the identical twins would jump around the corner within the next second, armed to the teeth with a variety of baby product missiles.

He was gasping with effort by the time he managed to stand upright.

The sweat was pouring off his skin, he was shaking all over, his heart was slamming madly, yet still he hadn't spotted the twins, and he started towards the main doors thinking for the first time there was maybe a chance he could get out of this place alive.

Coconuts and cucumbers, apples and pears, oranges and lemons, lettuces and tomatoes: a whole variety of fruit and vegetables littered the entire fresh produce aisle, and David had trouble making his way through the mess without falling on his arse again.

It was as he was passing a young ugly blonde busy with the banana fixture (several bunches now gaily decorating her head and hanging off her outstretched arms), the twins once more outwitted him.

They stepped out from the checkout area and advanced.

Doc Marten Man took the left-hand half of the aisle (separated in the middle by several displays stands once laden with fruit and veg), the limp-dicked guy the other. Together, they indeed seemed a truly formidable force.

They were absolutely identical, even down to the size of their cocks. Their shoulder-length dark hair hung lush and full-bodied from their heads, framing expressions of grim determination. The first one was now holding a bottle of Moët, while Doc Marten Man advanced unarmed.

Limp Dick Man caught David's eye, and fondled his wounded cock gently, his eyes promising horrendous revenge. He swung the bottle of champagne back and forth slightly.

Doc Marten Man was wanking himself off slowly, his cock erect once more (if, indeed, it had ever not been during the paperware battle).

Frantically, David looked around for anything with which he might defend himself. Or would the best option simply be to run again? But what about the skinhead muff-diver?

There wasn't exactly much point hanging around here however, with nothing more than a bunch of bananas as a weapon, so he turned around, and was about to sprint away when a roaring noise from outside the main doors stopped all three of them in their tracks.

As one, they turned towards the doors, and squinted against the glare of what seemed to David like a pair of floodlights.

Then, a moment later, the outside automatic doors slid open, the roaring noise increased in volume, and a dark black shape advanced into the superstore, the inside automatic doors sliding open to reveal the monster in all its glory.

If there'd been an opportunity to do so, David might have laughed out loud.

Instead, reacting as quickly as the twins were standing motionless, he raced past them towards the doors, and reached the black Mini Mayfair just as Danielle – hunched over the wheel, eyes wide – negotiated the vehicle into the shop with barely inches to spare.

The passenger door was pushed gently open, and a

wave of curling smoke wafted out. A voice from beyond the cloud offered, "Hey man, have a spliff, seems like you need one."

Diving headlong into the car, David started yelling mid-leap. "The fuck out'f here, get going, go, shit go go!"

"Go-go dancers man," Dusty said from beneath him, "surreal."

Crunching the car into reverse, trying to ignore the fact David was pawing her entire upper body in an effort to right himself, Danielle started moving them slowly backwards, careful not to knock the wing mirror on the doorframe.

Dusty pulled the passenger door shut just in time as they reversed through the inner doors, and gaped once more at the two naked twins standing in the supermarket in front of them. Then David almost kneed him in the face, so he put down the joint he'd been smoking, and tried to help sort him out.

In between trying to rearrange himself into a suitable position from which he could clamber into the back seat, David kept glancing up through the windscreen at the twins, who were now shaking off their initial bewilderment, and advancing rapidly. "Put your foot down for fuck's sake get us out of here!" he bawled at Danielle's stomach, and once more tried to get some leverage off something which didn't feel as fleshy as everything else he'd touched.

"Look, if I hit this doorframe, we'll be well and truly stuck, I just need–"

Limp Dick Man clambered onto the Mini's bonnet and put his bottle of Moët and Chandon through the windscreen.

David, Danielle and Dusty screamed in unison as splatters of safety glass speared inwards, and the champagne bottle was snatched out for another bash.

The hole was directly above David and Danielle, and it was clear by the look on Limp Dick Man's face just who it was he was after now. He was kneeling on the bonnet in such a way David could even see his cock start to get hard once more.

But Danielle had got the message.

They shot backwards and through the outer doors with enough force to knock Limp Dick Man back onto the floor. Immediately he sprang up again, and raced after them.

Swerving sharply to avoid the anti-ramraid concrete posts, Danielle used the wing mirror as best she could, looking over her right shoulder when David's head got in the way, and she was ready to turn the car around when Dusty screamed again and the champagne bottle hit the top of the windscreen frame and exploded.

It managed to put out the rest of the glass in the driver's side, and daggers of green joined the regular shapes of sparkling safety glass.

David felt champagne splash over the back of his head

and down his neck, but he had managed to find the driver's seat with his hands (admittedly they were between Danielle's thighs, but she seemed too preoccupied with driving to notice), and was starting to push himself up. Together with Dusty rearranging his feet, he managed to squirm between the front seats and into the back. He landed with his head in the right-hand footwell, and his feet against the left-hand window, but all in all, he considered it a great improvement.

Dusty was staring out the spider-webbed windscreen in disbelief as one of the naked twins, the one who'd thrown the bottle, started sprinting after their car. By the looks of things, if Danielle kept performing trying to turn the vehicle in the right direction, he would reach them in approximately two seconds. "Fucking get us out of here fucking MOVEMOVEMOVE!"

Crunching the car into first, she sped away as fast as the nine-nine-eight engine would allow, scraping the entire passenger side along the front-right wing of a new R-reg 'Papa?' 'Nicole.' 'Bob!' '*Eh*?' Renault Clio.

Behind and to the left of them, from one of the loading bays next to the cash machines, twin beams of spearing light illuminated the sprinting Limp Dick Man as a white Mercedes van exploded into life.

"Oh shit the other guy, he's after us, oh shit put your foot down!" Dusty was scrambling about in his seat, trying to keep an eye on both twins, and it was as he glanced back at the supermarket doors he noticed the dazed-looking skinhead wander out into the night. "*A-fuckin'-other one!*"

The skinhead's face was smeared from chin to forehead with what looked like a mixture of chocolate cake and blood, his glittering blue eyes creating an altogether un-settling image. Quickly taking in what was happening, he started towards Limp Dick Man – who had turned around and was busy clambering through the passenger door of the van – and reached the door just before Doc Marten Man stomped on the accelerator and they shot towards the exit.

Swerving the wrong way around the mini-roundabout, Danielle tried not to think how in hell she hoped to out-run such a powerful vehicle as the Mercedes, and flew off down the road as fast as she dared, remembering to avoid the hatchback David had so nearly slammed into.

Managing to right himself in the back seat, David twisted around and chanced a look out the window. The van had just driven over the top of the mini-roundabout, and was approaching rapidly. He turned back to the front. "You'll never get away from them in this!" he yelled, trying to be heard over the wind blasting in through the half demolished windscreen. "Why in hell didn't you get any-thing bigger?"

"Listen, if I realised you had this obsession with nut-cases–"

"I thought you said it'd be easier to drive," pointed out Dusty, "and you weren't very confi–"

"Thanks, Dust-bunny."

"Dust-bu–?"

"Oh fuck hold on!"

The Merc accelerated suddenly, and rammed into the back of them with enough force for their wheels to screech on the tarmacadam. David was knocked back down into the footwell. Danielle yelped, braked for the second mini-roundabout, then swerved to the left, towards the main road, just as the van shot forwards and almost hit them again.

"Main street, lose them on the main street, there'll be plenty gaps the van won't be able to fit through," David shouted from between the two front seats.

He noticed Dusty scrabbling around, looking for something on the floor, muttering repeatedly, "Joint-joint-joint-joint…"

As they bounced across not one but another two more mini-roundabouts in quick succession, Danielle almost cracked a joke about the road layout, but then started trying to work out the easiest route through the frozen traffic up ahead. Behind them, the van was gaining once more.

"Weapons, you get any weapons?" David suddenly bawled, remembering.

"No good," Danielle yelled back, "we got a few bits and pieces but – they're in the boot."

David scowled. "Ah, Jesus."

The van slammed into the back of them and slewed them sideways.

They bumped onto the pavement before Danielle could

get them back on course, and it was obvious from the screaming noise beneath David the bodywork had buckled, and was restricting the spin of the rear wheels.

"Better keep it in second or something!" he advised, then noticed she hadn't actually moved out of first. "Foot on the clutch!" he demanded, leaning over and yanking the stick into second. There was a lovely crunching noise, a revving of the engine, then Danielle let the clutch out and they sped forwards.

Narrowly avoiding several cars lined up patiently behind a set of traffic lights, she guided the Mini onto the wrong side of the road, then swerved back into the left-hand lane after the pedestrian crossing. Remembering David had had to drive on the pavement to avoid the blockage at the next set of lights, she swerved to the left, just as the Mercedes behind them slalomed through the crossing and advanced on them yet again.

The Mayfair bounced onto the pavement, the rear wheels still screeching, and once they were past the blockade, Danielle turned the car back onto the road.

Watching out the back window, David saw the van mount the pavement, slam into the frozen man on his way out the off-licence, then carry on along the pavement in an attempt to broadside them. Doc Marten Man had his window down, and was yelling and screaming at them as he yanked the steering wheel sharply to the right.

The two vehicles collided with a horrid scream of twisting metal and sheared paintwork, the rear window of the

Mini collapsing inwards on top of David, and the steering wheel was snatched out of Danielle's grasp as they were pushed sharply into the path of a frozen taxi.

Clearly not in the job long, the taxi driver was actually indicating, waiting to move into a one-way semi-circle of turning area commonly used as a taxi rank, so Danielle took advantage of the Mini's sudden change in direction, grappled with the wheel to regain some semblance of control, and shot down the exit lane and onto the paved walkway of Fore Street.

The shops lining the street were all closed at the time of the freeze, but there were still a few people who'd been wandering aimlessly around, and Danielle had to weave the vehicle around them, which proved slightly more difficult than she'd anticipated: by slamming into the side of them, the twins had successfully managed to fuck the steering. "I can't steer, the wheels're locked!"

"Just keep your foot down!"

"Joint-joint-joint…"

Diving onto Fore Street as quickly as she had, Danielle had managed to gain a few precious moments on the Mercedes, but now David could see it swinging onto the road and start thundering along after them.

"I'm going to have to… David I can't do this much longer!" She glanced back at him helplessly, so he leaned forwards between the seats and helped keep the wheel – now twisting and jerking around under Danielle's hands – locked dead ahead.

At the speed they were travelling, they reached the end of Fore Street in relatively little time, and bounced onto the tarmac of Market Place with the Merc still a good few car lengths behind.

"Across and down the hill!" David demanded.

"Joint-joint-jo– *gotyou*… light-light-light…"

"We won't be able to turn, we can't do it!"

Ignoring her, David kept them ploughing forwards – the screaming noise coming through the knocked out windows warning them the tyres wouldn't last much longer – and then with a force that almost knocked Danielle out the door, he tore the steering wheel to the right and guided them precariously down Hallstile Bank.

The Bank was steep, curved, and culminated in a busy roundabout at the bottom, but Danielle didn't dare let up on the accelerator: the twins had by now caught up again, Limp Dick Man hanging out the window and yelling incomprehensible mouthfuls of what she could only assume was abuse.

"Shit shit," David cursed, "the left, it won't turn to the left!" He'd tried yanking on it with both hands, but the wheel just refused to move. Whereas turning to the right was difficult, to the left seemed impossible. Unable to do anything about it, they mounted the right-hand pavement of Hallstile Bank, and it was more through luck than any judgement on David or Danielle's part they flew past a lamp-post with inches to spare, then bounced through the roundabout and over onto Alemouth Road.

"Into the Wentworth!" David instructed. The town centre car park was to their immediate right, so together they turned the wheel and flew over to where David could see a young couple frozen in the act of loading some groceries into the boot of a red Volkswagen Polo (as well as the usual Tourist Information Centre and public toilets, the car park also served a sports centre and yet another supermarket chain outlet).

The Mercedes rammed them.

This time, not only was there the sound of metal buckling and glass shattering, but of tyres exploding, axles snapping, and the general complete-fucking-up of their vehicle.

After the initial leap into the air from the impact and twin blow-out, the back of the Mini crunched to the ground before juddering across the car pack, eventually hitting the side of a Ford estate parked opposite the Polo.

"Out out fuck out!"

Dusty and Danielle didn't need to be told twice.

The white van slid to a screeching halt next to them, to their left, and slammed fully into the estate, demolishing the front-left wing and jerking the car sideways on its handbrake.

The twins and their skinhead had dived out even before the vehicles had collided, and already the skinhead had monkey-quick leaped onto the Mayfair's roof, and was jumping up and down and screeching excitedly.

David hung back a bit to help Dusty over the front seat and out the driver's door, but then they were running, forgetting the Volkswagen, forgetting the weapons in the boot of the Mini, just getting the hell away from there.

THERE WAS A FIVE-DOOR NISSAN MICRA FROZEN IN the middle of driving through the car park. An old lady sat behind the wheel, and was frozen chatting to her passenger, a young woman obviously bored out of her skull.

But David didn't really care about the occupants.

He reached the vehicle and tore open the driver's door.

Dusty and Danielle noticed what he was up to, Danielle screaming the warning, "Watch it David! The freeze, don't, the car'll react normally, stop–!"

The OAP was hardly out the door before David was clambering over her and launching himself into the driver's seat.

Granny face-planted the deck with an unfortunate

cracking noise, before the rest of her body finally left contact with the hatchback.

The vehicle immediately accelerated at a speed beyond anything David had previously experienced.

One moment it was frozen, then the next instant it was immediately travelling at nearly twenty miles-per-hour.

It slammed into the racing hippies about two seconds later.

Doc Marten Man was clipped by the wing and jerked away onto the ground, but Limp Dick Man hit the bonnet head-on and bounced forwards, spider-webbing the windscreen and rolling over the roof. The skinhead, running slightly behind his masters as he had been, managed to dodge out the way in time.

Inside the vehicle, David was struggling.

To have been sitting in a stationary car one moment and then a travelling one the next was proving something of a mindfuck. Physically it hadn't done much good, either. He could now add a distinct feeling of violent nausea to his list of complaints.

He still had enough presence of mind to grab the steering wheel however, and yanked it to the right while arranging himself into a more suitable driving position than the crumpled heap he'd landed in. Stomping on the accelerator, he guided the car around to where Dusty and Danielle were approaching. They reached the Nissan just as it skidded to a halt, and dived in the back, the frozen passenger still in the front seat.

Dusty seemed to be in shock, but Danielle was yelling, "Go! Quick! They're getting back up!"

David accelerated away, chancing a look behind him, and saw Limp Dick Man rolling around on the ground, Doc Marten Man hobbling over to help, and the skinhead bouncing up and down on the old lady, tearing at her clothes and screeching.

At the top of the car park, he yanked on the Micra's handbrake and spun the wheel, the dramatic skid he'd hoped would turn them all the way around sliding them only slightly sideways. Muttering, "Shit," he reversed a few feet, then shot forwards once more, heading back the way they'd come.

Danielle didn't think this was particularly constructive. "What're you playing at?!"

"Stopping these fuckers once and for all," he replied, his hands gripping the wheel tightly, his eyes fixed straight ahead.

The car was pointed directly at where Doc Marten Man was struggling to drag his twin to his feet. Nearby, the skinhead had mostly stripped the OAP, and was dangling her upside-down as best he could, her face crushed against the tarmac, her varicosed thighs gripped tightly in his hands.

By the time Doc Marten Man realised what David was

about to do, the skinhead had mashed his face between the granny's legs.

Limp Dick Man was rolling around in pain, inadvertently preventing his brother from dragging him clear in time. Doc Marten Man glanced down at him, looked up into the glare of the approaching headlights, then dived out of the way with only a moment to spare.

The Micra bounced over the writhing hippy at such a speed the front wheels left the ground. The engine whined for a moment – the wheels spinning uselessly in the air – before the car crashed back down.

The noises were horrid.

From inside the car, they could hear the thumping, the cracking, the squashing. The squealing and rattling of the suspension.

In the back seat, Danielle and Dusty could feel the bump and scrape of Limp Dick Man beneath their feet.

And then the screaming and yelling. Doc Marten Man bawling his rage. Limp Dick Man his agony.

David regained control of the spinning steering wheel, and guided them out the car park the way they'd come in.

Danielle turned around in her seat and watched Doc Marten Man cradling his twin brother's collapsed head in his arms, while nearby their pet skinhead kept chomping and sucking and biting.

David turned back onto Alemouth Road, and a few moments later the sickening scene had disappeared.

The roads this end of town had been quite busy at the time of the freeze, so David had to concentrate to guide the Nissan through the traffic, across the small roundabout outside Tynedale Park, and onto Haugh Lane.

As he slowly began to realise they were out of any immediate danger, he became aware of a number of aches and pains. Cuts on his face. A throbbing in the side of his leg. His endless headache, intensified by the unfreezing of the Micra. The swirling sickness in his stomach. "We're going to have to stop soon… I don't feel so good."

"I tried to warn you. About the car. Nonhuman material behaves normally when you touch it."

"I know. I just… I had to do something."

They drove in silence for a few moments, until David realised he was driving with no destination in mind. "Where should we go? I mean, what now?"

She caught his eyes in the rear-view. "I don't know David. I don't know."

Dusty started mumbling. "Home. I… I want to go home… home."

She turned to him. He was leaning against the window, his eyes fixed straight ahead. "It'll be all right, yeah? Dustsheet?"

He ignored her.

"Look," David began, "I got Rick's keys off him while I was in the supermarket – found the other half of the black card, too – so've you got any idea where he lives? I mean, it's a good a place as any."

"Well, we're in the right direction, anyway. Lives up near the high school."

"Okay."

They lapsed into silence once more.

David noticed she didn't seem to want to talk about the twin hippies and their pet skinhead. Which was maybe just as well. Especially the state Dusty was in. But it was daft just to accept their existence. There surely had to be a reason for all three of them surviving. Especially when they had obviously all known each other before the freeze.

Danielle started giving directions once he reached the top of the hill, and a few minutes later they were parked outside a moderately sized terrace house. David switched off the engine, glanced at the frozen still sat in the passenger seat, then got out. Danielle and Dusty joined him outside the front door as he started trying keys.

Danielle spoke up. "I'm not sure, but I think he shared with a couple of randoms."

"Right," David said, and grunted as a key turned and unlocked the door. He pushed it open, and ushered his friends inside. Once he'd shut the door behind them, he said, "I wouldn't mind looking through his room, you know, see if there's anything dodgy."

"Dodgy?" Danielle asked, taking in her surroundings.

"Well, anything to do with the black card. So if you and Dusty, I don't know, are you hungry or something…?"

"I think we should just stick together, don't you?"

He paused, then nodded agreement. "Yeah. Yeah, come on."

They headed upstairs. Both down- and upstairs hallway lights were on, which David assumed meant someone must've been home, so he led the way in case there were any frozens wandering around.

He needn't have worried. The upstairs landing was deserted.

There were three bedrooms, two of them locked, so finding Rick's room hadn't been as much of a chore as David had been expecting, but he still got a nasty shock when he walked into the unlocked room and found a frozen hunched over a desk and scribbling.

Once he'd unlocked the door, opened it, then flicked on the light, he went over to Rick's cluttered desk, while Danielle and Dusty sat themselves down on his unmade bed.

"Where the hell to start?" David asked them.

There was an absolute mountain of junk.

Papers, files, folders, booklets, rubbish, half-eaten food, overflowing ashtrays, a dust covered mirror, a few payslips from the supermarket.

And above the desk a noticeboard, equally crammed full.

A wonderfully grainy black-and-white 10x8" of an attractive girl David recognised as Becky had been pinned in the centre of the board, over the top of whatever was beneath. Someone (presumably Rick) had decorated the white border of the photographic paper with fluorescent yellow squiggles.

When David turned around, he noticed Dusty gazing longingly at the image. He waved his hand up and down in front of the photograph. Dusty looked at him stupidly. "You want to… knock up or something? I mean, if you think it'd help."

"David–" Danielle began.

"Come on, I told you, I feel like I've had the shit kicked out'f me, I need to relax."

Dusty remained motionless for a moment, then started digging around in his denim jacket pockets. "Joint," he told them. "Good. Good idea. Joint. Good…" He trailed off.

Danielle gave him a long look, then stood up and made to help David, who was starting to sort through the mountain of mess.

"Well if I do the desk," he suggested, "you could search the drawers or something, yeah?"

"Yeah, okay." She went over to the left-hand drawers, set underneath the desk, and opened the top one. In keeping with the rest of the room, it was stuffed full and completely unorganised. "Might be here a while."

David snorted. "I'm kind'f okay with a tedious job right now."

"What about this mysterious black card? Would've thought you'd be dying to join it together."

"Uh, yeah." He paused for a moment. "Well I just think we should wait, you know, see if we can find out something about it."

Danielle looked up from the drawer. "Freaks you out too now, huh?"

"Mmm. Yeah. Well Christ, after those twins and that… I don't know. How the hell they all survive, you know?"

"I'd wondered about that. Kind'f goes against what we've learnt so far, doesn't it?"

"Well seeing as we haven't learnt anything much at all so far…"

"No, but up until now it's all been random, hasn't it? I mean, we didn't know each other before tonight, did we? And no one else from the supermarket survived with you, none… none of my family survived. Yet those three. I just don't know."

"You didn't recognise them or anything, did you?"

"No. No… but I've heard of them. Well, the twin brothers anyway. Pretty notorious local family, from what I heard."

"So how the hell did they survive? I mean, what is it with this fucking freeze thing, why're all the nutcases surviving, and only a few good guys?"

Danielle smirked. "'Good guys'?"

He shrugged his shoulders, turned back to the desk. Sighed. "Christ. Let's just throw all the shit in the corner there, and dump anything interesting on the bed."

"Okay. Save us going through stuff twice, I guess."

They resumed the search, the pile against the wall gradually getting bigger and bigger, the pile on the bed non-existent.

It was as David was sniffing at the handheld mirror and creasing his forehead in puzzlement Dusty leaned over and handed him the unlit joint.

David raised his eyebrows questioningly.

"Looks like you could do with it more than me, man," Dusty explained.

He smiled falteringly, rubbed at his face with his free hand. "It's not that bad is it?" He glanced down into the mirror he was holding. A bloody cut on his cheek stood out against the darker muck of the dried blood Danielle must've missed. There were a few shards of glass in his hair. And the wound at the top of his forehead still looked nasty. He swapped the mirror for the joint. "Got your lighter there?"

"Here," Dusty said, passing it. He sat back down on the bed and looked at the mirror. Then he leaned closer and sniffed at it. "Christ." He started licking. "Bleuarrr! That's awful!" Contrary to his words however, he continued licking until the mirror was free of the pungent dust. "Hey that stuff *tingles* man!" He held out his tongue and waggled it around.

David sparked up, watching him with interest.

"Wha' i' mean when i' 'ingles?"

"I don't know," he laughed, exhaling smoke.

Danielle looked at them both, then at the mirror, and

tried to catch up. "Rick... the mirror... what, drugs or something?"

David shrugged. "Probably. Doesn't exactly matter I suppose."

"Matters to me," Dusty said, his tongue tentatively returning to the vicinity of his mouth.

Danielle was shaking her head. "No... Becky didn't, I mean she *wouldn't*... not if she knew–"

"Oh come on," David interrupted, resuming his search of the desk, "it's no big deal."

"You know..." Dusty began, "that stuff must've been pretty damned pure, man. I mean, you saw how much was there, yet I think I'm getting something."

David turned to him, took a drag on the joint, then asked, "You think he was dealing or something?"

"Come off it," Danielle interjected.

Dusty shook his head. "No idea. But that was pretty intense whizz."

David passed him the spliff. "Well well. Learn something new every day."

"I'm going to the toilet," Danielle suddenly told them, crossing the room to the door.

David looked at her. "Uh, you know I haven't checked it yet."

She stopped, realised. "If the light's on, I'll come back and fetch you, okay?"

He nodded.

She left the room, closing the door behind her.

"Nothing like a good joint," Dusty observed.

David smiled, then turned back to the desk to continue his methodical search. He found an old school timetable, an out-of-date UCI listings leaflet, some uncoiled and used typewriter ribbons, several pieces of paper covered in indecipherable scribbles, and not really much else. With a final sweep of his hand, he cleared the top of the desk, then kicked what he'd knocked off over towards the pile. "That was a waste of time."

"Would've thought the drawers'd be your best bet, anyway," Dusty advised, exhaling.

"Danielle hasn't found anything yet," he said, opening the top right-hand drawer.

"Speaking of Danni…"

"Yeah, she does seem to be taking a long time." He continued looking through the drawer.

"Reckon she's taking a dump?" Dusty wondered, passing the joint.

David smiled, raised the spliff to his lips. "I wouldn't know."

"Time of the month maybe?"

He snorted out a cloud. "Yeah, that'd explain a lot."

There were a few moments' silence as David smoked before Dusty spoke up again. "I really think she's taking too long, man."

"Come on, Dusty…" He looked at the younger youth, shook his head slightly. "Oh Christ I'd feel a right pervert checking on her."

Dusty shrugged. "What's wrong with being a pervert?"

David raised his eyebrows. "Know all about that, wouldn't you?" He took another drag on the joint, then passed it back. "Okay then, but if *I'm* not back soon, then there's no one else to check for you."

"Reckon I should come with you?" Dusty asked, his eyes wide.

David nodded. "Yeah." He gazed at the door. Took a step towards it. Paranoia overwhelmed him. "Fuck it I'm not going you do it she can bloody drown."

Dusty sniggered around the joint. "Drown?"

"Uh-huh. Drown."

The snigger turned to laughter. "You're crackers when you're stoned, man." He took a final drag on the spliff.

"Well something must've happened. Must've. Christ we shouldn't've let her go on her own."

"Oh yeah!" yelped Dusty, crushing the roach into Rick's overflowing bedside ashtray. "I'd've held her hand for sure!"

"Fucking come on this isn't funny–" His eyes suddenly widened. "Fuck, you don't think it's those hippy cunts again do you?"

Dusty's laughter was cut short. "Shit."

"Come on."

Dusty got up off the bed, and together they crept over to the door. David grasped the handle, and a moment later pulled it slowly open.

The hallway was just how they'd left it. The lights on, all the doors shut.

Beside him, David could hear Dusty breathing heavily. He stepped forwards. The bathroom was at the head of the stairs. Its door was shut.

Walking close to the wall, he moved towards it, Dusty matching his steps behind him. Glancing down the stairs before crossing to the door, David tried to see if the light was on inside, but with the hall so well illuminated it was difficult to tell. He stood next to the door, his hand raised, ready to knock.

Dusty was looking all around, eyes flickering every which way, then he turned to David and nodded sharply.

That was when they heard the intruder in the loft.

There was a soft thump, followed by several louder noises which could only have been footsteps.

The two youths stared at each other, faces bleached white, both poised and ready to run. But they remained frozen as the intruder started walking around again, this time dragging something behind him.

"It's them, it's got to be them, oh shit oh shit…" David's voice was quiet and panicky.

Dusty shook his head, whispering frantically, "No man, it's the creepy kid, that skinhead, he was just so scary, like a fuckin' monkey, got to be him."

"How did he get up there?"

Dusty shrugged his shoulders. "Can't see anything

in the hall," he said, turning around and scanning the ceiling.

David turned to the bathroom door and raised a trembling finger. "In there you think?"

Dusty started shaking his head as he realised. "Oh Danni… oh shit."

Looking down at the handle as if it was some strange animal, David slowly reached out and grasped it. The metal was cold. Closing his eyes and counting silently, he tentatively pushed down, ready to open the door.

"Do it," Dusty whispered urgently.

The door was lighter than David had imagined, and it swung open rather more quickly than he'd intended, but he needn't have worried: the bathroom was deserted.

Dusty let out a gasp of relief. "Can't see a trapdoor."

Stepping into the gloomily lit room, David peered around the back of the door.

Dusty watched as he tilted his head towards the ceiling. "Oh shit…"

David looked at him. "What do you reckon?"

The younger youth stepped into the room, and David pushed shut the door to reveal the open trapdoor, the yellow light spilling down, the lowered ladder. "What about weapons?"

There was another thump from the loft. It was quieter than before, and sounded much further away than the previous noises.

"No time," David informed him, and placed a foot on the lowest rung of the ladder. There was a small clang as his boot came in contact with the lightweight metal. "Better follow me up. Just in case."

"In case you need a hand?"

"In case the hippies've managed to get in the front door."

Dusty's face seemed to visibly drain of any remaining colour, and he almost pushed David up the ladders in his desperation.

The attic was cramped, dusty, and smelled of age and damp.

It was also incredibly silent. No rattling of pipes, no creaking of timbers. Just a few small clatters and thumps from the skinhead, and the noises David and Dusty were so desperately trying to avoid making.

They were crouched down next to the trapdoor, peering into the gloom. It seemed they were at the rear of the property, with the loft stretching away before them. There was only one bare bulb, which couldn't have been more than forty watts, hanging from a wire a few feet in front of them.

Beyond the light were shadows, and beyond the shadows was darkness.

That was where the noises were coming from.

Shuffling. Searching. Scraping of cardboard. Clomping of feet. Huffing of breath.

David looked at Dusty, then started off across the loosely laid floorboards.

They had just stepped past the light bulb when there was a much louder shuffling sound, followed by a grunt, then a continual shuffling, as if something heavy were being dragged across the uneven boards.

Dusty hissed, "Quick, back, to the side or something, hide…" He stepped out the way of the light, over to the side of the main boarded walkway. David darted over to the opposite side.

They waited as the dragging became louder. The skinhead was huffing with effort. In the gloom, David could make him out slightly. He seemed to be dragging a large box, about the size of a tea chest.

It was when he was about to step into the weak light from the bulb he fell over and squealed "Shit!" and landed on her front and almost broke her nose. Her dyed-red hair flopped around her head like a mutated money spider, and she looked up and said "Shit," again, just for the hell of it.

Dusty was the first to realise. "You had us shitting our pants!"

Danielle shrieked, leaping into the air, and swivelled herself towards him, eyes wide, face a mask of terror, and then David yelled, "What the fuck're you doing?!" and she screamed again and spun towards *him* and was so confused decided to crash to the floorboards once more.

The two youths stepped out from the shadows, hearts racing, and all but collapsed to the floor beside their friend.

Dusty caught David's eye, and started grinning. "Christ, man... Christ."

David nodded. "Yeah."

Danielle pushed herself up from the floor into a kneeling position. She clasped a hand to her chest and looked at each of them in turn, her breath coming in huge gasps. "Jesus fucking... *scared the shit out'f me you fuckers*!"

"We scared the shit out'f *you*?" David was incredulous. "We thought the skinhead'd got you or something!"

"Yeah Danni, how come you're up here?"

"I just..." she looked at him, catching her breath. "I mean, I thought Rick might have something up here, you know, something he'd kept in storage or whatever."

"Find anything?"

"Well I'm not sure. I mean, this box anyway. Got his name on, all taped up... I just thought we weren't having much luck in his room, were we?"

"Oh I don't know," Dusty commented, "I kind'f got something from it."

Ignoring him, David reached over and grabbed for the large cardboard box. It was fairly heavy, so he had to stand to drag it into the light. There was a sheet of white A4 sellotaped to the top, neatly felt-tip penned with an appropriate message:

RICHARD JAMES GREENHEAD
13C WHITBY AVENUE, HEXHAM NE46 3JJ
KEEP YOUR FUCKING HANDS OFF CUNTS

"Figured there might be something interesting inside," Danielle explained.

"Then why'd he keep it up here?" queried Dusty.

"It's not exactly covered in dust," David noticed. "Looks fairly new in fact. Probably he just put it up here a few weeks ago."

"Unless he only moved here a few weeks ago," Dusty suggested.

"He's been here years according to Becky."

"You still got the craft-knife?" David asked her, his hand outstretched.

"Yeah, somewhere." She dug it out and passed it over.

Trying to ignore the sticky-flaky feel of the nutcase's dried blood, David pushed the rest of the blade out and started slitting open that which Rick wanted no cunt to touch.

Christ knows why I'm bothering with this shite, there's no one I'd trust enough to read it, no one who wouldn't go completely mental having read it (at least, mental at me if not mental time-for-the-men-in-white-coats).

Suppose those same white-coat men would say it's some sort of therapy, getting it all down, off my chest, clearing my conscience, all that bollocks. Well I don't know. Don't give much of a shit either, to be honest. There's just something inside me, some burning or something, telling me to write, to type, to use this shitty typewriter and get down what I know before...

Before what?

Before I fuck up.

Before I make a mistake with the liquid card.

It's got me. I know that. I'm not one of your

typical twatfuck junkie wankers who can't even
get off fucking weed: shit get me another joint
or me head's gonna explode, what utter <u>cack</u>. Not
heard of something called willpower you wankers?
Self-awareness, to know when it's getting too
much, when it's time to stop? Mind you, most of
my so-called mates're headed in that direction,
so I shouldn't slag 'em off too much. Not that
they're likely to read this. But they're really
okay. Don't exactly need them to have a good
time, though.

Like I said, I'm in possession of a liquid
card.

And it's in possession of me.

It's not really alive. I used to think it
was. But what created it was alive, I'm pretty
certain of that. Alive when it created it, and
maybe <u>still</u> alive. Maybe watching how things're
turning out. What happens and who does what and
who has the balls to go all the way and who has
the intelligence to get out while they still
can.

Though mind you- shit phone, back soon.

*

Another day, another week, and even another
month if I'm not mistaken. It's just I've such a
busy life! Oh yeah oh yeah. Trotting off to
school in the morning, sitting around wondering
whether chewing razorblades would be more
enjoyable, then off to the supermarket in the
evening, wandering around <u>knowing</u> chewing
razorblades would be more enjoyable.

All the goopy blood sloshing around and
dribbling over your lips, the pain stabbing into

your brain and burning your head and numbing
your mouth.

But life's not as bad as it seems. I'm never
really bored. Never. I enjoy life. I have
everything. I want, I get. I mean, it's pretty
simple.

Oh fuck I can't be bothered actually. It's
bloody

02.12:13

in the morning, I've just got back from a
good night's shag and I need sleep. Of course, I
could always use the liquid card... See, I must
be getting better. Usually I wouldn't even think
about it. I'd just do it. But now I wonder. I
consider my other options. Think about it.

Then go and pause time anyway.

*

Just read back that last sentence. Good one,
good one. Of course it's not that simple.
Nothing ever is, really, at least not when
dealing with the liquid card. It's sort of like
a delaying of well not exactly time itself, but
the concept of time's existence. Like we believe
time ticks on in seconds and minutes and stuff
because that's what we know, what we've been
told, what we've learned. Only, like I said,
it's not that simple. It exists as a concept,
but its physical existence – the fact things
come after each other, moving ever onwards
towards something or other – doesn't have to
have anything to do with it. Which is pretty
obvious when you think about it, but think about
it you should. Actually you can go jack yourself
off in the bogs for all I give a shit (whoever

you are wherever you are whenever you are). But I'm typing this out for myself, and I want it all spelled out, explained as simply as possible.

Just in case one of these days my mind goes for a wander and doesn't quite manage to find its way back.

So anyway we're all physically aware of the passage of time, but conceptually it's a little less clear cut. Which is why the liquid card can do what it does.

Fucks the mind when you stare at it. The swirling colours the mixing liquids the sparkling depths. Hooks you and reels you in. Like all the drugs I've smoked and snorted (Christ even though I know no one's going to read this, it still makes me feel a twat writing that kind of thing), only hundreds of times more addictive. Because it's beyond a physical joint or line, beyond even sensation and experience. It's nothing you've ever seen before. Nothing you've ever been aware of before. It's freaky shit.

Physically, time carries on as normal. Conceptually, it slows right down. Almost stops. Pauses, if you like. It's a sort of delay. Delaying the conceptual existence of time. And meanwhile I have my fun. And meanwhile the liquid card eats away at my brain.

*

Just had to get you out and type this down. Properly pisses me off. Newspaper story - yet a-fuckin'-other one - about some twats who won the National Shittery and are so unhappy, got divorced, tried to kill themselves, all the usual sob-story bollocks (wonder how much the tabloids paid 'em): fuck me people must be so inconceivably <u>dense</u>. Are all people so fucking pigshit-thick? Jesus Christ 'money can't buy you everything I've got no friends no one loves me blah blah blah': how much shit is that?

Let me just put the story straight once and for fucking all.

I have everything I've ever wanted.

I don't have it, I go out and fucking get it.

And I love it.

Every physical moment.

It's what we're all striving for really, isn't it? Ultimate contentment. Yeah. I am ultimately content. And it is lovely.

I get a hard-on, I pull some smart lass's pants down and ram it in. I get hungry, I eat. I run low on funds, I go to a bank or shop and take whatever I need. I feel like driving a sports car, I find one, take it, then hit the road. I get some twisted idea into my head, maybe an idea for a joke, I just go out and do it. I fancy visiting a tropical island, I visit a tropical island. It's that simple. It's my life. It's wonderful.

Ultimate contentment.

He-hee, what a sermon! But no one to read it but me, no one to care but me.

School's getting so shit nowadays. I mean, not that it wasn't before, but I don't even seem to find it as amusing as I once did. And as for the supermarket, Jesus god when will someone just blow the fucking thing up? I suppose that's

the daftest thing about all this, that I still
stack shelves in a supermarket. But it's what
normal guys like me do, right? And I have to
appear normal.

I'm not sure how many liquid cards exist, or
even if anyone but the possessors know about
them, but if someone heard even a rumour... Well
that's not exactly likely, the fucking hold the
things have on you. You don't want to let it go
for anything. The card comes before everything
else. It's the way it is. The way it's always
been. And probably the way it'll always be.

*

Well shit so I can't even put aside a few
minytes evrry week to type this - diary? story?
load of bllocks? - on a regular basis, but no
one's perfect. In fact I suppose I'm juyst
lazty. I mean I'm knackered more-or-less all the
tim. And especiallytoday. My birthday, see?
Kind'f offf my tits at the minute, but I
thought, what the hell, I'll get out the old
clang-clang-clanger adn add a few sentences.
It's 19th September 1997 at

23.44:09

and I'm now eghteen. Well wekl. Actaully I'm
tio psised to think letr alobe tyupiee

*

Fucked a proper young un today. Christ I kind'f
regret it. But I only worked out her age
afterwards. You know? Christ. Wondered why there
was so much yucky mess.

*

Got some serious coke last Friday night. Serious
fuckin' stuff. Splashed all my mates. Even

170

suggested hitting the Riverside in Newcastle.
Then proceeded to tap up some minger. Yueerrrk.
But then... ah, but then...

And so it was that love entered the world of
Rick Greenhead.

Christ it was mental. We went back to
someone's house, kind'f a party, and there she
was. Properly corny: sitting on her own in an
armchair, this standard lamp next to her bathing
her in a warm yellow glow, and as coked-up as I
was it was as if she were spot-lit. I can hardly
remember the actual details of how we first got
together. But it feels like we were somehow
drawn to each other. I suppose everyone says
that sort of thing though. I don't know. Christ
this has never happened to me before.

And now we're together.

I haven't used the liquid card since.

Becky and Rick.

*

Oh yeah Becky and Rick.

And now Becky and Rick and the liquid card.

I couldn't help showing her. The card made
me. I'm sure of it. The thing has control of my
mind.

It freaked her out so much she pissed her
pants.

She was screaming her head off. Clinging to
me. Then when she saw the fuck-off wide grin the
card always gives me she stepped back. Away.
Screaming.

But then I gave it to her and she did it
herself and it enveloped her brain with its
existence and power and it was all soft and cosy

and cotton wool inside her head and she smiled
and then she grinned and she had so much fun and
it was beautiful.

*

Got a regular supply of that lovely lovely
cocaine now. Me and Becky. Snort it all up and
buzz in the head and then the liquid card.
Picking and choosing, pointing someone out and
jumping on them and using them and sometimes
wearing them out so much not even the liquid
card can get their conceptual perception of time
back to normal.

*

Fuck. Never thought I'd say this but I'm
depressed. Even with Becky. Even with the liquid
card.

I'm having some serious difficulty typing
today. I just sat and stared at the page for
about five minutes then. My mind blank. My eyes
unfocused. I just... it's lethargy, depression,
regret, confusion, everything all rolled up
together.

Becky's not here. She doesn't know about this
diary. If you can call it a diary with its
entries separated by days and weeks and months.
And I don't even write down what I did! Or not
much of what I did anyway.

Becky's not here.

*

This year is dragging on forever. It feels like
so much time has passed.

Of course, physically, it has.

Me and Becky have been using the liquid card
so much.

172

It's frightening, how much we rely on it. We don't even bother with the coke. All we need is each other. And the card.

The lovely card with its swirling liquids and delightful colours.

I'm looking at it now.

It's kind'f faded slightly over the past few weeks.

Me and Becky have been enjoying it to the limits of physical sensation and experience.

We are one with the liquid card.

It seems to be darkening slightly. Collapsing in on itself.

Slipped it back into my jacket pocket. It's safe now.

There's cock all on the television nowadays, don't you think?

"WHAT?"

"'There's cock all on the television nowadays, don't you think?'" David repeated.

"And… and that's it?"

"Ain't that enough, man?!" Dusty squealed. "Jesus Christ the guy was fucking… oh maan…"

"That's it Danni." He passed her over the final crumpled typewritten sheet.

"The guy was crackers, a nutcase, it's just coincidence, no one can fuck with time, no one." Dusty was shaking his head.

David had found the diary in a cardboard folder on top of the other contents of the box. It had been one of the first things he'd checked. The rest of the box looked full of several other folders and files, but from what he'd seen, it was mainly old schoolwork. As soon as he'd realised what he'd found, he'd read it out loud to Dusty and Danielle.

It had freaked them all out.

Now Danielle was shaking her head. She looked up from the papers. "Fucking hell."

David nodded. "Yeah."

"Okay, okay," she began, dumping the pages on the folder, "let's just suppose we take this at face value. That Rick Greenhead had some bizarre card-type thing which let him muck around with time. And that, somehow, when he and Becky both started using it, it, I don't know, overloaded, fucked up, and everyone died."

"Oh man," Dusty muttered.

"Why in hell didn't Becky mention anything? I mean, she'd been acting pretty secretive like I said, but if she'd just told me…"

"He said it was like a drug, didn't he?" Dusty remembered. "Said it had them both hooked. She wouldn't've been able to say anything even if she'd wanted, man."

"Yeah, but to think all this could've been prevented."

He nodded. "Yeah. Extreme."

David seemed to have come to some understanding. "Wait a minute," he interrupted, his forehead creased in concentration, "what was he going on about? Conceptual perception of time being different from physical perception?"

"Christ, something like that," Danielle agreed, "fuck knows what it meant."

"Well, what if when this card thing finally fucked up – and god knows how – what if it conceptually *stopped* time, rather than just physically delaying it like when Rick used it?"

"Or it used Rick," Dusty whispered.

Danielle looked at David. "What difference would that make?"

Dusty said, "Maybe it would mean like, watches and things would stop?"

"Exactly."

"But what about everyone dying? I mean, why haven't they just paused? Or stopped like the watches?"

"Because I don't think time has just conceptually *slowed down*. I think it has conceptually ceased to exist. Time has… died."

"That's rubbish." She looked at him. "I mean, we're still alive – and that's another thing – things're still happening one after another, time's still ticking on."

"As a physical sense of time passing, maybe. But conceptually I think it's kaput. I seriously think he's managed to fuck it where it hurts. Time doesn't exist anymore." He paused before adding, "As for why we survived, fuck knows."

Dusty had picked up the pages of diary, and was examining them closely. "'…the limits of physical sensation and experience,'" he quoted.

David and Danielle looked at him.

"And just what are the limits of human physical sensation and experience?"

Danielle shrugged. "Go on, surprise me."

"Sex and death, man," said Dusty.

There was the sound of breaking glass from outside.

All three of them leaped to their feet and looked around, eyes wide, hearts racing.

"Fuckfuck-hippiesfuck-monkeyshit!" Dusty yelled.

"Quiet!" Danielle ordered. "What do you reckon David?"

He shook his head. "No idea. Sounded like a few houses down, but could've been anywhere in this silence."

"Okay, Dusty grab that diary, let's get out of here, try and see what the hell's going on."

"All right," David agreed, stepping over towards the trapdoor. He let the other two clamber down first, making sure Dusty had the typewritten sheets clutched tightly in his hands.

Once they were all in the bathroom, David decided it would be easier to leave the access ladders down, and they walked quietly across the upstairs landing and over to a window which looked out onto the street.

There was nothing there.

"Safe to turn the light off?" Danielle asked.

"Should be all right," David replied, leaning over and flicking the switch. The hallway disintegrated into murky blackness. "Okay," he whispered, "yous keep a look out,

I'm going to check Rick's room for a weapon or something."

Danielle nodded agreement, her eyes fixed on the street outside.

He walked quickly back into Rick's bedroom, scanning the room for the likeliest hiding place. Surely he'd have been paranoid enough to have stashed a weapon somewhere? Just in case someone discovered his 'liquid card'? David opened the wardrobe and started pushing clothes around, checking to see if a baseball bat was leaning against the back corner, or if maybe an iron bar was lying amidst the pile of footwear at the bottom.

No such luck.

He was searching the bedside desk drawers for a handy butcher's knife when Danielle hissed from the corridor, "David! Quick! We've seen 'em!"

Joining them at the hallway window, he looked out onto the street.

More-or-less directly across the road, there was a group of tattered-looking men and women gathering around someone's front door. A moment later, the door was opened from the inside, and everyone trooped into the house.

"The guy got in through the window," Danielle explained, pointing towards a broken ground floor front window, which was hanging open.

David hadn't noticed it before, but now it was freewheeling into view, he muttered, "Christ," at the sight of a battered white Ford van stopping in front of the house. The driver put on the handbrake, then got out to join the guy who'd been helping push the vehicle down the slight slope of the road.

They leaned against the front of the van, smoking and chatting quietly.

"Fuckin' looters," Dusty whispered.

"Yeah."

"They were on this side of the road before," Danielle explained. "Next door. That's why we couldn't see them."

David looked at her. "You mean Rick's house is next?"

She nodded slowly. "Could well be."

"Well whyn't just leave now, then?" suggested Dusty. "Let's just get out, they need never know we were here. Huh?"

"I don't get it," David said, ignoring him, "they all look like they know each other. I mean, from before the freeze."

"Yeah, like from some hippy commune," agreed Danielle. "Or a bunch of Gypsies."

"Well how come they all survived?"

"Like I said before, man," Dusty replied, "sex and death."

"Come off it," Danielle told him.

"But it's true," he persisted. "It's like the time-fuck man said, 'the limits of physical–'"

"'–sensation and experience,' yeah we know." She shook her head.

"You know, I've been thinking about that," David revealed.

"Don't you start," she warned.

"No but listen." He turned to them both, his expression serious. "Time conceptually doesn't exist anymore. It's been conceptually destroyed, right?"

"But physically it still exists, yeah yeah, blah blah."

Ignoring her, he continued, "And when it happened, when it was conceptually destroyed – the freeze – most people died too."

"Any particular reason?"

"Haven't exactly worked that out, something to do with people being conceptually linked with time I suppose, I don't know... But I reckon I know why we survived."

"I'm waiting."

"Well think about it. What could counteract or bypass a conceptual destruction – a *nonphysical* destruction?"

She shrugged her shoulders. "Something physical, I guess."

"Exactly. The most extreme – or basic, depending on your point-of-view – physical human experiences. Sex and death." He leaned closer. "Physically time still exists. So those extreme physical experiences must exist, too. And, at the time of the freeze, everyone physically experiencing them..."

"Then they must still exist, too," she finished slowly.

He nodded, pausing before adding, "It's absolutely mad, mad stuff, I know. But kind of believable. Like, it's so simple."

"Dave Thornwood, professor of metaphysics for the new millennium."

Dusty offered, "The new millennium which, ah, doesn't actually exist anymore, right prof?"

He looked at them both, his head tilted slightly. "Up yours."

"Whoah!" Danielle suddenly exclaimed in amazement. "Look at what they're getting!"

David and Dusty turned their attention to the looters across the street. Two women were currently loading a huge screen television set into the back of the van, where the driver and his mate were busy sorting out the rest of the goodies.

Dusty shook his head. "Man, don't they know what's happened?"

David shrugged. "Either that or they just don't care. But there's sure as hell no point in getting half the stuff they've got." Under the orange glare of a streetlamp he could make out an array of electrical equipment, a load of furniture, and a pile of material he assumed was clothing. Maybe one more house and they'd have difficulty shutting the van's rear doors.

"What're we going to do?" Danielle wondered.

"I don't know. Stay here, I suppose. There's not much room in that van, I doubt they'll bother searching the upstairs."

"We could hide in the loft," Dusty suggested.

"Whatever. I'm going to check Rick's room again, if I can't find anything we'll each get a knife from the kitchen, okay?"

Danielle nodded, so he went back into the bedroom.

The bedside desk drawer still hung open. Inside were various pairs of underwear and socks. Not bothering to shut it, he got down on his hands and knees and peered under the bed. In line with the rest of the room, the space was cluttered and messy. Junk ranged from empty crisp packets and food containers, to a well-thumbed magazine David guessed was pornographic.

Instead of reaching for it, he grabbed at a metal tin sitting just behind the valance. Within easy reach of anyone who might be lying in bed, tripping out on paranoia, desperate for something with which to defend himself and his bizarre treasure.

The tin box was pleasingly heavy, and he lifted it onto the bed, undid the clasps, then opened the lid.

An urgent whispering from the hallway: "David, better get down to the kitchen if you're going!"

He smiled. "No need. No need."

He lifted the pistol out of the box and felt its weight, its metal construction.

Its power.

He pressed a button on the grip, and a long rectangle of metal dropped out the bottom and onto his lap. The magazine was loaded with shining silver bullets and, from its weight, David guessed loaded to capacity.

He slammed it back in like they show you in the movies and it went CLACK! and he grinned and it felt so damned good.

Danielle appeared in the doorway. "My fucking good Christ…"

David turned to her, still grinning. "The guy must've been an absolute headcase."

"Uh, don't you think you should leave it alone?"

"What? Who the hell's going to argue with you when you're pointing this at them?"

She twisted her face. "Maybe, but… well Christ just don't shoot anyone."

"Shoot anyone?" Dusty asked, appearing next to Danielle. "We should be so lucky, finding a gun– *oh fuck we've found a gun a real live gun oh shit*!"

"Where're the looters?" David snapped.

"Huh?" Dusty shook his head, tried to concentrate. "Er… just, just about to smash a downstairs window, I guess."

"Right. We hole up in Rick the Psycho's bedroom and lock the door, surely they won't bother if it's locked?"

Danielle nodded. "Yeah, that sounds sensible enough."

David got up and went over to the door, shutting and locking it as quietly as he could. As he turned around to ask if they should turn the light off, there was the sound of breaking glass from downstairs, directly beneath their feet. "Fuck." He turned the light off anyway.

"Hey shit," whispered Dusty, "where's the bed?"

"Quiet for god's sake, you too Danielle, no talking unless necessary, just stay on the bed, I'll be next to the wardrobe, opposite the door."

There were one or two shuffling noises as Dusty and Danielle found the bed in the impenetrable darkness, but David guessed they'd be muffled by the noises the intruder was making. It sounded like he was having difficulty getting through the window.

A moment later there was the sound of laughter from outside, more breaking glass, then a loud smashing and shattering from the room below. Then a very loud and very annoyed, "FUCKING HELL."

He leaned back against the wardrobe, the gun gripped tightly in his right hand. Even with the darkness disabling his sight, he still felt completely protected. He listened as the intruder unlocked the front door and let in his looter mates. They started searching the ground floor rooms, clanging and banging, whooping at something of interest, tearing the place apart for anything worth stealing.

Some part of him hoped they'd come upstairs, check Rick's door, break in.

Then he'd have to use the pistol.

Point it at them and chamber a round and the metallic noise would convince them it was real and then they'd be shitting themselves and maybe just maybe he'd shoot the fuckers anyway.

He felt so powerful in the dark.

"Sounds like they're coming upstairs," Danielle whispered urgently.

There was a heavy clomp-clomp-clomping from somewhere below and to the right of them.

Footsteps on the stairs.

Light started bleeding around the doorframe as someone switched the upstairs hallway light back on. David could hear one or two exclamations of anticipation. Then a much louder banging noise, almost right outside the door.

They were checking the bedrooms.

Half of him wanted to curse his continual rotten luck.

The other half wanted to grin widely.

"Shit this fucker's locked," from the hall.

"Kick the cunt dooon!" in reply.

David didn't know what to feel. On one hand, he felt a genuine, burning anger for anyone who could so recklessly and eagerly destroy another's home and property just for the hell of it, but on the other, everyone was dead, survival was now the name of the game, and maybe looting and vandalising was just their way of dealing with things too overwhelming to be dealt with rationally.

Christ, what would he himself be doing if he hadn't met up with any other survivors?

There were several moments of intense hammering as someone started battering the offending bedroom door. After a while, there was huge crunching noise, followed by several whoops of triumph. It sounded like at least four people were trooping into the room.

From the bedroom next-door there was a muffled, "Hey, I recognise this'n': proper bum bandit, wanders about our way sometimes."

"Them frozen fuckers freak me out," someone said.

David realised they were talking about the frozen in the bedroom, whom he'd seen sat at a desk.

After a moment's movement, there was a snort of laughter. "Yeah he suits that for sure!"

"What about *this*?!" There was a terrible crunching, smashing and splintering sound.

Followed by more laughter.

"Fuck that man's got telly on the brain!"

And then there were footsteps in the hallway and the noise of a handle turning, and it was Rick's bedroom door and the noise was so loud and echoey in David's ears and the handle-turner cursed and yelled, "This'n's locked too!"

"Found jack shit in that other locked one, fuck it," someone hollered.

"Aye howay, just leave it, see what the lasses've got from downstairs."

Clomping footsteps started their descent as another two sets headed across the hall to join them.

From outside Rick's door, the handle-turner once more lived up to his name and called, "Ain't yous two divvies in'rested in this 'ere locked door?"

"Everyone else fucked off?"

"Aye, reckon ol' Raw Man fucked his foot kickin' down the other'n'!"

"All righty, let's show 'em what we're made of!"

And they started booting the door.

David shuffled further back towards the wardrobe. He could hear Dusty and Danielle moving around slightly on the bed. Could almost smell their fear.

And his own.

He held the pistol out in front of him, gripped tightly in two hands, pointed at the door.

It sounded like all three of them were kicking the door simultaneously now, yelling and shouting and cursing with each blow.

The door took about three more coordinated kicks before David started to hear the splinter of wood.

"Couple more an' we'll 'ave it!"

In fact, it only took one more.

The door shot inwards and swung around to slam against the bottom of Rick's bed. The three looters stumbled about a bit, caught off balance, then stood in the doorway, silhouetted by the upstairs hallway light. It wasn't strong enough to creep too far into the room however, so David doubted they'd seen him yet.

"Get some light on the subject, lad!" one of them demanded.

The one nearest the wall trailed his hand around until he found the light switch.

He pressed it.

Rick's bedroom exploded with light.

David remained frozen, the pistol pointed at the three looters. In the periphery of his vision, he could see Dusty and Danielle on the bed. They too were motionless.

"Oh hey man…" the guy who'd turned the light on mumbled.

They all stared wide-eyed, the whites of their eyes standing out against the muck and dirt on their faces. David remained as frozen as he could. One of them stepped carefully forwards, slowly raising an arm. By the time it was horizontal, David could see it was shaking badly.

Fingers outstretched, the looter made to touch the gun.

A few inches away, he stopped. Whispered, "You think I should?"

Behind him, his mates were equally transfixed. "Don't…" mumbled one. "I mean… it might go off."

The first guy began to lower his arm. Nodded. "Yeah. Might. Might go off."

David's eyes were starting to water.

Time to make an entrance, he told himself.

He grinned.

Snaked his left hand on top of the gun and yanked back the slide and it went CLICK-*CLACK!!* and the three looters screamed in unison and one of them had the presence of mind to just spin around and get the hell out and ask questions later, but David wasn't really in the mood for questions so pulled the trigger on the pistol and the noise was absolutely incredible, deafening, the empty cartridge jumping out the breech and spinning away, the slide automatically loading the next round, and David pressed the trigger again and again the gun roared and again the guy in front jerked backwards and this time fell to the floor, while behind him the third guy was pissing his pants and staring bug-eyed as David pulled the trigger again but he was so shit-scared he didn't react like the first guy: the first guy knew what happened when people shot you – half of you ejected out your back and smeared itself over the wall and then you fell over writhing around in pain – the other guy knew this too but was so shocked rigid couldn't actually figure out what in hell to do, so just stood there as David once more exploded the room with light and smoke and noise and not much else really seeing as he'd aimed direct at the guy's chest and by rights there should be a massive hole through which you could see daylight but no there was nothing and David gaped at him and then something in his head went click and he–

–yelled, "*OH FUCKSHIT DANNI DUSTY RUN JUST FUCKING RUN THEY'RE BLANKS!*"

WONDERING WHETHER DIVING HEADLONG OUT of the window would be less of a suicidal manoeuvre, David pushed himself past the guy still standing in the doorway – still gaping forwards in disbelief, still shuddering in terror, still pissing his pants in fright – and raced through the hallway over to the stairs.

Where already there were people bounding upwards to see what the fuck was going on.

Behind him, Danielle and Dusty made their way over, looking almost as terrified as the guy in the doorway.

He pointed the gun down the stairs. *"Out the way or you're dead too!"* he bawled in his best shit-action-movie aggressive-lead-character bawl.

The leading looter looked up, dropped his jaw in disbelief, then more-or-less dived backwards onto those who were following. "*Shi'le'methefuckout!*"

The men and women soon got the message.

David negotiated his way through the last of the scattering looters, checking Dusty and Danielle were still following, then they all raced out the front door and back into the silence and cold of the night.

There were bits and pieces of loot strewn around the road and in front of the house, while the looters themselves were busy hiding behind their Ford van, which David saw hadn't moved from where he'd last seen it.

He turned to his friends. "Quick, into the Micra!"

"You cunts why'd you kill 'em, man?!" squealed someone from the vicinity of the Ford.

There was a communal intake of breath from the rest of the group as they prepared for what they no doubt thought would be a hail of bullets, but David just ignored them, and busied himself with getting the car keys out his pocket.

Encouraged by the lack of reaction, someone else shouted, "Whyn't fight like the fuckin' man you ain't, cunt?"

Danielle got into the back seat of the Nissan, while Dusty went around to the passenger door, remembered the frozen still sitting there, then got into the back as well.

David opened the driver's door and was about to get in when the sound of breaking glass behind him shocked him into spinning around, gun raised.

It was the first floor hallway window. One of the guys he'd shot was smashing all the glass out, yelling to be heard over the noise. "It ain't real, man! The fuckin' gun! It's fake, we're okay, it's not real, *fuckin' get 'em!*"

"Ah, shit," commented David, diving into the Micra and stabbing the keys into the ignition. A moment later the engine was ticking over, a moment after that he had it in first and was ready to take off, and that was when the first of the looters started appearing from around the van.

He floored it.

It was hard to see out the passenger side of the windscreen where Limp Dick Man had spider-webbed it, but he could hear the looters approaching rapidly. One of them managed to pelt a missile through the passenger door window, almost knocking the frozen out of its seat in the process, but by then the hatchback's tyres had got a grip on the tarmacadam, and they were off.

One or two objects bounced off the vehicle's roof, and one even cracked the rear window, but David was pleased to see no one had yet dived into the van and taken off after them. The dilapidated state the thing was in, it probably started rattling and threatened to drop to bits once it hit thirty, but all the same, another car chase was something he could do without.

At the end of the street, he turned up towards the high school road.

Dusty said, "That... was nuts."

Danielle agreed. "Absolutely... insane."

David seemed a little miffed. "Well next time, one of yous can think of something, stand there like a prick

192

shitting your pants wondering what in god's name you're going to do next. See how far you get."

"Okay David, okay." Danielle smiled. "But… a blank firer…" She dissolved into fits of giggles.

"Hey I thought it was still pretty cool," defended Dusty. "Scared the shit out'f me, anyway."

"Oh yeah, me too," Danielle agreed, "but… but… firing blanks!"

"Oh so that what's so amusing is it?" David muttered. "Christ."

He yanked the wheel around to the left, turning sharply onto the high school road, and roared up the incline.

"Where are you going?" asked Dusty.

"Yes where are you going?" Danielle parroted.

David shrugged his shoulders. "Thought we might find something interesting at the school."

"Hey come on man," Dusty protested, "I spend most of my time trying to get away from that place, you know."

"And I'm not exactly fond of it, either."

"Thought you said you were in sixth form?"

"So?"

"So why haven't you quit if it's shit?"

"Did you?"

"No," he replied tightly. "Persevered right to the bitter end, and what did I end up with? Fuck all." He shook his head, gripped the steering wheel tighter. The memories hurt. "Absolutely fuck all."

"Heavy," observed Dusty.

David slowed them down at the front gates, and turned onto the driveway, guiding the car around the twisting road up to the main entrance. It was a community high school, so would still have been open at the time of the freeze, night classes well under way, and there was even a ball game of some description frozen on the playground.

As he got out the driver's door, he looked over at the frozen players, barely illuminated by the weak floodlights. They were your stereotypical sporty types, all brawn and no brains, each wearing an expression of grim determination more commonly found on the average Rottweiler.

He turned back to the building itself. Its three storeys loomed above them. It seemed as if he knew each and every brick, was familiar with every aspect, every room, corridor, hiding place, out-of-bounds area, everything. How many years had he spent at the place? In how many ways had it shaped his life, formed his character? Twisted his personality, soured his views on the world?

The best years of your life.

Yeah well maybe so far, but Christ something would have to change sooner or later.

And of course it had.

He had tried to gut his supervisor.

And failed.

And been so emotionally involved in the physical experience of death (or near-death, anyway), he had survived the apocalypse.

The apocalypse of Rick Greenhead and his girlfriend, junkies to the end, hooked on the power of the liquid card.

And now David Thornwood was the new Possessor.

He suddenly laughed out loud.

Dusty and Danielle turned to him. They'd got out of the car, and were waiting for him to make a move.

He shook his head. "Just thinking about what Pricky Ricky wrote – you know, about him being 'the possessor' or something." He smiled. "Now I've got the card, what does that make me?"

"Not sure if you've noticed man," Dusty told him, "but that card's dead. The time-fuck nutcase said it was all colourful and stuff, hooked you in when you looked at it, but…" He trailed off.

"Yeah, I know," David agreed. "It's shivers-down-the-spine when you look at it sure, but nothing like what Rick was saying; no colours, no movement, nothing. It must be dead."

Danielle offered helpfully, "Might that have something to do with the fact he and Becky snapped it in half?"

"Why do you reckon they did?"

She shrugged. "No idea. Maybe they wanted one each. Maybe when it finally fucked up it somehow… exploded or something… Christ I don't know, and I don't think we'll ever find out."

David looked at her. Nodded. Because of course it was

true. How were they supposed to find out more? There'd been nothing but the diary to suggest Rick and his card had anything to do with all this. And that could hardly be constituted as proof the young lovers had destroyed the world. Ricky-boy was such a narcissist he might've just been typing out his bullshit fantasies, whittering on aimlessly, talking bollocks, writing a weird short story or something. Even if it were genuine, who was to know the exact date of the last entry? What had transpired between that time and the time of the freeze? With the diary all taped up in a box and put in storage, it would suggest the final entry had been a good few weeks ago, and that Rick didn't see himself bothering to add anything else in the near future. Why? Was it because, deep down, he knew he didn't actually *have* a future?

"Christ, let's get inside, I'm starting to get chilly."

They walked up the steps to the front doors, and stepped into the silent foyer. There was a portable blackboard set up between the entrance to the ground floor corridor and the main hall doors, informing visitors which rooms the night classes were being held in, and any other extra-curricular activities which were happening.

David pulled the blank firer from the ski jacket pocket he'd put it in, and held it out in front of him.

Danielle shook her head. "It does look pretty damned real."

"Suppose it's meant to," Dusty said. "But you think we'll need it Dave? In here?"

"God knows," he admitted. "Better safe than sorry though, I guess."

"So… what're we doing here again?" asked Danielle.

"I don't know. I mean, we haven't exactly got anything better to do and, well, maybe there're a few things we need, medical stuff, you know."

"Wow. Good thinking. The Medical Office is over there." She started off towards a door just a few feet along the ground floor corridor, which stretched away to their left.

"Yeah I, uh, did go to this school you remember?"

"Funny I never saw you around. You know. Bound to've both been here at the same time… some time."

"Me too man," Dusty piped up. "Hey, to think we could've all seen each other before this, maybe even stood in the same dinner queue or something." He paused. "Intense…"

They stepped into the Med Office, and David and Danielle started searching for a way to break into the locked supply cupboard, David replacing the replica weapon into a jacket pocket.

There was a large bench with a thin plastic-covered mattress against the far wall, and Dusty plonked himself down. He waited a while before asking, "So how come yous haven't mentioned anything yet?"

"What?" David asked, checking beneath the bed bench for a handy lock-pick or even handier crowbar.

"You know. About the freeze. Sex and death. How come

yous haven't asked what we were all doing? To see if it backs up the theory."

Danielle glanced up at him, and began, "I don't really think–"

David interrupted, "Let's just say, from what I know, it backs it up. Okay?" He looked up at Dusty.

Shrugging his shoulders, he said, "I'm not, you know, bothered about telling you. I mean, if you tell me what you were doing. Yeah?"

Smirking, but still trying to be serious, David shook his head. "No."

"Someone was trying to rape me, actually," Danielle said evenly. "Then, the freeze. I ran away. Screaming. Went into the supermarket. And there was David."

Dusty looked at her.

"Does that," she asked, waving a hand around, "back up the theory?"

"Uh, I guess sort of, I mean yeah, pretty much," Dusty mumbled, embarrassed.

"So then," she smiled humourlessly, "I've shown you mine, now you show me yours." She tilted her head to one side. "Or do I have to guess?" She was looking at him with a rather worrying glint in her eyes. "Let me see now... hmm – what can it be? – I know, you were hunched over with your cock in your hand and were busy tugging it back and forth, gaping with your stoned eyes at my best friend. Huh? Hit the nail have I? Or am I just *way* off?"

Dusty defended himself. "I don't think... I mean, there's nothing wrong with it, I'm not ashamed about it."

"Christ," Danielle breathed. "You really fucking were... Jesus you really were."

"Come off it, everyone does it man!" he yelped, getting increasingly agitated. "Ain't nothing wrong with it."

David felt it was time to lighten the mood. "Yeah, I do it all the time, and there's nothing wrong with *me*." He got up and stumbled around, feigning blindness, his arms outstretched. "Uh shit, I can't see, Christ – hairs on my palms, ahhh!"

Danielle shot him a look of contempt. "Grow up for fuck's sake. I'm talking about sexual harassment here, bloody peeping tom pervert–"

"Hey, I think that's a bit much," David warned.

"Ah, bollocks to it, you know," Dusty said, resigned. "So I was wanking over an attractive girl, wow-wee, now there's something you don't hear about every day, huh?" He huffed before continuing. "Anyways, all of a sudden she stops moving. Like I said, she was pretty het up about something, in a right state. Sounded like maybe she was screaming, too. Yelling stuff. Then, she freezes. Freaks me out a little – yeah, I was wrecked already – and just as I was about to... so I don't... well you know. No one was in, so I go downstairs, muck about with the–" Suddenly he stopped, eyes wide. "Hey shit, the cat, I was playing with the cat after the freeze."

"Surely it wasn't jacking itself off too?" Danielle wondered.

Dusty ignored her. "It'd been asleep in the lounge man, got the snip years ago, and I'm pretty sure it wasn't killing anything… how'd it survive?"

David turned to Danielle. "When we went to yours, you remember me saying I heard a dog barking?"

She creased her forehead, trying to remember. "Christ yeah. You… you reckon all the animals survived?"

He shrugged his shoulders. "No idea. Nothing to suggest they didn't, though: I mean, we've not seen any frozen, have we?"

She shook her head. "So how–?"

"It's got to be something to do with their perception of time," he decided. "I mean, like, it must be different from ours, right? So maybe, from an animal's point-of-view, there's nothing really conceptual about it, do you think?"

"So that means they wouldn't be affected by stopping – or destroying – time as a concept. Hmm." She nodded. "Logical… -ish. Sort of."

"I still don't get all this conceptual time physical destruction patter, man," Dusty complained.

"Well," David turned to him, "just think of it as the difference between our measurement of time – like seconds, minutes, weeks, years, all that – and the fact we're standing here without any clocks or calendars yet it's pretty obvious time – or something we know as 'time' – is passing. Right?"

"Uh, I guess."

"Well, what we're saying is time as a concept has been destroyed, while physically it still exists."

"So… which is which then?"

"What? Well which do you think?"

Dusty remained blank.

"Well what's a concept then?"

"Er… I don't, I mean, something in your head or something?"

"Right. So what's likely to've come out of someone's head? The measurement of time or the physical feeling of time passing?"

"Ah. Right. Well you didn't really say it like that before. I mean, physical feelings yeah, I got you. Right." He paused. "Doesn't exactly help us much, but yeah, I think I know what you mean."

"How do you know it doesn't help us?" Danielle asked. "We could, I mean, something could happen. We've got the thing that destroyed it in the first place, surely someone'll've survived who might know what to do? You know, based on the knowledge we have."

"Well, we'll just have to hope," David said. He turned back to the supply cupboard. "Still haven't got this thing open."

She shrugged, then stepped over to the door. "I don't know, think I might look for a key."

"In for a hell of a search, aren't you?"

"There's a key cupboard in the admin office."

"And the key for *that*?" piped up Dusty.

"If I can't find it, we'll just have to unlock it with your cock."

She left.

Dusty stared at the door, dumbfounded. "Whoah."

David tried to reassure him. "Wouldn't worry about it."

"But... my *cock*?"

Trying not to laugh, David leaned against the supply cupboard and commented, "She can't've meant it, she must know it'd be far too small."

"Oh yeah you are funny. Christ." He shook his head. "She wants to learn to chill, man."

He couldn't help but agree. "You got that right. Was like it with me too. I don't know. Maybe it's just... too much, you know? Shit, I'm surprised we all haven't cracked yet."

"I've been close, man. I don't mind telling you, like with her out the room, but... I've been real close. After the hippies and that fucking shaven monkey." He smiled. "Could've seriously done with a bucket after *that* carry-on."

"Yeah, know what you mean." He looked at the younger youth for a moment, sitting on the bed bench, his legs dangling, looking like he hadn't a care in the world. He asked, "So... what do you think we should do now, Dusty? I mean, after we get the bandages and stuff out the cupboard. What then?"

It was a while before he answered. "I... I just... I keep

thinking, why haven't the good guys survived, you know? Why aren't there any nice people alive? Like normal, good people, who don't take drugs, aren't peeping toms, don't run around with hard-ons and long hair, don't go looting the neighbourhood, you know? Where're all the people who usually survive disasters? The ones who help each other, fall in love with each other, sacrifice themselves for each other… Christ man."

"You said yourself. Sex and death. No one good gets involved in death, and as for sex… well maybe someone somewhere's trying to tell us something, huh?"

"Don't be ridiculous," Danielle said from the corridor. A moment later she rejoined them in the room. "Just because you're good doesn't mean your relatives don't die. Just because you're good doesn't mean you don't like sex. Anyway, who's saying us three aren't good?"

"Dusty was," David revealed.

Flustered a little, she continued, "Well, even so, there's probably loads of 'good' people who've survived."

"Then where are they all, man?" Dusty protested. "All we've seen are psychos and weirdos."

"I don't know, probably all together somewhere. You know, like everyone's met up, congregated someplace." She paused. "Someplace we're too dumb to find."

"Well we haven't exactly been looking," David said. "And who's to say anyone else is likely to be looking, either? Everyone'll just be as shit-scared and confused as us."

"I just think it's time we properly thought about what we're going to do, how we're going to survive," Dusty decided. "We just seem to run around bumping into all the shitheads and getting fucking nowhere."

"Okay Dusty, okay," Danielle said reassuringly, her earlier anger forgotten, "let's just get this cupboard open, sort ourselves out, then think about what we're going to do."

No one spoke for a few moments before David remembered, "You get the key?"

She held it up. "Yeah, no problems, was labelled and everything." She knelt down on the floor and unlocked the cupboard, then opened it up. It was packed full of a variety of medical supplies. "What do you reckon? Bandages, plasters, things like that, or do you want antiseptic stuff, paracetamol, what?"

"Christ," David said, "if the past few hours're anything to go by, we'd better take the whole fucking cupboard."

He had meant it as a joke, but no one laughed.

A few minutes later, Danielle had laid out a number of rolls of bandages, a cylinder of baby wipes, several packets of Elastoplasts, a bottle of Savlon, and two huge boxes of supermarket brand paracetamol capsules ("They're going to ban those big packets soon," Dusty informed David as he helped himself to a few. Then: "Oh. Shit. Not anymore they're not."). She placed the supplies into a plastic carrier bag, then shut the cupboard again.

She remained on the floor, leaning against the cupboard door, as David spoke from the bed bench where he'd joined Dusty. "It's weird, isn't it? Like, the whole school's just deserted. You can hear it – the silence – and feel this weirdo atmosphere. Like, potential sort of thing. I mean, I don't know, but it's as if something's going to happen, or is waiting for one of us to do something. Or no not really, it's more like the potential for us to do something is there, and it's as if we're… oh I don't know what the fuck I'm talking about."

"Neither do I, man," Dusty agreed.

"I think I do," said Danielle. "It's like a fantasy or something. Wishful thinking. That everyone in the whole school'd just disappear or drop dead, leaving you alone to wander around and do whatever you wanted."

David nodded, smiling. "That's exactly it. And now it's happened, it's as if your brain's reminding you of what you were going to do, saying, 'Aren't you going to? Don't you want to?'"

"Yous two have warped imaginations," Dusty decided.

"But it's more than just your brain doing it. It's as if the atmosphere is, like you said, *waiting* for us to do something. I don't know. It's weird."

David shook his head. "Scariest thing is, there really is nothing to stop us. We really could do whatever we wanted." He was speaking in a whisper now. "And what's absolute madness is it's not just the school, it's probably the *whole fucking world*. Just who's to stop us, who's to say what's right and wrong? Anything… we could do anything, and no one would care."

"Because there's no one *to* care," Danielle finished for him, speaking in an equally hushed tone.

They were silent a while.

Dusty tried to change the subject, a little uncomfortable with what his two older friends were trying to say. "Uh, and anyway man, you think maybe we should… I don't know, find a new car? Yeah. Find a new car, huh?"

"What do you think then?" David asked Danielle, ignoring Dusty.

"Is your heart racing as fast as mine?" she asked. She placed a hand on her chest. She didn't notice David watching it carefully. "I feel… excited or something, no, it's less than that, more like *potentialised* kind of. As if– I mean, the possibility is there, isn't it? My god, it really is."

David thought back to the freeze itself. "I remember feeling like this just after it happened. Like, I still didn't know why everyone was frozen, thought they were mucking around just to freak me out, but somewhere inside me it was as if I was *connected* to the atmosphere. I felt my heartbeat get quicker, felt excited but less than excited, yeah, that's exactly it." He shook his head.

"Can you guys quit this lark… man, you're starting to freak me out," Dusty admitted, flicking his eyes from David to Danielle then back again.

"Freak you out?" David asked. "Huh, you know exactly

what we're talking about, went even further as well…" He smiled at Dusty's puzzled expression, moved towards him and whispered, "Remember? Belly-button girl? 'Gone all soft babe'?" He leaned back and the grin widened and threatened to break into laughter.

Dusty was squirming. "Hey that was nothing like it, I mean it was, I was, there was… ah, shit."

"What? What happened?" Danielle wanted to know, looking at Dusty intently.

David suddenly jumped to his feet. "Anyone… fancy a wander?" He started across to the door.

"Hey wait man," Dusty began, "where're you going?"

He shrugged. "Just… exploring. You know. Maybe find something useful."

"I guess we'd better go with him," Danielle said, pushing herself up. Dusty joined her.

David started laughing a little. "Christ I feel so weird." He opened the door. "Come on."

They followed him back into the foyer, Danielle carrying the bag of medical supplies.

David was reading the blackboard. His eyes suddenly widened and he grinned. "Oh, yeah!" He started off down the side of the assembly hall, then up a small flight of stairs and along another corridor.

"What is it, man?" Dusty asked, struggling to keep up.

"Netball practice!" David called back.

Danielle shook her head. "Christ." She was still smiling, however.

Halfway along this new corridor, he opened a door on his left, and stepped into the sports hall.

It was deserted.

"Fucking bollocks," he told the room.

"'king bollocks, 'ing 'ollocks, 'locks, 'cks," the room replied.

Danielle reached him and clamped a hand on his shoulder. "What a shame, huh?"

He nodded. "Yeah."

Dusty squeezed himself into the room to get a better look. "Man, that would've been a sight to see."

Intensely aware of Danielle's hand still resting on his shoulder, David suggested, "Suppose we could try the changing rooms."

"Now that," Dusty said, "is one fucking top quality grade-A idea."

"Isn't that going a bit... far?" Danielle protested half-heartedly.

"No," said David.

"No," said Dusty.

She let go of David's shoulder, and the two youths pushed past her and headed along the corridor.

But then they stopped.

And so did Danielle, who'd been about to go after them.

Because they'd all heard the cry for help.

IT WAS WHAT DAVID AND DUSTY WERE LOOKING for. A young, innocent, attractive schoolgirl.

Naked.

They'd followed the sound of her pleas for help – "Is that someone? Hello? Anyone? Could you maybe, like, help? I'm… trapped, I, please…" – and found themselves on the assembly hall stage, having entered through the wings. The house tabs were open, and they could see there was no one in the actual hall. The voice seemed to be coming from the stage itself.

"Over here! Please help!"

"There," decided Dusty, pointing to a bunch of chairs which had been stacked high on top of each other. There were several piles, all jammed together, as if to protect or trap something beneath.

David stepped over, and called out, "Where are you?"

"Right under your feet!" came the reply.

David dropped his head to look at the floor. Barely detectable beneath the mass of metal legs and plastic seats was the outline of a stage trapdoor. "Come on you two, help me move these."

Danielle and Dusty started quickly tugging at the piles of chairs, dragging them well clear of the trapdoor. Now David could see it more clearly, he yanked at the final pile of chairs in his keenness, and accidentally knocked them flying. They clattered across the stage, just about bowling Dusty onto his arse.

The girl let out a little scream.

"It's okay, we'll get you out!" David assured her.

"What d'you think she's doing down there?" Dusty wondered.

"My friends thought it might be funny," she explained.

"Some friends," Danielle muttered, helping David to heave on the trapdoor handle. The door was quite stiff, but once they'd got it clear of the stage floor using the handle, they were able to grip the trapdoor itself, and pulled it all the way open.

A pale pale face stared up at them from the murky blackness with wide wide eyes. Two arms shot up towards them, hands open.

Dusty leaned over the hole and looked down. After some consideration, he asked, "You aren't… nuts, are you? I mean, you aren't suddenly filled with the desire to kill us all?"

The girl looked at each of her rescuers in turn. "Uh… no, not really. Not at all, in fact."

Dusty nodded, smiling. "Cool."

He grabbed a hand.

David grabbed the other.

Together they pulled her up out of the black and into the nightmare.

That was when they discovered she didn't have any clothes on.

She must've improvised beneath the stage, because she was wrapped in a mouldy sheet, but as they hauled her up it got snagged on something just beneath the trapdoor, and didn't waste any time in unravelling and dropping away, back into the dark.

The girl really was incredibly pale.

Especially when there was so much of her to see.

Dusty liked looking at her tits and her belly-button. David was pretty much focused on what was below.

The instant they let go of her hands and her feet touched the stage floor, she was running.

"Stop!" yelled David, Dusty and Danielle not bothering with words and already sprinting after her. A moment later he started off himself.

Dusty was really going for it. Belting through the stage door and off down the corridor like his life depended on it.

Danielle was a little uncertain of his motives. "She'll just be getting some clothes! The changing rooms, she'll jus– *oh shit the frozens!*"

She was right. Dusty watched as she dived into the female changing rooms and tried to slam back the door in his face. He booted it open and went in after her. "It's okay we just want to help!" he called, standing just inside the doorway. There was a shuffling sound from over near the showers. Perhaps a sob. "Oh come on, it's all right, we're not going to hurt you."

"Hu– hurt me?" she mumbled, shuffling around with what Dusty assumed was her clothes. "Who said, who said anything about *hurting* me?"

Dusty seemed confused. "Whay why'd you run?"

"*I didn't have any fucking clothes on in case you didn't notice!*"

"Okay, wow, right, fine…"

Danielle had joined him by now, and added her own assurances. "You'll be all right, don't worry…" She was quickly scanning the room for any frozens, but the place was deserted. Maybe they'd all gone home before the time of the freeze.

Suddenly, David burst into the room. "Where is she? Have you got her?"

Danielle shot him a look. "No we haven't 'got her'. She's

getting dressed. Like anyone would. Caught in that situation, I mean."

"You'll be all right, you know?" David called, if only to check for himself where she was.

"What's all this about *being all right*? Why wouldn't I be? Shit, it was a shock the sheet coming off and you two gaping at me, but…" There were a few more shuffling sounds, and then the sound of a bag being zipped up.

A moment later, she stepped into view, fully dressed.

David and Dusty once more started gaping.

Danielle pushed past them and smiled. "What's your name? I'm Danielle."

The girl shook her head. "No, look, it was canny you got me out and everything, but that's it, I mean, I need to get back home, things to do…"

David closed his eyes. This was going to take some time.

"Sorry," Danielle told her, "but I'm afraid – while you were under the stage – there's been… an accident."

She looked at her. "What kind'f accident? My parents, you mean? Are they all right?"

"Uh, well it's not just your parents… see, it's happened all over town. Maybe everywhere."

"What do you mean? What's *happened*?"

"I… I really don't know how to tell you this."

Dusty offered, "Maybe you'd better sit down. I mean, seriously. It gets pretty intense."

She looked at him, and then at David, and finally at Danielle. If she'd been wary before, she was downright suspicious now. She'd take any chance of making a break for it, David guessed.

He moved slowly backwards and leaned against the doorframe, blocking her main escape route.

She shuffled sideways, towards the changing area, and sat down on a bench. "I don't… I don't know what you think you're doing, but–"

Danielle got down on her haunches in front of her. "You sure you don't want to tell us your name? I mean, the weedhead's Dusty, the anorexic David, I'm Danielle."

"Shit, what is it with you? Names, names, names." She huffed, and then seemed to give up. "Kara. Kara Boyatt. But most people call me Karma."

Danielle tried not to make a face.

"Mmm, hilarious."

"Well if locking your friend naked underneath the stage appeals to your sense of humour, then I guess you might find it pretty funny, yeah."

"They were… oh they're not my friends at all. I'm…" She sighed. "I'm just one of life's losers. I mean completely. I'm a target. A victim. They say you're born a victim. It's in your eyes, they say. Well that's me. I was born a victim." She widened her eyes and leaned forwards. She was about six inches away from Danielle's own face when she asked, "See it? See it in my eyes?"

There were a few moments' silence before Danielle said, "No."

Karma leaned back. "Yeah well."

"What happened then?" Dusty asked. "I mean, how'd you get under the stage, man?"

"Bit on the slow side, is he?" she asked Danielle, then turned to the other two. "Netball practice. Afterwards, we all get changed. Only, I never get a shower, anything like that. I'm a victim. Getting a shower is not the done thing. A group of girls, they've got something in for me. They decide I'm having a shower no matter what. Off come the clothes. Under the tit-freezing cold water goes me. Then one of them comes up with the idea of locking me somewhere. The storage area under the stage is suggested. Down I go. Thump. They pile loads of crap on the trapdoor to make sure I can't push it open from below. Then, they just leave." She shrugged. "No idea how long it was until you came along. I fell asleep. Got woken up by you lot running around."

David seemed to have remembered something. "Is that it? I mean, nothing else happened? Before you fell asleep or whatever?"

Danielle realised what he was talking about. "Come on David, I think we've proved that theory a hundred times over. We don't need to embarrass her anymore."

"Embarrass me? What's he talking about?"

"Just… why you're still alive."

"Why I'm– hey come on, what do you mean? 'Still alive.' I'm not likely to be anything else, am I?" She looked at them incredulously.

"Actually," Danielle began, "that's what we have to tell you. The bad news. The shittest news you'll ever hear in your life. Guaranteed. And you won't believe it. You'll think we're crackers. But then you'll find out for yourself. Just like we did."

"Find out what for shit's sake?" Karma snapped.

"Cool it Danni," Dusty warned, "she's starting to freak."

"Christ, who wouldn't?" She paused before continuing. "Okay Karma. This is it... everyone's dead. Time has somehow stopped. Everyone's frozen in whatever position they were in when it happened. And they've all died. Except a few. People like us, like you, who were... doing something which affected the process or... fuck David, you're better at this than me."

"No, just hold on," Karma demanded, "just hold *on*. Everyone's dead. Oh yeah. Funny you lot aren't. Oh you're the sole survivors. Convenient. And time's stopped, has it? Yeah. You know–"

Dusty removed his watch and shoved it in her face.

"What's this?"

"Time's stopped, man. Not only stopped, but according to Professor Dave here, it's been destroyed."

She looked at the frozen digits. "Your watch is broken. Big deal."

"So's mine," said Danielle. "Frozen at exactly the same time as Dusty's." She held out her arm for Karma to see. "You got one?"

She shook her head. "Look, I believe you, yeah? Now if you just let me go, then perhaps—"

"What time you think it was when they chucked you under the stage?" David suddenly asked.

She seemed flustered. "I don't know, I mean netball practice finishes about half-seven, so… twenty-to-eight or something?"

"Okay then," he said, taking a deep breath, summoning up the courage to say what he needed to say. "Maybe ten, fifteen minutes after they locked you in… you started frigging yourself, right?"

There was dead silence.

Then Karma just about exploded. "*WHAT*?!" She leaped to her feet. "You *what*?" she hissed.

"Now do you believe us?" Danielle asked, rising to join her.

"Believe you? I believe you're a bunch of shitting nutters—"

"No man," Dusty interrupted, "we've met the nutters, got attacked by the nutters, that monkey fucker, now *he's* a nutter."

Karma stepped purposefully over to the door. She stood in front of David, hands on hips. "You're going to let me past, and you're going to let me past *now*."

David reached inside his ski jacket pocket and brought

out the replica gun. He didn't say anything, just smiled at her slightly and kept the pistol levelled at her chest.

In fact, no one said anything, not until Karma edged back towards Danielle, and sat back down on the bench.

"The only way you could've survived is if you were physically experiencing either sex or death," David explained.

"How do you know I wasn't killing a spider or something," she replied in a muted tone.

"Your cunt was red raw."

"Jesus David," Danielle gasped.

"Direct, man," Dusty commented.

"I think you'd just better put the gun away," Danielle suggested.

"Yeah," Karma agreed. "Away."

They all watched as he slowly replaced the weapon. Even though Dusty and Danielle knew it was fake, there was still some inherent power about the gun, an instinctive, media-fuelled feeling which made them cringe inside.

David lowered his head a little, seemed to realise something. "Okay, maybe that was a bit out of order, but out there..." He looked at Karma. "You'd never survive without us."

"T– try, try not to cheer me up why don't you."

Dusty walked over to another bench, sat down, and started knocking up.

Karma watched him.

"Just his way of dealing with things, Karma," Danielle told her.

"So… I mean it can't, it's not possible."

"We know. But it's happened. It's just coincidence we knew the person who… started it at all. That's why we know so much."

"What, someone *did* this, I mean, on purpose?"

"Well no, not really…"

"You still got Pricky-boy's diary?" David asked Dusty.

He looked up from the half-filled Rizlas. "Uh, yeah… somewhere." He reached into an inside denim jacket pocket, and brought out the A4 sheets, folded into quarters.

David stepped over and took them from him. "This," he began, turning to Karma, "is the diary of the person who ended up… destroying time. Obviously it doesn't explain much, we had to work most of it out ourselves, but… you can read it if you want." He passed it over.

Looking up at him, and then at the papers he held out in front of him, Karma paused a while before reaching out and taking the diary.

She began to read.

"Okay," Danielle said, turning to David, "did we work out a plan of action before?"

"Uh," he replied, "I think we were too busy losing it."

Danielle nodded, agreeing, "I reckon if we hadn't heard Karma, we'd be joining some of those nutters by now."

Dusty looked up. "Hey man, that's too…"

"But didn't you feel it?" she asked after realising he

wasn't about to continue. "Inside you, working its way up to your brain. Urging you on. Over the edge."

David nodded. "It was close. And just before too, pointing that fucking gun at Karma…"

"But at least, I mean we know what it feels like now… if it happens again, we can ignore it."

"Yeah," he agreed unenthusiastically. To have known how close you were to losing it, how close you were to degenerating into savagery.

It made David feel stupid and worthless and inherently *bad*.

Dusty was right.

There were no good people left.

He was about to say something about this when Dusty held up the finished joint and said, "A masterpiece, man," and all the lights went out.

IN THE BACK OF HIS MIND, DAVID HAD BEEN expecting something like this to happen for quite some time. No doubt it had nothing to do with the power station being currently unmanned, more a case of one or two nutters thinking it might be fun to set fire to a local sub-station or two.

But no matter how much he'd thought about it, nothing could prepare him for the absolute blackness which descended on them all.

First, there was noise.

"Fuck!"

"Hey man, just as I was about to spark up."

"Shit, what's going on?"

Then, silence.

He moved over to the glimmer of gloom coming from the changing room windows. He had to stand on a bench to look out, and almost tripped over getting onto it.

Outside, there was nothing but darkness. "Okay, looks like everywhere's been hit, all the streetlamps're out too."

"So... so that means there probably isn't anyone else in the building, right?" Danielle asked, her voice whispery and panicky.

"Uh, yeah. I guess."

"Look, what the shit is this?" Karma demanded, but speaking equally quietly. "I mean, why–? I thought most people had... died or whatever."

"Most except the nutters, man," Dusty supplied.

"What?"

"Sex and death, remember?" he encouraged. "No one good's going to have anything to do with either of them."

"What's bad about sex?"

There was a shuffling of material as Dusty shrugged his shoulders in the darkness. "Just what Professor Dave reckons, man."

"I didn't say that," Professor Dave protested, moving away from the window.

"Anyone know where there might be a torch?" Danielle asked.

"Haven't a clue, man," Dusty offered helpfully.

"Maybe try the secretary's office," Karma said.

"All right," began David, "no point everyone going, I'll–"

Danielle cut him off. "Forget it. Just *forget it*. We all go or no one goes."

"Seems like the sensible plan, prof," Dusty agreed,

"Will you drop this 'professor' bullshit?"

"Come on," Danielle said. "Where's your hand, Karma?"

"Uh, here… I think." She laughed a little. "Got you."

"Okay."

"Dusty, you ready?" David asked.

"No problems. Just–" There was the sound of several somethings tumbling to the floor. "Ah, shit."

David stepped towards where he thought Dusty was to help. "What is it?"

"Just me tabs, must've…" He started scratting around on the tiled floor. "Okay, it's okay, I got 'em."

"Right." David starting shuffling in the vague direction of the exit, his arms outstretched. He bumped into the wall, trailed his hands over the rough surface, found the door, and pulled it open. "I'll hold the door, let yous get into the corridor."

A hand prodded him in the stomach.

"Oops," said Danielle. A moment later she and Karma were through the doorway.

Dusty managed to walk through without bumping into either David or the wall. David rubbed the place where Danielle had touched him. The sensation was still with him as he stepped out into the corridor. He was pleased to see it was somewhat lighter the way they were headed, the skylights and occasional emergency light providing gloomy but precious illumination.

"So why've all the lights gone out again?" asked Karma.

"Nutters, man," Dusty whispered.

"Well, either that or the power just ran out," David offered. "But I'd guess it's pretty automated. So… who knows."

They were passing the side entrance to the stage when Danielle remembered, "The first aid bag. I left it in there."

"Okay, we'll never see anything in this," David decided, "we'll get the torch first, then maybe someone can run back for it."

Leading the way as he was, Dusty almost fell headlong down the short flight of steps at the end of the sports corridor, but Danielle was quick to grab hold of the back of his denim jacket with both hands.

"Whoah. Close one," he breathed. "Thanks, Danni."

They made their way carefully down the steps, then over to the fire doors leading to the main foyer. David pushed one open, and held it for the other two.

"Just a minute, just a minute…" he began, once they were all through. He was shaking his head, wondering what was bothering him. Something when he'd held the door open for Dusty and Danielle. Something… "Oh shit she's gone!"

Quick as ever, Dusty summed up the situation: "Ah, fuck."

"Oh no," Danielle said, "I had to let her go when I grabbed Dusty, Christ I didn't think to take her hand again, oh no–"

"Okay, it's okay, we'll find her. She can't've gone far. Do you want to risk trying to find a torch, or just run after her now?"

"We could do with some light, man," Dusty said.

"Yeah okay, come on."

"No," Danielle protested. "I mean, you guys go, I'll start looking for her, then you can catch up, right?"

"Hey, I thought you wanted us to stick together?"

"I do but... Oh, I knew she didn't believe us, knew she was just humouring us, Christ we should've *made* her believe."

"Come on, we couldn't've done much more than we did."

"But she's the only halfway sane person we've come across, I think– oh look I'm going after her, you get a torch, we'll meet up later." She moved back towards the fire doors.

"But how'll you know it's us, and not some... someone else?" Dusty wanted to know.

"You'll be the ones with the light," she said. A squeak of door hinges later and she was gone.

"We'd better crack on," David decided after a moment's silence.

"Yeah."

They started off along the side of the assembly hall, around into the larger section of slightly less gloomy foyer, then across to the main ground floor corridor. The admin office where the secretaries worked was the first door on the left. Dusty had to trail his hand over the wood to find the handle. The corridor stretched away to their right and dissolved into darkness.

Once inside, the light from the windows was enough for them not to walk straight into a desk, but it was difficult to make out anything else. They could be searching for hours.

"I reckon we're onto a loser here," David said.

"Yeah. It's pretty dark, man," Dusty agreed. He managed to find a drawer set into the desk, and yanked it open. The contents might as well have been invisible. "Fuck this, man. I can't see jack."

"Okay, come on, grab some of those papers," David instructed, stepping over to what looked like a small coffee table. He upended it, scattering junk onto the floor, and started kicking at one of the table legs.

"Destructive, man," Dusty decided, grabbing at whatever papers he could find.

Once he'd snapped the leg off the table, David picked it up, tested its weight, then went back to the desk where Dusty was creating as big a pile of papers as he could manage. David grabbed a few sheets and started wrapping them around the end of the leg. "You still got your lighter?" he asked.

"Uh, yeah – it's too shit to see anything with, mind." To demonstrate, he flicked the wheel and it burst into life – for about half a second.

Dusty was left blinking and more blind than he'd been before he'd used it.

But in the brief flare, David had noticed a Sellotape dispenser sat on the desk, and he started wrapping the tape around the papers to keep them stuck to the wood. Once he thought he'd got enough, and in the darkness it did look pretty medieval torch-like, he got the dodgy lighter off Dusty, and started trying to ignite the edges of the various bits of paper which were sticking out.

One or two caught, most didn't, but compared to the darkness, it was as if he had switched on a floodlight.

"Hey-hey, Professor Dave does it again," Dusty congratulated him, genuinely impressed, "MacGyver for the nineties!"

"You cheeky shit," David admonished, waving the torch towards Dusty, who stepped back, grinning. "Hey," he said suddenly, eyes gleaming in the firelight, "you reckon we should burn the school down?"

"Whoah, the man *is* in a destructive mood!"

"Right. Decision time. Use this to look for a proper torch, or just go after Danielle and Karma?"

"That Karma's a strange one."

"Yeah, know what you mean. 'I'm a victim, it's all I'll ever be,'" he whined, parodying her voice.

"Pretty good that."

"Would've thought you'd've jumped on her by now, though," David said, smiling.

"Huh?"

"Well, you know, you weren't exactly shy to point out what you thought of Danielle."

"Hey man, you must think I'm some sort of perv."

"Well now you come to mention it…"

They were laughing when they heard the ear-piercing shriek.

"Oh MAN!" bawled Dusty, leaping into the air.

David himself jumped up and around to face the office door, which they'd left open. His eyes were wide. The scream had been horrendous. A real shivers-down-the-spine screech of terror and pain.

It was impossible to tell whether it had been Danielle or Karma, or even if it had been female.

"Oh shit man, now what?"

"We'd better get the hell along there."

"The monkey, the fuckin' monkey?"

"Quit it with that monkey shit Dusty, you scare the crap out me every time you mention it!"

As quickly as they dared, they stepped back into the corridor and made their way through the foyer. David kept hold of the lighter in case the torch went out, a possibility which looked increasingly likely with each step: the papers underneath didn't seem to be catching at all.

Dusty was shaking as he walked. First the scream, and now the silence. Absolutely *anything* could be happening along there.

And most probably was.

They made it across the foyer, and pushed open the

sports corridor fire doors, David indicating to Dusty they should keep quiet from now on.

Once up the steps and into the corridor itself, the flickering, dancing flames of the torch quickly illuminated the fact it was deserted. David nodded towards the stage right entrance to the assembly hall stage, and they walked over.

That, too, was empty.

David could see the first aid bag Danielle had packed, so he stepped over and picked it up, passing it to Dusty for him to carry.

The further along the corridor they went, the heavier the silence seemed. David lit a few more pieces of paper on the torch, knocking away the blackened bits first. It seemed like it might be okay for the time being.

"Where's the likeliest place they went?" Dusty whispered.

"Haven't a clue," David admitted. "Maybe try the changing rooms again?"

"I guess."

They stepped silently over to the open door, and Dusty moved aside to let David and the torch go first.

The room was full of shadows, darkness, and flickering light, but not much else. David turned to the younger youth, his face creepily illuminated by the now-spluttering flames. He spoke in a whisper. "What the hell you think happened?"

Dusty shook his head, uncomfortable David didn't

seem to know the answers like he usually did. "I don't know man, anything, nutters, Karma went nuts, Danni went nuts, anything."

"Well... where next? The sports hall?"

Dusty kept shaking his head, and shrugged his shoulders too. "I don't know man, I–" He suddenly stopped moving his head, staring at something on the floor behind David. "Hey, I dropped my skins, too."

David turned around to where he was kneeling and retrieving the Rizlas off the tiled floor, and lowered the torch to check if he'd dropped anything else.

"Lucky I found them man, not that it would've been difficult getting another pack I guess, bu– ohhh." Dusty was staring at the wall just above the bench he'd been sitting on.

The mucky white tiles were splashed with red. David trailed his hand through one of the dark dribbling spots.

It was still wet.

He wondered who it belonged to as he wiped his fingers clean on his trousers.

"Hey Christ man, the showers!" Dusty pushed himself to his feet, then crept slowly around the end of the bench wall, and peered into the darkness of the showers.

A moment later and David was waving the torch around, illuminating nothing out of the ordinary.

"Shit, really thought I was onto something there."

"Okay, at least we know they were here. Or someone was, anyway."

They stepped back into the main changing area, David relighting the torch again before swinging it around for a final check.

He stopped swinging it when he saw the open window.

It was resting back against the frame, knocked off its catch, and in fact David wouldn't have noticed anything amiss had the window not been the one he'd looked out before.

And before, it had been closed, the catch securely in place.

Motioning for Dusty to follow, he stepped between the benches and over to the window. Once Dusty had joined him, he passed him the torch and the lighter, then stepped up onto the bench, and started slowly pushing open the window. Once it was fully open (and wide enough for a person to easily squeeze through, he noticed), he got the torch off Dusty, shoved it through the gap, then poked his head out and looked around.

The grass looked all shadowy and menacing in the glow of the flames.

And Danielle, leaning against the outside wall, her face upturned and staring straight at David, looked completely freaky.

He almost fell off the bench she gave him such a start. He managed to find his voice. "Are you… are you all right?"

"You find someone?" from Dusty. "Who?"

Slowly, Danielle nodded. "Okay."

He could tell she'd had a bit of a fright, so told her to watch out the way, then indicated to Dusty he should climb out.

David held the window open, so it was fairly easy for Dusty to clamber out and drop the few feet onto the cold ground outside. He passed him the dying torch once more, then the first aid bag, before wriggling snake-like through the gap himself, and squirming headfirst out onto the grass.

"I like your torch," Danielle said, once he'd righted himself.

"Uh yeah, thanks," David nodded, getting it back off Dusty. "We heard the scream, thought we'd bettern't waste time looking for a proper one."

"So what happened, Danni?" Dusty wanted to know, genuine concern in his voice.

She jerked her thumb towards the car park, along to their right, saying, "Might as well walk and talk. I want to get the hell out of here."

"What about Karma?"

She shook her head. "Gone." She started off, then, once she'd checked they were following, continued, "I came straight back to the changing rooms, calling out for her. She was in the showers, hiding, crying, the works. Screamed her bloody head off when I tried touching her. That must've been what you heard. Then she clobbers me one, starts clambering out the window. I climb after her, but by the time I'm outside she's away across the playground, screaming, bumping into the frozen football players and screaming some more."

"Whoah," Dusty declared.

David suddenly felt a little guilty at wiping Danielle's blood off on his trousers. Had he known it was hers, he'd have probably just kept it on his fingers. "Are you okay then?" he asked. "I mean, when she hit you? We found blood on the tiles."

"Blood? Uh yeah, I mean, I didn't know about that, but I guess… well nothing permanent, anyway." She sighed. "Christ, we should've, you know, *made* her believe, I mean…"

"It's okay. We did all we could. And if we didn't… well, we'll know for next time."

Danielle laughed a little. "Good one, David."

They walked the rest of the journey in silence. By the time they reached the car park, David's flaming torch had flamed its last and died. He lobbed it in the general direction of the football players. In the dark he couldn't tell if he'd hit anyone, but there'd been a pleasing fleshy smacking sound.

He reached what he thought was the Micra, and what was confirmed as the Micra when he found the driver's door unlocked. He held it open so the interior light would provide Danielle and Dusty with enough illumination to find the rear door handles.

Once more noticing the frozen in the passenger seat, David stepped around to the dented door, opened it –

diamonds of safety glass pattering down – unbelted the woman's corpse, then dragged it out and dumped it on the tarmac.

Just before clambering into the back seat, Dusty commented, "Brutal."

David shut the door again, then went around to his own door and got in. Looking at the mess of the windscreen, he wondered, "You think we should bother looking for a new car? I mean, this is pretty battered." He turned around to face them. The spider-webbed rear window was a bizarre backdrop to his two friends.

"I think we should just get going," Danielle offered.

"But where, man?" Dusty wondered.

"Yeah well I've been thinking about that. You know, what we were saying before?"

David and Dusty waited for her to continue.

"You know, about all the good people congregating someplace we're too dumb to get to."

"Hey, we'd go if we knew where it was," Dusty said.

"If there *is* such a place," David said cynically. "Who's to say all the good people're just too scared to do anything?"

"Come on prof, good guys always know what to do in disaster movies. It's all about sacrifice and determination and stuff."

"Yeah but–"

"Well as I was saying," Danielle interrupted, "I've been

thinking, and I reckon I know where most people might go."

"Yeah?"

"Yeah. The Metro Centre." She smiled proudly.

Dusty scoffed. "Never seen the good guys go shopping in a disaster movie."

"Fuck shopping," she said, "it's a big central place in the region, got to be the most well-known…"

David seemed to consider, then argued, "Yeah, but you saw what happened at the supermarket. Those places're heaven for nutters and the like."

"Well you know." She shrugged. "Maybe the good guys've found a way of dealing with that. Who knows?"

"Who indeed," echoed David mysteriously.

"I suppose it's somewhere to go, at least," Dusty conceded.

"Well yeah, bu–"

"Come on David, think about it. I reckon most people would want to meet up with other survivors. Right?" The two teenagers nodded. "Okay. Well, do you not think that's the most likely place? I mean, besides village halls and places like that?"

After a moment, Dusty said, "She could be right."

"Of course I am."

"I suppose it's a pretty famous place, yeah," David agreed. "Could be worth checking out." He turned around to face the front once more. "Might be a bit of a downer we get there and find the place trashed and crawling with psychos, though."

"Yeah well, we'll worry about that when it happens."

"At least it's something to do," Dusty repeated. "Something to aim for. You know. A goal."

"Yeah," David nodded. "A goal." He pulled shut the door, and the interior light plunged them into darkness. He started the engine, flicked on the headlamps

The frozen football players were shadowy and creepy.

They moved off down the driveway and onto the road.

Deciding the country roads would be less busy and less likely to be blocked than either the A69 dual carriageway or the more direct A695 route, he turned onto Allendale Road, then started off up Causey Hill.

They were silent as the car whined up the steep incline, but once they were heading east along the racecourse road, Dusty held up the spliff he'd made in the changing rooms and wondered, "Anyone fancy a smoke?"

David shook his head. "That'd just push me over the edge, Dusty."

"Edge of what?"

"Noddyland."

"Huh?"

"I mean I'm fucking knackered. A joint'd just send me to sleep." And it was true. The comfortable seat, the droning noise of the engine, the warmth of the heater. He hadn't noticed it before, but now he felt like he could sleep for days.

"You sure you should be driving, then?" Danielle asked.

He shrugged. "I don't know. Maybe we should stop. But maybe we should just keep on moving."

"I don't think I could sleep man, not after what's happened," Dusty admitted.

"Me neither," agreed Danielle, "but if you want to stop David…"

"It's okay, I'll be all right. Hopefully the good guys at the Metro Centre'll've sorted out someplace to kip."

"Still sceptical, huh?" Danielle admonished.

Beside her, Dusty sparked up, and exhaled a cloud of smoke. "Ahhh."

David turned the car onto the road for Slaley, and knocked the engine into neutral for the long descent to the valley bottom. The headlamps were powerful enough to make out anything in the road ahead, and travelling further into the countryside as they were, it was the only light for miles around.

He started wondering whether the whole region had been blacked out, like he'd first thought.

From the back seat, there was a slight coughing as Danielle started smoking.

The road reached the bottom of the valley, crossed a small bridge, then started steeply back up. David turned off at a junction, and headed along another B-road until they joined the main A-road. He could have probably got them to the next village via the country roads, but after that he wouldn't have a clue. He'd decided just to chance the more popular route. At least they'd missed the centre of Hexham.

Dotted around were several frozen vehicles, but they were spaced too far apart to cause any real problems.

Through Riding Mill, David put his foot down and made the speed camera flash. No one laughed, though. There were absolutely no signs of life from the little village. It was as if the madness in Hexham hadn't had a chance to reach this far.

For which David was grateful.

He had to drive the wrong way around the Broomhaugh roundabout. Frozen vehicles were blocking the normal way. He exited onto the Stocksfield road and floored it.

The road ahead was straight, wide, clear.

It descended slightly as roadside trees closed in and created a tunnel-like stretch of road. The darkness seemed to creep the trees even further towards them. Shadows flickered and danced just out of reach of the headlights.

He almost lost control when he one-handedly guided the car around the next curve.

It wasn't because he was doing eighty. Wasn't even because he was slowly falling asleep.

It was because there were about twelve figures standing across the road, dressed entirely in black, looking for all the world like a bunch of devil worshippers with their staffs and cloaks and hoods.

THE SKID WAS LOUD, LONG, WOBBLY.

The devil worshippers stood motionless.

"Holy shiiit!" whined Dusty.

Spinning the wheel left and right, the grip completely gone, David started to wonder whether it wouldn't have been better if he'd just rammed the figures. The way the skid was going, they'd be face-to-face with a frighteningly large tree in about two seconds.

He let up off the brake.

The wheels caught, jerking them in their seats as he tried to veer the Micra away from the right-hand verge.

The creepy fuckers still hadn't moved. But behind them, another vehicle's headlights lit up the night and backlit the worshippers, making them even more spooky.

Bouncing violently onto the verge, David finally got a grip on the steering wheel and attempted to guide them back onto the road. The car half turned, half skidded to the left, but the wheels caught on the high curb and ground the vehicle to a juddering halt.

In the back seat, Dusty and Danielle squawked as seatbelts sliced.

Once the Micra had come to a complete stop, the engine stalling dead, the devil worshippers started to move.

They broke their formation and raced over to the stuck Nissan, robes flapping behind them, hoods threatening to slip and reveal identities. Their clothes seemed to glow with the backlighting of the headlamps from further up the road. As they neared the vehicle, they started spreading out again, pushing and shoving each other to get into a position where they could encircle the car and the occupants within. Once they sorted themselves out, they held their staffs to the ground once more, stood motionless once more.

From this close, David could see the cheap material of the outfits. With the headlight beams shining so brightly, the robes looked almost transparent. The staffs were little more than dead tree branches, no doubt collected from the surrounding woodland.

There were shadows flickering from the direction of the headlamps.

He squinted to try and make something out, but all he could see was some people walking towards them, as slow and purposeful as the creepy guys had been quick and unorganised.

"The gun," Dusty hissed from the back seat.

David blinked. "The gun," he parroted, digging inside his ski jacket pocket and bringing it out. He didn't know how many blanks were left, nor whether the worshippers or the headlamp guys would be frightened away long enough for him to get the car moving again, but it was worth a shot.

He unbuckled his seatbelt, got ready to open the door.

The headlamp guys stepped into view.

Two of the worshippers moved out the way slightly, letting the three newcomers move closer to the trapped hatchback. There was a tall bloke wearing faded, creased leather, plus two security types, each dressed as if trying to out-do the other in chest size. The one on the left could have been pushing a good fifty inches, while the one on the right was so broad David decided he was just taking the piss.

Worryingly, all three of them looked vaguely familiar.

David wrenched open his door, got out and stood behind it, facing the new arrivals. He kept the gun hidden at first. "We don't want any trouble. Just, just let us through and everything'll be okay."

The leather leader grinned crazily.

The broad bodyguards stood menacingly.

One or two of the worshippers tittered, spoiling the spooky atmosphere somewhat.

"Look... just..." he mumbled.

"Point it at the sky and fire it!" Dusty hissed from inside the car.

David looked at him, then looked forwards again.

No one had moved.

So he raised the gun into the air and said, "Just fuck off or you're all dead!" Then he pulled the trigger. And again.

The flash of the blanks lit the scene quite impressively, at least momentarily. The massive noise echoed dramatically around the valley. The empty cartridges dived into the air. One of them hit a devil worshipper on the head. He jerked back a bit, muttering, "Fuckin' 'ell."

But apart from that, no one moved.

No one yelled.

No one ran.

No one did anything, in fact.

Until the leather leader started laughing.

And laughing.

And then David remembered where he'd seen him before.

Bounding up Rick's stairs to save his looter mates.

The devil worshippers rushed him.

TWENTY SHOTS. AT LEAST. HAD TO'VE BEEN. OR maybe he'd been mainlining it pure. He must've thrown up, too. Several times. And collapsed in an unconscious heap someplace. Someplace damned uncomfortable.

But he knew it wasn't true.

No matter how pissed you were, you'd have some difficulty in tying your own hands behind your back. Plus, not only did the side of his head feel twice its normal size, it probably *was* twice its normal size.

The devil worshippers had smacked his head so hard off the top of the Micra's doorframe he'd been unconscious before he'd even hit the deck.

God alone knew what had happened to Dusty and Danielle.

He tried opening his eyes.

Gave up.

Something had been wrapped around his head, covering his eyes, and from the sticky way it felt against his hair and skin, he guessed it wasn't a bandage.

He tried rolling over.

His arms were numb from where he'd been lying on them. He ended up face down on the floor. Blood started pumping back into his arms, making them ache and hurt. The rope had been tied tight.

He coughed.

There was shuffling from somewhere nearby. The sound of someone walking on carpet. Then kneeling down beside him.

He felt hands on his throbbing head. Clumps of hair came off along with the gaffer tape, but he didn't bother yelling. His brain hurt too much.

Then whoever it was pulled the rest of the tape off, away from his eyes.

That was when he yelled.

He soon shut up once he saw who it was, though. "What the hell?"

Karma gave him a lopsided smile. "Hi David."

She was kneeling in front of him dressed in a devil worshipper robe. Her hood was down, her hair bunched up inside it. The front of the robe hung open slightly, and he could see a little way down her neck and chest. She looked as pale as ever.

The room they were in looked like it had once been a kid's bedroom. Posters of manufactured one-hit wonders and assembly line Hollywood blockbusters covered the walls. Apart from that, the room was empty. No bed, no desk, no nothing. Just David and Karma. They were next to the wall opposite the door, regarding one another.

Karma said, "Roll over and I'll untie you."

He rolled over. She took out a knife from a pocket David hadn't realised was in the robe, and cut him free. He swung his hands around to the front, pushed himself into a sitting position, started rubbing his arms. He leaned back against the wall, grimacing with pain.

"Must've whacked you a good one, huh?"

He stared at her. Then looked down at his hands, which were itchy and aching with pins and needles. They looked almost as white as Karma. He could see where the rope had chafed his wrists. He took a quick inventory, noticing with a sinking feeling his ski jacket was nowhere in sight. He was still wearing his torn and bloodied work shirt, work trousers and boots. Apart from his head, and a slight sickness in his stomach, he seemed physically okay, if a little battered and used up.

Karma tried to smile again. She had put the knife, a sharp-looking thing with a wide blade, back in her pocket. "Raw Man's got a lot of questions for you. He's *sooo* interested in that diary I showed him."

David thought, Holy shit.

She shrugged. "Seemed a little mad to me, though. But

then I caught a glimpse of what they got from your jacket." She nodded. "Pretty scary. Seeing it. Because it makes everything true, doesn't it?"

He managed, "I guess so."

"Yeah. One thing I ought to mention though: Raw Man – that's our leader – he thinks it's your diary. And he thinks your pervert girlfriend is the girl you wrote about. And the stoner's one of your friends you coke-up every now and again."

David stared at her. Didn't blink. Felt his heart stop in his chest, his face drain of colour. "For fuck's sake…"

She grinned. "Didn't think it was true. But Raw Man, he just gets some idea in his head and won't let go. At least, that's what I've been told."

"What're you doing with them, Karma?" he asked, his voice whispery and scared. "Why're you here?"

"After your shitting girlfriend attacked me, I just wanted away from there. The school, I mean. I bumped into Raw Man's gang pretty soon after I started running. Like I told you, I'm a victim, so it wasn't much of a big deal. I didn't think they were going to keep me, at first. Couple of the guys kept saying stuff, you know, about what they wanted to do. But then Raw Man decided I should be part of them. And that was that."

"What's with the fancy dress costumes?"

She smiled. "They'd found a whole bunch of them in someone's house. Raw Man got really excited. He wanted everyone wearing one, so people would know we were all part of the same group." She shrugged. "That was okay by me. Victims aren't supposed to argue."

"I notice this Raw Man doesn't wear one."

"Well no. He's our leader. Everyone looks up to him. So he's got to be different. Plus a couple of other guys he has as security." She sighed. "We hit the road soon after. They'd managed to get hold of a bus from the station, and we headed over here. I think they'd just been camping out in fields before. But we found this place, and took it over. It's a farm. Pretty big. Near Stocksfield. Apparently they'd had their eye on it for quite a while. Raw Man set up a load of people at the roadblock, then told the van to go to the farm with the goods and get the place up and running. It's got its own generator, so we're okay for electricity. Maybe five minutes after we set up the block, you came along."

"Lucky us."

"Yeah."

"So why capture us? Why keep us here?"

"We didn't know it was you. We were just going to try and persuade you to join us. If you hadn't, well, I don't know. But when we saw who it was… I think everyone recognised you. And once we got you back here, and that card thingumy matched up with the story in the diary I'd shown them, well. It was all agreed."

"Agreed?"

"Yeah. Raw Man wants you to fix the card. Put it back together again. No one's touched it. They're all too scared. Raw Man wants you to do it."

"And then he'll no doubt want it back."

She shrugged. "Probably. I don't really know. I'm no one special. I had a job persuading them to let me guard you. Even then they locked the door after me. People know I'm a victim, you see. It's in my eyes."

"Yeah, you uh, keep mentioning that."

"I know. And your girlfriend said she couldn't see it. But she was lying. She saw it all right."

"How do you know?" he asked wearily.

"She wouldn't've attacked me otherwise."

He snorted. "Karma. She was trying to help you."

She shook her head. "No. I don't know what she said happened, but she attacked me. Kept whispering about it being a secret, about not telling you guys. Kept rubbing her hands over me. You know."

His smile started to falter. "Come on… she wouldn't."

"But she did. People kind'f go nuts when they know you're a victim. She grabbed at my clothes. I didn't bother pushing her away. No use fighting the inevitable. But then she shitting *bit* me. Really hard. I started screaming, so she pushed me away. Over to the windows. I opened one, climbed out, got away. I don't think she wanted to catch me. She could've easily grabbed me. But maybe that was her plan. To frighten me away. I don't know."

David was shaking his head slightly. "You know, I sort'f find all that hard to believe."

She looked at him for a moment, then stood up. She grabbed at the bottom of her devil worshipper robe and

248

started pulling it up her body. Slowly. David watched pale white shins lengthen and turn into pale white knees and then pale white smooth thighs. Karma had nice thighs. He looked at them carefully. But then she pulled the robe even further up, and his attention was distracted by her even nicer knickers. They clung to her body pretty tightly. He started to smile. He'd never been treated to a show like this before. Never. When he'd seen Karma starkers on the school stage, that'd been the first time he'd seen a real live naked girl in the flesh. And here she was revealing herself once more. It was starting to make him genuinely horny. Up went the robe. Her lower abdomen was smooth and flat – and pale. But it seemed to get a little redder the higher the robe went. Soon enough, David could see why. Just beneath her ribcage, almost at the centre of her body, there was a red and bloody mark the size and shape of a human mouth. He could even see individual gashes from what must've been teeth. They were quite small and had scabbed over pretty well, but must've been sticking to the robe slightly, because a few of them were starting to bleed. The blood trickled slowly down over her smooth pale skin, standing out dramatically.

"Do you see?" Karma asked.

"I see," he replied hoarsely.

"Do you want to… look closer or something?"

Closer. Yes. Good idea. He pushed himself off the wall and shuffled forwards on his knees.

He was now very close. He could feel her warmth. The

wound looked pretty painful. Some of the teeth marks were so darkly red they were almost black.

He was staring so intently he didn't realise she was still pulling up the robe. But then she raised it over her head and slid her arms out of the sleeves and it dropped to the floor behind her.

He looked up at her. Her breasts looked good so up close.

She was looking down at him with her victim eyes. "Don't you want to do anything?"

"Like what?"

"Like anything. I'm a victim remember. Take advantage."

"Huh?" But then he realised he would like to do something. Maybe something small. Her skin looked so very smooth. Touchable. And if she really didn't care... He reached out with his hand. His fingers brushed her skin.

"You can use the knife if you want," Karma suggested. She crouched down and searched the discarded robe. She found the knife, stood back up, and held it out for him.

He took it, looked at it, then back up at her. "What do you mean?"

"I mean I'm a victim," she reminded him.

When he didn't move, she reached out and took his hand with the knife in it, guiding it towards her shoulder. The blade prodded her skin slightly, and she dragged it down towards her breast, pressing a little harder the further she went.

David just watched, amazed.

The blade dug into her skin and slit it smoothly open. A moment later the wound began to well up slightly. She took the knife away from her breast, leaving a thin diagonal line running from her shoulder almost to her nipple. It got deeper the further down it went. Blood beaded over the edges and dripped a little across her skin. It actually looked quite... not exactly attractive, but... appealing.

He leaned towards it to get a better look.

Karma let go of his hand, took hold of the back of his head, then pressed his face to the top of the wound. She smeared him slowly down its length until he had his mouth on her breast. He brought his free hand up to her body and smoothed it over her skin.

She hissed slightly when he started poking his tongue between the edges of the slit.

But she kept holding onto his head. With her other hand, she took his knife hand once more, and once more guided it upwards.

This time they sliced open the skin across the top of her left breast, moving the knife horizontally. Karma hardly had to guide his hand at all. And he moved his mouth to the fresh wound with no prompting.

David tried moving himself around in his trousers a little. It was getting seriously uncomfortable down there. He'd never been this turned on in his life.

He started wondering how he'd feel if it was Danielle instead of Karma.

His heart leaped a little at the thought. His cock throbbed even harder.

He moved his head back and forth on her breast, licking the entire length of the bleeding slit, pausing to suck on her nipple.

He started settling down on his knees, moving slowly down her body, running his mouth over the scabs of Danielle's teeth marks. They felt bumpy and scratchy on his tongue. Karma's stomach moved towards him and then away from him with each shallow breath.

It felt wonderful to know Danielle's mouth had been where his was now.

He wondered if Karma had washed since the attack. He hoped not. He followed the trickle of blood from the bite wound down over her abdomen. Her skin and blood tasted nice.

He started wondering why in hell he'd never before really made an effort with this whole sex thing. It felt great to know you were wanted. Felt great to be able to share yourself with someone.

He sat himself down on his knees and found himself staring directly at her underwear.

The sight just about made him explode. He didn't dare shift himself around in his trousers in case the touch sent him over the edge. He had a feeling he'd be creaming his pants soon enough if Karma let him do what he wanted to do.

"Do you want me... lying down or something?" she asked quietly.

He looked up at her. It made him grin to be looking at her from such an angle, made him feel good. "Sure."

"Push me over. If you want to. Treat me... like a victim."

"Like a victim," David agreed, and pushed.

Hard.

She fell to the floor with a thud and a slight grunt of discomfort.

Then he was upon her.

He rubbed at her cut breasts with his hands, fresh blood welling up and smearing stickily over her smooth pale skin. He could see she was watching him, her eyes almost closed, her mouth hanging open slightly.

He grabbed at her damp knickers and started yanking them down her thighs, pausing a few delicious moments to gaze between her legs. She looked fucking great. He just wanted to dive in.

Then he remembered the knife, and cut her underwear off her.

He looked at her again. Her face was glowing with warmth. He almost gasped with relief as he freed his cock from his pants. She started rubbing her hands gently back and forth over the carpet as he positioned himself between her legs.

Chest heaving, heart racing, mind buzzing, he looked

down as his cock started pushing at her cunt. It felt warm and wet through his bell-end.

It was just too fucking much.

He managed to squeak, "Oh no," before he started gushing everywhere.

He just about had time to register Karma's eyes shutting fully when he heard the sound of a key turning in the lock of the door.

Still spurting, he tried moving backwards, tried tensing his muscles, but it was no use: he'd held off for so long, he'd been so turned on, it was just overwhelming him.

He rolled off Karma and groaned and started wanking out the rest of it, and another wave took him and washed over him, and he grinned and wondered who was about to get an eyeful.

The door opened and a devil worshipper stepped into the room.

He said, "Fuck me," and promptly turned around and left. He shut the door behind him.

David let out a long sigh, slowly getting his breath back. He tried to speak. "That… that's kind'f the story of my life."

After a pause, Karma replied, "No. You're not a victim. You're a survivor. It's in your eyes."

He had to laugh at that one. "In my fucking eyes," he echoed.

THE ROOM STANK OF COME AND BLOOD.

There was something else too, something unique David didn't recognise but guessed had something to do with Karma. It was all a pretty intoxicating, not unappealing mix.

He pulled his pants and trousers back up, not bothering to wipe anything down. There was nothing to wipe with, anyway. Karma pulled her robe over her head and straightened it out, leaving the hood down. She picked up her cut knickers, and was about to stuff them into her pocket.

"Uh," he began, getting her attention. "Is it... you know, I mean, can I have those?"

She looked down at them, then up at him. She was

smiling slightly, a kind of weird happy yet I-know-something-you-don't expression. "Of course."

He took them, rubbed them slightly, put them in a trouser pocket. It felt good to know they were there. He watched as she crouched down to retrieve her knife. She wiped it on her robe and put it in her pocket.

"What now then?" he wondered.

Instead of answering, she asked, "Did you enjoy yourself?"

"Of course. Yeah." Christ, it'd been the best sexual experience of his life (admittedly it was basically the *only* sexual experience of his life, but hey). "Did uh," he was almost afraid to ask, "did you?"

She smiled her smile again. "Yeah. Shame we were interrupted."

He nodded.

"Come here."

He stepped over. They stood face to face. She leaned forwards and kissed him, causing some residual sensitivity to zing an electric shiver through his body.

Then she slid the hood of the robe over her head, walked across to the door, and knocked loudly.

A moment later it opened slightly, and a devil worshipper (possibly the one from before) tentatively poked his head into the room. He made a motion with his head which might've been a nod, then pushed the door fully open.

Karma stepped outside, and David followed.

The worshipper asked, "Isn't this one, you know, meant to be a prisoner or something?"

Karma shrugged. "Not really sure. I take it Raw Man wants to see him?"

"Oh yeah. You bet. Desperate to see what that card thing does."

David muttered, "Christ."

"Come on David," Karma said, offering her hand. He took it, and they started off down the hallway.

The devil worshipper called, "Hey wait up!" He pulled the door shut, then scuttled after them. "Aren't we, like, supposed to be treating him, you know, badly? I mean, like a prisoner?"

Karma and David ignored him. They reached a wide, curving staircase, and started down. At the bottom was quite a large room, possibly a lounge, empty save for a few bits of rubbish. Karma guided him over towards what looked like the front door.

Outside, David was surprised to see it was daylight.

In fact, he was pretty much bowled over.

The sun was hidden behind a bank of light grey cloud cover, but all the same it was daylight, a breeze was rustling the grass, birds were twittering, animals bleating, it was normality, everything was okay, things were going to be all right. He turned to Karma. "What... I mean, how long've I been here? What's happened?"

She smiled sadly. "Nothing's happened. Nothing's changed. It's just daytime. Late afternoon. You got caught sometime last night." She shrugged. "Your guess is as good as ours as to what time. As your friends pointed out, time doesn't seem to work anymore."

David once more looked at the sky. It was reassuring to see it again. Last night had been eternal darkness. Daylight had seemed an age away. There'd even been times when he thought he'd *never* see it again. And the birds and animals, had he and Danielle been right about them, had they all survived the freeze? "Are all the animals alive?"

"Oh yeah. All of them. Well, apart from the ones Raw Man ordered for everyone's breakfast. It's pretty weird."

He looked around, taking in his surroundings. The farmhouse looked very large, an old stone building which towered behind them. Directly in front was a well-trimmed lawn, divided by a rough track he guessed was the driveway. It ran parallel to the house, and ended in a gate over to the left, just in front of a huge outbuilding, probably a barn. Beyond the drive was a few more feet of lawn. Surrounding it all was a fence which joined onto the driveway gate. Beyond the fence, fields.

More outbuildings were hidden to the right of the farmhouse, behind a Northumbria Route 685 coach which had been parked there, facing back down the drive. He couldn't really see any further that way; besides which, he was more interested in what had been built on the lawn the other side of the drive, in front of the left-hand barn.

He had wondered where the furniture from the farmhouse had gone. Now he knew.

The bonfire couldn't have been less than twenty feet wide, and was piled high with a staggering range of items. Sitting there like a bunch of traditional Bonfire Night guys were four flumped frozens – two adults and two children – guarding their belongings for evermore.

Karma pointed to the barn. "Come on. Raw Man likes staying in there."

They started across the lawn.

The closer they got, the more agitated the worshipper became. "I really think we should have him, maybe, kind of *in pain* or something."

"Well whyn't walk the other side of me?" David suggested. "So it looks like you've got me in between yous."

The worshipper nodded vigorously. "Yeah. Good idea." But he still wasn't satisfied. "Maybe... uh, maybe if you didn't hold hands?"

Karma and David let each other go.

They reached the drive and walked along, over to the barn. David kept looking at the huge bonfire, the frozens on top.

But then they reached the outbuilding, and he could see inside through the large main doors.

The leather leader he'd seen on the Stocksfield road was sitting in what could only be described as a throne, his two bodyguards guarding either side. Several worshippers were also standing around, behind the throne. Sitting near the left- and right-hand walls of the barn were the rest of the group. Two floodlights had been set up above and behind Raw Man, illuminating the space in front of him, but the majority of the worshippers remained in the gloom of the darkening day, and they really did look quite creepy.

Heads turned as the trio stepped into the barn proper.

Raw Man grinned as they approached.

They stopped a few feet in front of him, and he motioned for Karma and the worshipper to leave. Karma went and joined the row on the right, the worshipper the one on the left.

David suddenly felt alone and apprehensive.

Raw Man softened his grin into a smile of welcome. "Mr Greenhead I presume. I've been looking forward to our meeting."

"My name's David."

Raw Man raised his eyebrows. "Your wallet says otherwise, Mr Greenhead." He picked up a wallet from his lap: Rick's wallet, which had been in David's jacket. "Richard James Greenhead, your wallet says. Eighteen years old, your wallet says. But, ah, I think your diary tells us more."

"Listen, I took the diary and the wallet off this guy I know–"

"Come on. Remember my men found you in your bedroom, along with your two friends. You can't deny any of it."

"No, really, I took his keys when I got his wallet, found his diary in his house–"

"Then what, may I ask, do you have to say about this?"

He turned to the worshippers standing behind him, and one of them took a step forwards holding a tray.

A tray upon which lay the two broken pieces of the liquid card.

The barn had been quiet before, but now the silence was almost unnatural. The two black pieces held everyone's attention.

Including David's.

"The liquid card," he said pointlessly.

"Of course. Your liquid card. The card which – if I'm not mistaken – had uh, just a little something to do with all this?" He gestured vaguely with his arm, but David knew fine well what he meant.

"I swear it wasn't me: Rick, he's the one, he did it, him and his girlfriend."

Raw Man waved a hand for him to continue.

"It must've overloaded or something, you know, with the both of them using it, I don't know, but somehow it actually *destroyed* time – our concept of it, anyway – and everyone just… died." He lowered his head slightly. It sounded limp even to his own ears.

But Raw Man said, "Yes, I kind'f managed to work that out for myself." He smiled. "But it's nice to know I was right. Anyway, the thing is Rick, well, we seem to have a bit of a problem." He paused, looking intently at David.

"Problem?"

"Rivalry. They call themselves the Metro Centre People.

They've been broadcasting on the Metro FM wavelength, trying to recruit more members, reassure people of other survivors, things like that. But it seems like everyone's headed their way, with or without hearing the broadcasts."

"Christ." Danielle had been right. The Metro Centre. Who'd have thought?

Raw Man grinned again. "Funny, I thought that's where you were going."

"Well we didn't hear it on the radio or anything. Danielle just suggested it, you know, as someplace to go, a goal sort of thing."

He nodded, as if he understood fully. "Well, obviously I'm not too happy." He raised his arm, taking in the rows of worshippers. "I've been busy building my own little following, creating my own 'People'. The People of the Liquid Card, if you will."

At first, David had thought Raw Man was a pretty regular guy, if a little megalomaniacal. Now he realised the man was just plain bonkers. "Come on for Christ's sake, look at it, it's dead, Rick fucked it for good, it'll never work…"

Raw Man smiled happily. "I knew you'd see it my way."

David was shaking his head, looking at the man incredulously. But inside, his mind was in turmoil. What if just joining the liquid card *did* work? What then? Raw Man would be almost invincible. And these Metro Centre

People, were they a bunch of crackpots too? Or were they really the good guys David had strived so hard to find?

"Are there any... conditions you might need? For the rejoining? Darkness? More light? A room indoors?"

"What've you done with Danielle and Dusty?"

"Who, Rick?"

David scowled. "My... girlfriend, and the... the coke-head, where are they?"

"They're quite safe."

"I don't rejoin it without them."

Raw Man laughed a little. "I didn't mean *those* sorts of conditions, Rick. I did actually consider it, but I'm afraid it's just too risky. Sorry." He shrugged a kind of 'hey man, I did my best' shrug.

"I'm not doing it without them."

"Come now Rick. Take a look around. What're you going to do which wouldn't have about thirty people overpowering you?" He sniggered a little as he thought of something. "You can't rely on your toy gun now."

There was some laughter from the devil worshippers, and even one muttering of, "Scared me shitless fucker," but it soon died down. Raw Man was staring at David expectantly.

"What... what happens when – if – it rejoins?"

"Well, first you're going to tell me a little bit about it and how to use it – before you rejoin it – then afterwards I'll call back everyone from the roadblock, we'll load the coach, maybe have a little celebration, then take off for the Metro Centre." He smiled. "We'll want to join the Metro Centre People. We'll want to start a new life. We'll be so grateful we've found more survivors. So helpful and keen to work. But, of course, once we're all settled, well, unfortunately there's going to be a little slip-up in time, and I shall become the new leader, and the survivors shall join the People of the Liquid Card."

"But what happens to me? And my friends?"

He nodded. "Don't worry. As long as you join our family, you won't be harmed."

David snorted, but didn't say anything.

Raw Man peered forwards, looking outside at the last of the afternoon light. "Time for the bonfire, soon." He returned his attention to David. "It would be nice if you could rejoin the card before we light it. So we have something to celebrate."

"Look… all I know about it is what's in the diary. So whyn't just… just pass me the fucker and let's get it over with."

Raw Man grinned. "All right Rick." He gestured for the devil worshipper to take the card to David.

The worshipper stepped rather clumsily over, and offered the tray. David reached out with his hand. A voice seething with anger suddenly hissed, "No fucker makes me piss my pants and lives, got it cunt?"

Fingers inches from the broken card, David looked up at the worshipper. The hood covered the man's entire face, so after a moment's hesitation David snatched the two pieces from the tray, and watched the worshipper stagger back to his original position.

The pieces of the liquid card felt tingly in his hands. But they looked completely and utterly dead.

No way were they going to join together.

Holding a piece in each hand, he raised them up in front of himself so Raw Man could see clearly, and started moving them slowly together.

There was shuffling from the devil worshippers as the pieces neared each other.

When they were still a good few inches apart, David found he couldn't push them together anymore.

It was like trying to join the wrong ends of two magnets. They counteracted each other, their force so strong it was an effort to keep the pieces correctly aligned.

The crowd was starting to mutter and mumble, now.

Even Raw Man looked decidedly edgy.

David himself was starting to sweat, and not just with the effort. Twilight seemed to have fallen within the space of a few seconds. The birds and animals had all gone silent.

There was a roaring noise from outside.

A worshipper or two leaped to their feet.

But David recognised it as an engine, and a pretty clapped-out one at that. It whined and chugged and banged.

"Some new recruits," Raw Man said, the quiver in his voice betraying his apprehension.

"I can't," David began, pushing even harder, "it won't let me, they must've done something, I just–" He suddenly gave up, unable to hold the position anymore. He turned around as the roaring noise increased in volume.

The bashed-up white Ford van whined along the driveway and juddered to a halt in the loose dirt in front of the gate. Now it had stopped, David was aware of another noise coming from inside the vehicle: a banging and clanging and screaming and yelling.

The back of the Ford was jerking back and forth as if someone were throwing something around in there.

Instantly both driver and passenger dived out the front of the van and raced over to the barn. They looked like they were running for their lives, and the one who'd got out of the passenger side was sporting an ugly wound on his neck.

"Fuck fuck shit!" the driver was yelling.

Raw Man jumped to his feet, and most of the worshippers did the same, one or two going to the wounded man's aid. "What's going on?" Raw Man boomed.

The driver raced past David and fell to his knees. "We got them at the roadblock, they just, they just went *fucking insane*, we couldn't control them, they killed everyone! and Micro, he'll die too! oh fuck!"

David turned back to the van. It was still rocking violently back and forth on its suspension. He wondered just who the hell they'd caught in there.

The guy whose neck was gushing blood (Micro?) had

stumbled to the floor of the barn, and was now rolling around as several worshippers tried to save his life.

"Who's dead? Who killed them?" Raw Man was screaming.

"The freaks in the van!" the driver screeched. "Oh fuck don't let them near me *just don't let them near me*!"

"Christ," Raw Man muttered, clearly disturbed by the driver's reaction. He turned to his two bodyguards, pointed to the van. "Better go check it out." The two men removed wicked-looking hunting knives from their puffer jackets and gripped them tightly. The blades gleamed under the floodlights. They moved off, faces as expression-less as ever.

Even though no one seemed to be paying him much attention, David once more tried rejoining the liquid card. Once more they repelled each other. Their power was extraordinary.

The bodyguards reached the back of the van.

One of them started pounding on the door in an attempt to get whoever was inside to calm down, but the noise merely sent the captives into a further frenzy. The one who hadn't knocked looked at his partner a little worriedly. Then they each gripped a door handle and stood to the side of the van, ready to swing the doors open simultaneously.

The driver saw what they were up to and bolted, screaming. A few of the worshippers with Micro started shaking their heads. One of them leaned over and closed the corpse's eyes.

The bodyguards nodded a countdown: *one, two… three!* and swung open the van doors.

Instantly the two captives leaped out of the vehicle and bawled their freedom. One of them started bouncing up and down on the ground, screeching and screaming.

"FUCKIN' MONKEY-SHITMONKEY-MONKEYSHIT!" yelled a devil worshipper.

David snapped his head towards them. "*Dusty?*"

In turn, the surviving hippy twin swung his head towards David.

Doc Marten Man didn't even pause for breath. Just exploded into a scream of rage and hatred and raced towards his nemesis.

Devil worshippers scattered and yelled.

The skinhead monkey dived on top of an unprepared bodyguard and brought him to the ground. The other one just seemed to be standing in shock. He didn't even move when the monkey started battering his mate's head against a rock in the driveway.

Suddenly, David pushed the pieces of card together with as much force as he could muster. Even then, he could've sworn they hadn't forcibly touched, only fleetingly come into contact, certainly for no longer than a split second.

It proved to be quite long enough, however.

The shatter of light from the card temporarily blinded him.

It shot outwards and speared into the air, colourful and

magical, mesmeric and beautiful, dazzling the devil worshippers and stopping Doc Marten Man in his tracks.

Blinking back tears, David squinted to see what the light was doing. It seemed to flicker and dance in the air as if it was alive, then sparkle and radiate around in regular formations as if it was just a reflection of something.

Then, all of a sudden, it seemed to decide upon a destination and glittered away, out the barn and towards the drive.

The monkey had the bodyguard's head gripped in his hands, and was jumping up and down on his back, using his victim's own momentum to pound his face into the rock with each downward thrust.

Above him, the light of the liquid card quickly accelerated and finally found what it was looking for.

It disappeared into the carefully stacked bonfire and was lost from view.

A few moments later the bonfire exploded.

Three of the four frozen guys were propelled into the evening air like rockets. Furniture shot outwards and disintegrated. Flames leaped joyously high.

Doc Marten Man started racing forwards once more. Two foolhardy worshippers brought out knives and advanced. A moment later he was on top of them, punching and kicking and stamping.

One of the flying frozens slammed downwards into an escaping devil worshipper and almost tore off his left arm, shattering his shoulder. The other two found less destructive landings, one on the drive, the other the barn roof.

The remaining frozen on the bonfire started to kizzle and fry and burn.

Treating anyone who cared to look to a grand view of the bodyguard's pulverised skull, the monkey dragged him upright, and with a screech launched him towards the rapidly expanding bonfire. He clapped and whooped as flames started licking at his victim's clothing.

Dusty found David.

He pulled his hood down and whined, "Fuckers took away our gear man, and just when we could do with a smoke." The side of his face was a mass of red-purple bruises. "Let's get the fuck out."

He grabbed hold of David's arm and led him further into the barn, where they could see Raw Man disappearing through a door.

Behind them, Doc Marten Man was still stomping and kicking, and looked like he was prepared to carry on all night. The monkey had raced after the scattering devil worshippers, and had disappeared somewhere towards the farmhouse, along with the surviving bodyguard.

The bonfire was burning incredibly intensely, lighting the scene with flickering shadows and a yellow-orange glow.

Some flaming furniture had tipped over, and was resting against the Ford. Something which could have once been an armchair had actually found its way inside the barn, and was busy persuading anything even remotely combustible to join in the fun.

Dusty reached the door and yanked it open, pushing David through ahead of him. As he turned, he realised another devil worshipper was with them, so he ushered him in too. With a final glance to check the hippy guy hadn't noticed, he followed the others inside, shutting the door behind them. They found themselves in a large kitchen, and Dusty discovered the devil worshipper had been Karma, whom David was currently smiling and grinning at.

"Come on man, that monkey means business!"

David laughed in spite of himself, then turned to his young friend. "You any idea where Danielle is?"

"Fuck," he cursed, remembering, "one of the bedrooms, she refused to have anything to do with Raw Man, went pretty mental really."

"Went mental," Karma agreed. "She likes doing that."

"Right. Karma, try and keep a low profile, me and Dusty'll get Danielle, then we'll meet you in that van, okay?"

There was a deafening explosion from outside, and the farmhouse seemed to shake on its very foundations.

"Sounds like the van's up the arse," Dusty decided. He started off along the downstairs hallway. Glancing back to make sure the other two were following, he headed into the lounge and then up the curving staircase.

David had taken Karma's hand, but once they reached

the upstairs hallway they could hear the screams of panic and shouts for help, so he let go. Someone was screaming feebly from inside the nearest room, and he looked in to see a bunch of devil worshippers untying an elderly-looking woman. They hauled her over their shoulders and made for the door.

David got out the way to let most of them leave, but grabbed one by the arm and yanked back his hood. "The girl who was with me! Where'd you put her?"

The worshipper, a middle-aged man wide-eyed and frightened, pointed further down the hall and said, "Down there!" He started shaking his head. "Forget about her – the baldy kid, he's got her! there's no hope!"

Dusty and Karma were already ignoring his warning. David pushed him away and went after them.

There were another two locked doors, the door to the room David had been kept in, then another door, this one slightly ajar. The frame looked smashed and broken around the strike plate.

Someone inside was moaning in pain. Someone else sounded like they were slurping up the last of their milkshake through a straw.

Dusty and David looked at each other. David suddenly realised they had nothing to defend themselves with. But it was too late now.

The monkey had got Danielle. They had to save her.

He pushed open the door.

THE HINGES MUST HAVE BEEN WELL OILED. THE door opened silently, and swung all the way around to bump gently against the inside wall.

On the opposite wall, Danielle was leaning against the large window. Her wrists had been tied to the curtain rail. The ropes looked taut, the knots tight, her arms stretched and bearing most of her weight. She hadn't exactly been stripped, but her clothes were torn and tattered, her skin bloodied and scratched. There were a few bruises on the side of her face, too, on the same side as the ones on Dusty's. Her legs were spread, her feet resting on the carpet a couple of feet from the wall.

Between them knelt the monkey.

Heat rushed to David's face. Embarrassment. Anger.

But most of all jealousy.

And hatred for the monkey. The fucking monkey who'd taken what David wanted.

He hadn't even realised until now how much he cared for Danielle, but standing in the doorway and watching this, he was overcome by a sense of loss. As if something had been snatched from him and tainted.

At least Danielle, barely conscious, didn't appear to be hugely distressed. Her eyes were shut, her mouth open slightly. She was breathing noisily, making a grunting sound with each laboured exhalation. And her body looked completely limp, unable to escape the violation of the monkey-man and his mouth.

From downstairs there was the noise of breaking glass, of snapping wood, of crackling flames. The light of the liquid card was hungry.

There was also the noise of an old, knackered-sounding engine turning over and then rumbling into life. The coach. Raw Man and his People were moving out slightly earlier than planned.

David didn't need reminding time was running out.

If Raw Man and his worshippers reached the Metro Centre People before them, and if it turned out they were genuine, then…

Karma reached inside her robe pocket and brought out her knife. She handed it over.

He and Dusty stepped into the room simultaneously. David walked across, the knife gripped tightly in his hand.

He looked at the blade, then at the monkey. His skinhead was moving up and down and from side to side. He didn't even seem to be pausing for breath.

It felt too easy just to stab him.

All they'd been through trying to get away from the depraved little fucker, and it ended as simply and callously as a knife in the back.

Dusty shot him a look, and David just shrugged, gesturing with the knife, so Dusty moved behind the monkey and leaned forwards, ready to grab him by the shoulders and yank him away.

David got into position, gripped the knife tighter.

Still outside the door, Karma suddenly spun sideways and looked down the hallway. She started pointing into the room, and was maybe about to say something when the surviving bodyguard appeared and punched her in the face and she disappeared from view.

David and Dusty turned to the door, David with the knife raised, but when they saw the expression on the guard's face they both took the sensible option and moved the fuck out of the way.

The guard grabbed the monkey – who immediately started screeching and screaming – by the back of the neck and the back of his jeans and hauled him away from Danielle.

Moving quickly to her side, David cut the ropes from her wrists and, her eyelids fluttering open briefly, she collapsed into his arms.

Which was a good thing, because the bodyguard had just launched the monkey towards the window.

The skinheaded little shit hit the glass with his flailing arms and sailed through, thrashing and screeching his annoyance, glass shattering everywhere. There was a moment's further screech and scream and smash, and then a thump.

The bodyguard walked over to the window and leaned out, looking down.

Dusty yelped, and in a rush of adrenaline or stupidity shouldered the fat fuck in the arse and pushed him over the edge.

Unlike the monkey, he was silent on the way down, but still managed to make a noise when he hit the deck.

Dusty peered out himself, keeping an eye on his own back, and looked down. The monkey was nowhere in sight, but the guard was busy brushing himself down. He didn't seem best pleased. He looked back up at Dusty and roared.

Both little shit and fat fuck had landed in a bed of pretty-looking flowering bushes.

Dusty looked back at David and suggested, "Time to go, man."

Danielle seemed to have fallen into a stupor, so David half carried half dragged her across to the door.

Karma was sitting on the floor in the hall, crying. Her nose looked like it had been broken.

"You going to be okay?" David asked.

She looked up with red eyes and nodded slowly. Then

she looked behind him at Dusty, and stuck out a hand for him to help her up.

They hobbled along the hallway, the stench of smoke and burning wood strong in the air, and reached the staircase. Smoke floated and drifted around the room below.

"Think we should risk it?" David wondered.

"Better– uh, better use the back stairs," Karma suggested, snorting blood down her devil worshipper robe.

They continued on until they reached a second staircase, this one much straighter and smaller. The rumbling of the engine was a lot louder this end of the farmhouse, and David realised the coach was probably right outside, idly waiting for passengers.

He adjusted his grip on Danielle and started down, stepping sideways so he could see ahead to where he was putting his feet. Although she was pretty heavy, it felt great to have her in his arms. To be carrying her (or sort of carrying her, anyway), holding her body close to his. Even if she wasn't entirely conscious.

And the state her clothes were in made it something extra special.

If he turned his head far enough, he could see the dark hair between her legs, matted with monkey spit.

Her face was the nicest part, though. It was battered and bruised and dirty, but her eyes were closed gently, and her breathing seemed to be getting back to normal.

It was actually kind of a turn-on seeing her so beat up. Especially after what he'd done with Karma.

He wondered if he'd get a chance to do something like that with Danielle.

At the bottom of the stairs, there was a hallway stretching along to the left, along with what looked like an outside door on the right. Dusty stepped past him to the door and tried the handle. It wasn't a proper outside door, but opened into one of the outbuildings David had seen behind the coach.

The lights were on, and instead of a barn, he could see it was more like a garage or workshop. It was full of tools and workbenches and machines, its walls lined with metal shelving heavy with screws and nails and aerosols and chemicals.

There was also a mud-splattered Land Rover parked skew-whiff to the half-open garage door.

David waited by the entrance while Dusty and Karma checked it out. The doors were already unlocked, the keys on a bench near the open bonnet.

He went over and pushed Danielle through a rear door and onto the muddy back seat. Karma got in after her, and started rearranging her into a vaguely upright position.

As David stepped around to drop the bonnet, Dusty pushed the garage door fully open, letting the light from inside spill out onto a short track leading to the drive.

The Northumbria coach was parked over to the left, its engine now rumbling away at a higher pitch, and it wasn't long before it started edging forwards, onto the drive. Dusty raced back to the 4x4 and got in beside David, who had switched on the headlamps and was trying to start the engine.

It roared into life just as the coach trundled along the driveway in front of the garage, and David stuck it in first and got ready to follow.

As if from nowhere, a sprinting Doc Marten Man and his pet monkey streaked down the drive in front of them and after the bus.

"Christ man, those fuckers never give up?" Dusty wondered.

Raw Man's devil worshipping People, already panicky and seemingly crammed inside the coach to capacity, now went into a complete frenzy at the sight of their pursuers. The vehicle was rocking on its suspension as it struggled to gain speed, and David watched one of the windows near the back of the bus crack under some impact.

He crept the Landy out of the garage so they wouldn't lose sight of the coach, and although they were looking to the right, what was happening in the opposite direction soon grabbed their attention.

The barn Raw Man had met David in was by now completely destroyed. Flames gushed from nearby farmhouse windows as stone blackened and wooden beams collapsed. The Ford van now resembled some scorched skeleton, prehistoric and futuristic in equal measure with its fossil-like structure and mechanical innards. And next to it the remains of Raw Man's celebratory bonfire, now nothing but a pile of glowing embers and smouldering ashes.

"You uh," began Dusty, turning to David, "you didn't by chance accidentally on purpose drop Rick's card back there, did you?"

David smiled slightly. "No such luck."

"Didn't think so." He focused his attention on what was going on further down the drive, at the hippy and skinhead as they ran alongside the bus punching its sides and jumping up against the windows, scaring the shit out of everyone inside. "You think the driver'd've stepped on it by now."

David turned back to the scene. "Mightn't even know how. Plus it's completely overloaded." He looked over his shoulder. Karma was busy wiping Danielle's face with a cloth she'd found. Her own face could've done with some attention, too. It was red and swollen and smeared with blood and snot.

He not only felt sorry for her, but also a strange need to protect her somehow, to sort out her problems and tell her everything would be all right. "Hey," he said softly. "You sure you don't want me to go back and get something for your nose? Looks pretty bad."

She tried a smile. "Looks a lot better than it feels, then." But she shook her head. "We'd better just get away from here, David."

He nodded. "Yeah. Okay."

He moved the Land Rover forwards again, and turned onto the driveway.

Up ahead, the coach was on a section of track running

parallel to an area of rough, unfenced land. David accelerated and prepared to overtake.

The monkey and his master were busy grappling with the coach door, which they'd somehow managed to prise open. Several devil worshippers were desperately trying to yank it closed again. The vehicle still didn't appear to be doing much more than ten miles per hour.

By the time the 4x4 reached it, the monkey had clambered up the coach door and was heading for the roof.

David swerved onto the adjacent grass, and bumped the off-roader past the other vehicle then back onto the drive. He glanced back to see the monkey leaping around on top of the bus roof, Doc Marten Man struggling to pull himself up after him.

As he kept increasing speed, the bus slowly disappeared from view, and the last image he had in the rear-view mirror was of the two nutcases smashing their way into the bus through the sunroofs.

"Wouldn't like to be on that coach trip," Dusty noted.

"And they reckon public transport's improving nowadays," David agreed.

Dusty turned around in his seat and asked, "How's she doing?"

Karma nodded. "Guess she'll be okay. Few cuts and bruises, nothing serious."

"It's good of you to, you know, help her," David said.

"Yeah well. She's not someone you should treat as a victim."

"She's not likely to… try anything is she? When she wakes up?"

"Who knows."

"Why would she?" Dusty wanted to know.

"Apparently she went a bit nuts in the changing rooms. You know, when we went to get a torch?" He waited for Dusty to nod before continuing, "Well Karma says Danielle kind'f… you know, attacked her."

"I thought it was Karma hit Danielle?"

"Is that what she said was it?" Karma said, shaking her head. "Victims don't hit people. They *get* hit. Or shitting bitten."

"Bitten?" Dusty asked, looking at David.

"Uh, yeah." He slowed the vehicle to a halt, having reached the end of the long farm track driveway.

"It's right here, I think," Karma said.

He swung them onto the road and accelerated away. They were travelling along a bumpy B-road, surrounded by grass verges and hedges and trees. Night had by now almost completely fallen, and the headlights illuminated the road ahead and reminded David of last night, when they'd been stopped by the devil worshipper roadblock. He wondered how different things might be if he hadn't used the back roads to get them out of town. Maybe the main road would've been clear enough to get them to the Stocksfield road ten or fifteen minutes earlier. Of course, he wouldn't have met up with Karma again, wouldn't have… done anything with her. And after all, they had – eventually – got away from Raw Man and his fanatical plans. And no one was exactly *seriously* injured. Maybe things had actually turned out for the best.

"Shame we've got no gear left, man," Dusty sighed.

"Maybe the Metro Centre guys'll have some."

"We're going there?" Karma asked, surprised.

"Shouldn't we be?"

"You do realise that's exactly where Raw Man's headed?"

"I reckon he'll have his hands full a while with that fuckin' monkey, man," Dusty decided.

"But still…"

"Well it's where we were headed when we were stopped by your roadblock," David explained. "Danielle just reckoned it was the most likely place all the good guys'd head to. So we thought we may as well. Give us something to aim for, something… well fuck, something to *do*. I mean, what happens now? How d'you go about restarting the human race, you know? Hopefully there'll be at least some halfway sane people there."

"I could do with meeting people like that," Dusty admitted. "You kind'f get bored with the psychotic cult leader type after a while."

"Anyway," David continued, "if the Metro Centre People turn out okay, then we really don't want Raw Man getting there before us and telling them who he thinks we are – and what he thinks we did."

"I don't mind being known as a cokehead, man."

"Danielle might have something to say about being known as my girlfriend, though. And don't forget Raw Man reckons it was me and her who ended the world."

"Mmm," Dusty conceded. "Guess that mightn't go down too well with these Metro Centre guys."

"Who says we ever have to meet them?" Karma asked tentatively. "Who cares what they think? We could go somewhere, anywhere, just... live, start again or something, I don't know."

"Start our own 'People'?" David asked, smiling.

"No. Just... *live*. A new life. I don't know. It's... weird."

He glanced over his shoulder to look at her. She was sitting behind Dusty, leaning forwards on the edge of the seat, her head hung low. "It's best not to think about it," he advised, turning back to face the front.

"We're going to have to, sometime. We can't just let other people think it for us." Her voice suddenly hardened. "The Metro Centre People. Shit. It's almost as bad as the People of the shitting Liquid Card."

Out the corner of his eye, David saw Dusty looking at him, his eyebrows raised quizzically, but he shook his head slightly for him to drop it.

Even though what she was saying was true.

Even though he totally agreed with her.

But it really was best not to think about it all too much. It really was best just to get on with it. To live each moment as it came. Especially with people like Doc Marten Man and his monkey running around.

"There's no point anymore," Karma kept on in that same cold tone of voice. "Honestly, you may as well drive this thing off the nearest cliff."

Dusty sighed out loud and shifted in his seat a little.

"You read the books, watch the films – they're all shit. Utter shit. Full of people who care. People who can shrug off their old lives and get on with their new ones. People who don't whine about what they've lost. Or even *who* they've lost. Well it's shit. None of them get even close. None of them tell you about this feeling in your guts. This feeling of… *emptiness*. None of them tell you how useless you feel. How there's nothing left inside you anymore. How there's no point anymore. No point in anything for anyone."

"Karma–" David began.

"Don't bother," she interrupted. "I'm finished with the acting. Finished with the brave face. Shit it all. I'd rather be dead. I'd rather be shitting dead."

"Jesus *Christ*," hissed Dusty, shifting further in his seat to look out the window.

They were travelling down a steep hill, and David could see a bridge he recognised at the bottom, so he started slowing them down, pressing hard on the brakes. Just beyond the bridge the road joined onto the main A-road, and he deliberately skidded to a halt at the junction, just to let certain people know he was a little pissed off. He put the Rover in first, and was about to move off when he realised he was more than a *little* annoyed, so knocked it back into neutral and turned around and leaned between the seats to get close. "Okay then. Everything in that kid's bedroom, you were just acting, huh? Putting on a brave face? Wanting to die?"

She shook her head slightly and muttered, "I didn't mean that."

"Well what exactly did you mean?"

She glanced up at him. Her face was streaked with tears. Her nose looked angry and sore. Her eyes were even redder than before, and her whole body was jerking slightly with silent sobs.

He felt a weird tightening in his chest, and immediately wished he hadn't snapped at her.

Then she shrugged her shoulders, turned away from him, and leaned against the rear door window.

He slowly shifted back around, his head down. After a moment, he put the Landy back into first and started east along the A-road.

They were silent as they travelled through Stocksfield.

The frozen traffic was quite heavy, but there were no real problems. As he weaved from one side of the road to the other, David tried to distract himself by looking for any signs of life. But with the night so dark, and the streetlamps all out, it was difficult to distinguish anything other than the road ahead.

After a while, Dusty shifted in his seat into a more normal position. He glanced over at David and wondered, "So what happened to you, man?"

David was a bit startled. "Huh?"

"I mean when the freaky guys got you. We saw you get taken down, then they dragged you away." He shook his head. "Me and Danni just kind'f realised it wasn't worth the fight. Sorry, man."

"All worked out okay in the end, I guess. I didn't wake up 'til just before you saw me. Karma was the one guarding me. She told me what'd happened, what Raw Man'd planned. Then someone knocked on the door, and we went down into the barn." He shrugged. "You know the rest."

Dusty agreed. "Yeah. Could've really done without seeing that fucking monkey again."

David suddenly burst out laughing. "I couldn't believe it when that bouncer guy chucked him out the window."

"Christ yeah," Dusty said, remembering and smiling. "He fucking *launched* him into space, man!"

"Then you shouldered the bouncer out!"

"You should've seen his face! He was *not* pleased."

David's laughter fizzled out as quickly as it had arrived. "Shame it hadn't been a tenth floor window."

"Mmm, know what you mean. You get the impression that monkey doesn't want to let this one lie."

"Same with the hippy. And Raw Man. And his bodyguard bouncer. And the looters I pointed the gun at. And the rest of the devil worshippers. And… Christ." He shook his head. "I reckon we could *seriously* do with meeting some good guys around about now."

"Doubt we need to worry about the devil worshippers.

Though I thought we were all supposed to be monks. Anyway, most of them are just like me and Karma, forced to join in with it all. You saw them in the barn, they were shitting themselves."

"So what happened when they took you and Danielle back to the farm?" David asked. "What they do to your face?"

"Well, at first I wasn't having much to do with them. I answered a few questions, but most of the time I hadn't a clue what they were talking about. Stuff about Rick the Prick and the card. After a while I realised who they thought we were and I couldn't stop laughing. The guy doing the interrogating wasn't impressed." He shrugged. "Thought he might've broken something at first, but I think it's okay." He touched the bruising carefully. From what David could see, it looked swollen and painful. Dusty continued, "Danielle got the same sort of treatment. But she just wouldn't let up. Kept having a real go at this one bloke. I guess he just lost it. Let her have it big time." He paused. "She was unconscious when they dragged her upstairs. Then they brought in a robe, chucked it at me. It wasn't exactly a tough decision whether to put it on. You know?"

"Yeah," David nodded. "I know." He glanced over his shoulder at Danielle. "You think she'll be all right?"

"I don't know man. I guess. But Christ, what was that monkey *doing* to her? He just, uh, using his tongue or… you think… you think teeth were involved?"

David tried not to cringe. "I... I don't know," he croaked.

"Maybe Karma should check or something. Make sure there's no blood."

"Maybe."

"So you've still got the card," Dusty said, suddenly changing the subject.

"Yeah," David nodded. "Still got it."

"You see the light–?"

"I saw the light."

"How–?"

"I haven't got a clue."

After a pause, he ventured, "You think we should destroy it or something?"

David glanced at him. And realised his friend probably had a point. He'd only rejoined it for a split second, if that, and the destruction it'd caused had been immense. What sort of power could it wield if it was ever fully restored? And if that power fell into the wrong hands? Raw Man had explained in no uncertain terms just what he planned to use it for. And if it was as addictive as Ricky-boy said it was, then how long before even the Metro Centre People fell under its influence? "Maybe we should, Dusty," he said quietly, "maybe we should."

He slowed the Land Rover down, crossed over a round-about, and started along the Prudhoe industrial estate road. There was a thirty-miles-per-hour restriction, but David was soon zipping along at nearly twice that. He braked for the next roundabout, and they started climbing the valley once more.

"What happens if these Metro Centre guys're just as nuts as Raw Man?" Dusty asked.

David shook his head. "I don't know." He glanced back at Karma. She was in pretty much the same position she'd been in before. He hoped she was managing to get some rest. "Maybe Karma was right, you know."

"Didn't realise you were the suicidal type, Dave man," Dusty said lightly, but with an edge to his voice.

"I didn't mean that," David told him, and he could hear his friend sigh quietly with relief. He wondered why Dusty was so edgy talking about depression and suicide. "I just meant what she was saying about starting a new life. Just going somewhere and starting again."

"Sounds like that's what everyone else's doing, anyway," Dusty agreed.

"God knows where we'd go. Or what we'd live on. Or what we'd do."

"Start again, I suppose."

David suddenly laughed. "Me and you can flick a coin to see who's Adam, and Danielle and Karma can flick for Eve."

Dusty snorted. "Yeah. We'd need a snake, though."

"Zzzz-itt!" said David, mimicking the sound of a zip being lowered. Then they were both laughing.

After a while, they started getting closer to the city, and David had to concentrate to get them through the frozen traffic. More than once or twice he had to bump onto the pavement or swerve quite violently, and Karma was eventually jolted awake.

David watched her in the rear-view as she sat upright, leaned forwards to check where they were, then turned to Danielle to see how she was doing.

Coasting down the slope to the Blaydon roundabout, David noticed several vehicles with their doors hanging open, and there were even one or two flumped frozens strewn across the road. A young-looking frozen was hanging from a road sign, its trousers round its ankles. Nearby, a Ford Fiesta had run off the road and slid to a halt, digging trenches in the verge. Across the river several fires were burning, buildings or vehicles he wasn't sure, but it all served to remind him just how many people had in fact survived the freeze, and how many had descended into savagery.

He negotiated the busy roundabout carefully, then continued along the A695, now parallel to the River Tyne, towards their destination.

The Metro Centre was a huge two-storeyed labyrinth of shops and attractions – ranging from mammoth department stores and the largest indoor theme park in Europe, to small, unique businesses and high street names – all housed together in one super shopping centre, over thirteen years old and still the largest of its kind in Europe. Living just a few miles away, David didn't exactly think it was anything special, but it was certainly convenient, and if you happened to like shopping there was more than enough to keep you occupied. It was divided up into coloured quadrants with corresponding car parks, and David had got used to using the Red car park, one of the south-facing entrances, generally regarded as the 'front' of the Centre. Unfortunately, even though it was the main bypass for Gateshead and Newcastle, this stretch of the A1 was still only a dual carriageway, and together with the fact it was the most direct route into the incredibly popular centre, meant traffic was usually nose-to-tail around the clock. To avoid the no doubt impassable carriageway, David turned east onto the A1114, which would take him into Metro Park West and the Metro Retail Park, two groups of super-sized, warehouse-like and regular-sized buildings, separate to the main mall but part of the same Capital Shopping Centres conglomeration. Usually this entrance was nearly just as busy, but tonight David was puzzled to see the road was absolutely clear.

A few moments later, he found out why.

The roadblock was on the other side of the first round-about, just before the A1114 crossed the River Derwent.

He would have shat his pants anyway, but the fact it was about fifty by twenty feet of wrecked cars and dangling frozens, blocking four lanes of tarmacadam plus a good portion of verge, made it all the more terrifying.

"WHAT HAPPENS NOW?" DUSTY WHISPERED, gazing up at the grisly, towering barricade.

"I think we're about to find out," Karma said, leaning between the seats and pointing.

Several uniformed men carrying torches had appeared around the right-hand side of the roadblock, and were marching along the exit lane towards the roundabout where David had stopped the 4x4.

Even in the dark, it was obvious their uniforms were a pick-'n'-mix job, mismatched, torn and tattered. There were young boys and old men walking side by side. None of them appeared to be armed, which came as something of a relief, but they didn't exactly look like they were about to invite everyone in for tea and biscuits.

"What do you reckon?" David asked.

"Just say we want to join the shitting Metro Centre People," said Karma sarcastically. "Simple as that."

"What if they're *nutters*, man," Dusty whined at David.

"No… I don't think so. That roadblock, for starters." He shook his head. "It's too organised for nutters."

"It's made of dead people!" Dusty practically yelled.

"Only because they were in the cars. Too much trouble to get rid of them. They must've cleared the roads around the Centre, used them to build the blocks."

The makeshift soldiers were marching across the round-about, now. David wondered if he should get out. He decided he felt safer inside, so wound the window down instead.

The leading pair stepped up to the off-roader, and one of them leaned towards the window, his torch pointing to one side. He looked physically weary and tired, yet mentally alert and watchful. "You're wanting to join the Metro Centre People?"

David smiled with relief. "Yes. Yes, all of us."

The man now raised the torch and shone it across at Dusty, then into the back seat at Karma and the still sleeping Danielle. "Looks like you've been in the wars." He narrowed his eyes slightly, perhaps puzzled by the devil worshipper outfits. Then: "The unconscious one, she hurt bad?"

"We're not sure, uh…" He turned to Karma.

"She'll be okay," she said.

"Right. We'll get her sorted out in the first aid centre."
He stood up straight again, then turned around to say
something to the rest of the troop. Two of the younger men
nodded and raced back the way they'd come. "Okay, the
lads're off to get a stretcher, if the rest of you'd just like to
follow me?"

David turned to Dusty, and after a moment's eye
contact, they both opened their doors simultaneously.
David got out and closed the door behind him. He was
soon joined by Dusty and Karma.

The soldier nodded. "Okay." He turned around and
started back towards the roadblock. When they were about
halfway there, the two soldiers who'd ran off reappeared,
pushing a proper-looking wheeled stretcher between them.

As they came closer, David couldn't help but stare
upwards at the towering blockade of metal and flesh. It
was genuinely unnerving.

Maybe Dusty was right.

Once around the back, they were marched over to one
of two waiting vans. The leading soldier stood back, allowing two of his colleagues to move forwards and open up
the back doors. "In you get, they'll take your friend in the
other one."

"Shouldn't we wait for her?" David wondered.

"No, they'll take her straight to the MediCentre."

Not having much choice, they stepped up into the back
of the vehicle and sat themselves down on the seats which
lined the sides. Outside, the soldier said something to the

remaining men, then ushered one of the youngest looking ones into the van before climbing in himself. He pulled the door shut and went to the front to speak to the driver.

The engine rumbled into life, and they were soon on their way.

The young soldier was sitting next to the rear doors and holding onto a strap dangling from the roof. He very much looked to David like he was guarding their exit route.

The original man sat down beside Dusty. "You been on the road for long?"

"Hey man," Dusty began warily, "Dave's the man who knows, not me, no way."

The soldier raised his eyebrows. "Okay." He turned to David. "I take it you're Dave?"

"David, Dave, whatever."

"Wratten," the soldier said, and extended a hand.

David took it, and they shook. Wratten's grip was firm, his skin as cold as the night air.

"That's Dusty and Karma," David told him, pointing.

"Pleased to meet you all."

Dusty nodded, Karma managed half a smile, both of them still on edge.

"The other one's Danielle."

"Right." Wratten nodded. "What happened to her, then?"

David shrugged. "Didn't agree with someone. Should be okay, though."

"Right," Wratten said again. "No one we should be worrying about? I mean, they're not in pursuit or anything?"

"Oh." David made a face. "Now you come to mention it…"

The soldier moved back towards the front of the van. He looked over his shoulder and asked, "How many? You could describe them?"

David lowered his eyes a little. "Er, maybe… forty or fifty?"

Wratten almost lost his footing. "Forty or–" He grabbed onto a ceiling strap and quickly regained his composure. "Okay, so they're… what? A gang or something?"

"Yeah. They'll all be wearing those robes Karma and Dusty've got on. But there'll be a leader. Name's Raw Man. Plus these two other guys, complete psychos, one of them wears nothing but a pair of DMs, the other looks like a shaved monkey." He suddenly started laughing – Wratten was looking at him very strangely. "I suppose it does sound a little…"

"Far-out?" offered Dusty.

Wratten looked at him. "You can say that again." He turned back to the driver, then after a few moments returned to his seat. Now it was his turn to look wary and suspicious of his fellow travellers.

David shrugged a little. "I swear. They're heading this way."

"Should've knifed that monkey when you had the chance," Dusty said, shaking his head at a wasted opportunity.

David watched as Wratten narrowed his eyes, and he started wondering what the man was thinking. "Listen," he began, waving his hand back and forth to show the soldier he'd got it all wrong, "we just got caught up in it all, you know? I mean, nothing was *our fault*, you see?"

Karma could obviously tell David was struggling, so tried to change the subject. "Uh, Mr Wratten, where exactly are we going?"

"Ah well," he said, turning to her, "usually we'd take you to the first aid centre too, get you cleaned up, make sure you're okay, but, uh, considering the circumstances, I think it might be best if you met with the Centrefather straightaway." He paused, shaking his head. "We've been working around the clock ever since the disaster, and I don't mind telling you we haven't yet picked someone up we can't figure out." He smiled, shrugged. "Until you four."

"What do you mean 'figure out'?" David asked.

"Well, most people just want to join up because there's no one else to turn to, nowhere else to go. I mean— well, you obviously know the extent of the disaster?"

"Worldwide," said David.

Wratten started. "Well I hardly think that's the case, but it's certainly—"

"Hey man," Dusty interrupted, "trust him. If Professor Dave says it's worldwide… then it's worldwide."

Wratten gave him a long look before turning back to David. "Anyway, most of the new recruits are honest, hard-working people looking for a new home in this new world." He shrugged. "Unfortunately there're some who… well, like your 'Whore Man' and 'shaved monkey' who are–"

"Nutters," supplied Dusty.

"Yeah. That's right. For want of a better word."

"So how do you… deal with them?" David wanted to know.

The young soldier next to the door snorted. "'Deal with them.' Yeah, as if we'd do anything like that." His voice was high-pitched, almost squeaky, and betrayed his age.

"Oh quit it, can't you?" Wratten demanded. He looked back at David. "The Centre People don't believe in destruction. We just want to make the best of what we've got. Live our lives happily and peacefully."

"You should hear the noises in there, man," the young soldier warned. "You should listen to the fucking *noises*."

"*I said shut it*!" bawled Wratten, leaping to his feet and almost cracking his head off the top of the van.

The soldier stared back impassively.

After a few moments, Wratten sat back down. "We don't want our new recruits frightened off by scare stories, do we?" he said in a shaky but controlled voice.

David and Dusty exchanged a look, and Dusty mouthed, 'Nutters.'

"Okay," Wratten said after the van started slowing down, "I think we've arrived."

The vehicle came to a complete stop, and the soldier guarding the door opened it and got out.

David followed, along with everyone else. It felt good to be out in the open.

They were in one of the main car parks, the Green Quadrant by the looks of things, just in front of the Marks and Spencer entrance. The floodlit car park was almost empty, save for a few vehicles parked in the end lane, plus one or two next to which the van had parked. It looked like someone had started systematically removing all the cars.

David wondered where they'd all gone. Had they all been built into roadblocks? The A1 ran mostly parallel to the Centre after all, and there were many side roads and other service roads which led to the vicinity of the buildings. "So you've blocked off all the routes leading here?" he asked.

"That's right. We just wanted to make sure we were relatively safe in case… well, just in case. Plus it gives us a chance to monitor the new recruits. You know."

"The nutters?" Dusty enquired.

"Mmm," he agreed. "Come on, the Centrefather set up his main operations base in here." He indicated the Marks and Spencer building, and all five of them made their way over.

300

The van started up again, reversed out of its parking space, and moved off.

"Will Danielle be along soon?" David wondered.

"The MediCentre is in the Blue Quadrant," Wratten informed him. "I'll have her sent here if she's okay, otherwise we can head over there afterwards."

"So who's this Centrefather guy, man?" Dusty asked.

"The founder of the Metro Centre People." He sounded quite proud, as if he were describing the achievements of a loved one. "There are rumours about him having caused the disaster himself, but that's just rubbish."

"Wouldn't be surprised," the young soldier commented.

"You know," Dusty began, "this Raw Man guy Dave was telling you about, and this Centrefather, I'm kind'f getting a similar vibe."

"Well I'm sure you'll be able to make your own judgement, soon enough."

"So how'd he survive the freeze, man? Sex or death?"

"What?"

"The disaster. The freeze. The only way you could've survived–"

"Leave it Dusty," David interrupted. "We don't want to confuse things."

"You mean you…" Wratten mumbled, trying to figure it out, "you know something about the disaster?"

"Hey man," Dusty told him, "we know *everything*."

The young, highly strung soldier shook his head and

might've muttered, "Pissing hell," then stepped forwards and set off the motion detector for the entrance double doors.

They slid apart to reveal a pair of soldiers standing guard. They seemed more relaxed than the others, were dressed more casually in jeans and camouflage jackets. The younger of the two raised his eyebrows in greeting at Wratten, and went over to a computer set up on a nearby desk.

Wratten waited for everyone else to step into the building before walking in himself.

The soldier behind the computer beckoned the new-comers over. "Rainhead said there were four," he said to Wratten.

"Other one's off to the MediCentre."

"What about these three?" He regarded them critically. "Looks like they could do with a check-up."

"Uh, I thought it best they see the 'father, first. Special case."

"Special case?"

"*Very* special, you ask me," the soldier who'd accompanied them in the van butted in. "Like, special fucking needs special."

The computer soldier shrugged. "Okay. Names?"

David shook his head. "What?"

"Names and ages please, and I'll give you a reference number. We just want to keep tabs on how many people're living here, that's all. Just makes things easier."

"Er, well… David Thornwood, nineteen." He felt like he was signing up or something.

"Next."

Dusty stepped over to the desk. The soldier wrinkled his face at the devil worshipper robe, but didn't comment.

"Uh… Dustsheet, I guess. Sixteen. But I get called Dusty. For some reason."

The soldier typed in the information, then said, "Okay."

Karma stepped up and told him her name and age, then he typed a few more things and a nearby printer started whirring.

"Right, there you go." He handed over three labels, printed with their names, ages, and reference numbers. David's was CM25, Dusty's CM26, Karma's CF39.

Dusty slipped his into his robe pocket and wondered, "This mean I'm the twenty-sixth Metro Centre Person?"

"Twenty-sixth male. Within this cycle."

"Cycle?" asked David.

"Between dawn and dusk, or dusk and dawn," supplied Wratten.

"So this is cycle… C?"

"That's right," he nodded. "Between the time of the disaster and this morning was A, today B and tonight C."

"Simple as pie," the soldier from the van said sarcastically.

"What happens when you run out of letters?" Karma asked quietly.

The computer soldier shrugged again. "A2, I guess."

"So how many people are here, in total?" David wanted to know.

"Uh, there was less than a hundred in the first cycle, then maybe twice that or more today, and seventy-odd tonight. There'll no doubt be more tomorrow, especially now we've got the Metro FM broadcasts going."

"Anyway, thanks for that Seedman," Wratten told him, "we'd better be on our way." He nodded goodbye, and started off further into the shop, David, Dusty and Karma following closely behind, the young soldier from the van staying with the other two.

Usually this end of the Marks and Spencer building was full of shoppers milling about and looking through clothes rails, but now it was almost empty. All the stock had been cleared, along with all the frozens. Cash desks stood out like landmarks. One or two mannequins lay on the floor, stripped and broken. The different levels of flooring used for displays and sectioning departments within departments made the shop look uneven and disorganised. The other half of the store still looked functional, though from what David could see of the food hall, its shelves seemed depleted and some were completely empty. Furniture had been scattered around the household department, with most of the displays either incomplete or removed. He assumed Seedman's desk had belonged there at one time.

He also noticed the anti-ramraid shutters were down, sealing off the main mall entrance.

Wratten marched over to the restaurant and coffee shop.

As they came closer, David could hear conversation and laughter from within, all sounding rather normal and mundane.

It made him feel slightly optimistic about everything.

As if there might be a way of surviving this mess, and the man who knew how was sitting somewhere inside a supermarket caff.

They walked into the coffee shop, where there was a group of men and women sitting around a table in a cloud of blue haze. It really did look incredibly *normal*.

"Wratten!" somebody said and stood up, punching his head through the cigarette smoke cloud.

"Oh do shut up and sit down Imobaum," someone else said, grabbing the tall man and yanking him back down.

There were three men and two women, the Centrefather immediately obvious sitting imposingly at the head of the table. He stood up slowly, and turned to greet his latest new recruits.

He could've been in anything between his late twenties and early fifties. It was the movie star looks that did it for David. You couldn't really guess the age of a person who looked like they'd just stepped out of their personal Winnebago on a Hollywood film set. There were lines and a ruggedness which suggested age, but the overall impression was of youth and vitality. He seemed ready for anything, eyes intelligent and searching, hair neatly in place, mouth curving upwards into a smile of genuine welcome and warmth.

Makes a change to be smiled at rather than leaped at, David thought. He stepped forwards and extended a hand.

The Centrefather took it, and they shook. "You must be David?" His voice was quite light and laid back, but David could tell it carried authority.

He nodded, and stepped aside to introduce Dusty and Karma.

The 'father noted their robes, and wondered, "At a fancy dress party when it happened?"

"Uh no, not really, man," Dusty said, shaking his hand then moving quickly out the way.

"Shitting long story," agreed Karma, stepping up and shaking.

"Well, from what we hear, a rather unique one, too?" He was addressing Wratten.

"Yes sir, I thought it best you saw them straightaway. Their friend was unconscious when she arrived, she should be with the doctor now."

"I see." He seemed to consider something, then stepped back and offered the newcomers a seat. The table wasn't exactly very big, but the others shuffled around to accommodate them, and they were soon sitting comfortably, being offered coffees, sandwiches and cigarettes.

At the pack of Regals, Dusty wondered, "Nothing a little strong–?"

David elbowed him slightly. "These're the good guys, remember?"

The Centrefather seemed amused at the reference, but

let it pass. Instead, he started introducing the others. "This is Imobaum, my right-hand man," he pointed out the tall man who'd greeted Wratten, "next to him Jonson, he and Wratten are in charge of security," he indicated a young man in a camouflage jacket, "then Jazz," a woman in her thirties caked in make-up and a ridiculously colourful dress, "and Black," a small, shy-looking woman currently having difficulty keeping her eyes open, "my right-hand women."

David and the others nodded greetings, and the men and women all nodded back, except Black who nodded off.

It felt weird to be sitting there. Everyone was much older than David, making it seem like a staff meeting or something. He felt out of place and uncomfortable.

"Now I know this may seem a little strange," the Centrefather began, as if reading his thoughts, "especially after all you must've been through since the disaster, but you must understand we all feel the same way, no one has ever been through anything like it before, experienced anything like it, or even heard of anything like it."

David picked up a sandwich and agreed, "It can get a bit mental, yeah."

"Especially when you've got guys setting up their own People left right and centre," Dusty chipped in.

"I understand you're on the run from someone?" the Centrefather asked, unperturbed by the sceptical comment.

"Quite a lot of someones, sir," Wratten said. "Forty or fifty members, one leader, and two... nutters?"

"*Absolute* nutters," Dusty said, nodding.

Imobaum laughed a little, and shook his head. "We get a lot of them."

"And they're definitely heading this way?" the 'father wanted to know.

"Oh yes," said David. "They're going to befriend you, become part of your People, then... do something to get rid of you, and persuade everyone to join their own People."

"Their own People?"

"The People... ah, the People of the Liquid Card."

"Mystical," commented the soldier, Jonson.

"They all wear the same habits as those two," Wratten said, indicating Dusty and Karma, "so they shouldn't be hard to spot."

Jazz leaned forwards and asked Karma, "So were you two... part of them?" She had a voice as rough and gravelly as a ten pack of Regals in half an hour.

"Not by choice, man," Dusty made clear.

Karma merely shrugged. "I'm just one of life's victims." There were one or two nods around the table, as if this was perfectly understandable.

"So what exactly do you know about this, uh, disaster?" David wondered after gulping down the last of his coffee.

The Centrefather refilled his cup before answering. "Well, there're a number of theories, ranging from organised government apocalypses to the revenge of Mother Nature."

"We've had about twenty sets of people screaming

about what they know and how they knew it was going to happen," explained Imobaum. "Harmless, most of them. Then there're those who did it themselves. They caused the disaster: by accident, on purpose, because Aunt Edna's budgie died, because they thought it might be laugh, because the voices in their head told them to. Most of those are harmless, too. But not all of them. Oh, and there're loads of religious freaks, blaming everyone *except* themselves."

"So what *happens* to these nutters, man?" Dusty asked. "We'd love to know how to deal with them."

"Uh, maybe we'll come to that in a minute," Imobaum said, shifting in his seat slightly.

The Centrefather explained, "If we're to start a new life in which we don't make the same mistakes we did in the old one, then we cannot allow ourselves to kill or destroy or harm."

"Well hey," Dusty said, smiling, turning to David, "I doubt Rick and Becky wanted to punish everyone for breaking the twelve commandments or whatever it is, huh?"

"Er, yeah," David agreed, uncomfortable.

Wratten waited a moment before speaking. "You seem to... know something about all this, or have guessed something. Like before, you mentioned how we'd survived. Care to elaborate?"

"There's no need to push them, Wratten," the Centrefather admonished.

"Especially if everyone's got their own theory," David said, trying to get the heat off. He didn't particularly relish telling these authoritative adults how some horny teenage junkies wrecked their world.

"Most of them are just *dying* to tell us," Wratten went on. "You seem rather reluctant. Rather – maybe? – guilty?"

"You what?" Karma snapped angrily. She suddenly didn't look anything like a victim – or like someone who had given up on life. "Listen, we aren't answerable to anyone, we don't need to be here or stay here, or take shit from people looking for someone to blame."

The table was quiet for a moment, and David had time to feel really quite proud of her.

Then the Centrefather shook his head. "We don't want to blame anyone. We aren't even searching for answers. We just want to start afresh, get on with this new life in this new world, surviving as best we can." He nodded. "That's what we want to do – survive. And help others survive, too."

There were nods of approval from around the table. Even David felt a little touched, glad to be with someone who cared.

"Okay," Wratten said, relenting. "It's just... it's as if we're running out of time, as if something's about to happen, or something's about to change. I don't know."

There was silence.

David broke it.

He said, "We aren't running out of time. There's no time to run out of anymore." He took a deep breath. "Time has been conceptually destroyed."

The Centrefather nodded. "I know what you mean. There's something missing from our everyday existence. Time. Or time as we knew it, anyway. Did Wratten tell you about cycles?"

"Yeah," he nodded. "From dawn to dusk is one cycle, then dusk to dawn another."

"That's right." He looked around the table. "All our watches had stopped at the time of the disaster, in fact there were no timepieces left at all. We thought it best not to use the old, defunct measurement of time, so we came up with cycles."

"So… what else do you know?"

"It's all guesswork, really," he admitted. "We simply discuss our theories, air our views – if we need to make a decision, we just go with the most logical explanation."

"Conceptual destruction isn't exactly logical."

"No, but neither is the disaster itself. We knew there had to be something… outside our realms of under-standing about it."

"I used to work in a supermarket," David began. "Shelf stacking. You know, nothing too taxing. There was this other guy there too, Rick the Pr– uh, Rick Greenhead, never did any work, totally full of himself, thought he was the dog's. I always used to wonder why. And last night– I mean, during cycle A, we found out." He shook his head. "This is going to get complicated."

"Just do your best David," Imobaum encouraged, obviously interested, "if we don't understand, we'll ask at the end."

"Well, Danielle – the girl you sent to the infirmary – wanted to check on her best friend, see if she'd survived. But when we found her, she was frozen like the rest. Only she must've been screaming her head off. And in her hand was one half of something called a liquid card." He held up a hand, expecting a barrage of questions. "I don't know anything about it other than what I'm telling you, okay? It's difficult enough…"

"It's okay, take your time," said the Centrefather.

"Well I recognised it, because Rick had been holding the other half. And *he'd* been screaming when he froze, too. So we went back to get it, and grabbed his house keys as well. That's when we met up with the hippies and monkey. They were just trashing the supermarket, spotted us and started chasing us around town. I managed to run one of them over, then we headed up to Rick's place. And found his diary, which told us about the liquid card – it had the power to delay the conceptual existence of time." There were mutterings and whisperings around the table, but he tried to ignore them. "Which obviously… well, you can imagine what he got up to."

"You still have the diary?" Jonson wanted to know,

forehead creased in puzzlement, eyes piercing with scepticism.

"No. We met up with Karma, gave it to her to try and convince her, then Raw Man got her, and… well anyway. Thing was, Rick met up with Danielle's friend Becky and must've fallen in love. So he showed her the card, and got her hooked too."

"He said it was like a drug," Dusty pointed out. "Like he knew he shouldn't be using it, but it had him, had control of him. That diary got pretty heavy, man."

"He didn't really write much more than that, but we guessed the card must've overloaded or something, and when they tried to use it, instead of just delaying the concept of time, it *destroyed* the concept of time. And because most people are linked to time as a concept… well, it destroyed them, too. And just like when the card worked properly, they stayed frozen. Only this time they died. Like time."

"So how come so many've survived?" Imobaum asked in a hushed tone.

Dusty shook his head. "Maybe you'd prefer not to hear this bit, man."

"Say as much as you want," the 'father said.

"I'm telling you man, this isn't going to make you feel too great."

"I think we should be the judges of that, don't you?" Wratten said impatiently.

"Right then," David began. "Even though it's been conceptually destroyed, time is still physically moving on, right?"

"Right," agreed Imobaum.

"Okay. So, the only people who've survived are those who were conceptually linked with time, but who were physically…" He trailed off.

"Spit it out Dave, man," Dusty encouraged mischievously.

"It's the two base human physical experiences. Sex. And death."

The table was silent for a moment. Black had her head in her hands. David wasn't sure if she was thinking about the implications of his words, or if she was still asleep.

Imobaum started shaking his head and muttering. "Incredible… incredible…"

But Wratten wasn't impressed. "Come off it. The only way you could've survived is if you were shagging someone or killing them?" He smiled incredulously. "I think I prefer the one about the holy ghost going rogue and revealing itself to the sinners, and its face was–" here he adopted an exaggerated Irish accent, "'so terrifying they froze in terror and diiied.'"

"Yes that was a good one, wasn't it?" Jonson agreed conversationally.

"I really couldn't care what you think, to be honest," David snapped, suddenly angry. "It's the truth. You don't believe it, then fuck off."

"I believe you David," the Centrefather said quietly. The rest of the table turned to him. Wratten for one looked very surprised. The 'father explained, "It's too profound to be anything other than the truth."

"That's how we figured there were no good guys, you know?" piped up Dusty after a moment. "Uh, until we met yous of course," he added a little too quickly.

"I don't think we set out to be the 'good guys' Dusty," Imobaum said. "We just wanted to set up a place so people could meet other survivors, join together and struggle through as a group. And from the responses we're getting, it seems like that's what everyone wants to do."

David was nodding. "Yeah. Danielle didn't even hear the broadcasts, she just somehow *knew* this was the place to be."

"And everyone Raw Man stopped at his roadblock was heading this way, too," Karma added.

"So obviously," the Centrefather began, "from what you've experienced, you think there're a lot of survivors?"

"Well, at first me and Danielle just thought it was us two, you know? But then we met Dusty, then the twin hippies and Raw Man's bunch of looters." He shrugged. "I think there're a lot of survivors, yeah, but compared to the amount of people alive before the freeze... well, next to nothing, really."

The 'father nodded. "Yes, you can't really imagine the scale of it, can you?"

"I think we're jumping the gun a little, here," Wratten

interjected. "We don't even know the extent of the disaster."

Across the table, Jonson was nodding. "For all we've tried to contact other cities, even other countries, we could just be the only ones affected."

"You know that's not true, Jonson." Imobaum shook his head. "We've been monitoring the terrestrial, satellite and cable channels around the clock. Most of them've shut down by now, but the live broadcasts – the presenters were just as frozen as everyone else."

"Porn channels!" Dusty suddenly exclaimed, then looked around the table embarrassedly.

But Imobaum shook his head at that, too. "I don't know there're any adult channels transmitting live shows. Or at least not at seven o'clock on a Monday evening."

"You'd have thought someone might've tried to contact others though, wouldn't you?" pointed out Jazz. "Like we're doing through the radio?"

"Well, maybe it's just a matter of time," Imobaum conceded.

"What do you think David?" the Centrefather asked.

David shrugged. "I don't know. But from how Rick described the card in his diary, well, I just presumed it was the whole world."

Wratten scoffed. "Come on. Think about what you're saying."

"Okay everyone," the 'father began, "it's pointless continuing this discussion, and the way I see things, it

316

doesn't make much difference anyhow. We're all here, now, this thing has happened to us, we have to deal with it, live through it. That's all that should concern us for the moment."

"Yeah," Imobaum agreed, "we'll get nowhere arguing. Do you want to tell David and his friends a little about how we've tried to make the place work?"

"I suppose you must know more about it than me, actually," he joked, though David noticed he wasn't smiling much.

"Well the thing is," Imobaum said, looking at David, Dusty and Karma proudly, "we wanted to make a sort of 'mothership' thing. A home base for the immediate aftermath, where people could live and work, get sorted out, familiarise themselves with their new world. It wasn't much of a decision to come up with this place: both the Centrefather and I used to work here."

"So – wait a minute," Dusty requested, "how many of yous knew each other before the freeze, then?"

"Just me and Imobaum," the Centrefather revealed. "Wratten worked here too – no prizes for guessing in what capacity – but we didn't know each other. Jonson, Jazz and Black were just the first survivors we found who wanted to be part of the team."

There were various nods and agreements from around the table, and after a moment Imobaum continued. "There're over four hundred separate shops and restaurants, most of them big enough to house a lot of people. Obviously we're trying to keep most of the food and clothes shops up and running, plus some of the restaurants, but that still leaves hundreds of places. Plus all the buildings over in the Retail Park and along that way. Hopefully we won't be running out of space for a while yet."

"We were pretty surprised when people started turning up and we hadn't even started broadcasting," Jazz explained. "I mean, there were quite a few from inside and nearby, but I mean from even further afield. Most of those early arrivals Wratten and Jonson recruited as guards and soldiers, got them kitted out and everything. Then the others started setting themselves up in the food shops and things, got busy sorting stuff out. People like having something to do. Keeps their minds off the disaster itself, I suppose."

"Yeah," Imobaum agreed. "Although the first job we had to do had kind'f the *opposite* effect."

"It was part of something we're calling the sweep," the Centrefather said. "Sweeping up the... mess."

"You mean the frozens," guessed David.

"We had to sweep the mall first, obviously," Jonson said. "Me and Wratten organised most of it, going through and getting rid of them. I can't remember whose idea it was to use the cars as roadblocks. But that was next on the list."

"But where did you put them all, man?" Dusty wondered.

"Where *didn't* we put them, you mean," muttered Jazz.

"They're kind'f dotted about the place for now, true. But we couldn't decide on one location. You know, the best place to cremate them or whatever. There's some industrial chillers… but most of them are piled up in the overflow car park. Just for the time being, you understand."

"Moving the cars was another problem," Wratten said, taking up the story. "And then building the barricades themselves. But there were a couple of construction vehicles we used to stack the cars up high. It worked out pretty good."

"Well it sure scared the shit out'f me," Dusty confirmed.

"Not that they were exactly *supposed* to scare you," Imobaum told him. "But if you'd come here wanting to, you know, vandalise the place or something, then we wanted you to think twice."

"Mr Wratten says you've had quite a bit of bother," Karma pointed out.

"I think you'll find it was Jaxon doing most of the talking, thank you," Wratten corrected quickly.

"That one wants to learn to keep his mouth shut," Jonson snapped. "But as you've no doubt learned," he continued, his voice softening, "there're one or two people running around thinking they can do what the hell they like. To them, this current lawlessness is heaven sent. We've had to work hard not to let them near."

"But surely some of them wouldn't go nuts 'til they were inside the building, right?" Dusty wondered.

"Well…"

"We've worked something out which we think suits everyone," Imobaum said quickly. "Well, mostly everyone." He looked around uncomfortably. None of the others offered to help. "Well it's temporary. Sort of."

"No it's not," the Centrefather contradicted. "It's perfect. All our problems in one place. Out the way. We can't touch them, they can't touch us."

"What is it exactly?" David wanted to know, a little spooked by the Centrefather's words.

"Just… a place." Imobaum removed another cigarette from a packet and sparked up. "You know."

Black suddenly jerked awake next to Karma. She looked around groggily, recognised her surroundings, then dropped her head forwards once more.

Jazz shrugged. "We've not had much chance to sleep since the disaster."

There was the sound of hurried footsteps from the coffee shop entrance. David turned to see the young soldier from the van, the one Wratten had called Jaxon, racing towards their table.

He came to a halt next to his superior. "Sounds like those weirdos've arrived, sir. Lookout says he's got a coachload about five minutes away."

"Right," Wratten and Jonson said at the same time, pushing out their chairs and standing up.

"You don't know whether they're armed at all?" Jonson asked David.

"Wouldn't've thought so," he replied, shaking his head. "Like I said, they're here to befriend you."

"Okay." He turned to the Centrefather. "Suppose we'd better get out there."

The 'father nodded. "Fine. Try and persuade the leader to speak to us first, on his own or with a couple of others. Keep the rest in the coach, but make sure they're out of danger."

"No problem." The three men turned and walked hurriedly away.

No one spoke, at first.

But after a few moments, Jazz muttered, "Those two really piss me off sometimes."

"We have to have security, Jazz," Imobaum defended, crushing his cigarette butt into an ashtray.

"But do they have to be so…?" She didn't finish.

The Centrefather turned to David and his friends and asked, "Do you want to be here when we talk to the leader?"

Dusty shrugged. "I don't mind, man. The moment you lay eyes on him you'll know he's nuts, so I doubt you'll be chatting for long."

"Wonder where the hippy and monkey got to," David said.

"Who?" the 'father asked.

"The two proper nutters," David explained. "No way they'd try and negotiate or try and befriend you. They'd just barge right on in screaming and yelling."

"Yeah," agreed Dusty quietly, remembering the havoc at Raw Man's farm.

"Well, Wratten's men'd be sure to pick them up if they did," Imobaum said confidently, reaching for another cigarette.

The Centrefather nodded. "Yes. There's no doubt about that." He looked around the table, noticed the empty cups. "Well then. More coffee anyone?"

WHILE THE CENTREFATHER STARTED REFILLING cups, Jazz trotted off to get more sandwiches.

David gulped down a mouthful of coffee, then realised he'd forgotten to add any milk or sugar. As he heaped sugar into the cup, he noticed his hand was trembling, scattering grains over an impressively wide distance.

The Centrefather noticed, too.

"Guess I'm not looking forward to meeting Raw Man much," David admitted.

The 'father nodded slightly, but had a preoccupied look in his eyes.

David didn't like that look.

After a while, Jazz returned with a huge foil tray of sandwiches which not only varied in fillings, but also size, shape, colour and texture. Everyone except David, the Centrefather and Black extended hands.

While the others were munching and slurping away, David had time to think it was all quite civilised – or as civilised as you could be in what had so far been nothing but an uncivilised world – and for the first time in a long while he was starting to feel a little optimism. Maybe Dusty was right. It would be obvious Raw Man was off his rocker, the Centrefather would sort him out, organise his followers to join the Metro Centre People, and things would be all right. Maybe the hippy and monkey had leaped off into the jungle of Newcastle (and David didn't even want to think about what it might've been like trying to survive the past twenty-four hours in that urban sprawl), never to be seen again.

Jazz was wafting an egg sandwich under Black's nose, getting no response, and it was after she shrugged then stuffed it into her own mouth the clomp of approaching boots started echoing into the restaurant.

They all turned to watch Raw Man, the surviving body-guard, a lone devil worshipper, Wratten, Jonson, Jaxon and an extra soldier stride into the room. Raw Man and his men were in front, Raw Man grinning cheesily, his security guard frowning creasingly, and the devil worshipper scuttling along and trying to keep up with his master's huge, confident strides.

Behind them, the four soldiers eyed the newcomers warily, watching for any false moves. But it was obvious

Raw Man wasn't about to try anything. He was smiling too much, the performance already well under way. He looked to David like someone who knew he'd got what he wanted before he'd even asked for it. It was worrying to see him so confident.

He stopped at the bottom of the table, the opposite end to the Centrefather, and spread his arms.

The 'father nodded curtly, and told him to take a seat. Raw Man seemed a little miffed at the off-hand welcome, as if he'd been expecting fanfares and speeches, but he took the seat without complaint. The guard and worshipper stood either side of him, a few steps behind.

For the first time he looked directly at David. His words were casual, but his eyes gleamed with revenge. "Rick. I thought we were meant to be travelling together."

David shrugged. "I had a better offer."

"Well," he conceded, "perhaps you made a wise decision after all. Our journey wasn't exactly… *comfortable*." His smile slipped a little, and he looked over his shoulder at his companions, who shuffled nervously.

David guessed the reason for their fear: one long-haired hippy and one skinhead monkey.

The Centrefather coughed a little, and started to introduce everyone.

"No, no," Raw Man interrupted when he realised what the 'father was doing, "let me." He turned to David again. "This is Rick Greenhead, destroyer of time and all life which depended upon it. Next to him are his two coke-addled friends, not exactly destroyers themselves but, ah, what a coincidence they both managed to survive." He made a show of looking around the room, but in reality he'd taken it all in when he'd arrived. "I presume you have Becky, his girlfriend, stashed somewhere. She really was a nasty piece of work. No wonder you've hidden her away." He concluded with, "Together, she and Rick screwed up the world." After a short pause, long enough for everyone to digest what he was saying but not long enough to let doubt creep in, he turned back to the 'father. "I presume you must be the esteemed leader of the Metro Centre People, the Centrefather I'm sure I've heard you being referred as, these gentlemen standing here–" (Wratten, Jonson and the two soldiers), "must be part of your security detail, and these final three... your deputies?"

The 'father nodded slowly. "Correct."

There was a slight pause before Dusty pointed out, "I wasn't too sure about the first bit, man." He shook his head. "I mean fine, think I'm a cokehead if you want, but Dave here sure didn't destroy the world or anything."

"Well I'm actually quite interested in that," Wratten butted in, stepping forwards, an edge to his voice. "Seems to me our new friends here might not've been telling us the whole story."

David had to twist himself around to look up at the soldier. "Come off it Wratten. You mightn't like us much, but–"

"That's right Rick. I don't much like you. But I was

prepared to go along with your story for the time being, even if it was a little ridiculous." He sighed, as if with genuine regret. "But not now. Not now I've heard Raw Man's side of things. Not now I've read your fucking diary."

"Hey what, that's not–"

"You fucking degenerate!"

He might've been in an awkward position, twisting himself around and looking up, but David knew when someone was about to belt him one, and quickly pushed his chair backwards while simultaneously skittering out of the line of fire.

"You fuck," Wratten cursed, stumbling. He hoofed the chair out the way. "I had kids you fuck. Daughters. Eight and ten years old. You fuck."

"Wratten!" the Centrefather bawled, leaping up out of his chair and raging. "Get yourself under control man!"

The soldier stopped where he was, eyes blazing. He looked monumentally pissed off. "How can you stand there and defend someone like this?" he hissed.

"Because I haven't got a clue what you're talking about, that's why," the 'father replied. "I haven't seen the diary yet, remember? I haven't heard Raw Man's story yet, remember?"

"Well maybe it's high time you did," Wratten snapped, stepping back a little, making a show of regaining his composure.

"Yes," Raw Man agreed. He looked all smug and

pleased with himself. "Maybe it's time you did." He motioned for the Centrefather to return to his seat.

And as much as David found it difficult to accept, it was obvious who was in control at that moment.

He stepped over to retrieve his own seat from where Wratten had booted it, and replaced it in front of the table. He made sure it was at an angle which would allow a quick getaway, then slowly sat down.

There was a moment of silence. Then Imobaum ventured tentatively, "Coffee anyone?"

The Centrefather shook his head sharply. "I think we should just get this misunderstanding sorted out as quickly as possible, don't you?"

"I hardly think 'misunderstanding' even begins–" Raw Man started.

"Well maybe someone wants a sandwich," Jazz interrupted. There was silence. "Marks and Spencer's best," she added hopefully.

The Centrefather hung his head a little. Though it was obvious Imobaum and Jazz were just trying to calm the situation, it seemed it was having the opposite effect on their 'father. "Please continue," he told Raw Man after a few more moments of tension.

"Well," Raw Man said, looking around the table. "It seems you good people have been somewhat... misinformed." He let his gaze rest on David, Dusty and Karma. "I don't know what story you've been fed by these three, but I can assure you they are not who they claim to be."

"Oh give it up why can't you?" David demanded. "You can't expect–"

"Shut it Greenhead!" barked Wratten, stepping closer.

"You got it all wrong, man," Dusty whined. He glanced at David and flicked his eyes towards the café entrance. He wanted to make a run for it. Which probably wasn't such a bad idea.

"Come on now," the Centrefather told them, "let Raw Man have his say."

"My little group didn't know what'd hit them." Raw Man gazed first at Imobaum, then the Centrefather, then moved over David, Dusty and Karma to rest his eyes on Jazz, then Black, who was either asleep and pretending to be awake, or awake and pretending to be asleep. "The disaster – it destroyed us all. We were turned into… scavengers."

David couldn't believe how theatrical the man was being. It looked like Wratten and the soldiers had been won over already; it wouldn't take much to convince the rest. And then…

And then he and Dusty and Karma would be taken someplace. Someplace Imobaum and everyone didn't want to mention. Someplace where the soldiers guarding it could hear strange noises from inside.

He looked over at his two friends. Dusty was shaking his head as Raw Man kept whittering on about what a traumatic experience he and his looter pals had been through, while Karma was sitting facing straight ahead, staring at not much in particular and every so often blinking slowly, back into victim mode. Everyone else around the table seemed riveted by whatever bollocks Raw Man was spouting. Even his bodyguard and devil worshipper were standing seemingly transfixed.

"Then who should arrive but this young lady," Raw Man was saying, gesturing slowly towards Karma, who didn't react. "Obviously she'd realised Rick had gone too far. Realised how dangerous he was, realised she had to get out before it was too late. We offered company and warmth and relative comfort. And to back up her incredible story, she'd brought with her a rather strange and frightening document."

There was only one main exit David could make out. And Wratten, Jonson and their two mates were standing in the way. Then there was Seedman and the others at the Marks and Spencer entrance. Beyond them, the soldiers stationed at the roadblock. Beyond *them*…

…what?

What was left of the world David once knew?

Not fucking much.

And to be frank, there hadn't been much of one to start with, at least from what little David had seen of it. What future was there? Whatever petty punishment the Centre-father had lined up for him? Or a life in a world where time didn't exist, where men rampaged as beasts and order rampaged as chaos?

He closed his eyes and thought of sleep.

"It was only by chance we heard your radio broadcasts. But it was as if our prayers had been answered. There was someone out there with the same ideas as ours, someone who wanted to help people rebuild their shattered lives, shattered in the name of nothing but sex and drugs and the pursuit of physical pleasure."

"Sounds a good enough reason to me," commented Jaxon, the squeaky-voiced soldier from the van.

Jonson made to elbow him sharply, but the younger man had anticipated the reaction and already stepped out of reach.

Raw Man turned his attention to the soldier. "Not if you'd seen what I have, son. Nothing is a good enough reason for the suffering and pain I have witnessed." Here he slammed his fist against the table. "Nothing!"

David had to honestly suppress an urge to burst out laughing. There'd probably been less melodramatics in Danielle's A-level drama project. But it was obviously getting through to some. If it were possible, Wratten looked even more tense than before. And Jazz and Imobaum didn't exactly seem the sceptical outsiders he'd hoped they'd be. Only the Centrefather appeared emotionally unaffected... though it seemed to David he was busy calculating and reaching his own, personal conclusions.

"And this young man here," Raw Man gushed, indicating David, "is the cause of all that suffering. All that pain and death. The catalyst of the apocalypse, I give you *Rick Greenhead*!"

"Fucker!" Wratten screamed, leaping forwards.

"Sir, sir, quick!" A clattering of footsteps and screeching of words.

David tried the chair pushing backwards trick again, but Wratten simply kicked it forwards and would've ploughed it into David had he not managed to get out the way in time. As it was, the chair crashed against the table, spilling cups and sandwiches and waking up Black with a start.

The footsteps soon revealed one of the soldiers from the Marks and Spencer entrance. "Sir, the two undesirables you told us to watch for, sir, they're in, they broke through!"

Raw Man jerked out of his seat as violently as if the chair had just exploded. Behind him, the bodyguard tensed up with anger, then thought better of it and started looking around for a handy hiding place. The devil worshipper simply yelped and made a dive for the nearest makeshift weapon.

"Monkey-monkey-monkey," Dusty babbled, sliding around in his seat and grabbing hold of Karma who looked at him, startled.

Wratten seemed to forget about David once he realised what had happened. "They *broke through*?" he bawled, turning. "You fucking incompetents, how did they break through my defences?" He advanced on the messenger, fists raised and face twisted in rage. "*How could you let them break through*?"

"I... I'm... don't, I'm just telling you what I know sir, I'm–"

Disgustingly, David could actually see the spurt of blood from either side of Wratten's fist as the soldier's nose detonated under so much force. The man dropped to the floor heavily and vertically, as if a trapdoor had opened beneath his feet.

Wratten turned to the extra soldier standing next to Jaxon. "You, with me! Jonson, I'll take care of our uninvited guests, you sort out this lot!" He snarled at David, then grabbed the soldier with no name and ran for the exit.

"You fucking get them!" Raw Man suddenly screamed after them. "You fucking get the fuckers, the fuck– *their heads*! I WANT THEIR HEADS ON A FFF– FUCKING! FFFUCKING FUCK! FUUCK-AAHHH!" He was jerking his arms from side to side, his whole body shaking with uncontrolled rage. Then he proceeded to pound his fists against the table, shattering coffee cups, plates, sandwiches and ashtrays with equal ease. Now his feet were joining in with the attack, as he lifted them up and stomped on the floor in time with his fists on the table. Both bodyguard and worshipper were by now brandishing weapons – the guard his hunting knife, the worshipper a rather unconvincing plastic fork – but next to their ballistic master they looked so pathetic and helpless.

No one made a move to calm him, however.

Even David began to realise he posed no great threat. He was merely throwing a tantrum. A rather violent and impressive one admittedly, but it would prove to be as ineffective and pointless as the toddler's it resembled.

Dusty and Karma had since got out of their seats, and were now huddling close to David.

"Anytime you want to run man, just give the word," Dusty told him.

David looked around. Everyone seemed transfixed by Raw Man's performance. Even Black had decided to give consciousness a try for the duration. If they were going to attempt to escape, there would surely be no better opportunity. "You think? You really think they were taken in by... by *him*?" he asked, indicating the grown man currently screaming and bawling and jumping up and down on his chair and tearing at his clothes.

Dusty shrugged. "Knowing our luck."

David snorted. "Yeah, that'd be right." But then he shook his head. "Look guys, what've we got to lose? I mean, what's left out there?" He looked at Karma before he continued. "Maybe we should give this Metro Centre People thing a chance. Fuck Raw Man, they'll sort him out, do whatever they do to the nutters. I mean, does living in HMV the rest of your life sound so bad?"

"I'd prefer an Ann Summers shop, to be honest," admitted Dusty.

"Don't think there is one," Karma informed them, and shrugged a little at David's questioning look.

"Well, the underwear department of Etam or Top Shop, then," Dusty continued.

Still looking at Karma, David smiled. "Yeah, that'd do."

After a moment, he became aware Raw Man was actually screaming words now, rather than just a meaningless growl. A few seconds later he realised it was that pseudo-poetic title he'd used before: "*–apocalypse Rick Greenhead catalyst of the apocalypse Rick Greenhead catalyst–*"

Just as David wondered if the intelligible words might indicate his anger was about to focus itself and also become coherent, Raw Man jumped from his seat onto the table and half stepped half slipped his way to the end. There he stood, towering above David and his friends, face flushed bright red, arms and legs trembling, chest heaving.

"I want this man to pay." He spoke in a loud and flat monotone which somehow made his words all the more demanding. "I want this man punished. I want this man in pain. I want this man *dead*."

The Centrefather stood up.

Throughout the commotion he had remained in his seat, watching events impassively. "Maybe we should all just sit back down." The sentence was not the suggestion the words indicated.

Raw Man looked at him, then looked down at himself and around at his audience. He nodded. "Forgive me. I get a little upset occasionally." He turned and walked back along the table, returning to his seat.

David and his friends remained standing, however.

The Centrefather didn't seem to care. "People have always puzzled me," he stated simply. He looked down at himself, shuffled a little on his feet.

Out the corner of his eye, David noticed Imobaum looking up at the 'father warily, as if he'd heard something like this before and hadn't been happy with the outcome.

"The way they carry on, like life owed them a favour, like the world existed only for them," the Centrefather continued. "Like we used to think the Sun orbited Earth. Ignorant, immature, tunnel vision thinking." He raised his head, and looked at Raw Man.

The devil worshipper leader stared back as neutrally as possible. This was somewhat hindered by his recent outburst – his chest was heaving up and down with effort, his leather jacket was hanging from one arm, his face was glowing deepest scarlet, sweat was sluicing down every visible patch of skin – but still he made a valiant effort to keep up the impression.

"Most people get 'upset occasionally.' In fact, if we were honest with ourselves, most of us get downright pissed off just about every other minute of the day."

"Hey man," Dusty whispered to David, "take a chill pill."

David covered his laughter with a short sharp cough.

The Centrefather glanced in their direction, then continued. "But we learn to live with it. Control it." He paused.

Imobaum took the opportunity. "You know, I'm not

sure if we should be going into this right now." The Centrefather looked at him, challenging him. Imobaum waved a hand at Raw Man. "Raw Ma– er, Mr Man… uh, this person here has brought up some valid issues, and I think they're important enough to be dealt with immediately. Other… problems can wait."

"I'll second that," Raw Man coughed, his throat parched from his screaming fest. He reached for his coffee cup, then remembered he'd smashed it to pieces. He leaned over, grabbed an unscathed one still half full, drained it. "The less time we spend on pointless philoph– phill… thinking the better."

"David?" the 'father barked. He spun around and faced the three youngsters. "Or Rick or whatever the *hell* your name is? What do you think?" He leaned forwards, ignoring the rest of the table. "Shall we deal with the *valid issues* now, or just carry on pointlessly philosophising?" He blinked. "Hmm?"

Dusty swallowed. Karma lowered her head. Even David had trouble keeping his cool. The Centrefather was about to lose it. His eyes blazed fire. Muscles in his face twitched with repressed rage. The control he'd been about to talk about was obviously at breaking point.

"Philosophy's good with me," David whispered. Beside him, he could feel Karma nodding agreement.

"And me too," Dusty added quickly. "Philosophy, straight down the line. All the way, man. No problem."

"No problem!" someone echoed loudly.

They all turned to see Wratten striding towards them, the soldier with no name scampering awkwardly behind him. "A challenge, that's what it was! By Christ Jonson you're going to wish you'd been there. Out there in the thick of battle!"

"You get them?" Raw Man snapped, leaping out of his chair again. "You get the fucks, the *fuckscuntsfucks– YOU GET THEM*?!"

Wratten slowed to a halt before the table. "Oh yeah. We got 'em all right."

Now they were closer and motionless, David could see both soldiers sported pretty ugly-looking war wounds. There was a gush of blood drenching Wratten's upper arm, his clothing torn near the shoulder, splats from the wound decorating his face. A monkey bite? The soldier with no name's neck and jaw was red and scraped, drying blood caking his nostrils and lips. A stomping Doctor Marten?

Wratten grinned and bared his teeth. He held the expression for a few moments.

Then suddenly started barking.

Shouting out the sound, jerking his head forwards, spittle spattering, eyes blazing.

David and Dusty looked at each other and blinked.

Jonson seemed to understand, though. "The dogs," he stated simply.

Wratten stopped barking. Drool was foaming between his teeth and over his chin. He kept grinning. "The dogs. Came from nowhere. Attacked us *all*. Must've been a pack of ten, fifteen at least. Much more than last time. And hungrier. Starving. Got the baldy fucker a good one on the leg. Should've heard him *squeeeal*!"

"Christ Wratten, you're behaving like a fucking savage," Jazz snapped.

And, standing there staring at her, mouth still open and grinning, covered in blood and spit, he pretty much *looked* like one. He kept staring as he continued. "Not even our boys could keep this lot down. But we all knew what to do. Scarpered in all directions. Dogs on our heels. Dogs on the hippy and slaphead. Dragging the fucker by his leg. Shaking him all over, his fists battering down."

The soldier with no name let out a hollow groan and collapsed. On the way down, toppling forwards, he let everyone see what the problem was: the back of his head had been bitten, half scalped, blood and mush and matted hair decorating the glistening bone of his skull.

"You fuck!" Wratten exploded. "Stand to attention! You've returned from battle victorious! Up you fuck!"

But it was obvious he was going nowhere. He remained motionless, maybe two or three feet from where the messenger whose nose Wratten had pancaked still lay unconscious.

Just as Wratten seemed about to grab him and drag him to his feet, the Centrefather spoke. "You just let the dogs have them?"

Wratten looked up, grinned. "It was tempting. But no. Most of the pack ran after us lot, only two or three kept up the attack. Those two freaks soon got the upper hand."

"You mean you let them escape?" Jazz spat, disgusted.

"Don't be so fucking stupid. The dogs sorted them out. We just had to go in afterwards and clear up the mess. The baldy lad's leg's fucked, the hippy's had half his hair torn out. We've got them trussed up and ready for… well, whatever."

"Good work," the Centrefather said.

Wratten beamed. "No problem sir."

The 'father looked down at his team still sat around the table. "If we're all in agreement, I think our only course of action is to send them where we normally send those of a… disruptive nature. Yes?"

"Definitely," said Imobaum.

Jazz and Black both nodded.

"And, in addition, I feel it would be beneficial if Raw Man and his friends joined them, together with David and *his* friends."

"Uh, hey man–" Dusty began.

"Shut it!" screeched the Centrefather. "You've had your say, presented your case. Now let the jury decide." He turned to Imobaum and the two women. "Well?"

David tried to catch Imobaum's eye, but he kept looking away sheepishly. After a moment he nodded his consent.

"Seems like the best idea," Jazz agreed.

"Fine," muttered Black, the only word she'd spoken.

"I feel you're making a rash and foolish decision," Raw Man said, his voice hard and threatening.

"I hate to have to agree with him, but I'm not so keen on the idea either," David admitted. He indicated Karma and Dusty. "We're just kids, we've not caused you any harm, we just got caught up in this whole thing, surely you can see that?"

The Centrefather looked at him impassively. "Sorry David. Rick. Whatever. The decision has been made." He started to smile, then took a deep breath and screamed, "*ASDA… IIIT… IIIS*!!"

"Yah-HOOO!" Wratten howled, leaping into the air and racing out of the café, bawling orders to his men at the shop entrance.

Raw Man got to his feet. "If you'll excuse us, we'll find our own way out." He turned to his men, motioned for them to get the hell away.

Jonson and Jaxon jumped into action, bulldozing into Raw Man simultaneously and slamming him to the floor.

Meanwhile, a whole gang of whoops and screeches were coming from the shop floor, steadily increasing in volume as Wratten and his men raced towards the restaurant.

"'They're coming to take us away, ha ha,'" Dusty chanted.

"I know," David said. "And they really are. Time to fucking peg it." They belted away from the table towards the food counter, David hoping for an entrance to a preparation room or kitchen or something. They'd almost reached it when he realised Karma wasn't with them. "For fuck's sake!" He skidded to a halt, looked back to see she simply hadn't moved. "You go ahead, I'll get her!"

Dusty nodded.

But that was when the soldiers reached the coffee shop.

It was obvious these men had been part of the hippy skinhead starving dogs fight. They were wild-eyed with battle adrenaline, bloody with wounds, and crazed for more action. Six of them raced towards David and Dusty immediately. The rest piled towards the table, Jazz, Black, Imobaum and the Centrefather quickly stepping out of the way.

David tried skirting sideways, but the leading soldier simply kicked his feet out from under him, and he plummeted to the floor.

Behind him, Dusty was surrendering. "Okay man, whatever you say, I'll come quietly– OUFFF!" The men sent him crunching backwards, sprawling against the food counter, slamming to the floor.

Rough clawing hands grabbed David's body, spun him onto his back, snatched at the nearest available limb. Man-handled upwards, yanked and stretched spreadeagled into the air, waist height, chest height, head height, higher. Raised above them like a trophy, the soldiers shouting their victory. Turning his head one way, he could see Dusty rising to meet him. The other way, and there was Raw Man and his two men stretched out and struggling, captured animals. And Karma, compliant as ever, getting hauled into the air, more men than necessary clambering to grope her and hold her aloft.

Wratten was on the table, jumping around in parody of Raw Man's outburst. "Aaand… quick… *MAAARRRCH!*"

The soldiers started moving, marching forwards, jerking David up and down, battering and confusing him further. From what he could make out, Jonson and the soldiers holding Raw Man were in the lead, followed by the bodyguard, then the devil worshipper (whose high-pitched squealing and squawking was providing constant background noise), then Karma, and finally Dusty and David. Dusty was babbling "Oh man oh man!" repeatedly, while behind him the Centrefather and Imobaum fell into line.

"Black and me'll just stay behind and clear up," Jazz offered.

"A woman's work is never done, huh?" Wratten yelled, grinning, before jumping off the table and bringing up the rear.

David tried keeping his head up to see where they were going, but the soldiers' marching was so spasmodic it was difficult to make out much. They left the café and moved into the Marks and Spencer shop proper, and from what he could tell were heading over towards the Metro Centre mall entrance. This was confirmed when he first heard then saw the metal anti-ramraid shutters start clacking upwards.

It took a while for them to creep up the runners towards the holdings above the entrances. It made everything seem rather theatrical. Especially with the sudden hushed whisperings coming from the mall. David got the impression using these doors signified some special event.

There was a final click and the shutters locked home.

THE JOURNEY THROUGH THE METRO CENTRE shopping mall's Green and Red Quadrants was surreal to say the least.

When Imobaum and the Centrefather had described the place as their 'mothership,' David had imagined survivors making the best of a bad job, pulling together and making do with whatever they could salvage from shops and restaurants and services.

Instead, when the groups of soldiers and their victims moved from the M&S store into the mall, they were stepping into a completely new and self-contained world.

The first thing David noticed was the tiled flooring. Or rather, the lack of it. It was difficult to make out what exactly it had been replaced with – his head dangling down as it was, and the soldiers' marching bouncing him all over the place – but it looked like a deep covering of some flakes or other, like wood shavings but less uniform, soft bark-like scraps you sometimes saw covering the ground of rural playparks. But someone had made sure the connection with nature and countryside would never be fully realised: as much of the material as possible had been painted or dyed an infinite number of horribly garish and clashing colours, giving David the impression he was floating over a bastardisation of the colour spectrum itself.

Jonson led everyone around the right-hand side of an escalators, glass lift and water feature combination (the moving stairs frozen and buried beneath more coloured covering, the fountain switched off and the water a pissy-shitty colour), and past what had once been an electrical store.

As David's group of soldiers marched by, he managed to see inside.

There were a number of flamboyantly dressed people hanging around the entrance, gawping unselfconsciously at the passers-by, while behind them another group were huddled around a display of televisions, all playing the same crappy-looking film. A rattle of dubbed machine gun fire suddenly exploded out of the television speakers, and was followed by the requisite corny one-liner.

The pre-recorded noise focused David's attention on the other noises coming from all around, the yells and screams, music and laughter, chugging of machinery and yelping of animals. Plus Wratten's manic "LEFT RIGHT LEFT RIIIGHT! AAAND LEFT RIGHT LEFT RIGHT!" and the devil worshipper's constant screeching, as well as a soldier's sudden shout of disgust, "This fucker's pissed his pants!"

They moved further along, passing more shops and stores, gutted and seemingly untouched alike. Of those emptied, most had been completely transformed, and only a few bore any resemblance to their previous incarnations like the Dixons electrical store. Survivors had created homes and shelters of startlingly original appearance. Sheet glass store fronts had been covered with paints or materials, murals depicting – David guessed – scenes witnessed over the past two cycles. There were montages of the frozen dead (some in positions so obscure and extreme they were surely only representational), scenes of intense battle, images of love and hope, loneliness and desperation.

From the glimpses he got through the doorways, David could see the shops had been furnished as outlandishly as the Dixons survivors had been dressed. Colourful materials adorned the walls, ranging from tapestries and drapes to tea towels and clothing; furniture was of varying designs and styles, some the latest metal industrial minimalism, others time-scarred antique oak and mahogany, others as plastic and cheap as any child's make-believe toy set.

Usually there were several fake traveller wagon style handcarts set up the middle of the mall gangway, small businesses offering jewellery and other knick-knacky items, several snack food stalls, plus the usual display stands for services such as the AA and the National Lottery. However, since the Metro Centre People had moved in, all these had been removed, clearing the gangway as much as possible, leaving it blocked only by the occasional water feature or access to the first floor mall, enabling Wratten's adrenaline-buzzed soldiers to move their struggling captives through the Centre with speed.

In fact David was travelling so fast he was missing half the sights.

He could only lift his head up to look for a few moments before feeling dizzy. He caught glimpses of raggedly dressed children jumping up and down a staircase, sliding down the bannisters to land unharmed on the multi-coloured floor covering. A man and woman busy creating their own personal mural: a scene set against a jet-black sky and a blood-red ground. They themselves were dressed in nothing but paint. A larger group of survivors than he had yet seen, standing outside what had once been WH Smith, watching as two men hacked away at the one remaining shop sign. A final wrench and it relented, crashing to the floor, the onlookers whooping with glee, the shop now their home.

The troop was now approaching Town Square One, where the Green Quadrant turned into the Red, and another wide aisle gave access to the north half of the Centre. They continued west, moving around the Square, where a number of survivors were busy being organised into smaller groups by an elderly woman. A fat man whose face was invisible beneath a dense covering of hair kept jumping up in front of her and shouting. It looked to David like the group were about to go through the shopping mall with several empty supermarket trollies.

It was as David's captors tramped into the Red Quadrant walkway he heard someone shouting out, and come running towards the troop. From what he could make out, it was the fat hairy man, bounding past Wratten, Imobaum and the Centrefather and leaping up at Dusty.

"Hey man chill, hey man," Dusty was whining.

The man merely bawled more incoherence before moving forwards and yelling at David. Up close, the man was even fatter and even hairier. Spittle flew from his lips as he let loose another barrage of nonsense. Then he moved onwards to torment Karma.

His yelling hadn't gone ignored by everyone, however.

Up ahead, under the pink and blue HMV sign, David could see maybe three or four similar looking survivors approaching the original fat-and-hairy. They shouted at each other for a moment, then together advanced on the troop. One of them stepped up to David, jogging along to keep up with the soldiers' marching. The corner of a pillow or cushion was sticking up out of the collar of his loose-fitting jumper. His facial hair was a mass of colourful wool and string and fluff which had been sellotaped to his skin.

"ROO-ARR HAH HUH?" the man yelled somewhat

unconvincingly. His entire beard shifted from side to side as he shouted, and a few strands of wool drifted to the floor. His stomach also started to sag a little, until he shoved a hand underneath his jumper and pushed it upwards once more.

David decided not to even bother thinking about it.

The wannabe caveman moved on.

Closing his eyes and letting his head loll as far backwards as he could without it being too uncomfortable, David tried to blank his mind of any unwanted thoughts. Any ideas he had of where the soldiers were taking him, any plans he had to escape, any visions of life beyond the freeze. He concentrated on trying to calm his breathing and heartbeat. He even tried ignoring the battering his body was taking being jigged about by the soldiers.

After a while, the troop slowed their pace before coming to a complete halt and standing to attention.

Up front, David could hear Jonson speaking to someone. He opened his eyes and tried twisting himself around to get a better look, but he couldn't see much. There appeared to be some sort of wall or barricade just after what had once been Littlewoods.

Soon enough, the troop moved forwards once more, and he could see the entire width of the aisle had been blocked off, apart from a small doorway. Boxes, wooden boards, broken furniture and other junk had been piled up next to a staircase, the crossover on the first floor mall providing an additional barrier against whatever lay beyond. The troop was slowly moving through the door-way, where two more soldiers had been stationed: one by the door itself, another sitting behind a desk and staring at a laptop.

Beyond the barrier there was no colourful flooring. Just bare tiles, scuffed and stained.

It was cold. It was gloomy.

The noise from the rest of the Metro Centre was muffled. And drowned out.

By the screaming.

By the shouting.

The whooping.

Shrieking.

They had reached the end of the Red Quadrant.

An exit to the outside world lay only ten seconds' sprint from where they were now, blocked off by another huge pile of miscellaneous rubbish.

And in front of them, what had once been an Asda supermarket, closed and abandoned since December 1997, now empty, empty and dark, empty save for the endless sounds of torment coming from within.

"Aaand... DROP!" screamed Wratten, and the soldiers dropped.

David managed to grab hold of a soldier's leg to slow his descent, but still cracked his knee a good one off the hard tiles. Behind him he heard Dusty yelp in pain, while in front it seemed everyone else was faring just as bad.

"ABOUT TURRRN... AAAND... *MARCH!*"

The soldiers started clomping off towards the barrier, then back into the mall. On the way, maybe two out of every three men gave the captives on the floor the boot. The final soldier stomped on the back of Dusty's leg then disappeared through the doorway.

Remaining were Jonson, Jaxon, Wratten and a number of less formally dressed soldiers stationed at the abandoned supermarket entrance. A moment later Imobaum and the Centrefather, who'd been waiting outside the barrier, stepped through the doorway.

"The lads are dealing with the hippy and slaphead," Imobaum announced. "Should be here in a tick."

"Right," Jonson nodded.

There were a few minutes of relative silence as David and the rest of them pushed themselves up onto their feet, nursing various wounds. The devil worshipper limped over to where Raw Man was snorting blood out of his nose in long, sticky streams, and a moment later was joined by the bodyguard.

David and Dusty made their way towards Karma, who was having difficulty standing. Together, the two friends helped her to her feet.

"Thanks," she muttered, stepping close to David. He found her hand, gripped it tightly.

Dusty shook his battered head. "Man, we're in some shit."

David nodded. "Tell me about it."

The screams from the deserted supermarket seemed to

be getting louder with every moment. Every once in a while there was the sound of something smashing.

Raw Man stepped forwards, and appealed to the Centrefather. "You've had your fun. You've shown us who's boss. Now just let us go." He paused to shake his head and snort out another wad of blood. He swallowed. "You just show us the exit and we'll leave quietly. No trouble. You've made your point."

The walk through his Centre didn't seem to have calmed the 'father's anger one bit. "I thought we understood each other. We both seemed fairly sure of our aims and goals, wanted the same sort of thing. But whereas you have failed, I will succeed. My People will strive. There isn't any room for men like you. You have the vision, but no means to realise it." He stepped closer, indicated the supermarket entrance. "Beyond those doors is hell," he stated simply. "An infernal nightmare not of my making, but – as all the best living hells are – *of its own occupants' making*." He grinned, and David found himself wondering how on earth the man had ever convinced them he was anything other than insane.

The soldier who'd been on the laptop outside the barrier suddenly came scurrying through the doorway. "Sir, medic says he's got a right lunatic, half destroyed the MediCentre, cut up a nurse pretty bad–"

"*RIGHT*!" the Centrefather screamed, spinning around on his feet. "Any fucking more psychos out there?! Any killers lurking nearby wanting to join us? Rapists, arsonists, fucking paedos? Anyone?" He seemed about to continue, but then managed to control himself. "Okay son... call the MediCentre, say you'll send some men to escort the patient over here."

The soldier nodded affirmation then disappeared.

The Centrefather now turned to David. "The more the merrier, huh Dave-Rick? What do you say?"

"I say anyone wanting to be god is going about it the wrong way sending people to their deaths."

The 'father paused a moment. After a while, he started to smile. Then he returned to his original position near the barrier.

Dusty had been thinking. He whispered conspiratorially, "Hey Dave, you know this sex and death thing?"

"What?" David answered, distracted. It was hardly the time, and if Dusty still didn't understand, it was unlikely he ever would.

"No, hear me out, I reckon I'm onto something, say the bad guys were all involved in death, right?"

David shrugged. "Rape isn't death, but that's bad."

"Yeah but... oh." Dusty looked deflated. "But surely–"

"Not everything has to fit neatly into place. You can't just say death is 'bad' and sex is 'good' because who's to say what's good or bad?"

"That theory could lead you down all sorts of avenues of thinking," the Centrefather interrupted, eavesdropping.

"It's not just a theory," Dusty protested.

"Well, that remains to be seen." He considered for a

moment. He seemed genuinely fascinated. "Think of all the questions it begs, though. It challenges everything we've ever thought about ourselves, our purpose, our meaning."

David said, "We know."

"Makes me feel… quite small, and almost… pointless." There was a sudden scream, much louder than those coming from the abandoned supermarket, and he turned around to look through the barrier doorway. "Ah. Here they come."

Doc Marten Man and his pet pussy-eating-obsessed monkey were looking a little the worse for wear.

The hippy hardly suited that description now, most of his hair torn out by the roots, his scalp bloody and raw. When the soldiers dropped him, he let out a squeal of pain.

The skinhead was no less distressed. His left leg was bloody and limp and missing a chunk of flesh, and his whole body kept shuddering uncontrollably.

They were both trussed up with thick rope, the knots viciously tight, so they weren't about to go anywhere, but nevertheless just about everyone shuffled back about two or three steps. The soldiers who'd carried them about-turned and marched off to some other duty.

"Just one more," said the Centrefather.

"I think I can hear someone now," Imobaum told him.

David tried to listen, but the screams from the super-market and the pounding of his own blood in his ears from the sight of the hippy and monkey were overwhelming him. It was only when Imobaum, who'd been gazing out of the doorway, started nodding and pointing, did he become aware of a high-pitched growling spitting noise.

Whoever it was they'd taken from the MediCentre sounded pretty pissed off.

"And here he is, the final degenerate," Wratten announced gleefully, as another group of his soldiers trooped through the doorway and dumped their captive onto the tiles.

The first thing David noticed was that he was in fact a she.

The second thing was that she was Danielle.

The final thing was that she was more than just *pretty pissed off*: she'd gone loco.

She'd also been trussed up, and was thrashing against her bonds, writhing this way and that on the floor, sliding all around, screeching and snapping and hissing and trying her teeth on the rope, then jerking her legs and arms back and forth in an effort to break free.

"Christ man…" Dusty breathed.

"Sir, that's the unconscious girl I brought in with those three," Wratten revealed.

"Becky, Rick's girlfriend," Raw Man said. "Told you she was a nasty piece of work."

"She's more than that… she's *out of it*," Imobaum decided, staring, fascinated.

David let go of Karma and took a step forwards. "Danielle…"

At first she didn't take any notice, just carried on sliding around the floor, jerking her entire body a good couple of inches into the air. But then he repeated himself, louder, once more, almost shouting this time, and she finally got herself under control enough to look up at him.

Her chest heaved as their eyes locked.

"What's... what...?" he mumbled.

She jerked herself forwards, indicating the ropes. Her arms were slashed and scraped. The bruises on her face looked worse than he'd last seen them. Her hair was tatty and sweaty. Her clothes, at Raw Man's farm already torn and half hanging off, were minimal to say the least. He had to concentrate to hold her gaze. He wanted to look at her heaving chest again.

Wanted to look at her legs, mucky and cut.

Wanted more than just to look.

He turned to the Centrefather. "Can't you do something?"

The 'father shrugged. "Of course. She wouldn't survive five minutes in Asda all tied up like a hunk of meat ready for roasting. Mind you, who's to say anyone'll last longer than five minutes anyway?" He grinned. "Because believe me, if you think these three have lost the plot, you haven't seen anything yet."

Jaxon approached without being asked, brandishing what looked like the bodyguard's hunting knife. First he prodded Danielle in the nose with the tip of the blade as a warning, then started slitting the ropes holding her legs.

Raw Man seemed to sense any hope of reprieve was

rapidly running out. "I've got treasures. Stuff you wouldn't believe. All stored away. Priceless gear." He took a step forwards. "It's yours. All of it. Just show me the door, and I'll show you the hiding place. No catches, you can have the lot. Just please…" He looked back at his guard and worshipper. "These two fine, take them with my blessing, but please, not me, just let me go, I'll disappear, you'll never hear of me again, and the treasure, all that treasure, all yours…"

The Centrefather held up a hand. "The decision has been made. I can't go back on a verdict."

"No please, not in there, Jesus you can't–"

"Come on man," David spluttered, starting to panic himself. "You can't just lock up anyone you think might get in your way." He shook his head. "No matter how nuts they are, you can't just forget about them, the problem won't go away."

"Unfortunately, that's where you and I will have to agree to disagree. At least we know where they all are, at least we know they won't be part of our People, won't be able to disrupt anything." He shrugged, smiled. "Look on the bright side, the guards reckon there's still people alive in there from early last night. You could survive for days, longer."

"Of course," Wratten began, a glint in his eye, "you'll have to make do with whatever *nourishment* you can scavenge, but hey, I hear it tastes just like chicken!" He burst into raucous, demented laughter.

The Centrefather shot him a look. "Imbecile."

By now Danielle was free, and Jaxon was starting on the monkey. The skinhead was struggling violently despite his trauma, and instead of just poking his nose with the blade, Jaxon slashed one of his nostrils open. After that, the monkey remained motionless.

"Full *Chinatown*, man," Dusty muttered to no one.

David had by now helped Danielle to her feet, and was trying to get a response. "You all right? You're not hurt too much? Danielle?"

"Okay…" she mumbled after a moment, "okay."

"Right your turn, you saw what happened to your mate, it'll be your cock if you try anything," Jaxon threatened Doc Marten Man, kneeling down and sawing at the ropes.

Behind him, the skinhead had pushed himself up onto his good knee, and was looking around in a daze, his nose running blood. He tensed up tight when he saw the bodyguard, and almost lost it completely when he realised David and Dusty were there too, but once he saw Danielle his eyes seemed to glaze over, and he just sat there staring.

It was horrible the way the little fucker was just gawping at her, David thought. And the fact he couldn't get the image out of his mind of that evil shaven blockhead rammed between her soft smooth thighs wasn't helping matters.

Doc Marten Man grunted in pain as Jaxon freed his legs, and moved into a sitting position. His face tensed with discomfort as he stretched his aching limbs.

"All right," the Centrefather declared, "it's time."

All but one of the supermarket guards stepped forwards and stood ready. Wratten, Jonson, Jaxon and Imobaum retreated to the barricade doorway.

The Centrefather looked at each of his prisoners in turn, nodding farewell. When his eyes reached David, he paused. "Sorry it had to end this way."

David stared back. "It's not just about me. You keep doing this to everyone you don't like, you'll eventually not have much of a People left."

The 'father smiled sadly, held his gaze for a moment, then moved onto Dusty.

After nodding to Karma, he stepped over to where Imobaum was waiting. He turned towards the barrier doorway and stepped through. A moment later and Imobaum, Jonson and Jaxon had followed.

Wratten looked over at his men and started grinning. "Do it." Then he dived back into the mall and a wide metal filing cabinet was pushed across the doorway, blocking it.

The guards advanced, while the one at the entrance started rolling up one of the bashed and dented metal shutters.

And the Metro Centrefather's hell was revealed in all its bloody glory.

THE SHUTTERS CLACKED DOWN BEHIND THEM and sealed them in.

It was then David realised with surprise no one had even tried to escape. The supermarket guards hadn't seemed very professional, and there were almost as many captives as captors, but not even the scalped hippy or hobbled monkey had made a scene.

Maybe everyone was just accepting things.

Or maybe they'd realised what he'd been thinking about earlier: there was nothing much else left for them in the world.

The deserted Asda supermarket looked huge in the semi-darkness, much more cavernous than the Marks and Spencer at the other end of the Centre (and it wasn't lost on

David the irony of the Centrefather running his empire from that upmarket store, while down here in lowly old Asda insanity reigned). From what he could tell, the shelving still remained to delineate the standard supermarket aisles, shadowy white structures skeletoning the shop, some bits smashed and removed but for the most part whole. The darkness prevented him from seeing much else.

Apart from the darting figures.

The moving shadows.

The creeping human shapes.

Most of the screams and noise had stopped at the sound of the metal shutters. No doubt the supermarket savages knew exactly what that had signalled.

The arrival of more victims.

Fresh meat.

Their group stood together, the animosity between them forgotten for a moment, as a series of howls erupted from the darkness.

"Okay," Raw Man began, edging backwards, "the fucker's had his fun, got us scared– *you hear that you crazy cunt*? We're scared, you've scared us, now let us go!" He turned around and started battering his fists against the shutters. "*You fucker let us out!*"

For one mad moment David thought the Centrefather was actually going to relent and let them free, but it was only the guards on the other side chuckling to themselves.

"What now Raw Man, what the fuck now?" the bodyguard implored, his eyes darting around the interior of the abandoned building, the devil worshipper clinging desperately to his arm.

There was suddenly a much louder howl than the others, and the entire supermarket fell eerily quiet.

And then Doc Marten Man and the monkey skinhead stepped and limped forwards and together let out a scream-howl-wail of pure rage and savagery.

A moment later they advanced, the scalped hippy racing to the left, in the direction of the original entrance, now boarded up and impenetrable. Leaping into the air, he dived onto what David had thought was part of the Customer Services desk. The section of desk let out a huge roar as Doc Marten Man's momentum tore it from the main structure and threw it across the floor. The desk jumped to its feet and advanced on its attacker.

Meanwhile the skinhead had limped away at quite an impressive speed in the opposite direction, into what had been George, Asda's clothing department. He'd got maybe twenty feet into the section when a number of clothes rails sprang into life and attacked.

"Christ, the place is fucking swarming, they're hiding everywhere!" David yelled, turning to his companions.

"Well how do we get out of this one, Rick my man?" Raw Man wondered, scorn in his words but panic in his voice.

David looked around, searching the abandoned building with his eyes.

Things seemed to be moving everywhere.

What he'd thought was shelving had grown legs and was advancing; what he'd presumed were checkouts had leaped into the air and screamed out loud.

He simply didn't know what to do.

Hide someplace was the obvious answer; he just couldn't think where. There were psychos all over the joint. "Hide…" he started muttering, "where can we hide?"

Dusty had to shout to be heard over the squeals of pain coming from the Customer Services desk. "Let's try and get down the other end of the shop! If no one sees us, they might think we're just hiding someplace this end?" He shrugged, shook his head.

"Okay, let's just do it," David said, looking around at Karma and Danielle for agreement. Karma was staring straight ahead with unfocused eyes, while Danielle was looking around the shop almost greedily, running her hands up and down her thighs, breathing harshly. It looked to David like she was about to completely lose it. Again.

"If we can get around the clothes section," the bodyguard piped up, keen to be making some progress, "we might be able to make it along the back wall, seems fairly deserted."

David looked at him. The burly young man was squinting where he was pointing, his face sweaty and serious. Maybe he'd realised it was time to forget the rivalry and concentrate on survival. "Okay." He himself looked around. "We'll cut across where the household stuff used to be, you think?"

"Right, good idea," the bodyguard agreed. He turned to the devil worshipper, who was still clinging onto his arm and whimpering. "Keep quiet, for god's sake." He grabbed at the worshipper's pointed hood. "And get that bloody thing off your head, you won't be able to see a thing." Crouching low, he started off towards the central aisle.

David motioned for Dusty to take Karma and follow. He turned to Raw Man, who had been watching the proceedings a little puzzled. "What about you?"

The devil worshipper leader seemed to realise he had little choice, but tried spinning it around to make out like it was him doing David the favour. "Rick. You've finally seen sense and decided to join up." He stepped forwards and rested a hand on David's shoulder. "It's great to have you with us." Although his words were still scornful, it sounded to David like he was just going through the motions: even he knew it was time to forget about whatever had gone before, and combine forces against the greater evil of the Asda animals. He started off after Dusty and Karma.

Danielle was still standing looking all around, grinning now, and when David stepped up to her, he had to hold her head in his hands to get her to look at him and acknowledge his presence. "Come on Danielle, keep it together. We're going to get out of this. Okay?"

She nodded slightly. Then grinned madly, opening her mouth and leaning forwards to plant a massive wet slop of a kiss on his mouth.

He jerked backwards slightly. He could taste her spit on his lips. It trickled down his chin and mingled with his sweat. He looked at her, confused. He could still feel the pressure of her mouth. His lips were tingling.

She kept grinning. Then skipped off, away after Raw Man.

David quickly caught up and grabbed hold of her hand. It was slippy with sweat and felt far too cold.

Over to the right and behind him, he recognised the triumphant squawking of the monkey. There was also a horrible wet smacking sound, as if the skinhead were malleting a huge steak for dinner. The noise sent shivers zinging down David's spine.

Up ahead, the bodyguard had turned into what had once been one of the household goods aisles. All around, the sounds of destruction and mayhem increased in volume as the hippy and skinhead gave the supermarket savages a run for their money. Behind him, David could hear metal shelving being torn from its brackets and launched across the centre aisle. Quickly he ducked down, and pushed Danielle over to a nearby tributary aisle. He made his way along next to her, while behind them someone screeched in terror and there was another crash of shelving.

The hippy yelled with glee.

It shocked David to hear him so close. He turned around to look.

Doc Marten Man was in the central aisle, standing over a heap of metal and limbs. With another yell, he leaped onto the pile of shelving and started jumping up and down. His victim's shrieks were high-pitched and deafening.

Even though he and Danielle were barely halfway along the aisle, David didn't think they'd been spotted in the darkness, so he started moving once more. They reached the back wall of the supermarket and turned left. Up ahead, there was a group of shadows waiting for them.

Raw Man was panicky. "We thought that long-haired fucker'd got you."

"Listen," the bodyguard whispered, "this isn't going to be as easy as I thought. There's openings to the warehouse all along this wall."

"There could be nutters just waiting to dive out and jump on us," Dusty explained.

"We can't turn back," David said, looking over his shoulder. "Those two're making so much noise they'll have the entire population down here soon."

"Suppose we could check the warehouse ourselves," the bodyguard conceded. "Maybe find an exit, the loading doors, whatever."

"I think our best bet's just to carry on," Raw Man suggested. "Get as far away from these freaks of nature as possible."

"Wratten and his mates'll've surely sealed up all the exits anyway," Dusty decided.

"Could be they didn't," David said, thinking. "Maybe they reckon the nutters they chuck in here are too out of it to try and escape."

"I think that's being a bit hopeful," the bodyguard said. He shook his head. "Anyway, we'd better get moving, wherever we're headed. We can't hang around here much longer."

"Okay," David agreed.

It now sounded like the hippy had found someone else to attack, while the skinhead was busy screaming and smashing something, so for the moment they were safe from them, but the howling from the supermarket savages had started up again, and this time didn't sound like it would stop. Although they were masking the sounds of their movement, David had no doubt most, if not all, were heading to this end of the building. "Come on, carry on along the wall, we'll just have to be careful past the doorways, we need to get the hell away."

The bodyguard nodded his agreement and started off with the devil worshipper. It was more intensely gloomy this side of the abandoned supermarket, and they soon dissolved into shadows.

The rest of them quickly fell into line.

David kept tight hold of Danielle's hand as they made their way along the wall. Instinctively he hunched over forwards, trying to make himself less conspicuous, but

Danielle was just wandering along as if she were in another time, and the supermarket around her was alive with life, buzzing with indecisive shoppers and bored shop workers. He was about to tell her to get down, but one look at her told him there was little point. Her eyes were focused on infinity, her mind almost as far away.

It saddened him to see her so fucked up. Especially after all they'd been through together.

But at the same time he found it kind of appealing.

It made her seem vulnerable. He wanted to take her in his arms, cuddle her, smooth her hair and kiss it, tell her everything was going to be all right.

But that wasn't all.

That was just a cosy picture in his head. And it couldn't hide what he really felt.

What he really wanted to do.

There was a squawk of terror from up front.

Danielle's mouth slackened, let loose a wad of spit. David turned forwards.

There was a gaping square of nothingness in the wall ahead. Shadows he knew were Dusty, Karma and Raw Man had stopped short. Two other shadows were directly in line with what he now recognised as a wide, open entrance to the warehouse.

David guessed it was the devil worshipper who'd let out the scream.

It was a wonder he'd heard it, the amount of primeval noises the savages were making.

And then he realised if he'd managed to hear it, then no doubt most of the supermarket had, as well.

He hurried onwards to Dusty, Karma and Raw Man, Danielle following obediently. "What's happening?" he hissed.

"Fuck all," Raw Man whispered angrily, "that fucker'd piss his pants at his own reflection, the mentals'll know where we are now!"

At the warehouse doorway, the bodyguard pushed the worshipper onwards, then ran back to where the rest of them were waiting. "We've got to run now, as fast as you can, but don't make any more fucking noise!"

David was about to ask what the problem had been, but the guard was already following his own advice, turning tail and scarpering. "Okay everyone," he addressed the other three, "you heard him."

They started off, Raw Man lifting his legs stupidly high into the air, trying to lighten his steps in order to keep the noise down. David might've laughed if they'd been any-where else. Instead, he quickly followed, dragging Danielle behind him.

As he passed the opening to the warehouse, the endless darkness where anything could lurk, he kept his eyes fixed straight ahead.

They passed the defunct dairy refrigerators, and moved to the end of the building where there was an alcove which used to house the pharmacy. All the way further down, at the bottom of the side wall (previously Asda's health and beauty section), another set of external doors had been blocked and sealed.

As far as David could tell, this end of the supermarket was deserted.

The bodyguard made his way around the pharmacy counter, and disappeared behind some empty glass display cabinets. He returned a moment later. "There's a little room back here," he explained. "Completely empty, reckon we should hole up in there a while?"

David nodded. "Okay."

"Hey," Dusty began, squinting in the darkness towards the main doors. "Those shelves're still full."

David followed his gaze. Just next to the blocked entrance, on the bottom wall, there were a number of shelves which, if he remembered correctly, used to be full of crisps and snacks (he couldn't help noticing these things in supermarkets after working in one for so long). On the top shelf, about six feet off the floor, there was a row of shadows. They weren't exactly uniform in shape, but they all looked about the same size. He wasn't sure, but taking a guess, he'd say there was at least ten or fifteen, maybe more.

The gloom at this end of the store gave no clue as to what they were, but all the same, the objects were rather unsettling somehow. As if he should know fine well what they were, and should even now be running very fast in the opposite direction.

"Think we should check 'em out?" Dusty wondered.

"Fuck that," Raw Man decided, "let's just get ourselves hidden, get our shit together, think of how the hell we're getting out of here."

Danielle snorted. "No one's getting out." Her voice was thick and strange, as if she hadn't used it for a long time.

"You can stay if you want, missy," Raw Man told her, "seems to me you'd fit right in, but I for one–"

"They're heads," she interrupted. She nodded towards the crisps and snacks fixture. "People's heads. Cut off. They're trophies. Hunters' trophies." She paused. "Your heads will be there soon."

No one said anything. Dusty, who'd been standing near Danielle, started edging away. Even David felt threatened by her words.

"Look," the bodyguard said, breaking the silence, "the sooner we get thinking the sooner we'll come up with a way to escape." He waved his arm in the direction they'd come from. "Those psychos'll be searching the place from top to bottom soon enough. We need to defend ourselves no matter what happens."

"Right," David agreed again. He was all too aware of the screams and howls and shouts coming from the other end of the abandoned supermarket. It sounded like the hippy and monkey had incited a riot. "Everyone, in there."

The bodyguard went back into the room, and the rest of them followed. David had to push Danielle in front of him to get her to move.

The room was small, square, gloomy, and completely stripped bare. There were even holes in the paintwork where posters had been ripped from the walls.

The devil worshipper sat huddled in a corner, whimpering and scared. Karma was also sliding to the floor. Her devil worshipper robe bunched itself up over the tops of her knees. Her skin was pale and white, and when David looked at it he felt churned up inside.

The bodyguard, Raw Man and Dusty stood around nearby. David went to join them after settling Danielle down on the floor, automatically standing next to Dusty rather than the other two.

The bodyguard was sweating profusely. "Best way to deal with this is defence, I reckon." He looked around for support. "If we can keep hidden in here long enough to sort out some weapons, then maybe some of us could scout for a better hiding place, or a way to get out."

Dusty nodded. "Yeah man." He seemed more energised than David had ever seen him. "There's got to be a way out, like a service exit or something, up in the roof maybe, or tunnels underneath the whole Centre for workmen and stuff."

The bodyguard considered. "There's got to be places like that around the mall, but I'm not sure about in here."

"Christ, there has to be something," Raw Man said in exasperation. "That mad old fuck couldn't've blocked off every escape route."

"Maybe not him, but Wratten and his buddies, man," Dusty commented, "they're totally getting off playing army boys."

David was feeling dejected. He wasn't sure if it had something to do with seeing Karma and realising what he'd lost, or seeing Danielle and realising what he could never have. It might simply be because the events of the past twenty-four hours (*a day, had it really only been a day?*) were catching up with him, but he was suddenly overcome by a sense of pointlessness.

Rick and Becky's freeze had destroyed the world.

There was nothing left.

It was kind of the opposite of what he'd felt in the high school. There, he'd been excited by the freedom to do what he wanted, a weird mixture of apprehension and, yes, horniness, mixed up in his chest and making him feel all nice and warm and glad to be alive.

But now he was thinking about the freedom and thinking what the fuck was the point.

And it was resignation and depression in his chest. Making him feel empty and cold and defeated.

"Got to get out, got to get out," the devil worshipper was chanting from his corner.

David suddenly whirled. "What the fuck for you numb cunt?"

The others looked at him, shocked.

He turned to them. "Come off it, don't tell me you don't know what I mean." He gestured wildly at the door.

"There's nothing for us out there in the world– the world? there's no world left anymore. Everyone's dead and gone, and the only ones left are too fucked-up to care. There's no *point* in thinking of a way to get out, because there's nowhere to get out *to*." He lowered his eyes at first, a little ashamed of his outburst, then thought fuck it and faced the three of them eye to eye.

Dusty spoke quietly. "Dave man…"

"Come on Rick, surely it's a little late for self-remorse and regret?"

David took a moment or two to realise what Raw Man was getting at. "Oh give up that *shit* would you?"

Raw Man raised an eyebrow, shrugged a little.

"You think that if you want," the bodyguard said, stepping forwards slightly, "but we–" he paused to swirl a pointing finger around the room, taking in everyone but David, "are getting out. There mightn't be much left, but by fuck surely anything's better than leaving yourself at the mercy of… of *that lot*." He now waved his hand back towards the shop floor.

"It… it was you," the devil worshipper muttered from his corner. He'd stopped mumbling when David had shouted at him, and was now staring up at him, his face streaked with tears, fear in his eyes – but now recognition, too.

"Yes you know it's him," Raw Man said, understanding, "that was why you wanted to come in with us. To–" here he adapted a defensive stance, raising his fists and squawking out his words in an exaggerated Geordie accent, "'sort the little focker oot like, howay then where is the cont?'" He looked at his follower with barely disguised disgust. "Now look at you. Pathetic."

But the devil worshipper wasn't paying any attention. "Made me piss me pants," he nodded, staring fixedly at David. "Fucker made me piss me pants."

"Oh for the love of *fuck*," the bodyguard snapped, "grow up a minute would yous?"

"No no," David protested, stepping towards the devil worshipper slightly, "let him have his say. Come on. So I made you piss your pants." He looked around, shrugged. "So what? What're you going to do about it?"

The bodyguard suddenly cut an arm in front of him, jabbing it in his path and stopping it just short of his chest. "What we're all going to do is calm down. Or at least, focus our anger on those lunatics out there." With his other arm, he once more pointed to the supermarket proper, where the screams and shouts and whoops seemed to be getting louder with every minute. "Just remember we didn't *have* to group together and pool resources. And seems to me if we hadn't… yous lot would probably already be dead." He held David's gaze for a moment longer then, assuming he'd got the message, dropped his arm.

"Come on Dave," Dusty said, "get it together, man." He glanced over at the devil worshipper, shook his head. "Fuck him man. He's not worth it. It's the hippy and monkey and their new pals we've got to worry about. Okay?" He leaned closer. "Okay?"

David nodded. "Okay." He wasn't sure why, but he'd suddenly wanted nothing other than an excuse to kick the living shit out of the bawling fuckhead on the floor. An excuse to completely lose it, to hell with self-control and trying to be sensible just get in there, let it all out and beat the little fucker to death.

"Well," Raw Man said after a moment. "If we'd like to get back on track?" He was trying to be as patronising as always, but the underlying apprehension in his voice was obvious.

The bodyguard was looking around. "I just… I just think our best bet's for two or three of us to maybe distract them fuckers' attention while the rest of us make a break for it."

"Right, well we're obviously running out of time and that's the only halfway sensible suggestion anyone's come up with, I say go for it." Raw Man looked at Dusty and David. "Any objections?"

David shrugged dismissively. "Fine. But you're wasting your time."

Dusty was more positive. "Okay, but we need to sort out some weapons, plus work out an escape route."

"Head for the warehouse, I guess," the bodyguard said. "And if that's a no go, at least it'll give us another hiding place."

"If a bunch of freakjobs aren't already hiding there," Raw Man said.

"Well, that's a chance we'll have to take. Or some of us will, anyway." He looked around the room. "How'll we decide who's staying and who's going?"

"I'll fucking stay," snapped David after a few seconds of awkward silence. "Give the fuckers something to think about. At least I'll go down fighting."

"Hopefully it won't come to that," the bodyguard said, "not if we can find some weapons for you, anyway. Okay, who else?"

"Well," Raw Man began, "to be honest, and I've thought long and hard about this, and am prepared to make the sacrifice… I want to get the hell out of here."

"I'm not too keen on staying either, man," Dusty revealed, glancing guiltily at David.

"Okay. Me and David'll stay." The bodyguard looked around at the devil worshipper, Karma, Danielle. "Yous take those three as well. They'll be no use here."

"Danielle should stay," David said. She looked up at him. Her eyes seemed even more glazed than before. But her mouth twitched into something resembling a smile. It made him feel good.

"Well, if you're sure…" The bodyguard looked dubious.

"Yeah. She should stay," David repeated, and Danielle smiled even wider.

There was suddenly a scream from the shop floor, much louder than the rest, followed by a crunch of metal shelving. He wasn't sure, but it sounded to David like it couldn't have been more than a few aisles away.

"Christ they're getting close," Dusty whispered. "What the hell are we going to do for weapons?"

Raw Man started grinning as something clicked. "Of course." He turned to David. "Rick here can tell us what we're going to do for weapons, can't you? Because you've already got all we need in your pocket."

David looked at him. "What're you talking about now?"

"Come on Raw Man," the bodyguard protested, "I thought I said to quit the petty shit."

But Raw Man ignored him. He kept staring at David, grinning his inane grin. And then commented conversationally, "It sure managed to completely destroy my farm, didn't it Rick?"

There was silence.

Dusty muttered, "Oh, man."

The smash of shelving from one of the aisles outside was repeated, followed by the unmistakable screech of the monkey. There was a scream, then a series of thumps and smacks.

But David wasn't having any of it. "No way Raw Man, no way… it nearly took *me* apart along with your farm."

The bodyguard shifted on his feet slightly. "Are you talking about what I think you're talking about?"

"The liquid card," Raw Man explained. "You saw what it did. Rick can make it do the same here. No one need stay behind. It'd provide cover enough for us all to escape."

"Hey that sounds good in theory, but I'll tell you again: *no way*. I didn't know what the hell I was doing last time, and nothing's changed since then, I still haven't a clue."

Raw Man extended an arm towards him, opened his hand. "Then I'll do it. You think it's all a waste of time, there's no point anymore? Fine. Us lot, we'd prefer to live." He stared at David, stopped grinning. "Hand it over, Rick. Hand over the liquid card."

"No. Forget it. You're mad." It wasn't just what he'd said, but David was also afraid of what Raw Man might do if – against all the odds – he *did* manage to escape. With the liquid card in his power (or he in its?) nothing could stop him. "Let's just stick to the original plan."

The monkey screeched triumphantly outside, slightly closer than before. He was soon joined by a whole chorus of deranged whoops and screams.

"Christ we'd better stop fucking about and get organised, guys!" Dusty demanded, and stepped over to where Karma and Danielle were sitting slumped against the wall. "Come on Karma. Time to get moving."

She looked up at him, defenceless and defeated. He held out a hand, which she took, and he hauled her gently to her feet. "Come on," he told her again softly, still holding her hand, "we're getting out."

"Forget it Dusty," David told him. "Just accept the fact we're all fucked."

"Don't you *start* that again, man!" he snapped back, and for the first time seemed truly angry with David. "You want to trick yourself into believing that, fine. But not me." He held Karma closer to him. "And not the rest of us."

David was taken aback. He'd noticed Dusty speaking with a lot more sobriety earlier, but now he was like a different person.

"'What's the point, what's the point?'" he whinged in angry parody, so unlike the carefree stoner he'd been David was speechless. "What's the point in life itself, what's the point in anything?" He shook his head. "You don't get to say shit like that. I've fucking seen it when someone's in the blackest pits of it, man. I've fucking seen it when their only option is… when they've…" He squeezed Karma closer to him. "You haven't even got her excuse, man. You're not a fucking *victim*. You haven't got the *right* to say any of that." His chest was heaving, his eyes glistening. He exhaled noisily. "Just… just get yourself sorted, man."

"Well said," Raw Man agreed after a tactful pause. "And once you've finished getting yourself sorted, Rick… the liquid card, if you will." He held out his hand again.

David looked at him, then back at Dusty. Then he tried the bodyguard, but got the same cold, stony stare. Angrily he thrust his hand into his trouser pocket. "There you power-mad twat." He brought out the two pieces of the liquid card and slapped them onto Raw Man's palm.

Raw Man nodded slowly, keeping eye contact. He closed his fingers over the pieces. Stopped nodding. Broke eye contact. Said, "Much obliged."

Almost involuntarily, David took a step backwards. He noticed the bodyguard had, too, but was covering the movement by turning around and trying to rouse the devil worshipper.

Raw Man was staring at the pieces with a manic glint in his eyes. David told himself the devil worshipper leader probably wouldn't be able to touch them together for long, but he knew that didn't matter: he'd only managed a fraction of a second, probably much less, and the damage had been colossal. What was more, Raw Man was a grown man, surely much stronger than David.

His sense of hopelessness was complete.

Now it wasn't a question of if he would be killed, merely how: blown to smithereens by whatever forces Raw Man conjured from the liquid card, or torn to pieces by whichever savages reached him first.

He heard Danielle grunting and shifting behind him, and turned to watch her push herself up into a swaying standing position. She looked dazedly around the room, her battered face darker and more brutal in the murk, her torn clothing more shadowy and tantalising.

And seeing her, he once more felt a gut-churning pang of loss, of what the freeze had teasingly offered him and then cruelly snatched away.

Raw Man had a piece of the liquid card in each hand, and was holding them out in front of himself, gazing at each in turn. "Finally," he muttered.

The devil worshipper made a break for the door when

he saw what his master was about to do, but the body-guard caught his shoulder and yanked him back. "He knows what he's doing," he told him uncertainly.

The screams from outside were dying down slightly for some reason, and Dusty stepped over to the door, leaving Karma with the devil worshipper and bodyguard. The room was actually behind the pharmacy counter, so he could – in theory – open the door, peer around the corner, and look into the supermarket without being spotted.

He was about to test this theory when something huge and heavy crashed against the wall, and the resultant shrieking of metal and shattering of glass made it sound like half the pharmacy display had been demolished.

"Jesus fuck, they're just outside," he hissed. There was a raging scream, so close Dusty almost had to cover his ears, then footsteps running away in the opposite direction. "They're so near man, they're so near…"

"No cause for alarm. Everything's under control." Raw Man grinned. "Everything's under control," he repeated, and started slowly moving his hands together.

"Christ you're crazy!" David snapped. "You're doing it in here?" He looked around the room. Everyone was standing a respectable distance away, but in such confines, who knew what would happen? "For fuck's sake, wait 'til we're on the shop floor!"

But Raw Man ignored him. In fact, everyone was ignoring him. They were all staring transfixed as those two pieces of jet black – so much darker than the surrounding gloom – glided slowly towards a seemingly inevitable joining.

He turned to Danielle, but she was probably staring at the card more intently than Raw Man. Dribble glistened over her bruised chin. He stepped up to her. "Danielle, come on, we'll make a break for it."

Raw Man was starting to sweat, now. The fluidity with which he'd been moving his arms was faltering as he encountered steadily increasing resistance. The pieces were still a good twelve inches apart, but his arms were already wobbling under the strain.

Dusty watched the snapped card, looked up at the concentration on Raw Man's face, and knew David was right. There was going to be some serious fireworks. He glanced back at the closed door, listened to the shouts and screams from beyond.

"Little fff…" Raw Man was mumbling between gritted teeth. He looked like he was having real problems. His hands wobbled up and down and from side to side. "You little… I'll do it… I'll…" His face was all sweaty and red, trembling with effort.

David suddenly grabbed Danielle by the shoulders and pushed her against the wall, desperate to shake some sense into her.

He could feel the heat from her body against his palms. One of his hands slipped and pushed the torn material of her top even further down her arm.

The skin looked dirty and sweaty.

He glanced up and saw she was still staring at the two black pieces.

It seemed like he could do anything to her and she wouldn't stop staring.

Do anything to her.

The Asda animals nearest the pharmacy had started howling, reacting as if by some bestial instinct to the powers which were about to be unleashed from within. They were soon joined by answering howls from the rest of the supermarket, building to an overpowering mass of wild screeching.

Dusty realised suddenly everything was resting on Raw Man and the liquid card.

They'd left it too late to search for any real weapons, too late to prepare themselves. If the pieces weren't joined together soon, the nutters would be all over them. He stepped closer, prepared to help Raw Man if he kept struggling.

But it seemed the devil worshipper leader was making some progress. There was only three or four inches between the pieces, now.

Then two or three.

Then two at the most.

Out the corner of his eye, Dusty noticed David pushing Danielle around for some reason, groping and grabbing at her roughly.

Raw Man's hands were tensed tight. The skin was white where he gripped the card as he moved the pieces ever closer together.

The howling from the shop floor was becoming more frantic as the entire pack started to gradually congregate, and was joined by the sound of some of them jumping up and down excitedly.

They had found their prey.

And were about to move in.

The liquid card couldn't have been more than an inch away from being rejoined.

Maybe another second or two and they'd have touched.

But suddenly Raw Man gave up. "It's almost broke my fucking wrists!" he hissed, jamming his hands between his legs and shaking with pain.

"Oh fuck, you can't stop now," the bodyguard implored, "just once more, just slam them together!"

Raw Man looked at him stupidly, his wrists and hands still burning with pain, sweat sluicing down his face.

The howling and stomping from outside seemed to suddenly intensify, underlining the urgency in the bodyguard's yelled words: "For fuck's sake *just do it*!"

And so Raw Man lifted his hands up, pointed the pieces towards each other once more, and jammed them together with all his might.

The pieces touched.

For a moment in time the liquid card was whole once more.

The light was blinding.

It was just enveloping the card itself at first, but then stabbed outwards and started to gradually engulf the entire room.

The two pieces snapped apart and clattered to the floor somewhere.

There were a few moments as Raw Man stared goggle-eyed at the light before he realised he hadn't actually moved his hands.

Yet the card had sprung apart anyway.

Trembling, the first daggers of pain rushing towards his brain, he raised his open hands in front of him. The wounds were only just starting to bleed. He'd been holding the pieces tightly in his fists, so the ragged slits were almost in the middle of his palms. He turned them over to examine the messy exit wounds.

Then, as the pain finally registered, he stretched his arms out to the light of the liquid card and started to scream.

The light danced and pulsated, splitting off into streamers of sparkling colour.

It held David in awe.

He watched as it seemed to caress the walls, sliding over their surface to leave them glowing and energised. It made him long to be a part of it.

From behind him, Dusty heard someone scrabbling at the door. He had time to snatch his gaze from the light and turn around before a bare foot powered through the wood.

He heard a yelp, and then the foot jerked upwards, as if its owner had just fallen over.

Dusty quickly moved to the other end of the room, pushing Karma ahead of him as he went, as behind them someone crunched against the door, shaking it in its frame. There were one or two more thumps before some genius decided to twist the door handle…

…and the savages flooded the room.

The brightness of the light revealed the pack in shocking detail.

Eyes were black with huge pupils, faces red and brown with human muck, clothes long gone. There was little distinction between sex, no hierarchy; they piled through the doorway into the tiny room as quickly as those behind could push those in front.

The light seemed agitated at this intrusion, colours mingling once more, twisting around one another to become one, as the onslaught began.

The devil worshipper was the first to go.

Two men grabbed his robe and stripped him almost instantaneously, as if there'd been a secretly loose seam in the garment. He was holding his hands out in front of him now, naked save for a tee-shirt and underwear, as an uncountable number of the beasts descended upon him and started to literally take him apart.

The bodyguard jumped over to where Dusty was standing with the other three in the far corner, any defensive action he'd planned forgotten.

Raw Man remained in the middle of the room, screaming at the light, his broken and bloody hands held out in supplication. Behind him, the devil worshipper let out a characteristically high-pitched squeal from beneath the mess of writhing bodies. Raw Man stopped his own screaming, and turned.

More of the animals were pushing themselves through the doorway, most of them falling over and squirming on the floor as their companions collapsed on top of them, but a few were managing to maintain their balance, and were coming for the survivors.

Raw Man stepped back as three bald savages rushed him.

Two went for his legs, the other his face, its jaw snapping up and down, its few remaining teeth clanking noisily together.

And all around them the light of the liquid card continued to circulate the room, searching, forever searching, leaving the walls and ceiling glowing with energy, sparkles like glitter hanging in the air and providing surreal backdrop.

Raw Man brought his hands together as hard as he could for the second time in as many minutes, this time to disable rather than enable. His fists connected either side of the toothy animal's head, crunching against its skull and dropping it senseless to the floor. Looking down as the other attackers chomped and clawed at his legs, Raw Man seemed to realise what had been lost in the chaos. "The card…" he started muttering, looking around frantically, "oh no the card…"

To the right of the doorway, the pile of savages who'd leaped onto the devil worshipper was getting pointlessly yet progressively larger. His screams had long been cut off, but this was scant reason not to continue the attack.

Something which may have been a limb shot out from beneath the pile and scooted across the floor, only to be eagerly snatched up by an animal whose own arm had been removed at the elbow. It brandished the gore-soaked object like a weapon, smacked it wetly against the wall a few times, gobbets of loose flesh spattering out the end, then seemed to realise what it was and tried attaching it to his stump.

Watching from the corner, Dusty grimaced as he recognised it was in actual fact the devil worshipper's lower leg, the foot broken and smashed and dangling. The animal waggled the extra limb up and down obscenely, grinned, then let go, and seemed somewhat dismayed when it dropped to the floor.

"The card… the fucking– where? where?" Raw Man had by now kicked the two bald beasts off his legs, and was stomping around angrily, eyes desperately searching the increasingly blood-smeared floor. He waved his arms in front of him as if he was clearing cobwebs, trying to see through the glittering colour in the air.

He was so intent in his search he didn't even notice when the disabled animal launched the devil worshipper's leg at him in disgust. It bounced off his shoulder and landed next to the two beasts who'd been attacking his legs.

They screamed with glee and began to chomp.

Dusty turned away.

He didn't need to see any more. The savages were everything he'd thought they'd be – and more. They would smash them all to pieces.

And Raw Man rejoining the liquid card had been a waste of time. The light was still floating around the room, leaking physical colour into the atmosphere and dying the very air. The walls seemed to pulsate with energy as the light swirled over them, searching, it seemed, for a conductor or something, like unearthed lightning.

And there was fucking Raw Man, jumping around the room still searching for the card, the one-armed animal bouncing up and down in front of him in parody. Dusty could hear the one-time devil worshipper leader's pleas even over the screaming savages: "Where are you? where? oh please, I need you... I need you! *I fucking need you*! *Where are you fucker*?!"

He looked back and noticed a group of potentially female savages enter the room. They might've been female once, anyway: there were one or two saggy bits on their chests and no sticky-out bits between their legs, which didn't necessarily mean much seeing as there were quite a few male-looking savages with nothing there too, but this group seemed more organised than the rest, staggered into the room without falling over, and ran screaming immediately towards Raw Man and the disabled animal.

One moment he was standing there pleading with the liquid card, the animal in front of him poised ready to jump on him, the next there was a mass of screaming thrashing savages, the one-armed animal lost in the confusion.

Perhaps because Raw Man had been the one to conjure it into being, the light of the liquid card seemed to pay special attention to this attack, swirling and gliding between the mess of jerking limbs and thrusting torsos, then surrounding the pile of bodies as a whole.

There seemed to be some trouble at the doorway.

A few animals had tried to get through side by side and stuck fast. The doorframe shook and crunched as those behind pushed even harder.

While it stopped any more savages getting into the room, it also allowed those already in to stand up, take in their surroundings, locate their prey. A few still fought amongst themselves, but most had stood and were staring, grinning at Dusty and his friends all huddled in the corner. The pile of female nutters – under which Raw Man's screams of endless pain could still be heard – was in the way, but that was all.

Unless you counted the light, still swirling and fluttering and colouring the air.

But Dusty wasn't about to rely on that to save his life.

"It's time to fight, guys!" he yelled, trying to quash his utter terror and summon the anger and rage he needed to confront the approaching maniacs.

"Oh fuck it all to fuck and back!" the bodyguard babbled, jerking his head from side to side, but at least making an effort to look prepared, stepping forwards slightly and raising his fists.

David tore his gaze from the light and tried focusing on the oncoming attackers. He'd been watching the light since it'd appeared, waiting for it to do something, *willing* it to do something.

But it wasn't doing anything.

It had painted the walls and ceiling a bunch of pretty colours, true, and had created an interesting enough distraction from the savages' horrific attack, but that was all. He was standing protectively in front of Danielle – who kept leaning over his shoulder and grunting in his ear as she gaped at the goings-on – with Karma pressed vulnerable and victim-like to his side. In front, Dusty and the bodyguard were preparing for the inevitable, but there was little short of a machine gun which could stop the approaching nutters.

It was shocking to witness such savagery in people.

All sense of rationalisation gone from their eyes as if it had never even been there, expressions so bestial and void of coherence, filled with dark, base, physical need. It was a complete perversion of the human species, of the intelligent creature it had evolved into, an irreversible regression into the animal it had once been.

The approaching psychos stepped around the pile still tearing at Raw Man's body, one or two stamping through the light and onto whatever was beneath.

Behind them, David noticed with dismay the group who'd been attacking the devil worshipper was starting to disperse, and look around for more victims. There was a mess of offal and skin on the floor beneath them, but most of the devil worshipper was in the hands of the savages: a foot here, an arm there, a necklace of intestines, a cloak of skin decorated with dollops of flesh, and, spiked on someone's hard cock, the worshipper's scalped and half-skinned head.

The savage had it gripped by the sides, where the ears used to be, his thumbs gouged deep into the bubbling eye sockets for extra grip as he rammed it up and down onto himself and roared his pleasure.

The cork of nutters stuck in the doorway let out an ear-piercingly discordant scream of agony as those behind gave one huge, final shove, and propelled them into the room, taking most of the doorframe and half the wall with them.

The ensuing influx of bodies was like a tidal wave of water.

The group of females were knocked away from their prize, pushed to the floor, battered and crushed. A few grabbed hold of Raw Man's remains and dragged him away, but most were lost in the mess of bodies. One of them had managed to tear Raw Man's smashed and bloodied left arm free from his torso, and raised it up in front of herself like a trophy. The fingers and most of the palm had been chewed or torn away, and she moved it roughly between her legs, at first rubbing it against her groin, then thrusting it upwards. Annoyed it didn't seem to be going anywhere, she started ramming it up against herself, hissing at each vicious thrust. Finally, it disappeared up inside her and she screamed.

At this new obscenity, the light started darting around the room, moving so quickly it was impossible to track with the eye. The colours dispersed behind it, scattering everywhere, drenching the room in a blend of coloured air and coloured glitter, making it difficult to see.

David knew then it was about to find whatever it had been looking for.

Dusty kicked out at the nearest animal who'd come careering towards the corner, pushed from behind. His foot connected with the man's nose and it spurted apart, the blood a glittery blue-green in the flittering light. The animal staggered backwards, and toppled sideways over another man who'd been biting and chomping at Raw Man's groin, his face rammed tight between the corpse's legs. Both men yelled in dumb, angry surprise. Further up the body, someone suddenly started jumping up and down on Raw Man's face. Someone else started picking up lumps of gut from the pile next to the door and launching them across the room. Someone had crawled spider-like towards the bodyguard and was starting to bite and claw at his legs. Someone else dived past Dusty and tore at Karma's hair. A lot of someones started fights with whoever it was most convenient to start a fight with. The woman bouncing up and down on Raw Man's amputated arm screamed in ecstatic pain as one of her breasts was bitten in half. The men who'd fallen at Raw Man's groin were beating at each other's erections.

And then the light of the liquid card disappeared into the throng of bodies at the doorway and everyone stopped.

In that timeless moment, David had time to warn, "Get dow–" before the entire room exploded.

There was a blinding rush of intense white light, all the glitter and colour now vaporised into that one compact central light source, and then the room started to simply drop to bits.

The light was followed by a wave of burning heat, almost unendurable, and the first wall crumbled.

And then the ceiling.

And then another wall.

Those savages not initially blown apart started screaming as masonry tumbled down to crush and trap them.

There was the snap and crackle of electric fire, then a *wooosh!* of billowing flame as it seemed the very air itself ignited and turned the room into an inferno.

If there had been chaos before, now there was nothing but pandemonium.

Building materials crashed down, savages screamed as bones broke and skin split, walls simply weren't there anymore.

David couldn't see anything.

He was blinded by light, by smoke, by dust, by fire, by running bodies and falling brickwork.

The only thing he was aware of was a waft of cool air on his side. It had blown in after a particularly huge crash and smash and chorus of screams, but he wasn't sure–

And then he realised.

Enough of the walls had collapsed to provide access back into the abandoned supermarket.

Incredibly, Danielle was still clinging onto him, and sounded even more excited than before. He couldn't feel Karma anymore, and he couldn't see Dusty or the bodyguard.

Quickly, he grabbed hold of Danielle's hand, made sure she was holding on, then headed towards the cool air, back into the supermarket. Blinking back tears, he could sort of make out a pile of rubble in front of him, and stumbled across it, desperate to escape.

Behind him, Danielle tripped and almost took him with her, but he managed to get her to her feet, and half dragged her the rest of the way.

The pharmacy counter had been obliterated, and he limped over to a nearby aisle. Crouching down against the shelves, breathing heavily, he turned to Danielle. She was grinning madly, looking back, the fire reflecting spookily in her eyes and making her face glow orange.

He followed her gaze, and gasped with relief as he recognised a familiar shape stumbling through the wreckage. "Dusty!" His voice barked out rough and weak, but Dusty looked up and made his way over.

Behind him, a group of struggling savages fell into view, and David watched his friend turn back, spot something, and start towards the group. "No! What–?" But he couldn't manage anything more before starting to choke and retch.

Dusty started punching at flailing arms, kicking at naked torsos, and finally grabbed hold of what he wanted: the shoulder of someone's puffer jacket.

It was the bodyguard, his head bleeding profusely, his jeans half torn off.

He stumbled to his knees, the savages' grip lost, and Dusty quickly helped him back to his feet. "Keep moving, got to keep moving!" The fire had spread from the doorway to engulf half the room, and thick black smoke was gushing out at him, making his eyes water and his throat burn. They stumbled over to David and Danielle, collapsing next to them. "Got to…" he mumbled.

"Karma," David croaked, his hand held up before him to shield his eyes from the glare and dust as he looked back at the room, searching.

But the bodyguard was shaking his head. "That's how

they got me... I tried to stop them, I..." He suddenly groaned loudly, turned away from them, and vomited onto the floor.

"Christ... we need to... we've got to..." David was looking around, his eyes red and watering, searching for any means of escape.

"Come on." Dusty was pushing himself to his feet, stumbling around, but then fell to the floor once more. "Ugh, the smoke, keep low."

"The warehouse," the bodyguard suddenly remembered, spitting out wads of blood-streaked bile, "head for the warehouse."

Flames were clawing at the ceiling of the supermarket now, David saw, while the surviving savages had found the hole in the wall and were busy crawling through, coughing up blood and blinded by smoke.

There was something else he'd noticed, too.

Not all the Asda animals had been in or near the room when it'd exploded, it seemed.

Down by the blocked supermarket entrance, hanging around the shelves with the decapitated heads, was a group of shadows.

A group of shadows who were staying back for the moment, wary of what was happening, but who would soon shrug off their fear and come searching once they realised there was still victims to hunt and kill.

He pushed himself to his knees, let out a huge croaking cough, then warned, "We'd better start moving... there's more of them." He indicated the group he'd just spotted, who were even now starting to edge forwards, albeit warily.

"Oh god no," the bodyguard moaned, continuing to spit long strings of drool, but then quickly pushed himself into a crawling position.

Danielle was still staring greedily at the burning room, so David squeezed an arm. "Come on. We're going now."

She turned to him and laughed. Then looked at Dusty and the bodyguard and laughed at them, too. Noticing the bodyguard's head wound, she reached a hand towards it in curiosity, then moved forwards with her mouth as if to kiss it better.

"Hey what–?" he protested, but she had hold of the back of his head, and was moving closer to lap at the leaking blood and press her lips to the ragged gash. "Yuch, that– hey!"

"Come off it Danielle, for fuck's sake," David snapped.

Then she chomped into the wound.

"YAA-FUCK!"

She jumped forwards, toppling the bodyguard over backwards, sucking at the fresh spurt of blood, biting then chewing on the lumps of flesh she'd ripped off.

David grabbed hold of her torn shirt, but only succeeded in completely shredding it, so he pushed himself forwards and grabbed her around the middle, trying desperately to pull her away from the screaming body-guard.

And then he thought fuck this.

And raised his hands to her breasts and *squeezed*, yanking her forcibly backwards, feeling her hard nipples against his palms.

She let out a squawk of pain and frustration, her jaws gnashing up and down, blood spitting into the air, before collapsing backwards onto David.

Dusty moved over to the bodyguard, glancing back warily at Danielle; warily at David too, after seeing how rough he'd been with her.

The guard's head was now leaking blood all over his face and into his hair, but he seemed more troubled by the attack than the wound. "She's one of them! She's fucking one of them!"

And it certainly seemed that way, with her screaming and writhing away on top of David, struggling to get free of his grip.

Each time she wriggled, she seemed to be gyrating herself against him, and David had time to wonder if she was doing it on purpose when she started jerking her elbows backwards and inwards, trying to connect with his sides. "Stop it man!" he yelled. "Just calm it, get off us– *fuck*!" He had to let go. She was jabbing her elbows down simultaneously on either side of his chest, starting him off coughing and retching again. He could hardly breathe.

She sprang away on her knees, then turned around to face him, hissing hatred between bloodstained teeth.

It was the hate more than anything.

More than the fact she'd attacked the bodyguard, more than the fact she'd hurt him physically.

The hate.

He scrambled to his feet and launched himself at her.

She tried dodging to one side, but he caught an arm around her neck and spun himself sideways, knocking her onto her back and clambering on top of her. He brought his knees down onto her arms, on either side of her head, and sat on her breasts. She kept struggling beneath him, kicking her legs up high, trying to connect with his head. He held her wrists tight, clamped them to the floor, and grinned down into her bruised, bloody, smoke-stained face.

By god she was the most beautiful thing he had ever seen.

Dusty was screeching. "Fucking get it together yous two! They're coming! The nutters are coming!"

David looked up. Even the maniacs who'd survived the explosion were now approaching. The bodyguard had started crawling along the aisle in the direction of the warehouse, and was looking back expectantly.

Dusty gave David a final, pleading look, then shot off into the gloom.

Danielle had taken advantage of the moment to get her breath back. She was spitting up half-chewed splats of flesh. "*Fucker*! you're such a *fucker*! such a *fucker*, *fucker*, *fucker*–"

David snorted. "That's all it's about?" He slid down her body slightly, then started rubbing his groin forwards against her breasts. "That's all you want? A good *fucking*?" He started repeatedly raising her wrists off the floor then slamming them back down. "All you want? A good *fucking*? a good *fucking*?"

"*Fucking*! *fucking*! *fucking*!" she echoed gleefully, in time with every slam of her wrists and thrust of his pelvis.

"FUCKING!" he roared into her face, "*WANT YOUR FUCKING CUNT FUCKING– FUUUH-KING CUUUNT*!!"

She started bucking beneath him, thrashing her hips high into the air as he let go of her wrists and tore at his trousers–

his fucking supermarket work trousers that FUCKING SHELF-FILLING SHITHOLE

–and this cunt was going to get the fucking of its life it was going to get it get it: he freed himself, his cock now hard and huge, and she screamed at the sight of it, lunged forwards with her head desperate to bite and chew and suck but he jerked backwards, sitting on her legs now, tearing at the last of her clothes, ripping them away and there was her cunt bruised and scratched like the rest of her body, and her breasts big and scuffed and red and the nipples hard, and he lifted his fists into the air and brought them down on her tits, one fist for each, crushed them against her ribcage and she screeched but her mouth and eyes still wide and grinning, she fucking loved it the *cuntslutwhore* she wants it *hard* and he skimmed further down her body and rammed his head between her legs, his mouth on her cunt, his tongue poking inside, teeth scraping outside, and then *chomp* just what she fucking wanted him to do, and he could hear her screaming even though her thighs had clamped against his ears and her fists were battering the back of his head, then her legs spasming open again, and he pushed himself up, spitting and hissing blood, and thrust his cock towards her and there was nothing for it but brute force and he rammed himself into her mess of blood and flesh and *FUCKED*–

And then a high-pitched squeal belonging to only one thing.

From the top of the aisle, Dusty and the bodyguard both turned back and started yelling. "*Shitmonkey fuckmonkey*!"

The group of explosion survivors had been edging in Dusty's direction, with the bunch of nutters who hadn't been affected by the blast aiming for David and Danielle, who were doing… god alone knew *what*… about halfway down the aisle. It was this group the squealing was coming from, and Dusty squinted through the smoky gloom to see the hobbling naked skinhead break away from the pack and stumble towards David and Danielle.

Beside Dusty, the bodyguard's initial fear had been replaced by another emotion. "That shit-sucker," he was gasping, staring at the racing monkey, "that dirty shit-sucking fuck killed my brother, killed my brother, *killed my brother*!"

And Dusty realised he was talking about his fellow bodyguard, whose head the monkey had pulverised at Raw Man's farm. Whether they had truly been brothers

Dusty wasn't sure, but the bodyguard was stepping forwards now, blood-drenched face set in an expression of rage and determination, eyes gleaming with the need for revenge.

"Don't try it, they'll kill you!" he warned, but the bodyguard either ignored him or simply didn't hear him. And inwardly, he was ashamed of himself for wanting to run away again, run from the monkey, the monkey who'd been chasing them for so long, who'd never given up, never run, never fucking let them alone; and maybe the bodyguard was right, maybe now was the time for revenge, now was the time to get that scrawny skinheaded little shit and tear his fucking balls off, smash his fucking face, break his fucking bones–

He was moving before he even realised he'd made a decision, racing to catch up with the bodyguard. His fists were bunched up by his sides. "That monkey… that fucking monkey…"

And then the bodyguard was joining in, "fucking monkey–" now in unison– "fucking monkey *that fucking monkey THAT FUCKING MONKEY*!"

–and under him the bitch was loving it so much, jerking around, clenching her cunt around his cock as he *FUCKED* and *FUCKED* and leaned forwards to chew her face and bite her tits as he kept *FUCKING*–

The monkey limped onwards, endlessly screeching, then stopped as he caught sight of Dusty and the bodyguard, who were running now, yelling their war cry as they passed the horror of David and Danielle, heading away from the shelving – and then ploughed straight into the skinhead.

The guard used his bulk and momentum to spin the little fucker around and twist his arms up behind his back, allowing Dusty to start raining down the blows.

It was that smarmy fucking face which sent Dusty into a complete rage.

Just smugly sneering at him, daring him to try anything, like every schoolyard bully who'd ever tormented him, look at the loser layabout stoner with the suicide sister. "*MONKEY FUCK!*" he screamed, his arms moving in a blur, his fists powering against that ugly fucking face, against anyone who'd ever hurt him; smashing into it, blasting and crunching and slamming into it *and it felt wonderful–*

–wonderful as he thrust his fingers into the hole he'd bitten in her breast, gouging out lumps of flesh, digging deep, prodding deep, then punching it, punching, slipping out of her bloody cunt and moving up her body and slamming his cock into the flesh of her breast, ramming it inside, a new untainted cunthole, and she was screaming with delight, clawing at his stomach and digging her own holes, reaching around to his arse and scratching at him there as he thrust and thrust, gripping the torn tit in his hands as she poked her clawing fingers deep up inside him and they screamed in unison.

The bodyguard was just as desperate for revenge as Dusty. He dropped the monkey onto his back, pushed Dusty out the way, and started to stomp. The fucker would pay.

The fucker would pay.

The little shit was squealing and squawking under his boot, but he kept stamping, crunching bones and bursting flesh, then Dusty was next to him and joining in, going for the cock and balls as he kept going for the face.

She wanted him in her mouth, she wanted him deep down her throat, her fingers were jerking in and out of his bloody arsehole making his cock so hard, and he rammed his hands into her mouth and opened it wide, scraping at the insides to get a grip then yanking it open, slamming down with all his might and cracking the jaw, and her throat was all bloody and raw and fleshy and warm and he jumped up from her chest and landed on her head, his cock down the back of her throat, his hands forcing her mouth further apart, her hand splitting his arse open, and his cock was so hard and he was bouncing up and down on her face and the scalped Doc Marten Man was standing in front of him, drenched in blood and wanking himself off, but instead of fear there was joy as David leaned forwards and took the hippy's huge cock in his mouth and bit it, while simultaneously slamming Danielle's broken jaw closed on his own cock, feeling her teeth burying into his flesh, and he felt the blood in his mouth as Doc Marten Man started screaming with delight and pounding his fists against the back of David's head, drilling his skull onto his lacerated cock and David had time to think–

sex and death that's what it's all about Dusty was right

–before the hippy fell forwards and pushed him off Danielle, a chunk of his cock in her mouth, the rest of it geysering blood high into the air, and the three of them collapsed together in a final embrace, desperately holding onto each other as their lives slipped away, the fire reaching them seconds later–

–and Dusty didn't know how the hell he'd got away but the bodyguard was screaming as the pack surrounded him and the monkey's mashed corpse, and they rushed him and Dusty couldn't look, there was smoke and tears in his eyes and he felt a searing heat above him as the ceiling *whooshed!* with a flood of upside-down fire streaming across this entire section of supermarket, and he could feel his skin tightening and blistering as the screams of the savages erupted from the inferno and there was light bursting from behind him and rainbows in the air all around as a gush of water drenched him and brought him to his knees; but the light, he could see it now, moonlight and now floodlights and he had to reach it, he had to make it, the water streaming around his feet, spraying behind him but the fire so out of control, had to reach the light, there were people, shouts and screams of normal people, not savages, the savages burnt and cooked behind him, he had to reach the people, he had to reach the light, he had to survive, he had to make it, and then drenched by a power-ful stream of water but he *would* make it, he *would* survive, he *would* reach the light, stepping through piles of debris and human matter, stumbling out of hell and into the light, people stepping back but someone caring rushing forwards with a blanket, and there was the Centrefather staring shocked wondering what the fuck had gone on, and there was the crazy Wratten but it was okay: he was out, he was in the light, he was alive and–

EJECT

sf

22121997–25091999

Printed in Great Britain
by Amazon

41061888R00239